Third Party Candidate

Alstair Press

Published by Alstair Press
228 Park Avenue South
New York, New York
10003

This is a work of fiction. Names, characters, places, and incidents either are the product of the author's imagination or are used fictitiously. Any resemblance to actual persons, living or dead, or locales is entirely coincidental.

ISBN: 0-615-22825-9
ISBN-13: 9780615228259
LCCN: 2009923306

Printed in the United States of America
Visit www.amazon.com to order additional copies

Alstair Press

Visit www.booksurge.com to order additional copies.

For my wife Julie the kindest and most understanding person I know, and to my father Wade, to whom I owe everything. Also, special thanks to my sister Donna who has helped me so much.

The problems that exist in the world today cannot be solved by the level of thinking that created them.

Albert Einstein

Prologue

January 8th 2012
La Pesca, Tamaulipas Mexico

Darkness had fallen but the temperature still hovered at ninety-eight degrees in the Chihuahuan desert. The oppressive heat invaded the back seat of the small Volkswagen Beetle barreling across the desert. The air-cooled engine mounted behind Ali's back radiated waves of heat into the small confines of the car. Perspiration trickled down his neck into his sweat soaked T-Shirt. For some reason it hadn't occurred to him how hot it could be in Mexico during the winter months. With his limited Spanish, he listened intently to the car radio blaring over the road noise. The weather forecaster was predicting unseasonably hot weather for the state of Tamaulipas. Ali had spent so much time in Germany as a student, he had lost much of his indifference to heat.

"*¿Cuánto aún más a la ciudad?*" How much further, Ali asked impatiently because he couldn't yet see the lights of the village only the inky blackness of the desert night.

After traveling more than twelve hours, he knew they had to be closing in on the small fishing village by now; if not, something was terribly wrong.

"*Dos millas,*" The driver said as he wrestled over the small steering wheel jumping from pothole to pothole as dust bellowed from behind the wheels.

It wouldn't be long now, he thought. Ali would meet his fellow freedom fighter in the small out-of-the-way fishing village of La Pesca, a perfect jumping off point to the United States. It would offer them a clandestine starting point where they could slip into the country unnoticed by the authorities.

"No será largo ahora, hay las luces de la ciudad," The driver said, as lights began to twinkle in the distance. The man in the back seat welcomed the news as he strained to see his first glimpse of civilization in more than twelve hours of crashing about in the back seat.

Ali didn't respond to the driver; there was no need. Just the day before he had been secretly flown to the foot of the Sierra Madres from Columbia. The small twin-engine plane had flown mostly over water, no more than fifty feet above the white caps, to stay under the probing radar beams that reached far out over the waters of the Mexican Coast. The plane had landed on a gravel airstrip in the desert laden with a load of cocaine destined for the streets of the United States. The landing was rough with the desert airstrip barely illuminated with the flickering lights of smudge pots. The plane had slammed down hard on the gravel with rocks hitting the aluminum fuselage and making a frightening noise that seemed more like a crash than a successful landing.

Ali Al Rubaie would fit the general description of most of the Arab terrorists listed on the FBI's most wanted list. He had dark thick wiry hair closely cropped and a distinct Arab nose. His black eyes were set far back into his head with heavy, thick eyebrows. At just under five-feet, five-inches tall he wasn't a particularly imposing figure, but there was a deadness in his dark eyes, like most men who kill for a living. Even though Ali wasn't Pakistani, he had trained in one of Pakistan's most elite commando forces, the *Sindh Rangers*. In the years before Pakistan was an ally of the United States, he had been jailed and tortured because of his harsh criticisms of Pakistan's political leaders. After escaping from prison, he joined Al-Qaida and fought in Afghanistan as the United States invaded the country. Then to avoid being captured he crossed Iraq into Syria and linked up with Al-Qaida operatives there. This invasion and unsuccessful war against the Americans had led him to seek new ways to inflict serious blows directly against the United States at home, where it would hurt the most.

Like many Al-Qaida cell members, he took part and planned assassinations, bombings, and recruitment. His real name had never been known to anyone, not even to Al-Qaida operatives. He had lived most of his life with names no one could recognize or compare to a photograph and that was how he had stayed alive. At the moment, the only weapon he was carrying was an Israeli boot knife. This was a special weapon to Ali; he had taken it off a dead Marine in Afghanistan years before. Ali speculated that it had been a souvenir to the young Marine, too, probably taken from a Taliban freedom fighter. The double-edged black carbon steel blade was his favorite weapon. Besides, if he were to be caught with any kind of firearm in Mexico it would land him in a filthy Mexican jail for years. But knives were different down here; everyone carried one and the authorities didn't seem to mind.

The mission was much too important to jeopardize by being caught with a gun in a country where firearms were strictly prohibited and punishable by imprisonment. At the same time, he couldn't allow himself to be captured by any government, and he carried cyanide capsules to ensure that didn't happen. He never thought of himself as particularly heroic for being unwilling to be captured alive. He felt giving his life for Allah, even before the attack, would still result in his martyrdom, and Ali would easily choose martyrdom before giving his enemies the satisfaction of capturing him. He had vowed to his handlers never to be captured alive!

This mission was to be his last. A last glorious attack where he would heroically die to ensure his mission would be successful. He would personally detonate the device, then wake up almost immediately afterwards in the splendor of paradise. Infiltrating the land of the great Satan and setting off the most lethal blast in the history of the war would be well worth dying for and would make him the most important martyr in history. The misery to the American people would be unparalleled, Allah willing.

"*¿Adónde vamos?*" the driver asked, as the car passed the first dilapidated building of many that lined the dusty main street running east to west through town.

"*Al Puerto,*" Ali said to the driver. He would meet up with his partner, Tan Gaddam, at the local harbor. Together they would be smuggled into a small coastal town in Texas where a car would be waiting for them.

The Volkswagen slowly drove up the main street, which ended at a crumbling concrete wall that served as the harbor dock for the local fisherman. As Ali unfolded out of the back seat, the soft warm breeze of the Gulf of Mexico covered his face with a blanket of moisture. It seemed twice as humid standing next to the water's edge, and he instantly felt even more sticky and uncomfortable. The driver popped the hood of the small Volkswagen and struggled with the Ali's large bag.

"*¿Necesitas ayudar?*" Ali said wanting to help the driver with the bag. He didn't want the driver to talk about the trip later, so he tried to be helpful to win his trust. Ali wanted to be nice but knew Pesos would be more effective at convincing the driver to remain silent about his trip to La Pesca.

"*¡No, No, yo lo tengo!*" The driver said as he pulled the bag out by himself with a toothy smile.

Ali pulled out a wad of Pesos and counted out to the Mexican driver 2,200 in various denominations. Ali then asked the driver if he would just forget all about his trip to La Pesca and offered him another 1,500 pesos tip.

"*¡Si, yo nunca he estado en La Pesca!*" The driver said eagerly as he grabbed the rest of the money from Ali's hand. "I've never been to La Pesca," he said in Spanish, smiling broadly and displaying a single gold front tooth.

The driver hurried back to his car, jumped in, and sped off quickly down the dark street before the strange Arab man could change his mind about the sizable tip he now had safely folded in his grimy shirt pocket.

After the car was gone, Ali picked up his bag and walked down the filthy dock past some old fishing boats rocking in the darks swells. The whole area reeked of decaying fish as the humid breeze churned the smells into a reeking odor that nauseated Ali. The smell was so bad that he tried to breathe through his mouth and not his nose, to save his olfactory glands from sending the message of how bad it was to his brain.

A man approached him from the opposite direction. "*Señor Valachi?*"

"*Si,*" Ali answered. He was traveling on a forged Italian passport, and Italian was a language he spoke fluently.

"*Do you speak English*?" The man asked with distinct western drawl, like a cowboy from an old western movie.

"Yes, I do," Ali answered. The man was now within a few feet of him. Ali could see him clearly. He was of Mexican decent but dressed like an American with a white button-down collar shirt, blue jeans, and deck shoes. He was a big man probably weighing ninety kilos, and the shirt was soaked under the arms with perspiration.

"Great, my Spanish isn't that good, sir. My name is Dave. My folks never spoke a lot of Spanish to us kids, wanting us to be English speaking Americans not Mexicans," He said, as he stuck out his rather large mallet-like hand to shake. The two men shared a clammy handshake as they met face to face.

"Where's your boat?"

"Right down here out of the lights," the man said, as he turned and started walking back down the concrete wall, which doubled as the sidewalk, towards a darker area of the harbor.

Ali felt uncomfortable about following the man into the darkness, because it could be a trap, but as long as he kept the man in front of him, he knew he would be able to control things. Ali felt confident he could quickly reach his commando knife that was tucked away in his right boot. This wouldn't be the first man he had killed with it and he would do it again, quickly and efficiently, if he had to.

"Your friend is already here!" The man said as he walked along in the darkness not sensing the real danger behind him.

Ali relaxed a little knowing Tan had made it safely to La Pesca. That meant they could leave immediately. It would be dangerous to hang around the Mexican town until morning, too many prying eyes and too many questions.

"How soon can we put to sea?"

"We need to get the hell out of here tonight, I told the locals I was just here for fuel and I didn't check in with the authorities or anything. Things could get a little sticky if anyone traces me back to this sort of thing, I could lose my boat, you know?"

Out of the dark, a sleek white fishing boat appeared tied along the wall. As they walked up to the stern of the boat, Ali could make out the name lettered in gold "*Adios Amigo*" Corpus Christi, Texas.

"Let me help you there, sir," the man said as he reached for Ali's bag.

"No, thanks I can take care of it."

"Suit yourself," the man said as he hopped on board and quickly went up a teak ladder that led to the Fly Bridge.

Ali jumped into the cockpit after him and slid open the door to the salon as one of the powerful diesel engines smoked to life, coughing at first, and then settling into a low rumble vibrating the entire boat.

As he entered the salon, he saw Tan sitting on the settee. Suddenly, the second engine coughed to life. Black smoke billowed from under the stern lacing the boat with diesel fumes.

"*Al Ham dulilah,*" Tan said, praising Allah, then jumping up relieved that his fellow *Holy Warrior* had finally arrived.

"Yes, Allah has truly blessed us, but this will be the most treacherous part of our journey, my brother."

"*In Sha'allah,*" Tan answered softly, knowing Allah must will their actions.

"Yes, Allah has truly blessed us and he will help us now."

"We will make it, God willing," Tan answered softly.

Tan was a thin Asian man in his mid thirties. He was Malaysian and a Muslim. He had been handpicked for this mission because of his technical skills. He would be responsible for assembling the weapon that even now was being smuggled into the United States in separate components. A nuclear weapon so compact and dangerous that they would be able to drive it to ground zero and destroy buildings within a three mile radius leaving a deadly radioactive plume that would kill thousands more. This unprecedented attack would weaken and possibly break the will of the American people, hopefully for good.

Captain Dave, after releasing the dock lines, eased both Caterpillar engines into gear and the Sport fishing boat lurched forward, then began slowly idling out into the darkness of the harbor. Within a few minutes, the boat had cleared the small port and was speeding Northward in the Gulf of Mexico plowing through dark seas with no running lights.

Across the Gulf of Mexico, Americans slept comfortably, unaware of the imminent danger that was speeding its way through the porous south Texas border.

I

February 23rd 2012
Boston, Massachusetts

"I'll do this thing, God willing—" The young Asian whispered over the splattering rain soaking his sweatshirt. Gray storm clouds scudded low overhead while cold rain fell in sheets cutting his visibility to just a few feet. Syed hoped the sudden downpour would obscure his face from the cameras that might be focused on him. The rain was his friend today. "Thank you, Allah," he whispered. The package he was ordered to retrieve had arrived the day before to a small apartment house mailbox in Boston's China Town. The box was hidden from view in a remote hallway in the rear of the apartment building. All he had to do now was pick it up. *There wouldn't be any more to it than that, just get in and get out*, Syed tried to convince himself for the second time in less than a second. The apartment wasn't rented, so the mailbox wasn't being used. The flat cardboard envelope had been postmarked in Vancouver from an address that didn't exist. This seemed to be a perfect place to smuggle information into the US. He wasn't a seasoned terrorist but he was convinced this was the perfect spot, but he hadn't been asked what he thought, just ordered to pick-up the package.

"Please protect me from the evil eyes of the great Satan, Allah," he whispered, as he began to cross the flooding street. He jumped over the rushing water to avoid soaking his feet. He then moved quickly across to the other side looking both directions to avoid the traffic. As he jogged through the water, a thought quickly came to him. *If I get caught, I will have failed my first mission for the Jemaah Islamiya. I can't let that happen. Please don't let that happen, Allah...*he pleaded silently. This was his second trip to Boston's China Town and knew that most of the Chinese locals lived in small apartments above their businesses. It was a complete community, not just a business district, which was critical to his mission. Due to the large number of Asians living there, he would blend in easily. The drop off location had been chosen carefully so he wouldn't look out of place and make it difficult for the authorities to pick him out in a crowd. Even though he was Malaysian, his ancestors were mostly Chinese, but that didn't guarantee the FBI wouldn't recognize him. Syed was becoming nervous, his heart was pounding, his senses screaming; he had never done anything like this before, but that didn't mean he couldn't. Without wanting to, he began to visualize himself opening the mailbox and being swarmed by angry FBI agents, screaming with their weapons drawn. He could only imagine what his parents would think, since they were proud immigrants of the United States. If by chance he was caught, his family would certainly attempt to understand what had happened to him, maybe where they had gone wrong, but he knew they would never condone his actions; but that was okay, because he reported to a higher order now.

Syed didn't live in Boston; weeks earlier he had received a key, which had been addressed to him in New York. The key would allow him to pick up his first assignment from the JI. He looked around nervously, again, to ensure that no one was watching, then he inserted the small brass key into the lock. The gritty tumblers inside the mechanism grinded after the key entered the small elongated hole. The lock gave way, and he slowly opened the hinged door, glancing from side to side. Inside, Syed found a brown envelope. He pulled it out quickly and stuffed it into his jacket pocket. His eyes darted back and forth, again, searching for the FBI agents who might be lying in wait to spring out from every direction. To his relief, nothing happened. He stood there for a minute, while disbelief set in, then he slowly walked back into the pounding rain. It was midday and car horns were echoing as drivers attempted to negotiate the wet streets, but no one seem to be interested in him. He had pulled it off! *I've defied the FBI*, he thought, now smiling confidently holding the package close to his heart.

He had watched the area for most of the morning to ensure the apartment building hadn't been staked-out by the authorities. He was now convinced he hadn't been followed, but Syed wasn't taking any chances and had forced himself to watch the area for hours to ensure he was alone. The additional surveillance had probably been a waste of time, he thought, but that's how he had been trained. To be wary of everything and everybody. It wasn't until he safely opened the envelope and had transferred the contents to another place for safe-keeping did he begin to relax. All he had to do now was drive back to Logan Airport, board his flight back to New York, and he would be safe, safe to carry out whatever plan he was asked to execute. After all, if anyone were tracking him, he would already be on his way to jail. This was a dangerous business, but he had been well trained and his confidence was now growing. The coded DVD was mixed among CDs in his black leather case. To look normal, he put the headphones around his neck that were connected via *Bluetooth III* to his Sony MP-8 media player located in his right coat pocket. To anyone watching him, he looked just like any other young college student flying out of Logan. He boarded his flight to New York without delay and arrived at JFK at 4:05 PM. After leaving the airplane and entering the terminal, his confidence began to fade. The young terrorist was beginning to imagine potential threats everywhere. Every businessman reading a newspaper seemed to transform before his eyes into an FBI agent. He tried not to make eye contact with anyone, trying to be calm, walking at a normal pace. He had watched too many Hollywood spy thrillers where suspects walked too fast, with agents walking even faster behind a fleeing suspect before apprehending him. He forced himself to stop at a newsstand to purchase a copy of the *New York Times*, but he didn't want to appear hurried or rushed. But standing in line, waiting to pay, he became more nervous and agitated. He couldn't help it. *I could have been out of the terminal by now*, he thought. But instead, he stood patiently behind an elderly lady slowly counting change out of her change purse. "Hurry up you old fool!" He said in a language no one was likely to understand. He could feel his heartbeat quicken as beads of sweat began to trickle down his forehead and into the slits of his twitching eyes. *Maybe I haven't beaten them*, he thought. Finally, after what seemed an eternity but in reality was only a few seconds, he paid for the *Times* and walked casually towards the exit.

The DVD was an imitation of a popular movie DVD, but one track of the colorful disc had encrypted information burned at the end of the movie. The authorities would have to find the encrypted data at the end of the disc just before the credits, no easy task. The hidden code would be extremely difficult to break by any intelligence agency because of the multiple layers of code written in Arabic. The encrypted information would direct him to his actual assignment for the JI. Syed was committed, spiritually, to perform any act, even if it cost him his life, because he had pledged his future to Allah. He was now a major player in a much larger drama that would require him to make great sacrifices in his blind obedience to the will of God. Syed was committed to bringing down the great Satan, so his life was a small price to pay.

March 16th 7:50 p.m.
New York

In his small apartment in Brooklyn, Syed placed the DVD in his laptop and began to run the de-encryption program. He was nervous and excited and tapped the first two fingers of his left hand on the small desk by his bed.

"Come on, Come on!" he whispered, demanding the program to decode quicker.

Syed was born in the United States and raised in California. Three years before, at the age of eighteen, he had moved to New York City to study engineering. During his junior year he had taken a trip to Malaysia and ended up staying for six months. His family had indulged him mainly because he would be staying with family and reconnecting ties between their extended relatives. Once in Malaysia, Syed traveled from Kuala Lumpur to Kuantan on the South China Sea. There he met distant cousins. It was there that a man named Amar, who was a member of JI, befriended him, then later recruited him into the Islamic resistance group. The trip back to Kuantan was more than just an extended vacation, it was like finally coming home. In his ancestral home he was not just another Asian kid living in a society dominated by white Christians and Jews, where he was often mistaken for Chinese rather than Malaysian. In

Malaysia, he was like everyone else. No one thought of him as different. He was just Syed Badawi a Muslim, a man. Syed, with Amar's help, had quickly assimilated into not just the Malay way of life but also the JI. Amar helped Syed learn the reasons why the organization existed. He then became intellectually involved and emotionally connected to the causes of the JI. For the first time in his life, he was proud of his ancestry and who he was. His life in the West was a disappointing experience; it had been a difficult life for him. It was difficult because of the enormous pressure exerted on young Asians in the States to fit in. In high school, there was always pressure to act like an American kid, dress like them, talk like one. At home it was different, his family had expected him to act like a Malaysian. He found it hard to get along in both worlds, at least it had been for him. Sure some of his Asian friends loved their lives but he didn't. In Malaysia, all of the strife and unhappiness melted away, all the uncertainty was gone. It wasn't long before his friends just saw him as one of them, not as an Asian-American, not as someone different that needed to assimilate, but a true believer, a brother, a Muslim.

He joined the "Jemaah Islamiya" because it was something he could do that would demonstrate to his friends in Kuantan, especially Amar, that he was worthy of their friendship. Syed wanted to find a way to make America pay for their actions around the world, policies that hurt innocent Muslim women and children. Together, these two ideas merged into a willingness to support people who were like him, the people who had so willingly accepted him. The whole idea of exacting vengeance against America had become a strong attraction to him, something he felt he had to do. Syed was convinced it was his destiny. It was obvious that even in far away Malaysia the West had negatively impacted the lives of the people. Kuala Lumpur was as "Westernized" as any country in the world. The tall glass buildings, the bumper-to-bumper traffic, and the "*Americanized*" dress of young people on the streets convinced him the JI needed to stay in power, and if he could help in some way, he would, God willing. This he had solemnly pledged to Amar.

Over the wonderful, dream-like months he spent in Kuantan, he was slowly indoctrinated in the ways of the Islamic resistance organization. Over time his hatred for America had grown. Tan began to slowly change. He changed from a man who didn't like the ways of the West, to a man who hated America and all it stood for. Slowly, over time, as he learned more about the goals of the terror group, he suddenly felt an overwhelming need for an outlet to express what he now believed in his heart, that America was evil and beyond redemption. He understood, accepted, and internalized the basic beliefs of the organization. He was acutely aware that it might require his own martyrdom but he decided privately to approach that only when that time came. Syed was certain that Allah would reward him for his actions if it ever came to that. His conversion was now complete. He was "born again" to die for Allah.

As he waited for the encrypted message to be decoded by his computer, he noticed the images of smoke and chaos streaming across on the plasma screen of his television. He pushed the mute button to find out what had happened. The voice came from a female reporter near the scene describing what she termed a "terrorist attack," which angered Syed because he believed the United States government was the terrorist, not the Freedom fighters. Apparently, the attack had taken place just minutes before in London, another shopping mall. Good, he thought, another success, another martyr has spoken. It was just another statement to the West that they will pay for what they have done! He was part of this now, Syed knew, watching the black smoke billowing skyward.

There would be no going back, he thought. Syed was afraid, but determined. He had sworn to God that he would support the attacks that would free all Muslims from the iron grip of the West. The Americans and the British deserved to die.

The Muslim world he had grown to know in Kuantan with his brothers of the Jemaah Islamiya, was beautiful. It was a way of life that provided a welcome respite from the decadent West and all of its meaningless trappings! The high mountains dropping down to the South China Sea was the most awe-inspiring landscape he had ever seen, a land of dreams and the goodness and the sanctity of Islam. The beautiful highland lakes and rainforests high in the mountains were so different from the hell he experienced in the filth-ridden, rat-infested city of New York. This Muslim land of Malaysia represented everything that was good and the JI wanted to protect their Holy Land from the West. He had been assured that his afterlife would be attained if he dedicated his life to fighting for Islam.

Syed heard the computer beep over the sound of the television. He again hit the mute button, stopping the sounds of chaos being described in such detail by the reporter. The computer hadn't completed the decoding! "What's wrong now?" Syed read the message blinking on the screen, "Cannot Decode.".

He sat there thinking. This was the program he had been given by the JI to decode. How could it not work? His mind was lost in thought about what he might have done wrong loading the program, and he had decided to go into the control panel and delete the program so that he could reload it. "It had to be something I've done incorrectly," he said, talking to himself. "How could I have failed?"

As he worked on the computer, Syed heard muffled voices outside in the hall of his apartment. Spooked, he quickly ejected the plastic disk from his computer. He then hurriedly placed it back into the black leather case on a nearby table. As he pushed the mute button again on the remote to restore the sound back to his television, he switched the channel. There was a light knock on his door, just one.

At first he decided not to answer at all. He was sure now that he must have been shadowed by the FBI, tracked like a dog back to where he lived! But he knew the FBI had to identify themselves first, didn't they? So it had to be someone other than the authorities, but he wasn't expecting company.

"Who is it?" Syed asked.

"Friends from Kuantan—"

Syed relaxed. Just the sound of the name of his faraway home made him feel at ease.

"Can we come in?" One of the men asked.

"We have a message from your friends there."

"What message?" Syed asked not feeling comfortable about letting strangers into his apartment.

"It's about the code, we're with the JI too, let us in, we can't talk about this in the hallway," he whispered.

Syed relaxed more when he heard the Cantonese accent of the second man.

"Okay," he said, as he unlocked the door and opened it. Two men, one was an Arab and the other Cantonese, quickly walked past him to the center of the room both looking around curiously. Both men appeared to be about the same age, in their mid thirties, and dressed in jeans and sweaters. Neither man had facial hair.

"So what do you want?" He looked into the dark brown eyes of the Cantonese man. They were ordinary enough, but Syed thought for a moment he thought he saw fear. Why would he be fearful? he wondered.

"There was an unfortunate mix-up; you were given the wrong software for decoding," the Arab man said, his eyes darting around the room quickly, searching.

"I know! I have already attempted to decode it, but it won't work!" He said anxiously.

"Where is the DVD now?" The Arab man asked slowly and cautiously.

"Over here," Syed said and started over to the case to retrieve it, relieved that the problem was not his after all. But before he could take his second step, he felt a terrible pain in the back of his head, then another one, equally painful. He saw the red throw rug on the floor come rushing up to his face as he hit with a heavy thud. He could still hear voices from somewhere above him, but they now seemed far away, muffled. He lay face down on the rug unable to move and with no feelings in his legs and arms. The next thing he saw were black shoes just inches from his face, but moving away as if in slow motion.

As Syed's limp body lay sprawled across the dirty apartment floor, the Arab man straddled him at the waist, then pulled Syed's head up far enough to get his knife under his throat. With one quick slashing movement the blade cut deeply into his throat severing the jugular vein. He then stood up and left the paralyzed man lying in a rapidly expanding pool of blood. Then the murderer took a DVD from the back of the case and put it in the empty spot where the encrypted one had previously been. Next, he took the laptop computer and put it in its case and threw it over his shoulder. Both men then backtracked through the apartment making sure they hadn't touched or left anything behind. Carefully they opened the door enough to see if anyone was in the hall. Assured that no one was watching, the two men quickly left the rundown apartment and the lifeless body of the young man, dying on the floor.

The last fuzzy images in Syed's mind slowly began to vanish; it was the image of the beautiful green waters of the South China Sea lapping on the sugar white beaches of Kuantan. His muddled mind couldn't figure out what had happened to him, but strangely, he felt alright and unafraid. Syed was aware he was lying on the floor of his apartment but couldn't remember how he'd gotten there. He made a feeble attempt to move, but the effort didn't seem to pass the thought stage. He wanted to get up but couldn't muster enough energy to even try. The last thing he felt was the cold air from the hallway rush up and surround his face as the door closed across the room, then again his fading mind's eye flashed back to the green mountains falling to the South China Sea. It was all so beautiful. His last thoughts of Malaysia were real, vivid, in his mind as his life slowly slipped away.

2

March 17th 2012
Montgomery, Alabama

Liz, Doug's wife, handed him coffee she had just finished pouring into an oversized crystal cup.

"There, that's your third and last cup, if you're still interested in cutting back," she said curtly, casting an impatient look at him.

"I promise, that's it," Doug said as he smiled at her.

"I honestly hope so. You'll be bouncing off the walls if you drink one more." Liz then turned and walked back through the arched doorway, but just before closing the door, she looked back at him and smiled, the same beautiful smile he had fallen in love with so many years before. Almost ten years his junior, she was still slender and beautiful as the day they had met in Mobile, a chanced meeting that had changed his life forever. As a former Miss Alabama, she was still petite and attractive as she had ever been, with short auburn hair and sultry green eyes. Doug watched her, in all of her beauty, as she disappeared behind the large wooden doors that led into their home. After she was gone, Doug turned his attention back to his estate and the red pea gravel road that ran through a thousand acres of green Alabama pastureland. The gravel drive climbed a small wooded hill and ended in a circular drive at the steps of his contemporary mansion. For a moment, he lapsed back into his most private thoughts, marveling at the beauty surrounding him. He was enjoying the briskness of the early morning, silently standing, spellbound, and soaking up the beauty of the moment. The pastoral setting he had created for his new home brought him a great sense of satisfaction as he cast his eyes down the long drive before closing them to feel the cool morning air hit his face. This had become a ritual of sorts following his retirement from business and politics; however, enjoying his mornings quietly had become increasingly difficult of late. Since agreeing to run for President of the United States there hadn't been much time for the former Governor of Alabama to enjoy *Ferguson House*, and its comforting sanctuary. He had been tempted out of retirement by a new political party, founded by several disgruntled congressional leaders in Washington. Doug saw possibilities in the new party beyond his achievements as governor. Stumping across the country, attempting to introduce voters to these new possibilities was a high priority at the moment. Primary season was in full swing, and he was committed to exerting all the energy and influence needed to do well in the primaries and thereby convince voters that he, a third party candidate, was viable and could actually win the presidency. The whole thing could be a mistake, he pondered silently, sipping his coffee again, but if it was a mistake, it was one he had to make.

The Freedom Party, as it had been chartered, was composed primarily of congressional leaders from both sides of the philosophical aisle. Its founders had painfully cobbled together a coalition of powerful congressmen who held fiercely to their belief that the two-party system was failing the American people. Could he really make a difference, Doug wondered? It didn't matter now because he was committed to putting every bit of energy he could to win the Presidential election, no matter what the outcome and how difficult it might be.

Like the many third parties that preceded it over the course of two centuries, the Freedom Party was a political oddity, and like its predecessors, its leadership consisted largely of dissatisfied politicians who no longer felt they could make their voices heard.

At the age of sixty-three, Doug enjoyed a slim, powerful build that hadn't changed much from his days as a Marine captain serving in Viet Nam. Standing a tad under six feet, with a broad chest, he still looked like a Marine. His choice in clothing today, a blue and green plaid madras shirt and blue cotton trousers, made him appear more youthful than he was. He still boasted a thick crop of black hair, and he knew from experience that his good looks could be counted on to attract a large segment of the female vote.

As he often had, since retiring, Doug reflected on the path that had brought him to Ferguson House. He had graduated from a private military academy in the south with a degree in economics, but most of his business acumen was acquired from his father, Jack, an "old school" investment banker from the days before leveraged buyouts, junk bonds, and e-commerce. Before his father's death, they had built a successful oil tool company that was the source of his considerable fortune that now allowed him such a comfortable standard of retirement.

He had to be crazy, he thought. He had control of a successful business, a great family, and financial security. Despite the comfortable retired lifestyle he had envisioned and created for himself, he had said "Yes" to the Freedom Party anyway. Knowing it might not rank among the smartest decisions, he had agreed to spend an enormous amount of his precious time and a part of his personal fortune running for President.

Doug tried to put his decision into more abstract terms to make it seem more palatable, but that was difficult, because the time and energy involved were very real, very far from abstract principles. The belief that his country needed him was forcing him to sacrifice the time that was supposed to be devoted to his wife and kids. But he was burdened with the knowledge that his family and his children's families would need a place to live, a place to live free of terror, however, where they could prosper and grow old in peace. Right now, his country wasn't providing for that kind of future. It was a country on the run and in its panic was retreating from the basic ideals that it had been created to defend. Leadership, if it could be called that, came from partisans who couldn't put their differences aside and couldn't cut their dependency on the international companies that funded campaigns and thereby affected political decisions. Washington seemed to have no idea how to protect the average American citizen from the terrorism that had been growing for more than a decade and seemed to be reaching a horrible grisly crescendo.

Tony Landry, known as "Tony" by his friends, because he grew up deep in the heart of Cajun country, had just finished positioning a copy of the *Washington Post* and *New York Times*, both neatly folded in half, one on top of the other, in the back seat of the Chevy Suburban. It was part of Tony's job to make Doug's life a little easier in simple ways as well as in complex planning. The Ferguson's were much more than just an employer. Tony had worked for Doug for eleven years, which included four years at the Governor's Mansion. The Ferguson's were like family.

Tony enjoyed his position as administrative assistant and bodyguard, especially his role as a bodyguard because it was like being a college linebacker again, just a little more deadly. He was officially on the payroll of Ferguson

Industries, although he rarely set foot in the company's spacious steel and glass headquarters in Mobile. Over the past month, he had speculated privately what his role would be if Doug overcame what seemed to be impossible odds and actually became the next President of the United States.

Tony had had a stellar football career at the University of Alabama where he stood out as a middle linebacker for the *Crimson Tide.* He was fortunate to have met the Governor at a golf outing for the football team sponsored by his company. Even though the Governor hadn't attended the University he was a steady supporter of the school, as he was with Auburn. That night, the two men just happened to be seated at the same table at the Cottonwood Golf Club for dinner and Doug had taken an instant liking to the young man. Tony Landry was articulate, that is if his Cajun accent didn't throw you off, a good student, and an easygoing guy off the football field. Doug had a knack for finding good people and hiring them. Tony had proved to be just that. After graduation, he had become Doug's personal assistant and bodyguard and was certainly built to do both jobs. With the exception of going off to do two tours of duty in Iraq with the Marines, he had remained in the employment of the Governor.

Unfortunately, Tony's father had died when he was just thirteen years old, and during their association with each other, Doug had become not only Tony's employer, but over time, his surrogate father.

Tony made a final check inside the Suburban to see if there was anything else he could do to help the governor get through his day a little easier, some small thing that would make a noticeable difference. The interior smelled sweet with leather and Tony made sure everything inside was just like the Governor would want it. From where he stood, nothing looked out of place, except maybe the newspapers. Tony again changed the position of the papers slightly to ensure that their position on the right side of the back seat seemed more symmetrical. The former governor liked everything in its place, nice and neat, not that he would ever mention anything to Tony about such a small detail, but taking care of small details like that had rubbed off on him. One of the things Tony had learned in his years with the Governor was that having a plan was important and having an eye for the smallest of details could serve a person well in business and politics. The state of Alabama had been run with that same eye for detail when Doug was the governor, and Ferguson Industries had always been operated that way. Tony had often rationalized that this orderly way of doing things was extremely important in achieving success. He compared it to shooting a handgun the way he had been taught by his father. To be able to hit your target and score a kill you had to make sure that you were aiming at the kill zone and nothing else. You had to aim at that one area on your enemy's anatomy that would drop him dead in his tracks. If you got caught firing off rounds in the general direction of your enemy it could cost you your life. Rounds had to be placed accurately in combat conditions or you would pay for your mistake. Tony had seen the results of poorly aimed first shots in Iraq where terrorists, many times young boys, had quickly pulled their AK-47s into firing position rattling off rounds wildly in the general direction of the enemy, then moments later a lone marine sniper would pull off a single round that sliced through the poor fellow's heart at four hundred yards. Yeah, he had seen the relevance of being exact in the real world, a world where your survival depended on planning and training, and the smallest details. With the government's official policy of appeasement, after an ineffective policy of chasing terrorists around the world, and the loss of the war in Iraq, Tony's marksmanship had become more important at home.

Tony finally closed the door of the SUV assuring himself that all was as near perfection as he could make it. He took a folded towel off the shelf and wiped the front windshield to get the dust off that had blown in under the garage doors over night. The governor would be driving today. That was another trait that Tony had grown to respect. Doug always liked to drive his own vehicles. He was a perfectionist but not pretentious. Just like the Suburban, it was the only vehicle he drove and he preferred to drive himself wherever he went. It wasn't unusual to see Doug on television driving himself around with his campaign manager seated next to him. His handlers hated it because it didn't look Presidential. It angered Tony when these talking heads, these so called editorialists on the major networks, made negative comments about the governor's habit of driving for the cameras. In their opinion, it was a ploy to get votes. However, those who knew Doug were never shocked when he took the wheel. The simple truth was he didn't have the patience to let anyone else drive, he was always in too much of a hurry to do that. Tony laughed and thought, if the impossible became reality and Doug became the next President of the United States, he would see him drive himself to the inauguration. In fact he would probably show up, an unfashionable, twenty minutes early.

As Tony turned around, folded the towel, and placed it back on the shelf, the shoulder holster that held his Glock 31 discreetly under his windbreaker slipped out of position up under his muscular ham-like bicep. This wasn't the first time this had happened. It would take a minute to pull the German made automatic pistol down to a more comfortable position under his left arm. It didn't help that his large chest took up most of the room inside the windbreaker. Tony personally liked the Glock 19, which was a smaller version of the popular 17L because it was a compact weapon and more comfortable to wear. However, times had changed, and one bullet per opponent seemed to make the odds a little more in favor of a one-man army, which was what Tony was expected to be. So when Glock introduced the new 31, he had switched. He was convinced the .357 Magnum, in the Glock automatic configuration, was more in line with the threat level that existed today. It had taken some time to get use to shooting the higher caliber handgun, but being a member of the Montgomery combat shooting team, he got plenty of practice. The 31 had a standard trigger pull of five pounds per inch, but Tony's Glock had been technically altered down to the bottom limit of only two pounds of resistance, making the weapon much more responsive to his expert touch. His shooting team, "Striker One," had placed second in the "Peace Keeper Challenge" the previous year against the best combat shooters in the country, including teams from the military. Tony's father, Jimmy Landry, had been one of the best gunsmiths in the state of Louisiana who taught his son how to handle a pistol at an early age. He drilled into Tony's head that a gun was like no other thing on earth; it was one of those rare objects "that if you ever really needed it and didn't have it, then you would probably never need it again," he would stress to his son. So Tony had grown up enjoying marksmanship, especially with a pistol. This love and respect for firearms along with his natural athletic abilities made him a pretty damn good bodyguard by anyone's standards. The Corp had liked his shooting ability well enough and wanted him to make a career of the Marines, but Tony had bled enough for his country having been wounded twice in the Middle East.

Doug walked into the garage just in time to see Tony, all two-hundred, forty-five pounds of him, twisting around trying to pull his holster down under the crimson windbreaker. Even though he hadn't played football for years, he looked as if he could still step on the field tomorrow and make an immediate impact in a football game.

"Don't tell me that cannon is giving you trouble again," Doug said, as he watched Tony squirm. "Can I make a suggestion here?" Without waiting for an answer, Doug said, "I'd suggest you buy a bigger windbreaker or a smaller handgun." This wasn't the first time Doug had seen his six-foot, four-inch bodyguard struggle with his new Glock. It seemed like every time he bent over or sat down he had to readjust the larger pistol.

"Yeah, you're right, I'm thinking a new holster. But I'm not giving up this weapon."

"I hope you get it figured out before it goes off and blows a hole in something." Doug said, grinning.

Doug was as knowledgeable about the Glock 31 as his bodyguard. He knew there was very little chance of it going off accidentally. The Glock had three safeties to prevent the weapon from discharging accidentally. He also knew that Tony wouldn't have a round in the chamber and would also have all three safeties engaged, and that was enough to make the Glock safe. Doug didn't like the idea of having to carry loaded weapons around but, like most elected officials, the reality of serious threats had become a way of life. Without secret service protection, he had refused it for the time being, opting for carrying his own .45 caliber Colt Automatic in the glove compartment. This was the same pistol he had qualified within the Marine Corps. The reliable Colt had always served him well in combat and he didn't have any reason to think it wouldn't now. Unlike Tony, he didn't feel the need to invest in new technology for self protection. A .45 caliber round at thirty yards was as lethal as any weapon in the world.

"Give me a second." Tony said, as he made a final adjustment to the leather harness. He leaned his large frame to the right while stretching and lifting his left arm even higher. Finally, after everything was back in place, he straightened up and pulled the windbreaker down around his narrow waist.

"There! I'm good to go. What's our schedule look like this morning, boss?" Tony said as he walked toward the vehicle.

He had just returned the night before from south Louisiana where he had visited with family and enjoyed some nightlife in the bayou country. He liked to go home as much as possible when he was not required at Ferguson House. Tony still had family in Louisiana and loved to attend the fish fries that always seemed to be planned when he was coming home. He still enjoyed hero status in his hometown where he had played fullback and linebacker for his local high school. When he was a senior they won the state high school football championship and nobody had ever forgotten that. But there were still a few LSU hardliners in town who never really forgave him for playing football for the University of Alabama, but he was still their native son, a Friday night hero and Saturday afternoon legend.

"We've got a meeting downtown with Party leaders," the Governor said as he swung in behind the wheel and cranked the SUV's V-8 engine.

"I guess I'm riding shotgun again?"

"You mean elephant gun don't you?" he said, smiling at Tony. "Why don't you relax? I bet you were up late the last few nights," Doug said, as he began to back slowly out of the garage. After they were out on the driveway, Doug pressed the button on the remote that would automatically shut the garage door.

The Suburban rolled down the road that led to the gate kicking up a small amount of white dust. The tires made a familiar crunching sound in the gravel that reminded Tony of his own rural home.

"What's the meeting about this morning? Is there some good news I need to know about?" Tony was still trying to find a comfortable position in the car seat, shifting his weight back and forth and pulling his windbreaker down.

"Not really, actually just the opposite, we're not doing too well at the moment; you've probably seen some of the television coverage about our poll numbers, right?"

"Yeah, I think I read in the paper that we are under five percent?"

"That's probably accurate. The reason is, our message isn't getting through, and I think we're not attracting enough mainstream media coverage. The media has nothing to gain by giving our party a fair shake when it comes to airtime. Honestly, if we're going to get this campaign on track we have to have the media on our side, and right now they're not on board."

"Don't you mean the media geeks who can't sell air time by covering the Freedom Party?" Tony complained. He wasn't a big fan of the media. He had always felt that he had been unfairly criticized by the national sports media while playing football at Alabama. It had always been, "Tony Landry should have done this or he should have done that, "...and the *Tide* might have won the game," or "...if Landry hadn't dropped that crucial interception the *Tide* would have beaten Auburn by more than a touchdown!" Like he ever had a choice about dropping an interception! Most of this criticism came from people who never played the game and got their kicks out of acting like they really knew something about playing football.

"So you don't think we're getting a fair shake in the media?" Doug said, toying with Tony, knowing he didn't like the media.

"You're asking me if the media is giving you a fair shake. You've got to know you're asking the wrong boy that question, Gov!"

"Yeah," Doug said. "I thought I'd get your juices flowing in case we meet some bad guys this morning!"

"Hell, don't say that, I might have to let Heir Glock out of his cage!"

"Heir Glock, huh?" Doug said with a wry smile.

Doug passed through the gates and took a quick left hand turn, then accelerated onto the black asphalt road that led to Interstate 85. Tony glanced into the rearview mirror and saw steam coming out of the exhaust. "He should have started the engine and let it warm up a little," he reminded himself.

3

March 17th 2012
Montgomery, Alabama

Doug stepped into the bright sunlight from the cool shade of the multi-level parking garage. He began walking at a breakneck pace east towards Montgomery's Plaza Hotel hoping not to be seen. This was one of those rare times for the former-governor when he didn't want to speak to the media. His Party's political fortunes weren't going all that well, and Doug didn't have a lot of good answers for pugnacious reporters who might want to ask questions. He was confident that Cliff, his campaign manager, had kept information about the meeting from leaking out. This would buy some time to hammer out some responses to explain the disappointing numbers. Tony was walking fast, trying to keep up, quickly scanning the street in both directions. His concern wasn't the threat of reporters but instead one of those disgruntled political goons that liked to leave messages about their desire to kill his boss. As he swept the area, the only person in he saw was a man standing on the corner about fifty yards away selling newspapers.

"No threat there, "Tony thought with all of his senses fully alert.

"Nice Day. I wish we could play golf," Doug said as he stepped up on the curb quickly closing the distance to the hotel.

"Dream on, Governor! I'd take playing a round of golf any day over another stuffy meeting!" Tony said, as he scanned three-hundred and sixty degrees. He always got a workout walking with his boss. Doug never walked slowly, always at a fast pace that had to be about the same speed as those Olympic walkers, Tony thought. Not only did he have to make sure that the Governor was safe but he had to do it all at a breakneck pace, he didn't like that part. Heavy breathing affected his aim and a good aim was everything in firing a pistol.

"Hey, Tony, I've got a history question for you. Here it is— Did you know that Alabama was one of the first states to secede from the union?"

"I think I knew that. I'd bet my home state wasn't far behind," he said, keeping a sharp eye for trouble in all directions.

"That turned out to be a big mistake, didn't it? You know, pride goes before the fall. All of those hotheaded Confederate patriots underestimating the enemy and over-estimating their own military prowess. That war proved that some really smart people can make bad decisions sometimes—"

"I agree with that. There are still a lot of bad feelings lingering today over that war." Tony spotted a hooker walking the street a block away. *No harm there*, he thought.

Without looking back, Doug said, "that's something we should never do, just assume things. In my opinion, the mistake the Confederacy made was they didn't properly size up their opponent and assumed they were right. Of course, this is the same mistake that's made by one side or the other in wars. We all know now that's what happened when Japan bombed Pearl Harbor; the Japanese didn't accurately size up their opponent."

"Yeah, that one cost a lot of lives on both sides," Tony said with his head on a swivel, scanning back and forth continuing to look for threats.

"I'm wondering when this is all over, say a hundred years from now, who will the historians say misjudged their opponent in this war. Will it be radical Islam or us?"

"I sure hope it's us," Tony said as he sucked in a gulp of air still chasing the Governor down the sidewalk.

"Okay, I'm going to change the subject to something more interesting. Did you know the writer F. Scott Fitzgerald once lived right here in good ole Montgomery?"

"Yeah, I knew that—"

"They say F. Scott loved it here. I wouldn't disagree with him. This town is still a great place to live," Doug said, as he entered the lobby of the Plaza Hotel.

Having grown up in Montgomery Doug knew every street, back alleyway, and building in the city. As a kid, he rode his bicycle down the same streets he had just walked. The hotel hadn't changed all that much since then. His meeting with party officials today would take place in a small suite at the Plaza, the same place he used to meet when he was running for Governor, years before.

The original founders of the party were already waiting in the hotel, including the man that had started it all, Senator Ben Atchison.

Walking in, Doug was relieved that no one was standing in the lobby, so they quickly slid unnoticed into the elevator. John Tolbert, a trusted political ally in Alabama politics, had already called him on the cell phone with the room number. When Doug had suggested John's name as his Vice Presidential running mate there was very little opposition, especially when Doug made it clear he wouldn't run without him. John had served as his Attorney General when he was governor and was the founding attorney of Tolbert, Johnson, Rasmussen, and Hobson, one of the most prestigious law firms in the state. This Alabama native was among the most powerful political operatives in the South. Both men had met in college in their *Knob* year at *The Citadel* and they had become lifelong friends. Together they had forged a political bond that had served both men well. John had welcomed the opportunity to run for the Vice Presidency with his old friend. Unlike Doug, John seemed much older than his years, short at barely five-feet, five-inches tall and pudgy. His once jet black hair had now turned silver gray and had thinned considerably on top allowing his shiny scalp to show through. He had never stopped wearing suits, as most lawyers had, in favor of more casual and more comfortable dress. Like Doug, he had amassed a sizeable fortune that ensured his family would be taken care of long after he passed on. Now, all of that hard work was in jeopardy, he believed, with terrorists now operating on US soil with impunity.

Ben Atchison, the founder of the party, was a United States Senator from South Dakota and had been the first legislator to decide that something had to be done to try and take the country in a new direction. That direction would be to take the government back from those who wanted it operated for big corporations rather than for the people. At one time, Washington politicians could get away with policies that favored the lobbyists, but the country had never been in this kind of danger before. The status quo, the business as usual attitude, was no longer in the best interest of the people. There were too many outmoded foreign policy decisions that were now getting American citizens killed. So with no reservations, Ben had acted upon his beliefs. In Ben's mind, the policies of the United States helped terrorists, like sending foreign aid to countries that aided and abetted known terrorist groups. Ben had enjoyed an outstanding career in the Senate and had served on the Senate Foreign Relations Committee, which, for years he had chaired. It was through this committee that he had followed a single-minded, but decidedly conservative, philosophy on international relations, which eventually led him to lose his Chairmanship. He was considered an obstructionist and was simply removed from the committee by his own party!

The other two founding members of the party had shocked their parties when they deserted and joined the fledgling Freedom Party. All three legislators had caused chaos within their respective parties when they decided to leave.

Bart Foster was a Republican and a United States Representative from Houston. Leonce Collins was a Democrat and a four term United States Representative from a district in Northern Louisiana. Although there were more party members from both sides ready to make the switch, some were still waiting to see how things would work out before throwing their political weight to the new party. With the exception of Bart, the men that founded the Freedom Party didn't represent many of the larger congressional districts in the country. They were a collection of intelligent politicians with excellent political credentials. A young, unknown campaign manager, Cliff Morris, hired on to handle the political campaign and its organization. He was a young, smart, energetic Yale graduate that had worked for some of the real players on the national political scene. Doug believed his positive attitude about winning and keen intelligence and political instincts would pay off. All agreed that Cliff had done an above-average job thus far in their organization. The disappointing poll numbers, over the last few weeks, were starting to take its toll on all of them, however, but no one blamed the young campaign manager.

Doug followed Tony down the dingy hall to Suite 318 and knocked once. Leonce opened the door.

"Come on in, Governor, we've been waiting for you." Leonce was a tall, dark-headed North Louisiana gentleman rancher. He owned and operated a ranch that bred fine cattle with several prize bulls, but cattle breeding wasn't the source of his fortune, it was land, land that his family had owned for generations. The general population of Northern Louisiana were very different from the folks who lived in the southern part of the state. Northern Louisianans were more like the people from the piney woods of East Texas than their distant cousins, the Acadians in southern Louisiana. The Collins family was politically active in North Louisiana where they understood the electorate. With Leonce's father and grandfather serving in the United States House of Representatives it had always been a foregone conclusion that he would do the same.

Everyone stood up and shook hands with the former governor.

"How's it going, Benny?" Doug asked his old friend who had been sitting in one of the fake leather chairs near the hotel window."

"Not bad, Governor, you look fit and ready for some campaigning. Have you had a chance to watch the news this morning?"

"Not yet."

"I'll let Cliff fill you in!" Ben said. "There's some damn good news for a change, Governor."

Cliff was slowly fumbling through a stack of papers as if he was alone in the room.

"Give me some good news, Clifford," Doug said, now changing his attention to his young Campaign Manager. He generally liked the young man; no doubt he was a whiz kid, but what was more important, he had his finger on the pulse of the new generation of voters emerging across America.

"Our poll numbers were wrong, or I guess they were wrong," Cliff said. "I asked a new independent polling company to set some of the polling questions up a little differently; they did a poll and the data doesn't agree with the data we've been getting. Actually, this new poll, when the right questions are asked of voters, give us between eleven and twelve percent among people who are eligible to vote! It's like those softball polls that come out of *Newsweek Magazine* when they want to push a candidate they like, but what we have here is real. Guys, voters are more concerned than we thought about the "same old guys" up in Washington running things. When you ask questions that address safety concerns, we have more underlying support than any of us knew. What's really cool is that the other two parties don't take us seriously, and I would wager they don't have this data."

"Let me see polling information," Doug said, as reached out for the deck of papers." He quickly thumbed through the first several pages.

"Where did you get this again?"

"M-Data Source," Cliff said, smiling at Doug over his *Nike* brand, popular, square framed glasses.

"Who are they?" Ben asked.

"They're some guys that I know at M.I.T. They started Monster-Data Company, and they specialize in finding out what people think, you know, the underlying stuff that most people don't get to."

"This is great news; so we know what's driving these numbers, right?" Doug asked looking over at Bart and winking.

"Of course we do!" Cliff said, as he punched the keys of his laptop.

"Have you been through these numbers, Bart?"

Bart Foster was an intelligent politician, a Republican, who kept winning elections in the Democratic stronghold of south Texas. He wasn't wealthy and had never been. He was an ex University Professor turned politician who had excelled in his transition, becoming more persuasive than he would have ever been in the classroom.

"Not yet, but it certainly looks like our polling was way off," Bart said, readjusting his glasses nervously.

"How could this data be so different?" Doug asked. "Ben, can we really believe this?" He continued, uninterrupted.

"Yeah, I think it's all those town meetings you're holding and following the Democrats around to their primaries. It must be having an impact. No third party candidate has ever tried that! We're speaking directly to their voters at every stop along the campaign trail! The other party brings their constituents out and we convince them that we're a better choice; we're also talking about things they don't want to talk about. What else could it be? It's just good old fashioned hand shaking and pointing out the obvious."

The Plaza wasn't the Ritz Carlton but it was just one of those places political meetings would have been held in the old days, not the sort of place a modern day reporter would expect to find a presidential candidate.

Leonce liked to smoke fine cigars. He pulled out a Cuban *Partagas Short* and, after fidgeting with it for several minutes, lit up. Smoke floated through the air and filled the room with its odor. Although Benny wasn't supposed to smoke anymore, he too pulled a cigarette out of his coat pocket, lit it, and took a deep pull. He then held the smoke in his lungs for a few seconds and finally, exhaled slowly. Gray smoke drifted above his head and hung near the ceiling like a quickly forming cloud.

"It's incredible that we're doing this well. There's no doubt there's going be media scrutiny of these numbers gentlemen. In fact, I don't think anyone will believe this kind of improvement. Look, I'm as afraid of good news as I am of bad, because the effect it can have on the campaign. If these numbers are real, we need to run with it fast and hard! If they are not, we need to low-key them, or risk not being creditable. But we certainly need to capitalize on our newfound success. Actually, we need to do it before we go to South Carolina and Michigan. If we feel like these numbers are real, I would be in favor of spending some well-placed media dollars in both of those markets!" Doug offered up for discussion.

Leonce was in charge of the purse strings for the party. The party's political war chest was not particularly impressive; in fact, it was down to only twenty million dollars. Compared to the reported campaign funds of the two other candidates, it was paltry in comparison.

"How much in Carolina and how much in Michigan?" Leonce asked as he put his cigar in the ashtray and opened his brief case pulling budget information out.

"Get with Cliff and see if we can find out what the other candidates are spending in the three-day run-up to the primaries and then top it! I want our message clear and stronger than anyone else right before the next polling data comes out," Doug said directing his attention to Leonce.

"That's a mistake!" Ben said. He was the oldest and most experienced politician in the room. He had been through numerous reelection bids and often didn't agree with Doug. He knew Doug was popular, but still he was only a state politician, and not very knowledgeable about National politics.

"I already know what you are going to say, Ben. If we use our funds too early all could be lost, right?" Doug didn't consider himself an amateur politician. He knew the political stakes were high and he felt this was the time to make a big splash, but he needed to stroke Ben's ego and defer just at the right moment to get him on board.

"Exactly! We won't have the money in the bank when we really need it!" Ben argued.

"Well maybe and maybe not. I think as we pick up momentum, the funding will come; you know I believe success breeds success. I know that's trite, but it's true. A lot of our financial support is coming from the internet and, as we gain momentum, I think that will only increase. Right now, I'm spending a couple hours a day corresponding directly to supporters via the net, and if you take a look at our contributions from this source, they're going up dramatically everyday—"

"How dramatically?" Ben asked, his interest now peaked.

"From about ten thousand dollars a day to about thirty thousand. Now I can't say with any certainty that this will continue if we lose some momentum, but right now contributions are strong."

Ben had computers, even a laptop, but he didn't use them very much. He found it hard to comprehend that people would send money to a campaign using a computer. It made him feel a little out of touch and insecure about what he knew about the election process these days. That's why he had these young guys around, he thought.

"So people around the country are pledging money on computers?" Ben continued.

"No, there not just pledging, they are transferring funds, baby," Cliff responded.

"So the party is getting the money right at that moment, like a wire transfer?"

"Old term, but accurate," Cliff said.

"So, this is not something we're projecting will come in, it's money in the bank?" Ben asked, as he smashed his cigarette out in a plastic ashtray and sat forward.

"Now you got it!" Cliff answered, smiling. "Take a look at this," he said, as he handed over two pages of financial data to the Senator.

Ben took a minute to study the columns of numbers on the printout.

"So, if I'm reading this right, we have banked contributions of over one hundred and fifty thousand dollars in five days?"

"That's correct, sir! A lot of this funding has been generated because all of us have been answering questions to potential contributors on line, and other "E" generated tools to stimulate contributions."

"With this kind of money coming in, I wouldn't oppose out-spending both parties in these next two states. What do you think, Leonce?" Ben asked, now changing his mind.

"I think it's the right thing to do. If we pick up more support, it will increase our funding drives." Leonce seemed to have already made up his mind; he was paying more attention to the burn on his cigar.

"What about the media then, Leonce?" Cliff asked.

"Let's do it," Leonce said.

"Cliff, let's find out what the others are spending and let's try to top it!" Doug said.

The meeting lasted just over an hour before each man left the room separately, leaving one by one, for the airport.

Doug looked over at Tony. "See it wasn't that bad, was it?"

"Hell no, not with news like that," Tony said scanning the lobby.

"Let's get some lunch. I'm starved."

"I'm for that Gov!" Doug said as they exited the hotel.

4

March 18th 2012
New Jersey

The two terrorists sat in a dilapidated office built inside the huge confines a rusty, deserted warehouse on the banks of the *Passaic* River. This relic of the past, a metal works facility, was now just a remnant of the manufacturing era that had long ago moved offshore. The building now served as a good hiding place for the two Islamic radicals who sat comfortably among empty packing crates covered with layers of dust. In front of them was the laptop computer taken from Syed Badawi, whom they had murdered; the encrypted messages had been decoded and both men were shocked at what they were reading. Not shocked that they were to carry out a devastating attack on the United States, but shocked at the actual target that had been chosen by their handlers.

"The streets of New York will flow with our enemies' blood, God willing." The Asian man whispered slowly as the totality of the message became clear and started to sink in.

"No, there will be very little blood, only dust and deadly radiation caused by the intense heat, my brother."

The thin Malaysian man, Tan Gaddam, had studied since childhood under radical Muslim religious Clerics in Malaysia. He had attended one of the many schools run by clerics that taught the radical side of Islam. The *Datuk School* was located in the lush, verdant hills that over looked Tan's hometown of Melaka. The school had been raided many times by the army in the days before the rise of the Islamic government. Tan had learned to hate the government that had been so friendly to the West. He had been horribly whipped with bamboo sticks more times than he could remember, then told to go home by government soldiers. But he had come back only to be tortured again and again for what he believed, the sacred word of Allah. He had also witnessed his teachers beaten for teaching the word of Allah and then thrown into jail, some never to return.

When the time came, Tan had jumped at the chance to infiltrate into the United States and work in a terrorist cell that would attack the infidels directly. He and Ali had been smuggled into America and their identities and identification papers had been carefully crafted; they simply assumed the identities of two other Muslim men who were citizens of the United States. As long as they stayed away from the airports and other sensitive checkpoints that were equipped with fingerprint and eye-scanning technology they would be safe from detection. Both men had been trained in Syria to assemble a small nuclear device with components that had been secretly smuggled into the United States. Other than their handlers back in Syria, Ali AL-Rubaie and Tan were the only two operatives in the United States that had knowledge of the attack. This nuclear detonation would be the most punishing attack to ever take place against the United States. This attack on American soil would be so damaging, so large in scale, so horrible, that it would overshadow every other disaster in American history.

Ali was from Syria and was an experienced fighter. He had taken part in numerous bombings and was in charge of the mission.

As Tan read the screen one last time, he was thrilled about what he had read but sadly recognized the fact that he was supposed to die in the attack. He would have to die because it had been ordered by his handlers; it was right there on the computer screen flickering in front of him. Even though he had prepared for this possibility, there had been other ways to carry out the plan, but apparently the planners wanted to take this extra measure to ensure total success. It would be the most devastating attack the world had ever experienced from Jihadist, and he was willing to die to guarantee the success of the attack. Since only he and Ali knew the details of the plan, total secrecy was ensured so there was a high probability the FBI wouldn't know what was coming. This would also provide that no one else could be interrogated to find out about the attack. Fortunately for them, the loop was now closed.

Both men were aware that any slip up could put the mission in jeopardy. That's why they had been forced to kill poor Syed in his apartment. He was expendable. Sure, it was an unpleasant act but a necessary one. Syed died as a Martyr for the good of Islam. What else could he want in this life? The plan called for only two men, dependent on each other, and in total secrecy, to carry out the attack. Tan was convinced that this one bold stroke, this one stab at the diseased heart of the infidel could crack the fragile American psyche. Tan and Ali had spoken for hours about how this single blow could drive Americans out of every major city in the United States, thus depriving the government of the necessary infrastructure to operate. The terror created by this attack would convince most Americans that living in the city, any city in the United States, would just be too dangerous. That was the plan, and the devastation of this weapon would make it a reality.

"These freaks, these sons and daughters of whores, will die by the thousands, God willing!" Ali said excitedly, after reading the message on the computer screen for a second time. Ali had been inspired by what he read, Tan thought, intently listening to every word. Tan had grown accustomed to the intensity that seemed to sweep over his partner now and again. After all, Ali was a volatile personality but able to fool anyone who came into contact with him into thinking that he was mild and meek, even a harmless man. But Ali was anything but harmless. He would not hesitate to kill another Muslim, just like he had brutally killed poor Syed. He would stop at nothing to further his aim of striking a devastating blow at the infidels. Their orders were clear, they had just been instructed to use the nuclear device they were assembling to blow up the United Nations building. The instructions also disclosed where the last and final component, the nuclear core, would be shipped and how. All they would have to do is secretly retrieve the component and complete the last phase of the activation process.

"I thought it would be the Empire State building or Madison Square Garden!" Tan said slowly "But the United Nations Building?"

"What does it matter? Half of the city will be reduced to radioactive dust, anyway!" Ali said as he took the DVD out of the computer, bent it in half with the force of his hands, and placed it in an empty coffee can. He added scraps of paper and wood that were lying around and took a single match, struck it, and dropped it into the coffee can. It wouldn't be long now, Ali thought, until the people of this sick and disgusting city would be burning in hell. He smiled as he watched the flames in the can flicker in front of him. The grounds of the United Nations and Manhattan would be useless for years in the future. These vile and unholy people who wanted to dominate the world deserved this horror, they deserved to die in this fiery hell, and they deserved their fate. It was fitting, Ali thought, that the infidels who had invented this technology would now die by it.

Ali continued to stare blankly at the fire flickering in the can and said, "this will be the largest attack ever made anywhere in the world, my brother, and we're the lucky ones who get to carry it out! Allah has truly blessed us…"

"Why do they want to detonate the bomb at the UN building? What's the purpose of this? They're not our target… I mean, there will be Muslims in the UN building?" Tan said cautiously.

"Its time, it's the next step, my brother. Without a doubt it's the next step! They will have to die for the cause of Islam. Besides, most of the Muslims who work there aren't on our side anyway. Ours is the true path of Islam. We can't allow weak non-believers stop us. The United States now controls the United Nations and they flaunt their power over the rest of the world and these so called Muslims help them do it. It will be a remarkable statement to turn the building into dust right before the eyes of the world." Ali still couldn't believe his good fortune. If he had been able to choose a target on his own, one that would have stricken fear in the world, it would have been the United Nations building. He now had orders to incinerate the headquarters of this bastion of stupidity. This was an attack against the entire West, not just the United States, but also the French, British, and all the rest of the puppets who bowed down to the American dogs"

"I think this is the most difficult target in New York that could have been chosen," Tan said apprehensively. "The UN building has better security than any other building in the city." He knew that Ali would not hesitate in killing him, too, if he even thought for a moment that he wasn't going to carry out his part of the attack.

"That's what makes it so special. If we can destroy it by making it ground zero, can you imagine the effect it will have on the morale of these infidels?"

Before Tan could answer, Ali said. "It will be psychologically devastating! It has to be ground zero and we will do it, God willing."

The acrid smell of burning plastic was starting to fill the room as the DVD melted in the flames.

"Take the hard drive out of the laptop and destroy it," Ali said.

"How should I destroy it?"

"Use the hammer from Syed's apartment."

The two men still had the hammer that Ali had used to kill him. The instrument of death had been washed and wiped clean with bleach. It was a precaution they had taken just in case, so there would be no DNA on it to connect them with Syed. The blood-splattered clothes worn by Ali had been dumped in a nearby storm drain. The plan was to dispose of the hammer in the Passaic River. No one would ever look there. Both men had worn leather-soled shoes. Leather shoes left very few identifiable tracks and were nearly impossible to trace. But those shoes were already drifting down the river, discarded like so much other trash that was in the river and would never be traced to them.

"Hurry up! Do it as fast as you can. We need to get rid of it. You never know when the authorities will break the door down and try to stop us. We don't want to leave anything behind they can use."

Tan was a slightly built and extremely intelligent man who knew the inner workings of computers. He had worked for a computer service company before being smuggled into the United States. In fact, he had dreamed of owning his own computer repair company in Malaysia before he had been assigned to train for this mission. Tan knew that this dream could never be realized, it wouldn't happen. He knew he couldn't survive the attack on the UN building, and he was resigned to his fate because it was his duty. His strength came from the way the Datuk School had indoctrinated him. He had come to believe that he was the powerful arm of Allah here on earth, here to swat the infidels with his power. When he was growing up, no one paid much attention to him at home. He wasn't considered acceptable by any of the girls in his hometown and had been ridiculed as a child because he wasn't big enough or strong enough to protect himself from the boys who bullied him. Except for his friends at the school, he had no others he could actually call friends. Outside of the school, he had been nobody, nothing but a miserable weakling, someone that others could push around. But after the attack, the whole world would know his part in this historic mission.

His photo would be flashed around the globe. His image would be feared and celebrated for all time, and he would use his brain, not his brawn, to accomplish this act of bravery. He would be held in high esteem and respected for his act in support of Islam throughout the Muslim world regardless of what they thought of him in his home town of Melaka.

Finally, after several minutes, Tan was able to get all the screws out of the computer so he could access the hard drive. Ali was in deep in thought, Tan noticed, probably thinking about some part of the attack plan, no doubt. He removed it from the laptop and set it down on the gray steel desk where he was working. He then methodically put the computer back together.

"Here's the drive," Tan said, standing and offering the drive to Ali.

"Just destroy it with the hammer where no one can read it."

"No, I'll throw it into the river." Tan didn't like taking a hammer and smashing sensitive computer parts into splinters. Computers were wonderful machines and, to him, simply throwing the drive into the river seemed a better option, after all the results would be the same.

Tan walked downstairs and out to the river's edge, being careful not to be seen. When he felt that he wouldn't be seen, he walked to the edge of the dock and tossed the hard drive into the turbid waters of the Passaic River. "There, it is done," Tan said quietly to himself. It just didn't feel right throwing a perfectly good hard drive into the water, but like other things that had to be done he did it. Tan took a moment to stand outside in the night air and think about the difficult task ahead of them. Nothing from this point on, next to his very own death, would be any more difficult than watching Syed being killed by Ali. Witnessing another human being struck with a hammer had been both shocking and repulsive. Unlike Ali, this was his first mission, and he had never been a part of killing before. Tan was committed and agreed in principle that it had to be done. Syed was a minor player, just someone to bring their instructions, nothing more. If there was anything about the mission that had caused him doubt, it was the killing of an innocent Muslim who only wanted to help. Although Tan had never met Syed before tonight, he knew he was a true believer or he wouldn't have taken such extraordinary risks to secure the secretly coded DVD. He wished the killing wouldn't have happened, but it did. Unlike Ali, Tan didn't think it was such an easy thing to do. For him killing another Muslim was difficult and unthinkable, but killing Syed had apparently been a part of the plan. Poor Syed should have been given the chance to choose the way he died, to have the glory of walking to his death and accepting it. Tan was now nauseated again from what he had witnessed. The whole scene kept coming back, the young Syed's blood soaking the rug and running off slowly covering the floor. The whole scene flooding his mind, the twitching body,

Syed lying on the floor, confused and dying. Tan had never thought he would have to kill Muslims. He had come here to kill Americans and he was having a difficult time understanding why he would have to kill more Muslims to do that. He secretly wondered, what would Allah think about the fact that he had killed Muslims?

Tan knew he must put Syed's death behind him and focus all his thoughts on the specific elements of the plan yet to be accomplished. Since the date of the attack was now set, just one part of the plan was left, to actually complete the final assembly of the bomb. All they needed to do now was install the core. That was it, then the bomb would be operational. The 23 kilograms of plutonium would be delivered somehow to a spot in the Atlantic Ocean five days from now where he an Ali would pick it up. It had been decided, by their handlers, that it was impossible to smuggle 23 kilograms of plutonium through any of their regular routes or into any United States commercial entry points. The US had stepped up its placement of nuclear sensing devices and now plutonium would have a high probability of being discovered. It had been calculated that there was a one-in-ten chance that the weapons-grade fission material would be found if it came in a cargo container. It would have to be hand delivered to them directly to have any reasonable chance of the core being smuggled into the United States. With thousands of miles of coastline on the East Coast, it would be virtually impossible to be detected if they were careful, Tan thought. As he stood in the cold night air, the next steps were running through in his mind.

Tan, while in Syria, had been told that the United States had concluded that a suitcase size nuclear device wasn't a real threat. So that kind of assessment would make their mission easier, the authorities weren't really looking for a nuclear device that compact. They believed this was simply impossible, because the amount of U-233 fissile material needed for a nuclear device could not be obtained. And they were right, but that was before China had become interested in the plan. It was before China decided to help the Jihadist for economic reasons, to help them in a way that no one could ever hold them responsible for. The bomb design that would destroy the UN building wouldn't fit into a suitcase, but it would fit nicely into a small delivery van. It had been designed to be as compact as possible but it still weighed four hundred pounds. The Jemaah Islamiya had purchased both the plan and the U-233 material from China. China's motivation had been simple, although China's strength in world trade was on the rise, there were always methods to speed things up. China viewed their clandestine support of the JI as a way to destroy the economic structure that made America so strong. It hadn't been China's first excursion into destabilization. They had supported Libya's nuclear program and Saddam Hussein's attempt to build a nuclear weapon as well. However, both attempts had ended in failures. Later they had lent support to Iran, which had enabled the Mullahs to develop nuclear weapons while Europe and the United States idly looked the other way, helpless to find a joint way to stop them. They had even helped North Korea, a risky strategy, since they shared a border. The Chinese never understood why the US, with its power, hadn't stopped either country from going nuclear, but believed it undermined their enemy.

The nuclear device that the Chinese developed and made available to the JI wasn't much different in design than the early W-54 Davy Crockett warhead or the 53 SADM (Small Atomic Demolition Munitions) produced by the United States Military. This tactical nuclear weapon had the explosive yield of ten thousand tons of TNT and used about twenty-three kilograms of nuclear fissile material to create the blast.

The two most difficult components of the nuclear device to smuggle into the United States was, of course, the plutonium but also the thin beryllium reflector needed to reduce the total mass of the system. This wouldn't be an easy task either. The reflector had been smuggled into the US directly from Malaysia in a container of metal lamps to be sold in a large discount department store chain. Free trade had its benefits. The nuclear device now sat partially completed under the foundation of the old warehouse. A concrete saw had been used to cut a rectangular hole in the warehouse floor. After the soil was excavated, and the sides of the hole shored up, Ali and Tan had stored the thermal nuclear device there, underground. The piece of the slab that had been removed was fitted so it could be slid back into place. With a little dirt swept back into the cracks, the hiding place was camouflaged from prying eyes. The plan was masterfully conceived, thanks to the policies of the US, which made them so vulnerable. Now the infidels would reap what they had sewn!

Tan suspected that the JI was allied with the Chinese, which was a strange partnership, he thought. He knew that the Chinese were bold and were no more afraid of shaping world affairs than the US had been during the last fifty years. Tan believed that every American citizen must know that their loss of power was inevitable, that war would eventually be fought on their soil. Surely, the politicians of America understood that if they could arm the likes of Saddam Hussein and other ruthless leaders in the world when it was in their best interest, then it would be fair for the Chinese to be able to shape policy in the same way. Tan believed there must have been dissenters in Peking who thought their actions dangerous and irresponsible, but apparently, their voices were drowned out in favor of those who wanted a new world order. It had been easy for him to figure out from the schematics that this bomb was the work of the Chinese. He then concluded that top planners in China believed that if the United States was able to track the plutonium back to China they had plausible deniability because China was only one among many countries that now that had plutonium U-233. If the nuclear material were somehow tracked back to them they would simply claim it had been stolen.

Tan believed the Chinese leaders must have come to the overwhelming conclusion that fighting a war to ensure world dominance was better fought through surrogates. It was just like the old days in Korea and Viet Nam. The new surrogates were the Jihadists who would attack and give up their lives for their cause, a cause that would help Chinese ambitions.

5

March 29th 2012
The Citadel
Charleston, S.C.

Outside, it was a brisk sunny day in Charleston; inside, Doug sat alone in a chair just left of the podium. He looked out over a sea of cadets as the President of The Citadel, Lieutenant General Marvin Adams, introduced him to the student body. This would be his first trip to South Carolina prior to the primary elections in June. McAllister Field House had been built long after he had graduated. Now he was back running for President of the United States. Every time he returned to The Citadel, memories good and bad came flooding back to him. He could recall all of the discipline of his first year as a Cadet Recruit. The Cadre, in their sacred quest to separate the weak from the strong, directed "Hell Week." All the self-doubt was the worst emotion Doug remembered as a "Knob, "as they were called that first year. He still remembered trying to shoulder the strict discipline that was handed down impatiently by upper classman, one rule at a time, Cadet to Cadet. Sadly, he recalled other young men, classmates, break under the stress, then opting to leave the Citadel knowing that the military way of life wasn't for them, their last emotional walk across the infamous quadrangle painted in the familiar red and white checkerboard pattern surrounded on all sides by the sandstone colored barracks. Those final last sad steps taken by poor kids who couldn't bear the constant pressure anymore had finally given up, heartbroken. Doug was proud that he had made it through all the trepidation and insecurity of that first difficult year when the Cadre used every trick in their book of cruel insults, to separate the weak from the strong.

As a military college, The Citadel was revered in the South as a place to learn discipline. Even after all these years, he still felt pride about going to the most prestigious private military college in history. Time and time again in Viet Nam, the discipline he had learned at The Citadel had kept him alive. He had also instilled trust in others, through tough discipline, which helped his men survive severe combat missions in the steaming jungles of Southeast Asia.

The Campus had changed, but old Stevens Barracks was still there. As a Knob, he remembered having to shine the brass plaque at the north entrance of his Barracks hundreds of times, where the sacred words of Robert E. Lee had been inscribed. He had never forgotten the quote: "*Duty is the sublimest word in the English language.*" In a political world so full of scandal and dishonesty, those words had served him well through the years.

Like most Colleges, even The Citadel had changed in small ways, but like the architectural design, the values of the college had never been tampered with. The indomitable tan colored walls of the buildings were the same. Tall, ominous fortress-like buildings still surrounded Summerall Field where the Corp of Cadets marched for Charleston tourists every Friday. Where pretty southern girls showed up to see their boyfriends march in their crisp grey and white uniforms. It was a place where accountability was still the most important issue on campus, and Cadets wanted to earn their rings. By modern American standards, it was a social enigma, a place where honor was more important than just getting ahead. It was a place where the improvement of self in many different ways was more important than merely improving in just a few. The Citadel, with its strict discipline and honor code, seemed to be an island in the middle of an ocean of chaos. A place frozen in time, clearly anachronistic, where beyond its gates the realities of life were very different than what they were inside. Perhaps this was never more evident than today, where more and more chaos prevailed, a world of fear, where acts of terror were dehumanizing the people of America, a place where no one was safe. But here, behind the walls of The Citadel, things really hadn't changed all that much.

Doug had graduated from the military college in the class of 1973. After leaving the school, he had served a single tour in the Marine Corp in Viet Nam. The war had been difficult for him because he had known so many young men that had died in a war Washington wasn't committed to winning. By the time he had made it to Saigon, the war had already been lost. So many young lives had been taken, and a war lost because of Washington politics. Future wars had been shaped by the government's failures in Viet Nam. Today, politicians were acutely aware that the people would never stand for long and protracted wars. The terrorists had also learned this since the days of Iraq. Any military engagement or campaign had to be quick and victorious or it would become negative political news to be exploited by one's political opponents, at home and abroad. As far as Doug Ferguson was concerned, it was America that had changed.

Of course, most people still wanted to be free, but very few were willing to lose their sons or daughters to preserve that freedom. That was the way it was, and that was the way it was going to be, until the problem with radical Islam was solved. But more and more people in America were unwilling to die for foreign countries that seemingly didn't care. The American ideology of "*all people want freedom*" wasn't at the forefront of American politics any longer. That idea had died a slow death on the battlefields of the Middle East. It had been replaced by a more practical view of protecting the homeland and letting others decide how they would be governed. This was despite the free elections in Afghanistan and Iraq. Those had come and gone and still the terrorist threat remained.

Finally, Lieutenant General Marvin Adams finished his splendid introduction of Doug Ferguson. Applause erupted as the Governor was given a warm cadet welcome.

"Good Morning," he said, as he looked out over a thousand crisply clad Cadets.

"Good Morning, Sir!" the Cadets answered in unison like thunder reverberating through the building. The entire field house then erupted again into wild applause for someone they considered one of their own. After several minutes the Cadets seated themselves.

"Gentlemen, the protection of our coveted Democracy will someday be in your hands! Your steadfast belief and dedication in freedom and our system of government will prevail…" Once again over a thousand Cadets stood and applauded demonstrating their support for Doug Ferguson.

"Well-Come-Back! Well-Come-Back! Well-Come-Back!" the students chanted in deep masculine voices as they clapped their white-gloved hands in unison so popular with Citadel Cadets when supporting one of their own.

Doug raised his hands in the air over the lectern and, with palms down, signaled the young Cadets to be seated.

"Today more than at any other time in history freedom for America is in peril. Americans are losing personal freedoms every day by those who oppose the very concept of freedom. The time has come to politely ask countries that support terrorists to stop! The time has come to politely ask the citizens of these countries that support terrorists to stop! Again, applause erupted this time with *"Give them hell! Give them hell! Give them hell!* The former Governor let Cadets go on for a minute because he enjoyed being back in front of such motivated and patriotic young men and women.

"Because we have lost freedoms that are part of the very fabric of our nation, I'm running for President of the United States as a proud member of the Freedom Party! A new Party that will stand up for the American people and their basic freedoms!"

After the applause finally died down, Doug continued. "When elected to office I will immediately organize a Terror Control Center or TCC, as it will be called, which will monitor nations who are suspected of supporting terrorism against Americans here or abroad. This new agency will be in contact with leaders of these countries on a minute-to-minute basis if needed to 'politely' ask them to take action against those who are plotting against the people of the United States!" Doug was starting to get into stride and felt confident about the speech. "The TCC will be an agency comprised of members of the appropriate branches of government that can respond to dangers immediately, not months or years later!" He continued forcefully while making constant eye contact with Cadets in the audience.

"My plan will put immediate and constant pressure on rogue regimes to round up their terrorist elements, immediately, or face the full power of the United States! In some cases, the TCC will respond with a range of offensive actions from mandatory financial sanctions to blockading the entire country and, of course, we will never pull the military option off the table. The difference in my initiative is that rogue nations will have only a matter of hours, not years, to make a decision. We will stop the diplomatic shell game and alliances that are made by other countries to undermine our freedoms!" Again, the speech was interrupted by applause, and Doug waited for the Cadets to be seated. "We will cut off aid to countries that receive billions of American dollars while failing to jail and prosecute terrorists who freely walk around their country. This message will be made with perfect clarity! Round up your terrorists or we will treat your country as an enemy of the United States. My administration will make it clear that if we have to utilize military force, it will not be in the form of a protracted war! We have lost too many brave American soldiers searching for terrorists in every dark corner of the world. When elected, it will not be the responsibility of our military to track down terrorists in countries on foreign soil. It will become the responsibility of the nations who support and harbor terrorist to now crack down on these groups. The world must understand that the American people and my administration will not tolerate attacks on our soil without immediate retribution.

"I will introduce legislation to put pressure on all fronts to change the behavior of these countries that support terrorists. The leaders of these countries will have fundamental choices to make. They can choose freedom for their people, the freedom to flourish with no worry of having the United States as an enemy, or they can choose to continue down their dangerous path of self-destruction. They can choose either option, but the consequences of an immediate response from the TCC will loom dangerously on their horizon. There will be no special list. Any country that we suspect is sponsoring or harboring terrorists will have the same appropriate sanctions put in place against them, regardless of whatever nations rise up in support of them. Some will say this is unilateralism and saber-rattling, but we Americans must protect ourselves from those who want to destroy us. It is time that we recognize, as a nation, that this Republic is in clear and undeniable danger. This danger can no longer be tolerated and begs for immediate action, not denials. You have heard it said that 'justice delayed is justice denied.' If I am elected to serve as your president justice will prevail!" The cadets erupted again into a thunderous ovation. Doug continued his inspiring oratory, playing to his receptive audience to those young men and ladies who would enforce this policy.

"I have a message for any country thinking of such an attack: Don't! We must ensure that our country is in a position where we can hit our enemies hard and leave them unable to strike back. After the War on Terror has been won, I will support a new international policy of less involvement in world affairs. Then, and only then, can we concentrate on building a better America. But not until these threats no longer exist." Again, applause broke out as more than a thousand Citadel Cadets stood and applauded. They supported a member of their own "*Long Gray Line*" as they called their graduates. On several more occasions, his speech was interrupted by applause. The speech lasted for a brief forty-five minutes. As he left the field house, it was to the sound of loud applause, then followed by the masculine chants of "Give'm hell, Doug!," "*Give'm hell, Doug*!" which echoed out through the open doors of the field house and could be heard at the far end Summerall Parade Field.

Doug was confident that this was one of the best speeches he had ever delivered. Most of the national media people were there to cover his speech. The new interest had been generated by growing poll numbers. Doug was making it more and more difficult for congressional leaders to explain their unyielding support for countries that were not cooperating in rounding up terrorists. Many people were now convinced that multinational companies, especially oil companies, had too much influence over the government. The average American citizen was beginning to believe that America was being sold out because of politicians' dependency on special interest groups.

The policy speech at The Citadel was the perfect political venue to send a simple message that terrorism was the number one problem facing the country in this century. Much had been done, much had been tried, but nothing had really worked. The speech had ended in a standing ovation by the Cadets. After shaking hands with the various members of the school's officer corps, he then unceremoniously departed for the city.

"Good delivery! Great speech, Chief," Cliff said. He was riding next to Doug in the black suburban as they exited *Lesesne Gate* and made a left on Elmwood Street.

"They loved you, boss." Tony added as he leaned forward from the back seat.

"It really felt good to get back here again. Was the message clear enough?"

"Yeah, I think so. Now we've got to hustle and start shaking "paws" in South Carolina; that needs to be a top priority. We also to need to stay on the heels of the Democratic candidates until the June primaries," Cliff said.

"How much time do we have before the CNN interview?" Doug asked, as he occasionally looked out over at the low-lying Ashley River.

"We have about twenty minutes." Cliff said.

As Doug drove the suburban down Lockwood Street toward the downtown marina, many memories came rushing back. He used to run this same route, along the Ashley River, during his daily workouts at the Citadel. Most Cadets ran this way to enjoy the scenery. Doug could still recall how calm and organized his life had been at the military school. All that had changed when he landed on a *Tiger Air* Boeing 707 flight to Viet Nam. Except for the weather, Charleston's geography resembled Viet Nam's. From the SUV, the low-lying marshlands and the brackish Ashley River seemed strangely similar.

Within a few seconds, Doug was lost in his thoughts. Inside the car it was quiet, the only sound was the constant hum of the tires rolling over the rough pavement. Suddenly, he was transported back to the war; he heard the whine of incoming mortar rounds and the controlled chaos of a landing chopper to evacuate the wounded. He couldn't forget the eerie stillness of the jungle after the choppers flew away leaving his platoon alone and vulnerable. Only after they pounded the air with their powerful rotors and disappeared over the canopy of the jungle did the animals resume their hollow calls. A soldier in Viet Nam quickly learned that the sound of the jungle was good. It was when there were no sounds that a solider had to worry!

"Are you thinking about your interview? I can help you prepare if you like." Cliff said, as he scrolled down the screen on his laptop not looking up to see if Doug had heard him.

"No, I'm not really thinking about anything." Doug said, not wanting to share his thoughts about Viet Nam.

After a moment of silence, he asked Cliff, "how long has it been since the last attack?"

"About three months. The last attack was on my mother's birthday." Cliff said looking up from his computer with interest.

"So it has been about ninety days, since these guys have blown something up?"

"Yeah, I understand the President is going to make political hay on this topic in the next couple of weeks, you know, saying his anti-terror programs are working."

"It's been too long!" Doug said slowly, as he turned the suburban on to East Bay.

"Yeah, I know what you're saying."

"It's been too long without hearing something out of these murderers. I don't think they've packed up and gone home…do you?"

"No, but maybe the CIA and the FBI are doing a better job. That's a possibility, right?"

"Maybe, but I think it's something else."

"I know what you're going to say," Cliff said, as he closed his laptop to give Doug his full attention.

"If my memory is correct we have averaged about one attack per month, right?"

"Yeah, I think that's accurate." Cliff confirmed.

"We are told that we have terrorist cells all over the country, probably some are our own neighbors, right?"

"That's what they keep telling us," Cliff said.

"So why have they stopped their attacks all of a sudden? I can think of two or three plausible reasons. One might be that the FBI has slowed things down like you said. Second, we've killed so many of them that there is a shortage of bad guys out there, which is highly doubtful. Or last, a much larger attack is being planned and they want to lure us into a false sense of security, you know, like the programs are really working."

"So this could be the calm before the storm, right?" Cliff added.

"Yeah, it could be..." Doug said, as he pulled the SUV up to the front of Charleston Place Hotel. The cobblestone entrance was typical of Charleston's beautiful colonel past.

The hotel lobby was small, a beautifully restored Charleston hotel. The building was very old and had been converted to a luxury, five-star hotel under the guidance of The Charleston Preservation Society. Tony got out of the vehicle first and walked around to the driver's door and then opened it for Doug. As he checked the front seat for his notes, he tossed the keys to him.

"Cliff, see if you can find out anything about the lull in action. These guys must have a reason to stop killing,"

Doug said, as he climbed out of the front seat looking at the old hotel he had stayed in numerous times.

"Done," Cliff said, thinking about sources that might give him that information.

"Nice place, Boss," Tony said, looking up and down the street for anything unusual, as he got out of the SUV.

"Yeah, I love it here. I wish we could stay longer. I could take you to some of the local watering holes where we use to hang out as Cadets."

"Probably not wild enough for me, Boss, besides, I'd rather go fishing early in the morning. I've heard the fishing is pretty good off Folly Beach."

"That would be nice, wouldn't it?" Doug said, as he hurried up the steps into the lobby.

"You know I agree with what you were saying; these bastards have stopped killing for a reason. I've been thinking about it too. You know, it's just like Iraq; every time you think you're going to get a lull in the action, they hit you. I feel the same thing."

Although Tony knew this was an important political outing, he was still excited about having visited his first military college. The Military College of South Carolina, The Citadel, was impressive and gave him valuable insight into his boss. No wonder he liked things neat and orderly! Tony thought the Marines had been demanding, but these kids could have given any military organization a run for their money, maybe even taught them a thing or two.

The interview was set up through a local affiliate in Charleston. The satellite linkup would be provided to the network and be a live feed to the interviewer back in New York. A conference room had already been set up with chairs and a table where Doug would be wired for the interview. Someone from the campaign staff had already put campaign posters behind the table and chairs so they could be seen during the course of the interview.

In the Presidential suite, John and Ben sat watching the large plasma screen mounted above the rustic fireplace. The image of Doug was clear and lifelike, as if he was sitting in the room. The news anchor was Kenna Adams, a highly rated news reporter with a knack for getting to the point. Ben was confident in Doug's ability to hold up to the rigors of the interview. He had prepped for the tough questions concerning the viability of his candidacy. It was the impression of both men that Ms. Adams had thrown Doug a couple of political softballs that he hit out of the park. As the two men closely followed the interview, the question they had both been waiting for, was finally asked. "Do you think the absence of terror attacks in the United States over the past ninety days means our intelligence agencies are doing a better job?"

"Well, I hope so," Doug said. "That's what we all want, of course, but having said that, I believe our government has a long way to go in solving this problem. Sadly, I believe we are only dealing with the symptoms, rather than the causes."

Both men had sat on the edge of their seats hoping he would be able to bring up their plan of a real-time *Terrorist Control Center.* As they nervously waited, the question came.

"What about your proposed TCC initiative? How could this possibly slow the spread of terror in this nation? As I understand, you are proposing a new government agency with intelligence, diplomacy, and the military under one roof so they can make real-time decisions. How would this work and why does the country need it? Isn't it just replicating other agencies?"

"Ah, there it is! Now the entire country will hear about our proposal," Ben said.

"Yeah, let's see what he does with it!" John said nervously.

"We can no longer deal with dangerous real-time situations over the course of weeks or even months. My proposal would put decision makers from all agencies in one room, at the same time, to deal with all international terror fronts simultaneously. In this way, we can utilize our intelligence to solve these problems with diplomacy, trade sanctions, or with our military forces. We can be in touch with terrorist nations in real time." Ms. Adams had graciously allowed Doug, the underdog third party candidate, the time to elaborate on his proposal for about two minutes.

"That's a home run, John!" Ben said. For the first time their party's most important political idea to control terrorism had hit the airways.

"I think he did a good job," John said excitedly, glued to the screen.

"Yeah, he did, now all we have to do is wait patiently and see what the other candidates have to say."

This whole idea was Ben's, not the specifics, but the idea of having a bold proposal that the other candidates would have to respond to, to throw an innovative idea out there and let the other presidential candidates respond to it. In this way, Ben believed his candidate could gain some semblance of legitimacy.

Doug was more than holding his own. He was coming across folksy, intelligent, and Presidential.

"I think Ms. Adams is somewhat enamored of our candidate," John said, smiling.

"I think you're right. She's giving him plenty of freedom to respond without asking more tough questions. We don't need tough questions right now, trust me."

Just as quickly as the interview started, it ended, leaving Ben and John satisfied that Doug had changed the political landscape, at least for now. All they had to do now was wait and see what the country thought.

6

March 29th 2012
Charleston, S.C.

The interview had the intended impact. Three of the four candidates had taken little time to respond to Doug's proposed shuffling of government resources. Their comments ranged from "impossible" all the way to "an irresponsible act" against the Constitution of the United States. For the past seventy-two hours, the idea of a twenty-four-hour manned TCC as it was now being popularized by the media, was becoming the main topic of the air waves. Bart was beside himself about the media coverage. A good idea had turned into an important political ploy, and now all the other candidates were responding to it. Doug was really in the race, now, since the entire fields of candidates had to come out with their own positions on the proposal. This was considered a radical new approach to counter terrorism and it was getting the kind of press they needed. The Freedom Party was now part of the legitimate political landscape, which it hadn't been before Doug's proposal.

Leonce had come to Charleston the day after Doug's national interview, which was carried by most of the cable networks. He had read a statement to the local press made by the new fundamentalist Muslim regime in Kuala Lumpur. According to the *New York Times* article, the Malaysian spiritual leader named Ahamad Al-Wahb, the leader of the extremist group Jemaah Islamiya, was quoted as saying "We must rise up and continue our vicious attacks against America." More importantly, this frightening statement was echoed by Najib Putra the new President of Malaysia. He was quoted in Kuala Lumpur as saying, "we must support our brothers to defeat the Great Satan." The intelligence community agreed that President Putra was calling on terror cells to attack American interests. This was a serious development. No government leader had ever come out and asked terrorists to attack, worldwide, at once. Leonce, as one of the official leaders of the Freedom Party, was speaking nightly about the deteriorating condition of international policies against terrorism. His down-home way of explaining how the United States was being sold out by the two-party system here at home, and why Europe didn't care anymore, was having an effect.

Doug had made it clear at the same local press conferences that the situation with Iran and Malaysia were typical of the kinds of problems the current administration either couldn't or wouldn't deal with. He had gone further in the interview than anyone thought he might by making an extraordinarily concise argument about why institutions like the United Nations couldn't deal with these kinds of threats and didn't want to. He also made the statement that "...the present administration wouldn't make any real substantive moves against the countries that were supporting terrorism against the homeland." Doug made the point that he was convinced that terrorists had been emboldened by the fact that they acted as individuals and couldn't be connected directly to specific governments that supported them. That was the crux of the problem, Doug had argued. Terrorists were being funded by rogue nations, but not officially. This was a perfect situation for the terrorists and those who supported them. Many, worldwide, now believed, and terrorists sensed that they were winning the war. Most terrorist organizations were convinced the United States no longer had the ability to carry out "Nation Building." More and more renegade governments were starting to overtly support terrorist actions abroad and doing so for one obvious reason, they felt the United States could no longer respond effectively.

The burden of proof that was necessary under international law was almost impossible to obtain, and any move to put sanctions into place or use a coalition of military forces against governments proven to be supporters of terrorist only ended in frustration. So terrorist groups capitalized on the clandestine support of the growing number of Muslim governments worldwide that were popping up like weeds to support individual terrorists. Even when rogue governments announced to the world they supported terrorism, they still couldn't be connected to actual terrorist activities. So their leaders were untouchable, no matter what they said publically. Of course, their words were meant to cause fear on American streets. It appeared too many that the most powerful weapon in the terrorist arsenal was the present administration's willingness to play fair and be accountable for actions against innocent people held hostage by the Mullahs in the Middle East. Since wars hadn't been won, appeasement was adopted by the current administration. The President's policy had only encouraged a more unified approach by rogue nations against the United States. Countries like France were so desperate for oil to feed their economies that any kind of sanctions on countries like Venezuela only served to drive up the price of oil and therefore be unacceptable to most of Europe. Doug believed that the United States was now in a box that was impossible to escape from, especially through appeasement. Because of the current situation, the President and Congressional leaders understood there would be no help from Europe on cracking down on countries like Iran, even though they supported the efforts of Islamic radicals. In fact, Doug was convinced that Europe's interest in cheap oil had even persuaded them to look the other way as Iran had developed nuclear technologies even when the missiles were going to be pointed right at them.

The Governor had traveled from one end of South Carolina to the other speaking about the threats on American freedom. Many of the people he met on the campaign trail had either read the article in the *New York Times* about Al-Wahb or heard about it. The comments made by President Najib Putra had left most people stunned, since attacks had rarely been supported by official governments before. The depth of the resolve of the Muslim world was just now starting to sink into the collective minds of the American people. It was clear to most that the war was almost over, and America had lost.

Although President Putra's statement was a direct threat to the United States, other Muslim countries had started to issue similar kinds of statements, although not as direct as his. It was an act of defiance meant to demonstrate solidarity and resolve among Muslim nations. The messages were clear: "are you ready to go to war with the whole Muslim world, two billion strong?" Just weeks earlier, Mullahs in Iran had issued similar statements that they were fully supporting, as a nation, the Jihad against the American people. The intelligence agencies had always known the real Iranian position, but what was different now was that the government itself was issuing war-like statements, emboldened by their new arsenal of nuclear weapons. Any attack against Iran could potentially shut down the region's oil supply crippling not only Europe's primary oil supply but mainland China as well. The whole globe had been turned into a chess board with oil rigs as its pieces.

At home, the economy had weakened and the debt had continued to grow as money got siphoned out of the economy to support the war and had weakened the dollar abroad. For the President to make a decision to attack another Muslim country seemed to be, even to the most hawkish of leaders, a folly. The government had learned, through one horrible mistake after another, that as soon as the war was won somewhere in the world, the real cost became the reconstruction of the countries that had been destroyed by the fighting. This cost, in hundreds of billions of dollars, had grown unacceptable to American taxpayers. "Nation Building" had become the number one reason for the failing economy of the United States. As if that was not bad enough, any chance of a free and democratic government after the war had to overcome the power struggles that invariably broke out between each Muslim sect. These various terrorist groups chose to murder each other, rather than settle their differences peacefully and come together to unite under one goal, to cripple the economy. It was a Catch-22 and no one seemed to have a viable escape from this conundrum, at least until now.

Doug sat at the antique cherry wood desk in his hotel suite watching TV. The CNN broadcast was about his TCC proposal and several analysts were discussing its pros and cons. He was, along with Tony, waiting on John Tolbert to come meet them for dinner. They had reservations at one of the finer Charleston restaurants. Ben and Cliff would join them later. Charleston was a comfortable place, and Doug was enjoying his short stay, but he was ready to get on to Michigan with a stop in

Montgomery in between. With their new strategy and momentum, he wanted to move quickly and start building a base among Michigan voters. There wasn't much time to get around the entire state of Michigan, and he wanted to get started as quickly as possible before the primaries began in earnest.

There was a single knock on the door.

"I'll get it. It's probably John," Tony said, as he moved towards the door.

Tony pulled his coat over his pistol but left it unbuttoned then opened the door.

"I have a note for the Governor, sir," the man said as he handed the large brown envelope to Tony.

"Thanks." Tony reached in his pocket to tip the young man. As he pulled his coat back the bellman saw the black pistol that was only partially hidden.

"It's isn't necessary," he said nervously. "Thank you anyway sir."

"Are you sure?" Tony asked, as he shoved a folded twenty-dollar bill towards him.

"Quite sure," he said as he turned and walked quickly away.

He closed the door then walked over and handed the brown envelope to his boss.

"I believe that cannon of yours scared the kid out of his wits; it wouldn't hurt to keep that Glock covered up around regular people," Doug said.

"Hey, that's my job, boss, to get respect. That's what I'm doing—"

Doug looked at the envelope from one side then the other. "It must have been hand delivered to the hotel, there's no postmark."

He carefully opened the folded flap on the end. Inside was a small piece of white lined paper and nothing else. He pulled the paper out and began to read.

> **I saw your interview on all the networks. You're right! Something needs to be changed. I hope you succeed. A large-scale attack is imminent! The government knows who is behind the potential attack, but no agency is doing enough to stop it. No agency is doing enough to prevent the attack! No bad guys in the cross hairs at the moment.**

"Tony, go down to the front desk and see if you can find out who delivered this—" Doug handed the envelope back to him and then folded the note and put it into his shirt pocket.

"Right away." Tony took the envelope moved quickly to the door and then disappeared.

Doug was confused for a moment about the contents of the note. His first thought was that it might be a political trick to undermine his campaign, or maybe some crazed schizophrenic blabbering about the latest voice reverberating in his head. But his gut told him it was probably someone on the inside, CIA or maybe FBI. If it was someone on the inside, that was the scary part.

Tolbert knocked on the door, after Tony left and let himself in.

"Take a look at this—" Doug said, handing the note to John. "I just got it a second ago."

"Hmm, looks like we have a talker on our hands, a whistle blower maybe—" he said sitting down on the sofa and studying the note for a couple of more seconds.

"So you think we might have a disgruntled insider?"

"Probably an analyst would be my guess," John said, handing the note back to Doug.

"What would make you think that?" Doug asked.

"No one else would write something like this. This person is upset. He is supplying information because no one is doing enough to stop what he believes is inevitable."

"What about a mentally deranged person who's a little paranoid at the moment!"

"Maybe, it could be a little of both," John said, shrugging his shoulders. "But I don't think so; this stuff happens a lot in state government as you know, some do-gooder trying to make things right."

"Yeah, but this is different. This person is taking a hell of a chance here. I mean if he really is an insider in one of the intelligence agencies or even the administration," Doug said. He folded the note in half and put it in his brief case for safe keeping. "This guy could do some serious jail time over something like this!"

"Well, what's a couple of thousand lives worth, if he really thinks he knows something? What kind of chance would you take to save innocent people from being slaughtered, especially if no one seems to be listening and you were convinced that something terrible is about to happen?"

"I see your point."

"Yeah, this guy obviously doesn't care anymore, if he is an insider. A hell a lot of people are fed up right now. I've seen that right here in South Carolina. People are afraid. It seems to me like whoever wrote this sees hope in our party for whatever reason. That's why he is contacting us. Trust me that's what this is."

"What about a political trick?" Doug asked.

"For what purpose, to get you to go on television and warn people, look like a fool in front of millions of people? No, whoever wrote this note knows the game isn't played that way, especially at this level. No, my guess is, that it's a frustrated insider trying to help us and at the same time get some self satisfaction."

"Okay what do we do?" Doug asked. He trusted John more than anyone else.

John finished chewing and swallowing peanuts he had been eating from a silver tray on the conference table. "Nothing at all; let's just wait and see what the guy sends us next—"

"What about just handing the note over to the FBI?"

"Hell no."

"Why not?"

"Because there is no political certainty of what would happen if you turned it over. There could be a leak to the press, then your opponents could say that you planted the message for political benefit. Hell, they could say anything they wanted. This whole thing could be too politically open-ended. No, we need to keep it for a while. However, I do think we should put the note in another envelope addressed to the FBI, and hold on to it for a while. You know, CYA," John said, as he threw more peanuts into his mouth.

"So it looks like we were about to send it to the FBI?" Doug asked.

"Exactly. It shows intent! Are you sure you don't have a law degree?"

"I don't need one. I've got you," Doug said, smiling.

"Let's just keep it around for a while longer. I also think it would be a good idea for you to go to the front desk, personally, and address the new envelope while the clerk is looking on," John added.

"I'll do that."

"You want a beer?" John asked. He had gotten up and gone to the wet bar in the room and was bent over looking at what brands had been stocked in the bar refrigerator.

"Yeah, I could use one. Let me have whatever you're drinking—"

As John checked the refrigerator, Tony returned from the front desk.

"What'd you find out?" Doug asked curiously.

"Whoever delivered the envelope must have left it at the front desk and disappeared. I also checked around with the staff and no one saw anything. A young lady named Judy found the envelope and sent it up."

"Did you ask around the lobby to see if anyone else saw anything?"

"There wasn't anyone in the lobby to ask. The place is as empty as a hen house with the door left open."

"I don't think this person was going to hang around waiting to be seen," John said, as he pulled a couple of bottles of Heineken out of the refrigerator and gave one to Doug.

"Yeah, I agree with John, whoever left that envelope here is long gone by now," Tony said.

"What about the house video cameras?" Doug asked.

"I'm working on that. There are plenty of cameras on the property, but none aimed at the front desk. I've ask the manager to check the rest for someone carrying an envelope."

"It wouldn't matter. This guy would have disguised himself," John said.

"You're probably right, but I would still like to see what the guy looks like," Doug countered. He couldn't get the note off his mind. It was an eerie reminder of something he already knew. It had been much too long without some kind of an attack.

7

March 30th 2012
Flint, Michigan

Doug relaxed in an antique yoke-back chair near the window as sunlight streamed in from outside. As he gazed around his surroundings, everything looked frighteningly familiar. This room appeared just like all the rest, lavish and comfortable, but of course, not home, and home is where Doug wanted to be. Traveling the campaign trail had him staying in an endless line of hotel rooms, which were melding into one. This suite had a spacious bedroom with an adjoining conference room with the usual theme-related décor. Here, in the state of Michigan, the hotel room was artfully decorated with paintings of the Chippewa Indians hunting the snow covered wilds of the Michigan peninsula. Doug's schedule was grueling, but that wasn't the worst of it, more personal criticisms were boiling in from his political opponents. His proposals were starting to gain traction and this was making him a lightning rod for criticism. It had always been hard for him to deal with political criticism, even in the past, but he reluctantly accepted it as part of the process and knew more criticism would be coming his way.

The phone rang, but Doug didn't answer it immediately. At the moment, he was caught up in his own self doubt, something that was relatively new for him, something he hadn't allowed for in the beginning. He stared at the phone a moment longer, as it continued to ring angrily. Then, finally, he leaned over and picked it up.

"Hello."

"Is this Governor Ferguson?"

"Yeah, who's this?"

"I'm the person who sent you that nice little note in Charleston," the caller said in a muffled voice.

"Why didn't you hang around? We could have talked," Doug said disarmingly.

"I couldn't, you know that…"

"Where are you getting your information?" Doug asked.

"I can't tell you that, but listen to me, I won't say this twice. I'm in a position to know. You have to trust me. I have information indicating there is going to be a large scale attack!"

"When?"

"I don't know the exact date but my guess it will be before the end of the year."

"And who is going to be responsible for this attack?"

"It will be an Islamic country supporting the attack, but terrorists will actually be responsible. My guess is the Malaysian government and probably instigated by President Putra!"

"Why don't you call the authorities? How can I possibly help you?"

"Let's say for now, they know all this, but they don't have enough information to act."

"Again, what can I do?" Doug said a little frustrated.

"I've studied your business— I know your company has operations in Malaysia"

"We did, but not any longer. We've pulled out. Too many complications, too much instability."

"You still have contacts there, right? Probably in high places...why don't you use your contacts to see what you can find out? I'm convinced their government is going to be involved in this."

Doug's impression was that the caller was knowledgeable and credible.

"Listen, I'm not sure what you want from me?"

"I think you can find some things out, that's all I'm suggesting!"

"How's that?"

"You know people over there that trust you. You can get information, just get it."

"Who are you working for?" Doug demanded.

"That's not important, but if you want to help me stop all this, and I believe you can, just use your contacts in Malaysia and try and get information you can use."

"I'm sorry I can't do that," Doug said emphatically.

"You will if you're serious about saving the lives of innocent Americans! You haven't had enough yet? We now have terrorists on our streets for God's sakes. We've got our own home-grown crazies, who aren't even Muslims, blowing things up to make a point. Hell, now even Hollywood is doing movies with terror themes and making millions as the American people suffer. Where does it all end, Governor, can you tell me that?" The callers voice was strained and passionate.

"Why don't we start by telling me who you are and then maybe we can work together on this," Doug pleaded, but the phone line went dead.

Frustrated, Doug sat for a moment with the phone still at his ear. Nothing the caller had said was untrue. Hell, it was all true. The major change in tactics by Islamic extremists was paying huge dividends and, at the moment, the government had no way of responding to it. He slowly put the phone back on the receiver and called a meeting at the hotel.

Doug immediately called John, Leonce, and Tony to his suite. While he waited, he watched a local television program that was reporting some new polling data. The results were good; apparently, he had picked up some new support. Two polls showed the party with around thirteen percent of the vote nationally if the election was today. It was clear to him, the TCC initiative was resonating among voters, not only in Michigan but across America. It was an idea that had taken hold because people were afraid and fed up. They desperately needed something to grasp that might stop the madness that was now at their backdoor steps. The idea of having a Terrorist Control Center that could act immediately anywhere in the world to save lives had given the party a boost. Later today, he would be holding a town hall meeting at the Farmer's Market. There he would take the time to outline his programs for agriculture, but he would save more time to defend his TCC proposal, confident his comments would make front page newspapers across the country.

Within minutes, all three men had arrived and were seated at the conference table waiting for Doug to begin.

"As you know, I received a phone call minutes ago apparently from the same person who sent the envelope in Charleston," Doug said, as he took a seat at the end of the long oak table. All three men could see he was worried. The drapes were open and sunlight was flooding in, seemingly contrasting Doug's demeanor.

"Well what'd he say?" Leonce asked, while pulling a legal pad out of his brief case.

"Basically the same thing! He believes that we are going to be attacked and that it will be the new Putra government who'll be responsible."

"Did he say where he was getting this information?" John asked.

"No, but he said the authorities knew about the possibility of an attack but didn't have enough information to act, or maybe politically don't want to act, because nothing can be confirmed."

"My God, who in the hell is this guy?" Leonce asked.

"He wouldn't say, but he claims he's connected with the US authorities."

"But he wouldn't say exactly who, of course," Leonce asked making notes.

"Pal, I really pressed him on it. Believe me, but he's not saying—"

"You know his phone number can be linked to yours here in the room, not that he would use a number that could be traced back to him," Leonce said.

"Yeah, I think we might need to bring in the FBI, what do you think, John?"

"Sure, but let's call Bart and Benny first. I want to know what they think."

"Damn right, they need to know he's made contact again." Leonce said, nodding in agreement.

Both men were immediately contacted by phone. After some discussion, they both agreed that it was time to call the authorities.

"What do you think Leonce, should we really involve the FBI or not? There might be some political consequences," John said, one final time directing his question to Leonce.

He might be a Bible belt cowboy from north Louisiana, but John had learned to trust his political sense. If there was anything they could gain politically from this it would be Leonce that would figure it out, and Bart was even better politically.

"I think what we have here is a young, intelligent guy that nobody is listening to at one of the agencies," Leonce said slowly, as he leaned back.

"That's what I'm thinking. Why's he giving us this information? Why not tell one of the other candidates?" John asked.

"Maybe he has. Maybe he is telling everyone who will listen," Leonce said. He dropped his pen on the legal pad and pushed away from the conference table. "That means we better do the same thing; otherwise, it could look bad for us down the road."

"I think he's telling us because he is being ignored by his superiors and he's not the kind of dude to take no for an answer," Doug added.

"Yeah, that's all great, but that doesn't answer my question, why us?" John asked.

"Just what he said, he wants help from Doug. He thinks the governor can find out things he can't, because of Ferguson Industries' history of doing business in Malaysia. He's working like a CIA agent if you ask me. Remember back in the cold war when businessmen suspected of being CIA agents were arrested in communist countries? Well, most of those guys were working with the CIA," Leonce continued.

"Can you get information?" John asked.

"We might be able to, it's possible," Leonce answered.

"Why not try then?" John asked.

"Yeah, I agree with John. If we could help foil some kind of plot it could only be good for the campaign. It might even put you in the front seat for once," Leonce added.

"There is certainly a high probability that the other candidates have been informed by our caller, right? If that is the case, they'll probably contact the FBI too. That means we need to contact them too. If we don't, it might appear that we don't care or, worse yet, that we don't want to cooperate with the authorities. We could leave ourselves open for all kinds of criticism for not doing the responsible thing," Doug said.

"He hasn't told anyone else, believe me. We would have heard about it by now," Leonce said emphatically.

"I really don't think it matters at this point who this guy has spoken to. If we don't inform someone in government, we could leave ourselves open to all kinds of political attacks if something bad happens," Doug said.

"As weird as that is, you're right," John added.

"If we do that, the information is going to stop. Make sure you understand this. The FBI will find this guy before we can use it to our advantage," Leonce warned.

"Well, at the moment, this information really isn't doing anyone any good, is it?" Doug responded.

"I think this guy might be trying to help us win the election too," Leonce said.

"That's a possibility, but what would he get out of it?" John asked.

"Satisfaction, job promotion, who knows?" Leonce answered. "But I think he wants to help us and save some lives at the same time."

"That's an even bigger problem, if some catastrophic attack does occur, and it is construed in such a way that we knew and didn't say anything, that would be a problem. If the guys on the hill found out I had prior knowledge, I don't think it would be very long before Congress started impeachment proceedings, if we happen to win this thing," Doug said.

"I'm not saying don't call the authorities," Leonce said defensively, sensing Doug wasn't going to agree with him fully.

"Are you implying that we shouldn't turn this guy in or not?" Doug asked.

"Not at all, I'm just saying there could be some political advantage for us, and at this point, we need any kind of advantage we can get."

"Now, that is something we can all agree on," Doug said, finally smiling at Leonce and breaking the tension.

There was a brief moment of nervous laughter from the group in acknowledgement of both the dilemma they were in and the obvious state of the campaign. A pregnant pause of silence followed. John noticed Leonce rubbing his face and staring directly at the floor.

"What's wrong, Leonce?" John asked.

John's question seemed to wake him from his self induced trance. "Here's what I'm thinking. Let's go ahead and turn it over to the FBI, but we need to keep good records of our conversations with them, I mean all of us. We need to cooperate fully because, obviously, that is the right thing to do, we all agree on that. No one in this room wants to see anything bad happen, but at the same time we aren't really responsible, either. But I would suggest that we look into these allegations on our own as well so that if something does happen, we can protect ourselves from any critics who might materialize along the way. Who knows, we might learn something that could help us in the campaign," Leonce added.

"How's that sound to you, Doug?" John asked.

"So you want me to cooperate with this guy?" Doug asked.

"It wouldn't hurt," Leonce said.

"Okay, I'll see what I can find out," Doug replied quickly.

Doug noticed Tony looking at him with a concerned look on his face. Up to now he hadn't spoken a single word.

"You have something to add to this conversation?" Doug asked. Everyone in the room turned their attention to Doug's bodyguard.

"Well, just this. If the Ferguson people start talking to people in Malaysia, you might become a target for these radicals. I mean we don't know if any of these people can be trusted," Tony said. "I mean your people or their contacts in Malaysia aren't professionals—"

"So you think it's dangerous?" Doug asked.

"Yeah, I think so," Tony responded immediately.

Doug thought about it for a minute, then smiled and said, "Then you will have to make sure nothing happens to me."

"Are you sure about this, Boss? This could get ugly quick. I don't think we can trust anybody over there with your life—"

"I don't think anything is going to happen, but if it does, we'll handle it." Doug knew there would be security issues by spying inside a foreign country hostile to the interest of the United States, but that was part of the game and accepted it.

"It's settled then. Let's get the FBI on the phone and get them out here—" John said.

"I'll do it." Leonce reached for the phone on the conference table.

8

April 5th 2012 12:30 p.m.
Flint, Michigan

Special Agents James Nelson and Tim Carlton entered the hotel suite looking around as if they had never seen a hotel room before or maybe not one this nice. Both were cordial as they shook hands with everyone. Agent Nelson was the senior agent. He was exactly what Leonce expected, he was middle aged, probably not one of the Bureau's best. Nelson's hair was cut close around the ears. He was wearing a medium-priced, charcoal-colored suit with a muted blue tie. He was close shaven with shades of gray just in front of his ears, and he wore gold-rimmed, oval-shaped glasses that made his eyes seem small and distant behind the lenses. His junior partner, Tim Carlton, was probably ex-military. It seemed obvious, by his physical proportions, that he was a serious body builder. He was one of those guys who didn't look comfortable wearing a suit; it just didn't fit right, too loose in some places and too tight in others, which wasn't all that uncommon for a man whose hobby was body building and who bought cheap suits off the rack. His hair was cut short and apparently had some kind of gel in it to keep it flat against his head. The FBI still wouldn't tolerate a Special Agent with spiked hair.

"You gentleman come on in and grab a seat. Can we get you anything to drink?" Leonce asked, indicating the wet bar.

"No, I think we'll be fine, Congressman," Agent Nelson said, deciding to stand rather than sit.

"Just call me Leonce. Are you sure I can't get you two gentlemen something?"

"No, we're fine, thank you. So, fill us in on the threats you've been getting," Agent Nelson said, directing his questioning at Leonce rather abruptly, something he had a habit of doing.

"Before we get to that, Agent Nelson, I would like to discuss confidentiality issues first," Leonce said, just as abruptly. He had questioned hundreds of appointees on various committees during his time in the House of Representatives, some were cooperative, some were not, and he knew how the game worked. If this was the persona the agent wanted to project, then he would project the same thing right back at him.

"Sure, no problem," Nelson said, recognizing the shift in the Congressman's demeanor.

"Since we are in the middle of a Presidential campaign, total confidentiality would be appreciated! We can't afford for any of this information to leak to the press.

"Sure, we don't want that either. Whatever we say here needs to be completely confidential!" Nelson said, as Special Agent Carlton nodded in agreement. They both had clearly received the message coming from the congressman that their rudeness wouldn't be tolerated.

"We asked you to come over, because we have been getting some information, from an unknown person, about a possible terrorist attack to be carried out sometime this year, an attack larger and more dramatic than anything else we've seen. This information has been directed directly to Governor Ferguson. First this note, then a phone call this morning at 9:30 a.m.," Leonce said, as he handed the envelope over to agent Nelson.

Both Agents listened intently but didn't seem to be particularly interested about what they were hearing. In fact, they appeared to be bored. Doug normally didn't make snap decisions about people, but he didn't sense a lot of interest being shown. It was the body language more than anything else. Sure, they might be very busy with all kinds of threats coming in every day, but not being interested in what someone like United States Representative Leonce Collins, a powerful member of Congress, was saying, was troubling.

"So you're the only one who's actually being contacted in here, Governor?" Agent Nelson said as he redirected his attention to the governor. He had finished looking at the note and handed it, along with the large brown envelope, to the other agent.

"That's right. This guy seems to think that I can help in some way," Doug answered, leaving out the fact that the caller wanted him to use his company to seek information. The one thing Doug didn't want was for Ferguson Industries to become a part of the investigation.

"Now, when did you get the phone call again?" Nelson asked with a stoic expression as he pulled out a small spiral notebook and made an encrypted note.

"He called about 9:30 a.m. on the hotel phone," Doug said, thinking that Agent Nelson either had a short memory or wanted to confirm that he agreed with Leonce's version of the timing.

"Okay, what time was it when you received the note here at the hotel?" Agent Nelson asked.

"It wasn't this hotel… I received the note when we were in Charleston campaigning."

"When was that?" Doug sensed his answer piqued Nelson's interest, and Doug knew why.

"That was on March 5th –"

"What time?" Agent Nelson asked still writing notes in the small spiral notebook.

"I think I received the note about the same time, around 9:30 in the morning."

"This guy seems to prefer early morning communication, doesn't he? By the way, how did he get the envelope to you?"

"He left it at the front desk where it was discovered then subsequently delivered to me."

"We'll send the envelope and the note to forensics and see what we can find out."

"That sounds good to me," Doug said, being supportive.

"Okay. Let me ask you an important question, Governor. Why didn't you call the FBI office in Charleston when you first received the note, or more precisely why didn't you report it then?"

He had prepared himself for this question because he knew it would be asked. Doug had decided to change his response slightly from what he agreed to with John to better reflect how he really felt at the time, which would also make his statement a bit more believable.

"Well, I had put the note in an envelope and addressed it to the FBI. But then, the more I thought about it, I guess I convinced myself it was just a hoax, you know, some kind of political trick to embarrass me, so I just didn't call."

"Okay, then we'll check things out, but I think your hunch is right, it's probably just a hoax, nothing more," Agent Nelson said, as he closed his notebook and put his pen back inside his left coat pocket.

"I hope you're right. This is serious, if it's a real threat."

"Here's my cell phone number," Carlton said, writing on a slip of paper and handing it to Doug. "If you get another call from this guy, just call me on my cell. When I see your cell number come up on my phone, I'll call our tech guys and activate a trace on the hotel phone wherever you are. But you'll need to stay in contact with me and let me know where you're staying so we will have the phone number you're speaking from.

"Okay I'll do that," Doug said.

"I'll set up everything this afternoon so we will be ready to go," Nelson said, stoned faced.

"I guess that's it, thanks for coming out," Leonce said.

As they started towards the door Tony met them at the door and opened it for them. Then the two agents left as quickly as they had come.

After the door shut and after a moment of silence, John said "That it? That's all they need to know?" he said, apparently disgusted with what he had just seen.

"Apparently...kind of troubling isn't it?" Doug said.

"Let me do what I do best and be a lawyer for a minute! These guys are going to begin a serious investigation and they start off with a short lackluster interview like that? What the hell is going on here? I'd question a Mississippi hooker longer than that even if I had a video of her transgression!" John said in his southern Alabama draw.

"I don't think our mystery caller is going to get much attention from these two," Leonce added.

"You know it seemed to me that they were a little noncommittal about the whole meeting, you know, like they didn't want to be out here," Doug said.

"Yeah, it felt like, 'Here we are, we aren't working on our important cases, why are you politicians bothering us?" Leonce added.

"Yeah, that was the same feeling I got!" John said still irritated. Doug was surprised and disappointed in a meeting that lasted less than ten minutes. Sure, Nelson had offered to trace calls, but they really didn't seem too interested. *Maybe they knew more than what they were saying,* Doug thought.

“Maybe they thought this was some kind of political ploy, a trick of some kind and that we were going to use it in the campaign and they didn’t want any part of it. You know these guys have been under a lot of pressure, lately, especially from all of us in Congress,” Leonce said.

“Maybe that’s it. But whatever it is, they didn’t seem to be too turned on by what we were reporting,” John chimed in.

“You know the FBI is pretty stretched out right now, maybe this is just how it’s done these days,” Leonce said, softening his position.

“I don’t know. It’s hard to believe that’s all they wanted to know from you.” John said, as he stood and peered out the window. “The whole thing is pretty troubling if you ask me.”

“At least they volunteered to trace the next call. That’s something, right?” Doug said.

“Doug, I’m still pretty well connected up on the Hill. If you want, I can make a phone call or two and try to get some more senior people working on this,” Leonce offered.

“No, let’s see what happens. It’s their job not ours now! Since they’re prepared to use wiretaps, I’m not sure what else can be done. But, what still bothers me is their freaking attitude. Don’t get me wrong, they’re probably pretty good guys, but ten minutes?”

John looked at Doug with disgust written all over his face. "Here's something that's bothering me; we're losing this war, and now it doesn't seem like the FBI has enough gas in their tanks to work these cases. I mean we're getting our asses handed to us, right? It doesn't seem to matter how many aircraft carriers we have or how many boots we put on the ground, it's never going to stop a single person from blowing up another person, and it never will. We've needed excellent intelligence and good border patrol to prevent that, right? But, what do we get? We get two guys that are either too tired or too overloaded or don't give a shit, and I'm not sure which it is."

"Yeah, things are bad; no one can argue that. At this point, it doesn't matter what our military does overseas, it won't help us here at home; it hasn't so far, no matter what the present administration claims! Terrorists keep slipping into the country and blowing people up and nobody seems to be able to stop them," Doug added.

"I would agree that we did have some limited success back in the early days with the preemption phase of the war, but once the terrorists got reorganized and new leaders emerged, they started winning the war. They are hitting us here at home where it really hurts! It doesn't take a lot of planning to kill a few innocent people at a mall," Leonce growled. "But, they're doing a good job of it."

Seeing John get so animated made Doug think about how difficult it would be for John to navigate, politically, in Washington politics. John was always known for his fiery personality, and he was accustomed to winning, not losing. Doug wasn't sure how diplomatic John would be as Vice President. Doug knew one thing for sure, he would have to keep a close eye on him because he'd always been capable of alienating people. Nevertheless, after thinking about John's personality for a second, he said to himself, "that's okay, there's a hell of lot of people in Washington that need to have a fire lit under their asses!"

"What did you say?" Leonce asked.

"Nothing, really, just ignore me if I start talking to myself," Doug responded with a smile. He wanted to avoid inciting more anger in Leonce.

An already agitated, Leonce added," the bad guys always dig a hole and pull it in after them. They just hide until we leave and then they pop out again and take control through murder, intimidation, and assassination. You can't win!"

"The reason we're losing this war is that we never hold the people responsible for this mischief accountable for their actions. No one holds these radical regimes accountable for what they are doing secretly! And as long as we don't, they'll fund and train these murders, and why not? They have nothing to fear from us!" John said.

"Tony, I need for you to run down to Mobile for me," Doug said.

"Sure, no problem, what for?"

"Go see John Bennet. Tell him I sent you and I want him to check some things out for me, but to keep confidential, and I want you to do it face-to-face, with no one else in the room."

"Okay," Tony said a bit confused.

"Tell Bennet I want him to start a secret dialogue with our contacts in Kuala Lumpur. Tell him we desperately need information on the JI. We need to find out if they have plans for a terrorist strike against us, we need to get someone over there to infiltrate their organization. It's a long shot, but who knows, we might find something out. Tell him about the caller and the threats. He'll know what to do. The old man is good at this kind of thing."

"Will Bennet need a phone call from you to get started?"

"Just tell him I can't make any phone calls and I can't write anything down, just tell him to do it, he'll understand."

"Would you do me a favor?" Tony asked.

"Yeah, sure, what is it?" Doug asked, surprised, because Tony rarely asked for anything, from anybody.

"Keep your eyes wide open since I'm not going to be around to protect you."

"I'm touched Tony, I didn't know you cared so much." Doug said, laughing.

"No, I'm serious. One of these days, some whacked out weirdo might take a shot at you, you need to be prepared, boss."

"I'll be fine, you just get on down to Mobile and get things rolling and get back as soon as you can!"

"You got it, but keep your eyes open, okay?"

"Don't worry, I have everything under control here."

Doug was certain John Bennet could call some favors in and capitalize on some of his company's past relationships. Ferguson Industries had been involved in the energy business in Malaysia for years and John had stayed in contact with many of the people Ferguson had done business with in that part of the world. John was President and CEO of the company, a trusted officer who had been with the company since it was founded. He was a man that could keep his mouth shut and work as an intermediary for Doug. His contacts worldwide were extensive, and he possessed a talent for finding out even the most closely guarded government and corporate secrets. This was the kind of information that was absolutely necessary to open new markets abroad. As an outside company doing business in Asia, especially in China, this was the only way new markets could be opened successfully. It was no secret that money could buy a lot of knowledge, and knowledge had always been the key to success. If there was something to all this, John Bennet would find out, Doug was certain of that.

2

April 6th 2012 3:26 a.m.
International Waters Atlantic Ocean

The rust-stained fishing trawler rolled in the dark seas over a hundred nautical miles off the coast of North Carolina. The Global Positioning System was showing the exact latitude and longitude that was secretly decoded from the DVD back in New Jersey. Their location was just a lonely windswept spot in the open ocean chosen for the rendezvous by smugglers.

The trawler had been purchased with cash by Tan as a fishing boat from a local fisherman. There had been no questions asked because Tan looked like all the other Asians who bought old fishing boats with cash to start fishing in the waters around the Carolinas. The old fisherman was more than happy to sell the boat for cash and avoid all the paper work. He didn't like the fact that these Asians with their strange customs were buying boats and fishing, but the old man was ready to get out of the business and desperately needed the money.

The plan was to rendezvous at this exact spot in the ocean precisely at 3:30 a.m. This night was chosen because it would be a near moonless night. Tan and Ali had been lucky, because the weather, for now, was cooperating. They were now in the Gulf Stream where any wind out of the northeast could end their trip rather quickly in this part of the world. A small swell was running out of the southeast, and the wind was only ten knots. As they motored in small circles, the old British-made diesel engine chugged along flawlessly below deck.

The plan was to pick up the plutonium core and travel back by boat to the Passaic River through the Intracoastal Waterway. Once back inshore they would only have a short outside passage from Norfolk to Sandy Hook then up to their secret hide-out in New Jersey.

The old radar antenna swung around in a monotonous circle at a constant speed above the wheelhouse, sending out a steady wave of energy that could search for any obstacle in the dark night around them. Inside, Ali stared at the green glow of the radar screen looking for a blip that signaled the ship they were meeting had arrived.

"I see nothing but waves on the radar," Ali said.

"They're late; we would see them by now," Tan said as he peered out of the wheelhouse into the darkness.

"I now have a target at two and half miles bearing ninety-six degrees magnetic," Ali said suddenly.

"Okay, go out on the deck with the flashlight and wait for their signal," Tan stayed at the helm and continued to turn the boat in wide looping circles.

Ali went outside on the foredeck and strained to see the vessel with his naked eyes. Whoever they were, they weren't showing navigation lights. Then, finally, a spotlight flashed a short beam followed by a longer beam of light, the Morris code signal for the letter "A." This was done three times in rapid succession. Ali flashed back the same signal and returned to the warmth of the wheelhouse.

"It's them, let's proceed slowly," Ali ordered.

"Where did they come from?"

"I don't know, they just appeared! I'm just glad they're here," Ali said as he hung on to one of the teak handholds just over his head as the boat rolled.

As the two vessels approached each other using their radar, the faint outline of the boat started to come into view.

"It's a submarine!" Tan shouted as he pulled the throttle lever back and slowed the trawler down to avoid a collision. The black shape of a submarine was now only about forty yards away and straight off their bow. The boat tossed up and down on the choppy seas as it approached the port side of the submarine.

Below decks on the Soviet made P-130 submarine stood Captain Andréa Saadak. Not only was he the Captain, but he also was the owner of this small ninety-foot sub named *Nadia*. The sub was one of the smallest that had been designed and operated by the Soviet navy during the cold war. With a small crew of ten experienced crewmembers it could be operated with very little cost and with the utmost in secrecy. Andrea had acquired the sub from *Rosoboronexport* the official arms dealer of Russia. The P-130 had been purchased for him, for a profit of course, by friends in Yemen. After a very short time, ownership was transferred to Andréa Saadak, who was a member of the Russian Mob "*Solsnctskaya,*" but the ownership of the submarine was his and his alone. The money to purchase the small sub came from a loan from Alexia Zabav, the boss of Solsnctskaya, but the loan had been paid off the year before. The small submarine had paid for itself in the first two years of smuggling operations and continued to supply a nice profit to Saadak and his crew. He worked with Solsnctskaya to support whatever illegal activities were required, as long as he was cut in for part of the profit.

Andrea had been in the Soviet navy, not as a Captain but as an engineering officer. This had all been before the collapse of the Soviet Union and the dark days afterwards. After not getting paid for several years, he was one of the first from the submarine corps to start looking for other work. He had a cousin in Moscow who offered him a job driving and working on trucks for a Vodka manufacturing plant with ties to Solsnctskaya. This was where he eventually met Zabav.

He had been given a job working on Alexia Zabav's yacht and they became trusted friends. Andrea had hatched the plan of buying the P-130 from *Rosoboronexport* and using it for smuggling. He was familiar with the P-130 and felt sure he could operate it profitably. Andrea believed this small sub was perfect to smuggle under the noses of any country, even the United States. He had explained to Alexia in great detail how submarines are almost exclusively detected acoustically, and unlike its huge nuclear cousins, a modern diesel-electric sub was difficult to detect in the open ocean. When the small ninety-foot submarine was submerged, operating on electric battery power only, it was almost impossible to locate. Zabav quickly saw the potential of having a submarine to smuggle drugs and agreed to help set up the deal.

Captain Saadak wasn't very particular about who or what he carried aboard *Nadia* for cargo, as long as the customer met his price. He had smuggled terrorists into and out of the United States. He and his crew had trafficked narcotics from Columbia to the United States and Europe by simply getting close enough to a deserted shoreline under the cover of darkness. Even if spotted by the Coast Guard, which had never happened, the vessels of the United States Coast Guard were not equipped to track him when submerged, so getting away would be simple enough. The range of the P-130 had originally been two-thousand miles but, since the submarine no longer carried torpedoes, the range had been increased to twenty-seven hundred miles by adding additional diesel fuel cells. Andrea had, as a part of his fleet, a Russian fishing trawler for support. The range of his submarine at twenty-seven hundred miles was not enough and the Trawler support vessel carried fuel and supplies for trips to Asia when needed. Nadia's homeport was a small port named Bata in the Bakassi Peninsula. The ownership of this oil-rich region that made up part of the border between Nigeria and the wilds of Cameroon was the perfect place to call home for her. Captain Saadaak was paying off high-ranking officials of both Nigeria and Cameroon for his safe haven. Politics were of no concern to him. He had allowed politics to direct his life for too many years. Now that time and that place were gone and he was determined not to be controlled by any political ideology again, none except those that benefited him personally—for profit!

Nadia was rolling in the swells after she surfaced in the black Atlantic Ocean. Captain Saadak had quickly made his way through the deck hatch and onto the deck after contact had been made. He had personally signaled the other vessel to come alongside. Below decks two of his crewmen were unbolting the dangerous cargo for transfer. The Captain was in extremely good spirits. His bank account would have a sizeable new deposit in just seven hours. The amount of one and a half million dollars would be in his possession for this trip. Not bad for a former engineering officer of the Soviet Navy.

Two other crewmembers had made their way from the cramped quarters below with dock lines to toss to the other vessel as it came alongside.

The two men below decks finally finished unbolting the long, narrow cylinder. It was so heavy it would take four men to move it aft to where it could be hoisted through the hatch and onto the deck above. None of the men knew what was in the cylinder, but they suspected it was some kind of bomb because of their instructions to handle it very carefully.

Captain Saadak could now see the forty-five foot trawler clearly as it came alongside the Nadia. The two men scrambled out of the wheelhouse and secured the lines that were being tossed over to them.

"Secure the gangway!" Captain Saadak shouted.

The aluminum gangway was unfolded and placed across the water between the two vessels and made secure. The large cylindrical steel case was hauled up through the sub's foredeck hatch onto the deck by five crewmembers. Not a word had been spoken between the two men on the trawler or the men on the deck of the submarine.

Ali was irritated that it was taking so long to get the component out of the sub and over to their vessels. He was as contemptuous of Russians as he was of Americans. The Soviet murderers had killed thousands of his brothers in Afghanistan, as had the Americans. He was proud that he could use one against the other in his plan to kill Americans. He only hoped after his own martyrdom that the JI would carry out an even more devastating attack on the Russians. All infidels deserved a similar fate.

The core material only weighed about 21 kilograms, but it was incased in a lead and steel-lined cylinder for safety. The entire cylinder weighed over 158 kilograms. This cylinder casing of over three hundred pounds had to be slid over the aluminum surface of the gangway with two men pulling lines that had been attached and two pushing from behind. Lines had been made fast to the deadly cargo just in case he rolled off into the sea. It was difficult work and, more than once, the men had to stop and shift their cargo as the two vessels continued to wallow in the lumpy seas. Finally, the plutonium 233 was aboard the trawler. Two of the Russian men helped Ali and Tan rig the heavy metal container to the boom of the fishing trawler and lowered it into the hold.

Then, as quickly as the Russians had come aboard they left. They had, with great haste, pulled the gangway back and pulled it back aboard the submarine. The tall Russian Captain, with a half grin, made a halfhearted salute to Ali as the large, black hulk started to move forward slowly. Ali made no effort to acknowledge the infidel Captain.

Below decks, Tan and Ali made the large cylinder secure to the deck next to the old rusty diesel engine. With large bolts already in place wide metal bands were placed around the cylinder and made fast. Then two engine-cooling hoses were placed on fittings that had been fabricated onto the cylinder. The large, black cooling hoses were not actually carrying any seawater to the cylinder but only appeared to do so to give the appearance that this was a reservoir of cooling water.

By the time the job was finished Captain Saadak was five miles away and about to go submerged. The sky was already getting light in the east and it would not be long before sunrise. It would be far better to run deep during the day until he was farther offshore to keep from being spotted by American air patrols.

As the sun rose above the North Atlantic, the fishing trawler was on course for the North Carolina coastline with the deadly core of plutonium on board. Now, the rest of the voyage would have to be made right under the noses of the Americans without being discovered. It would be a long and perilous trip but, Allah willing, it would be made.

10

April 6th 2012
Atlantic Ocean

"I'm going below for some rest," Ali said, as he walked in a zigzag pattern across the cabin. "Call me if you need anything," he said as he disappeared below.

"I'll let you know," Tan said.

The door on the starboard side of wheelhouse was wide open and locked. This would keep it from swinging back and forth as the trawler rolled in heavy seas. The fresh ocean breeze blew through the wheelhouse as the fishing boat wallowed in steep following seas. They were now on course for the barren North Carolina coastline plowing through the inky blackness. Tan had decided to run for Oregon Inlet between Nag's Head and Hatteras Island. It would have been a shorter voyage to Charleston South Carolina, but the recent terrorist attacks there had made that port too risky to enter. The chances of being boarded by the Coast Guard were much greater in Charleston than Oregon Inlet. The US Coast Guard station at the inlet would be less likely to board a fishing boat there, because the area was a small fishing port and both men felt this would be a safer choice. Tan was aware that Cape Hatteras could be a dangerous place for small boats. He took the necessary time to research the pilot books in great detail in preparation for the voyage. Sailing around Cape Hatteras could be dangerous for any size vessel, but it was a chance that had to be taken. Cape Hatteras was legendary for manufacturing its own weather conditions that overwhelmed vessels every year in its monstrous seas. Here, the northward flow of warm water from the Gulf Stream that collided with the cold North Atlantic waters near Cape Hatteras made conditions perfect for brutal storm development.

The little trawler was bouncing around in choppy seas still over a hundred miles to their west. Neither man had ever been there before but that wouldn't matter. With their GPS handling the navigation, it wouldn't be a problem approaching the coastline. With the data imbedded in the memory chip of the handheld chart plotter, they would be able to make a safe approach in almost any weather conditions. The United States Government, by providing such innovative technology, was actually helping them fight their war against the infidels. Like the warriors before them, they were simply using America's technology to their own advantage. In fact, the nuclear technology developed during the 1950s had been refined to a point where a small nuclear device could kill hundreds of thousands of people if placed in an area of dense population. Using the tools of the enemy to defeat him added a macabre sense of symmetry in Ali's mind.

Tan had been chosen for this mission, not just for his electronic knowledge, but because he was the son of a fisherman. He was at home on the sea. He had worked on his father's fishing boats as a young man. The sea had always been a place where Tan, being shy and awkward, felt at home. The wide expanses of blue water didn't frighten him. The peace and fury of the sea made him feel alive. He was aware of the dangers of Cape Hatteras and wondered aloud, "Will we be delivered to our destiny? I think so, God willing!" He whispered to himself. Tan knew Cape Hatteras was well known for swallowing ships larger than his own. But he wasn't afraid, Allah would surely protect them and they had a great deed to do in his name.

Ali was feeling the effects of his seasickness. It had been relatively smooth going out with placid seas, but following seas along with diesel fumes swirling around the cabin had combined to incapacitate him to the point where he could only lay in his grease-stained bunk and suffer. It must be part of God's plan for him, Ali thought. He would endure whatever hardships God placed in front of him, no matter how difficult, so he could kill the infidel Americans. This was his destiny, and he knew that no man could fight his destiny.

Tan began to notice low-lying black clouds building to the north lit by the occasional strike of lightening on the horizon. The scudding clouds were building like an ominous wall. The winds were starting to pick up from the southwest. As the storm grew more intense, the surface winds started to increase. The air was being sucked into the heart of the low-pressure system that was developing to the Northeast. Tan placed a cord with a loop in the end around the top of the wooden spoke wheel to hold the old boat on course while he closed the deckhouse door. The cold wind slapped him in the face as he stepped onto the deck. It felt good to be at sea again, even if there was a storm on the way. He knew that, this time of year, storms came and went in the evening, so they would just have to hold on until the storm blew through the area.

As the wind came up, the monstrous seas started to build out of the southwest but Tan knew they would soon turn and veer to the Northeast. From his experience as a fisherman, he knew the seas could grow and turn into a boiling cauldron as the two wave patterns started to collide against each other. These collisions sent spouts of angry dark seas skyward, the result of tons of sea water in the form of waves colliding with each other in mid ocean. Tan slowed the boat's speed and turned her into the wind to more effectively take the oncoming seas on the bow. He wanted to get this accomplished before it was too late to come about in the steep, menacing seas. Tan knew that, as the wind built, the seas could become too violent to turn his boat without causing extreme danger. What worried him now was what would happen when the wind finally shifted?

By now, the wind started to howl through the rigging of the fishing trawler. She was straining to climb the steep frothing seas but then effortlessly slid down the backside. At the moment she was comfortable enough. The winds continued to increase out of the southwest as more and more warm air was fed into the storm.

Tan had decided, as he had done before, to put his fate in the hands of Allah to deliver him from the dangers of the sea building around them. "Al Sha'allah" he shouted to the increasing winds that were now buffeting his small vessel.

"What's going on?" Ali said, as he made his way back to the wheelhouse. Vertigo was taking its toll on his weakening body, and he began to wish he had never stepped foot on the boat.

"It's a storm building to the north." Tan never turned around to look at Ali, he couldn't. The seas outside had built very quickly to steep, twelve footers, each came crashing in on the small wooden fishing boat with a loud thunderous crash.

Ali, sick and weak, returned to his bunk below. Before he could climb into his bunk, vertigo again took command of his body and he suddenly vomited. Tan started to worry about his dangerous cargo breaking loose from its mounting bolts. The core of the nuclear device was secured to the deck flooring in the engine room. If the heavy core and its container broke loose it could compromise the hull structure and send them and their boat sounding to the black depths thousands of feet below. Tan thought about how nice it would be if he were safely below the surface in the submarine owned by the Russian, down where things would be calm, far below the furious waves that were tossing their boat now. But, even though it was rough, Tan loved the fury of the sea and he knew they could survive this storm.

The seas were growing in size, and Tan suddenly remembered he had not lowered the trawl boards to stabilize the vessel in the turbulent seas that by now were crashing around the vessel. He yelled below for help but got no answer from Ali. Knowing that he was probably rendered helpless by seasickness, Tan again looped the rope around the top of the spoke to hold the boat into the oncoming seas. When he was satisfied that the boat was holding its own and staying on course, he opened the wheelhouse door and ran aft to lower the trawl boards. As he began to lower the starboard sideboards, a wall of white frothing seawater came over the bow and around the cabin. Tan was washed backwards. As he tumbled, he caught a cable on one of the aft wenches and held on. The deck flooded with water that quickly ran off through the scuppers. He pulled himself up and fought his way forward, as the bow of the boat started up the next oncoming wave. Then he stumbled forward, just in time to gain shelter behind the cabin as the next wave swept past and again flooded the aft deck with tons of water. Tan waited for just the right moment, then finished lowering the starboard trawl board. Then he cautiously lowered the port board by timing his movements with the onslaught of the waves, careful not to get washed overboard. After both were dragging under the water, he made his way back to the wheelhouse just before another wave rolled aboard. He could feel the tugging of the vessel against the submerged boards as they limited the amount of roll of his vessel, all the while the cables and rigging groaned with the strain.

Soaking wet and cold, he now stood dripping at the wheel. He desperately wanted to change into dry cloths, but didn't dare leave the wheel again; it was too dangerous. The sea state had grown much more perilous in just the few minutes he had been on deck. The boat would now need his constant attention to keep from being caught broadside to one of the steep breaking waves. If the boat was caught by one of these treacherous monster waves broadside, even with the boards down to stabilize the vessel, it still could be rolled and capsized.

Below, in his bunk, Ali sensed, even though he was completely disoriented, that things had gotten worse. In a state of half consciousness, he prayed to Allah to spare him from the wrath of the sea, not because he was afraid to die, but because he wanted to carry out his attack on the enemies of Islam. Even in his terribly sickened state he had enough determination to pray.

The air was full of spray, the sky was dark, and lighting illuminated the huge seas outside the cabin. He hoped that the old, wooden fishing boat could survive the night or they might die before being able to carry out their attack on America that had taken years to develop, a plan that would cripple the United States and weaken it to the critical point where the government would falter and fail.

The Trawler continued to crawl up the huge seas in the black of the night. The storm had been raging for hours, and the seas had now grown to thirty feet. A dangerous cross-sea had developed with ten foot swells running across the troughs of the larger waves at a right angle. The boat groaned as she struggled to the top of each wave only to be rolled on her beam-ends as she was hit by the smaller swells coming from the other direction. Tan fought at the helm to keep the boat heading into the large, breaking seas. Every couple of minutes, a wave larger than all the rest would rise up in front and Tan would advance the throttle to insure the boat climbed to the top of the wave. In spite of her age and questionable condition, the old vessel was holding her own.

This ocean was different from the seas he had grown up on in his country. The North Atlantic was cold and hostile and reminded him of New York City. He thought it was fitting that such a cold and hostile sea should border such a cold and hostile nation. He didn't really want to die tonight on the ocean, and he secretly admitted to himself that he didn't want to die in the bomb blast, but it was his destiny.

His father had always told him "you should not fight your destiny, it is Allah's plan for you." While in school, he had sensed that, one day, his destiny would lead him to fight those who wished to kill his faith, those foreign people who had always defied Allah and the Muslim faith and wanted it swept from the face of the earth like a plague. Now, here he was fighting the sea to get a chance just to kill those who wanted Islam to die. Allah wasn't making it easy on him to carry out his will, though. Tan thought of this night as a test of his determination to carry out the work of God no matter how difficult it became or how hopeless it seemed.

Suddenly, a larger swell in the cross sea slammed against the starboard side of the boat, knocking it completely on its beam. Since the wave didn't completely break, the vessel had just enough time to right herself before being hit by the next wave. Again, the boat shuddered and went up on her beam-ends almost going over completely and capsizing, but she didn't. Again, she righted herself and stayed afloat. Tan was knocked against the starboard wall; then, as the boat popped up, he slid across to the lower side of the cabin. He landed in a heap against the bulkhead. Between the time of the first and second waves, he had been able to stay where he was by holding onto the handholds built onto the bulkhead. The wheel had spun over to starboard all the way, and the boat was now presenting her beam to larger waves than he had ever seen. Tan struggled up and grabbed the wheel, spinning it back to port while applying more power. The boat answered her helm in time to present the bow to the next huge wave coming at her. Not having enough speed, it seemed that she hung on the very top of the lip of the wave for what seemed to be minutes before dropping down the other side. "That was close," Tan murmured. The trawler had almost fallen back, bow over stern, nothing any vessel could take without major damage and succumbing to the seas.

Tan started to hear a heavy thumping down below. At first, he thought it was the sound of the hull against the waves, but then he heard a clanking sound that was accompanying the heavy thumps. He knew it was the core breaking loose. There was no way he could leave the helm long enough to go down to the engine room and secure things.

"Ali, get up," Tan shouted. He then put the rope around the top of the wheel spoke to hold the course long enough to shout down to Ali.

At first he got no response. He ran back to the wheel again to work the boat into position to confront the next onslaught of water. The boat was rolling wildly from beam to beam again as the cross sea continued to strike her in the troughs of the huge waves.

He again ran back. "Ali, get up! We are going to sink!"

The words seem to appear in Ali's mind from nowhere. In his sickened state, it really wasn't words he was hearing; it seemed to be just light, random thoughts that were occurring in his mind. Over and over again…then he felt something pull at his shoulder.

"Get up we are going to sink."

Ali glanced up in shock and saw Tan's face just above him, but before he could say anything, Tan was gone, again. Ali guessed they were in serious trouble and dragged his weakened body from the bunk stepping and then falling with a thud in the vomit covering the cabin sole. The smell rushed up and into his nostrils and he wanted to puke again but fought it back; there's no time for that now.

Again, Tan appeared. "Come up and take the wheel!" He shouted again.

"Okay, Okay."

Ali fought his way up to the wheelhouse from the cabin below by holding onto the overhead handholds placed there for bad weather.

"Take the wheel and hold the boat into the oncoming seas," Tan screamed.

Ali grabbed the large, wooden wheel with both hands. The effects of the seasickness suddenly disappeared replaced by fright.

"I can't see anything," Ali yelled.

"Just watch the compass; the larger seas are coming out of the Northeast now. Just hold the boat at seventy-nine degrees.

"Okay, I'll try."

Tan disappeared below into the engine room. Going down through the cabin where Ali had been sleeping, he jumped onto the bunk, scrambling to the other end before jumping back down onto the deck to avoid the slick puke-covered floor.

As he entered the engine room, he switched on the light. The hot air and noise was oppressive. The diesel engine was screaming as it fought to turn the prop through the water. Tan was shocked to see that the large steel cylinder holding the core had broken completely loose from its mounting bolts. It was sliding back and forth between the side of the hull and the engine. The heavy cylinder was slamming against the engine's exhaust manifold every time the boat heaved to port. There was no apparent damage on the hull, but the engine manifold was leaking cooling water. A couple more impacts would probably tear the manifold right off the engine, Tan thought. He needed a way to secure the steel cylinder somewhere between the diesel engine and the hull and not get crushed in the process. The first thing he saw was a plastic milk crate full of pieces of oily wood blocks. He found four heavy blocks and waited until the cylinder violently rolled back against the hull, with a thud. He quickly sprung into action and placed the blocks under the cylinder. The blocks were just thin enough to get under the curve of the cylinder to hold it.

As the boat rolled again, the cylinder attempted to roll over the small wooden blocks. Tan had wedged himself between a deck support and the cylinder and held it in place with both feet. A coil of nylon rope swung above his head on a hook on the deck support column. He grabbed the rope and uncoiled it quickly. He then placed the end of the rope through a pad-eye that was welded on the top of the cylinder for lifting. He made the line fast, and then tied it to one of the wooden ribs that lined the hull planking. Another wave rolled the boat, and he again held the vessel in place with his legs. This time, he secured the other end of the line through the welded pad-eye on the other end of the cylinder and tied it to another rib. For the moment it was secure. Without resting, he found more rope and continued to tie the metal vessel to various strong points on both sides until it was secure. The boat was rolling madly and he was sweating profusely. His ears were ringing from the sounds of the diesel engine screaming at high RPMs. He decided for the moment that the manifold would hold and the bilge pump could handle the little bit of water leaking out into the bilge. He quickly looked around and noticed there wasn't much water in the bilge at all; she was a strong little boat and was holding her own, Tan thought.

As he fought his way back up from the engine room and through the lower cabin up to the wheelhouse, he found Ali still holding on to the wheel. He looked wide-eyed and fearful at every wave that broke over the bow.

"Let me have the wheel."

Ali turned and left the helm dropping down the companion way and back to his bunk.

As Tan again began to steer the boat through the monstrous waves, he was shocked to see a light on the horizon just to the east of his position. As the boat fell into the next trough, he lost sight of the light. His heart raced at the thought of being run down in the middle of the night by a ship. As the boat crested the next oncoming wave, the light on the horizon was actually the moon about to emerge above the horizon. The storm was almost over! He could see the storm clouds starting to break up and the moon starting to emerge between them just above the horizon. The little fishing trawler was about to break out of the quick moving storm that had passed over them; it was 3:32 a.m. It would take awhile for the seas to subside, but at least the worst was over and Tan breathed a sigh of relief; it looked like they were going to make it.

Tan recalled that the old fisherman who had sold the boat to them had said the fishing trawler had been built in Bath, Maine, and she was a sturdy craft regardless of the way she looked. The old man had been right, Tan thought to himself, as he continued to steer through the remnants of the fading storm. It might have served the New Englanders better if they hadn't built such a seaworthy vessel, because it had just saved the lives of two of America's sworn enemies that would bring more death and destruction to the shores of the infidels. Tan laughed as he thought about it. A broad smile came across his face as he guided the fishing vessel through the frothing seas, but he wasn't smiling at the New Englanders, but instead at the majesty of the sea he had just experienced. He felt alive, more alive than he had ever experienced. Allah had brought them safely through the storm and, soon, they would bring an even greater storm to the shores of the infidels.

11

April 20th 2012
Kuala Lumpur

The slender Malaysian slipped quietly down the hallway on the third floor of the aging Hotel Barclay on the outskirts of Kuala Lumpur's old business district. He was wearing a short-sleeved, white-silk shirt outside of his black, linen pants. His small, lean appearance was not especially threatening but, in reality, he was a skilled and dangerous killer. He carried a small, black-leather case with a zipper that extended on three sides, so it could be completely laid open to access the lock-picking tools within. He moved cautiously but quickly down the hallway making no sounds to give his presence away. The dirty carpet in the hallway smelled musty, but it was still thick enough to silence his footsteps. The Hotel had once been a favored destination for wealthy tourists, but that was long ago. The owners over the years had been determined to maximize profits and had let the Hotel Barclay fall into a shocking state of disrepair. It was now just another cheap place to stay for businessmen and students traveling in Malaysia on a tight budget.

The intruder was careful and confident. He was certain he hadn't been followed and moved cautiously in the shadows to keep from being seen. The hotel wasn't well lit because the owners believed they could save more money by going to smaller light bulbs that were more energy efficient. The effect of the dim lighting was grim and depressing, but it enabled the intruder to pass unseen to the fourth floor of the hotel. He hoped if seen, his facial features would be all but unidentifiable in such poor lighting. As he moved closer to room 409, he heard the unmistakable sounds of an unlocking door, then the door opened and a young Asian woman came out of the rooms just in front of him. The man stopped and turned away from her to hide his face. He began to act as if he were putting a key in the door adjacent to where he was standing. He was lucky that the young woman never turned to look in his direction and casually walked to the elevator leaving him alone. The intruder smiled, *she never even knew I was here*, he thought, then moved farther down the hallway. He chose the emergency stairway instead of the elevator; if he hadn't, he would have come face to face with the woman, someone who might have identified him later.

As he reached the door, he looked both directions to make sure the hallway was clear and then lightly knocked twice. He then took one step back and, with his right hand, pulled out a black 9mm pistol that was hidden in the back of his pants. The pistol had a three-inch silencer screwed into the end of the muzzle. To make sure no one in the room could see his weapon, he again put the weapon behind his back under his shirt. If anyone came to the door, his orders were to kill him, then take any information he could find in the room. Hours of surveillance of the room had paid off, and no one answered the door. The Arab man who rented the room had left as he had done on two previous mornings at approximately 9:15 a.m. The man then unzipped the black leather case and pulled out a small lock-picking device. In a few seconds, he had picked the lock and entered the room closing the door softly behind him.

The room was small with one double bed, and a small, carved-teak desk. It was typical of cheap hotels in the Far East, musty and not particularly well maintained. He noticed that the wallpaper was peeling away from the wall in one corner. As he looked around the room for a computer, he could clearly see the bed had been slept in. The pillows and sheets were in a state of disarray, and the whole room looked disheveled and dirty. He knew he would have to work fast. It was already late in the morning, and the Arab could return at any minute. The intruder was careful not to disturb the room; anything out of place would give away the fact that someone had been there. He wanted information, but he didn't want the terrorist to know he had taken it. After going through the hotel room several times, he had found nothing of interest, and certainly not what he was looking for. As he went back into the bathroom, he noticed a small drain tube coming through the ceiling tiles over the bath. He had seen this before; it was the drain for the condensation catch pan of the air conditioner unit mounted in the ceiling. This meant there was a space just above the bathtub. He pulled one of the acoustic tiles out and could see the bottom of the pan that drained the air conditioning unit. He quickly pulled another tile out. Dust floated down into his eyes, and he had to take a moment to clear them. He then continued his search with a small flashlight into the space above his head. Behind the dirty air conditioning unit, he found what he had been looking for. It was a laptop computer. He felt around it to make sure it wasn't booby-trapped and then carefully lifted it out of its hiding place.

He put the computer on the teak table in the room and pressed the power button. The computer quickly spun to life as the screen flickered on. He pulled out an external drive from his bag and started the process of downloading files from the computer. It was taking longer than the man had anticipated, and he began to sweat in the small, stuffy confines of the room. "Hurry up!" he said in his native Cantonese as he nervously tapped his fingers in rapid-fire fashion across both knees. Just outside the window in the streets below, the man could hear the honking of horns as cars tried to navigate through the morning traffic. He was painstakingly copying every file on the hard drive so he could sort through them later. He hoped that the documents would be somewhere on the hard drive. He quickly made some notes about the internal drive just in case he had to come back later and steal the drive itself. If it came to that, he would bring a replacement drive and take the one from the computer so the drive itself could be checked for deleted files. It would just be a matter of switching the drives, then downloading all the files back on to the replacement drive so the owner would not suspect his files had been stolen.

After copying all the files, the man put the computer back over the tub in the bathroom and put the tiles back in place. He wiped the bathtub clean of dirt and foot prints. He then checked the room carefully by mentally cutting the room into sections in his mind. He then checked each section quickly to ensure that nothing had been disturbed or left behind that would reveal that he had ever been there. Only after he was satisfied that everything was back in place did he go the door. He took a moment to listen for anyone who might be in the hallway. The man heard nothing and slowly turned the handle on the door and opened it. He quickly made his way out of the room, allowing the door to lock behind him, and walked casually down the hall back to the stairwell.

In a matter of minutes, he was back in the lobby of the hotel. He walked right out the front door without anyone paying much attention to him. He disappeared among the throngs who lined both sides of the street. He left without any trace of ever being there. The man walked briskly, turning down side streets periodically stopping to see if he was being followed. Once he returned to his small Toyota sedan, he sat down behind the wheel and sped away. As he drove down the crowded Malaysian streets, he hoped he had what was needed; if he didn't he would have to go back.

12

April 21st 2012
Carolina Coastline

"Are you feeling well enough to take the wheel?" Tan asked, as Ali made his way into the wheelhouse. His clothes reeked from the repugnant smell of regurgitated bile, which now covered the cabin floor. Ali's cloths were damp and wrinkled and clung to his clammy skin. To Tan, his partner looked more like a man on his death bed than a dangerous international terrorist prepared to kill millions.

"No, not yet!" He said weakly. Ali was drinking orange juice from a small can and looked disheveled and drained.

"I need to go below and take care of our cargo, in case we are stopped by the authorities."

"Okay, but just for a minute!" Ali said as he walked over, blinked from the bright sun that now flooded the wheelhouse. He took a couple of deep breaths, and then reluctantly took the wheel. His knees were weak and his head was still spinning, but not as bad as before. He found he was able to stand without heaving as he clutched the wheel.

The fishing trawler steadily made its way north on the Intracoastal Waterway system under bright blue skies. *This is better than the ocean,* he thought. The air was fresh and cool and woke him up. Ali was starting to feel better now, from the clean air he was now breathing deeply into his lungs. His strength was starting to return as the fluids began to replenish his body. He continued to sip orange juice as he steered the old trawler through the brackish waters of the Intracoastal Waterway. A noisy flock of white seagulls followed in the boat's wake dipping and diving for small fish in the prop wash looking for their morning breakfast.

Ali closely monitored the electronic navigation information that was displayed on the chart plotter just above his head. The navigation was simple. Ali just had to watch the small icon that represented the boat and follow the markers northward toward Virginia.

Tan went below into the small cramped confines of the engine room. He felt a hot blast of air hit his face and the smell of oil and old paint as he opened the small door that led aft. Once he entered, he saw the core and its metal casing were still tightly lashed in place and secure as he had left it. He untied the ropes to release the large casing so he could remount it properly. After struggling with the weight of the bomb core he was able to move and refit it next to the engine on its mountings. He carefully reattached the fake cooling hoses and cleaned the engine room to hide any sign that he had worked there. As he climbed the small steps back into the cabin Tan looked back to double check that everything looked normal. The metal casing that held the plutonium core had been disguised as a heat exchanger for the diesel engine. To the observer, the steel casing looked like just another poorly designed part of the boat's makeshift cooling system.

It was only moments later that Tan had taken the wheel back from Ali, as they continued to make their way north along the Intracoastal Waterway. Coming around the next bend in the waterway Tan encountered a large, white, motor yacht traveling south. The man steering from the fly bridge was smoking a big cigar and waved at Tan as the two vessels passed port to port. Tan stuck his head out of the wheel house into the fresh air and waved back at the man, then smiled politely. "He is probably a retired military officer who has killed Muslims!" Tan mumbled to himself. He instinctively turned the boat into the oncoming wake and took the waves on the bow, then turned back on course again. In the distance, coming down the waterway, was another vessel coming towards him at high speed. As the two vessels closed on each other, the unmistakable red stripe just aft of the bow wave came into view. It was the United States Coast Guard! "Why now, God?" He asked himself.

"Ali, Ali," Tan yelled frantically.

Ali came stumbling up the companionway. "What is it?"

"It's the Coast Guard! Hide! Go to your hiding place quickly, you only have a couple of minutes!"

Ali scrambled down forward through a hatch in the wheelhouse floor. Both men had agreed that being Arab, Ali would certainly raise suspicions, so they had made plans earlier that, if they were stopped by the authorities, he would hide below decks.

Ali made his way forward in the tight space below to the anchor locker. He pulled himself up and into the space where anchor chain and rope were stored. It was wet and dark and stank of mildew, but Ali burrowed forward under the weight of the rope and chain. He then moved massive amount of rope over to one side of the small "V" shaped compartment located in the bow and covered himself with a brown plastic tarp that the two men had purchased for just this occasion. He then pulled the tangles of rope over the tarp and his body. He was curled in a fetal position and finally pulled the final coils over his head, which was by now out of sight under the tarp, camouflaged from prying eyes. Tan could see the Coast Guard patrol boat slowing down. As the two boats neared, he heard the siren blast a short high-pitched sound followed by a voice over the loud speaker.

"This is the United States Coast Guard please slow your vessel and prepare to be boarded."

Tan pull the throttle back to idle. The ominous, gray aluminum US Coast Guard vessel turned smartly as it passed and quickly came up from the stern. Tan was overwhelmed with fear as he waited to be boarded. "Be calm," he whispered. "Nothing will happen."

"Fishing vessel just idle and we will come along your port side," a man's voice on the speaker said.

Tan's pulse was racing. He pulled on an old New York Yankee baseball cap over his head. The patrol boat easily caught up and pulled alongside. Three young coastguardsmen in dark blue uniforms and bulletproof vests quickly jumped aboard. The men carried AR-15 rifles and pistols. The patrol boat backed off and followed on the port side. A short, stout man who looked to be in his thirties, led the boarding party across the weathered decks to the wheelhouse where Tan was piloting the boat.

"Good Morning, Captain."

"Good Morning also to you," Tan spoke perfect English but made his voice sound like an Asian man who barely knew how to speak English.

"Are you alone?"

"Yes, I alone."

"Where are you going this morning, sir?" The Coast Guardsman said slowly.

"I go for repairs."

"Where are you going for repairs, sir?" The officer again said slowly, attempting to pronounce each word so it could be clearly understood. What a fool, Tan thought.

"I go first place up the road, soon as I see good place, I stop…" Tan continued to try to sound like a poor Asian fisherman hoping to convince the man he was harmless.

"What is your problem?"

"No big problems, fuel I think no good, use too many filters."

"Yeah, we all have that problem. Do you mind if we look around below?"

"No, you my guest, you look—" The officer motioned the two other guardsmen to start searching the vessel.

"Do you have your papers for this vessel?" The officer asked slowly and precisely.

"Oh yes, they right here." Tan pulled the papers from a drawer next to the wheel and handed them over.

"I see you just purchased the boat," The Coast Guard officer declared.

"Yes, and he no take care of fuel, cost me too much money!" Tan said excitedly.

"Sorry to hear that. Do you have any identification that can prove you are US citizen?"

"Yes"

Tan pulled out a US passport that had been carefully forged for him. Tan was remarkably cool through the questioning. He had practiced his lines many times to prepare for such a boarding. However, he knew the fake passport was probably not perfect. Tan's heart started to pound furiously in his chest as the man studied his passport. To his relief the Coast Guard officer handed it back to him, apparently approving of it.

"I'm having my men inspect your vessel. So just keep idling forward until we are finished, do you understand?"

"Yes, okay, no problem!" Tan said quickly, with a toothy smile.

"Sir, what's down here?" Asked one of the younger Coast Guardsman. He was smaller than the other man and had blond hair and blue eyes. Tan noticed his name was *Murphy* from where it was sewn on his shirt just above the pocket.

"That go forward to crawl space?" Tan said as he crouched and made a crawling motion with his hands continuing to act like a poor Asian fisherman.

"What's down there?" The guardsman asked.

"Just wires and rope and anchors, officer," Tan said and again motioned with his hands as if he was letting anchor line out...

"Okay, you mind if I take a look?"

"No, Sir, take good look."

The man pulled a small red metal flashlight out of his belt and shined it down below.

The Coast Guardsman went through the small hatch and then took his flashlight and pointed it all around the hull underneath the deck. The guardsman could see a bundle of loose wiring hanging down that resembled a giant cobweb hanging from above. The bundle of loose wire swung back and forth as the boat moved through the choppy water. As he moved forward on his hands and knees, he could see slivers of light passing through the deck, where there were small separations in the decking. He continued to crawl forward just above the smelly bilge, shining his flashlight from right to left. He stopped just short of the anchor locker and shined the light around the bow section and into the locker area. For just a moment, he thought he saw the anchor ropes move. The guardsman kept shining the light into the space for a moment longer but saw nothing else. It must have been the boat moving, he thought. He crawled backwards as his knees started to ache from the pain of the rough boards he was crawling over. He made his way back towards the hatch and again emerged from where he had started into the fresh air.

"Everything in good order, right?" Tan asked excitedly.

His heart was pounding. He was sure that his chest must be showing the palpitations of his rapid heartbeat. It seemed more like hours rather than minutes since the young man had disappeared below. The other man was searching aft the cabin and probably into the engine room, although Tan couldn't see him from where he was standing. At this point, Tan's instincts were screaming to him to jump from the boat and try to swim to the nearby shore. He could run and take his chances in the low lands of the shoreline to make his escape. Every nerve in his body was by now on alert! He felt like his body was coiled and ready to react. He told himself to calm down and everything would be okay. Tan wished the boat had been rigged with explosives right now. If it were, he thought, he could detonate the bomb at this very moment and become a Martyr. But it wasn't. He still had time to leap into the water and make his getaway, though. The shore line was close enough that the patrol boat could never catch him before he made it ashore. Before Tan could act the Coast Guardsman said.

"It would be a good idea for you to organize all that loose wiring and hang it properly."

"I know very much work to do officer!" Tan forced himself to say over the lump developing in his throat.

"You could get an electrical short down there and burn the entire boat to the water line."

"Yes. Yes, I know, very dangerous!" He said, as he nodded politely.

At the same time, the other Coast Guardsman emerged from the cabin in the aft section of the boat. He said nothing and walked past Tan out onto the deck and went forward and said something to the man who initially questioned Tan. "This is it!" Tan said to himself under his breath. "They probably found the core! They know something's wrong now!" Tan's senses were screaming for him to jump from the boat and swim to shore, but he didn't. The Coast Guardsman with the blond hair and blue eyes named Murphy now joined the other men on the forward deck. They spoke among themselves for a minute smiling and laughing, then the older one came walking back to the wheelhouse.

"Everything seems to be in order. My men agree this vessel needs a lot of work to be seaworthy, so I suggest you take care of some of these problems before this vessel catches fire and burns. We're letting you go on your way since you just bought the boat, but be sure and correct these problems as soon as possible."

"I know, many problems, officer. I take care…" Tan said feeling immediately relieved.

"Well, have a good day, and be safe out here." The guardsman said. He then pulled his portable VHF radio out of his pocket and called the Coast Guard Patrol boat back alongside and, in minutes, they were back aboard their vessel and speeding off to the south, and just like that they were gone!

Tan applied power slowly and started northward again, along the waterway, with his heart still pounding. They had been boarded and no one had discovered that they were carrying deadly plutonium on board. The Coast Guard hadn't been able to discover his human cargo either. All the Coast Guardsman seemed to be concerned about was his safety. How ironic he thought! It was as easy as his handlers had said it would be, easy if they followed their plan. These foolish Americans couldn't see what was happening right before their eyes! He wondered how such a stupid people, like these Americans, could end up as a super power. It was hard to understand.

The boat rocked gently from the small waves that were entering the cove from the larger bay that loomed just outside. The fishing trawler lay quietly at anchor. A single light bulb burned from just above the bunks in the aft cabin. It was cool and pleasant in the boat now that the sun had set and darkness had fallen.

"You did well, my brother," Ali said as he ate tuna from the can.

"God is with us and protecting us," Tan replied.

"Yes, he saved us from the storm and then from the infidels, God is great!"

The cabin was cool and the two men sat in their bunks resting from the ordeal over the past several days.

"We need to move quickly back to the warehouse before we are boarded again, we might not be so lucky next time," Tan said. He had his eyes closed, resting them, looking very relaxed now.

"I'll be glad to get off this boat! This wasn't a good idea. We could have been drowned in the ocean before we even had a chance to carry out our plan!"

"Well it's over now and we're making good time. We should be back in no more than five days, God willing," Tan said, as he stretched out on his bunk. The men had agreed to take four hour watches; if anyone approached they would probably use a spot light. If that happened Ali would go to his hiding place again.

"I'll take the first watch," Ali said as he climbed up the short stairs of the companionway to the wheelhouse. Tan turned on his side and went to sleep almost immediately from exhaustion. He was both emotionally and physically drained from the past several days.

Ali could see the far away lights shimmering across the bay from a small town. The wind was cool and blowing over the water. Ali could smell the scent of damp earth in the air.

He was in the land of the infidels but it was a strangely beautiful place. As he sat on the deck under the stars he promised himself that when the time came, no matter how beautiful this land was, he would destroy it and every living soul that he could. The boat swung on her anchor as the soft wind shifted from the east. Now, only a dark, tree-lined shore was visible barely a hundred yards away. The insects were chattering along the banks. As Ali closed his eyes, he felt he was back home on the riverbank near his childhood home, but as soon as those thoughts started to overtake him, he opened his eyes again. "No, I'm not at home!" He said softly to himself. "I will never go home again. I will be dying soon as a Martyr. I will be going to a world where it will be much better than this world," Ali assured himself. As he sat on the deck, he pondered his existence. His life had never been good, except for the killing he had done in the name of Allah. But soon he was going to have to leave this world behind, prematurely, but that was God's will. "To die for Islam was the will of Allah," he whispered softly to himself. If he was meant to die, then when the time came he would die. He would die proud and brave to change the world, to rid it of evil.

Ali thought about his two sons at home. He missed them and he knew they probably missed him as well. They were so young not to have a father, but they would grow strong one day and answer to the calling of Islam, if God willed it. Nothing would make him more jubilant, more proud than to have both boys die as Martyrs in this fight against the unbelieving. He only wished they were old enough to die with him now, he thought. At the moment, nobody at home knew where he was. No one knew what he was about to do. His sons might never know how brave his father had been, but that was in the hands of Allah too.

Suddenly, Ali could hear the sound of a small boat entering the cove. The boat was moving at a high speed but with no lights. Ali froze for a second, then slinked aft along the cabin. Then the boat suddenly slowed to an idle, and he could just make out the outline as it approached. The people in the boat were laughing and shouting over the sounds of the outboard motor. The boat passed within thirty yards of the trawler. Ali had slipped into the wheelhouse where he wouldn't be seen. As the small pleasure boat passed, he could make out the images of two men and two women as the boat continued to idle towards the nearby beach. As Ali watched, the boat stopped in the shallow water at the edge of the beach and all four people got out splashing and laughing as they went ashore. They were too far away for him to understand their words clearly. Ali could still hear shouting and laughing carrying across the dark water. Ali knew it was just a group of young people having fun, nothing to be concerned with.

He sat back and began listening to the sounds of happy people spending a night on the beach. Soon they built a fire on the edge of the water, and he could barely make out human shapes sitting around it. Anger started to well up from deep within. These people wouldn't be carefree forever, he thought. The sins of their government will be answered, and these young people will have nothing to be happy about in the future. Happiness will be replaced by more fear! Paralyzing fear that will follow them where ever they go. Ali's mind raced back to the Middle East where women and children could only relax for hours, not days, where death lurked behind every corner and from the air. Where the American military would guide smart bombs into towns attempting to kill militants but, instead, killed innocent people. And they call them smart bombs, Ali thought! They would pay for this, and he was determined to make them pay! With the will of Allah, he would change the minds of these Americans! He might indeed die in the process, but their lives would never be the same again.

13

April 30th 2012 9:30 p.m.
Washington D.C.

Stevie Dillon sat in her favorite blue flannel pajamas staring at the computer screen. Her third-story Georgetown apartment was nice enough, but expensive. On her salary living in Georgetown took quite a large portion of her FBI paycheck. She hadn't bought a lot of furniture so the apartment remained almost empty. Most of her furnishings were cheap and much of it had been left over from her college days.

Stevie didn't feel especially sexy waddling around in her pajamas and house shoes. But since she wasn't expecting company tonight she had chosen to put something on that was a little more comfortable to work in. It was already past nine-thirty and darkness had fallen outside. The room was dark except for the glow of the plasma display that radiated a blue hue that dimly lit the room. She had, from her exceptional memory, recreated several lines of the latest patterns of Arabic words that had been generated by the

FBI computers. As she sat there mesmerized by the stream of Arabic words. She tried to create meaningful sentences out of the code. So far the computers had been helpful but they hadn't been able to crack the code.

It had been over a month since the coded messages were delivered to the FBI and, other than some initial progress, nothing further had been decoded. The code was proving to be one of the most difficult the Bureau had seen. Stevie had augmented her prodigious memory with actual documents to be used at home, in reality a security breach. The FBI would never allow classified evidence to leave FBI headquarters. Once coded documents were received they were logged in as evidence, and in the case of national security, usually classified either secret or top secret.

To spend more time on the code and avoid being caught carrying classified information out of the Bureau, Stevie had created a clever word stream of her own. Lines of Arabic words were broken down to letters, and then assigned a specific number. In this way, Stevie had transformed coded pages into seemingly meaningless lines of numbers. Once the document was turned into pages of numbers, she simply put it a file folder and carried it out of her office. In this clever way, she had been able to smuggle some of the secret code home for more study. This was clearly against FBI policy, but she had broken the rules for a good reason, to try to break the code faster. "It wasn't that big a deal," she had told herself when she decided to take classified material out of headquarters. This must be the way a double agent operates, she thought, but I am using this information for the benefit of my country, she reassured herself as she worked.

As Stevie immersed herself in the strange code, she heard a squeaking sound followed by a grating noise. It sounded like metal sliding on metal coming from inside her bedroom. The bedroom was at the very back of the apartment more than thirty feet from where she sat. Then she heard the unmistakable sound of a window rattling. It took Stevie a minute to react, for the sounds to sink in. For a moment, she attempted to persuade herself that the noise came from next door. However, her instincts told her differently. But she still tried to convince herself it would be impossible for anyone to come through her bedroom window. The bedroom faced a vacant lot on the back of the apartment complex and was three stories above the ground.

Stevie slowly opened the drawer to her desk and pulled her pistol out. She had made a habit of placing her weapon in the desk when she came home from work. The Smith and Wesson 1076 was her personal weapon that her uncle Joe had given her after she graduated from Quantico. The old 1076 had been discontinued by the FBI years ago, but she kept it along with her service pistol for personal protection. She never left any of her firearms out in the open, because guests had a tendency to want to pick them up and ask questions. She flipped the frame-mounted safety, now making the trigger live. She paused as she poised herself and then slowly made her way down the hall to the door of her bedroom. The door was half open and the room was dark inside.

As she stood there in front of the door, Stevie wondered whether she should slide her hand in and turn the light on or just push the door back and walk in. She couldn't remember at the moment if she had left the light on or not. But, after a moment, she concluded that she had indeed left the light on. Her logical mind screamed that it was unlikely that an intruder could get into a third story window. But her training taught her that criminals can get into just about any place they want, no matter how impossible it might seem. She had made up her mind to slide her hand quickly inside and flip the lights on. As she moved forward, suddenly the wood flooring creaked under her foot certainly loud enough to be heard by anyone standing nearby. "Shit—" She said under her breath. She stopped and backed up several steps. She knew if someone was in her bedroom they would know she was in the hall. She had inadvertently given her position away; if someone was actually behind the door, they would have the drop on her. She decided to try something else.

"Come out, FBI!" She said, a little embarrassed about speaking into a possibly empty room. She moved closer to the door and pushed it gently open with her left foot while aiming the gun at the middle of the doorway, every nerve in her body was ready to react. Her hands were steady, but her mouth was now dry as she attempted to swallow.

"Come out with your hands in the air! By now Stevie had moved closer to the door. Since there was no response, she quickly reached with her left hand to flip the light switch on while she was still holding the pistol in her right. As her hand moved past the inside of the doorframe and into the room to find the light switch, the door slammed violently against her wrist trapping her left hand and part of her forearm!

She screamed in agony as the slamming door crushed her arm. She was trapped like a rat in a trap, a trap she had inadvertently set for herself. She instinctively pulled back with all her strength but couldn't free herself. The weight of the intruder on the other side was exerting an enormous amount of force against the door. Stevie struggled in vain again and again to pull herself free. Without really thinking she pulled her Smith and Wesson and started firing into the door, the deafening sound of the blast in the small hall area made her ears ring immediately, but she was sure she heard screaming from the other side.

The muzzle flash and smell of burnt gun powder filled her nostrils with an acrid smell. The spent casings fell all around her bare feet and bounced against the wall. One landed on the top of her bare ankle above her house shoe, and she felt the burning sensation as it rolled off onto the wood floor, with a clink. At that very moment, the door opened slightly and she lost her balance and tumbled backwards, landing flat on her back on the hall floor. She brought her pistol back up and leveled it at the door. Stevie expected the intruder to come rushing out at any second. She could see the door was riddled with bullet holes. The door suddenly slammed shut again and she heard it being locked from the inside. She half scrambled, half crawled backwards as fast as she could, back down the hallway back into the living room. Her heart was pounding furiously and her arm ached where the door had crushed it. Once in the living room, she grabbed her cordless phone and backed into the dining room and beside the hutch that had belonged to her mother. Squatting down, she quickly dialed 911. She rattled off what had just occurred to the operator and identified herself as an FBI special agent. By this time, she was gasping for air and her left arm continued to throb with pain and was beginning to swell. She had fired six shots and only had three left in the clip. Her other clip was in the drawer next to the computer but she didn't want to move just yet. From where she sat, Stevie felt confident she could kill the intruder with one shot. The Winchester Silver Tip 175 grain loads could stop anyone at close range traveling twelve-hundred and fifty feet per second. She decided to sit still and not make a move until help arrived.

A dark crimson blood trail led across the hardwood floors to the open window. Blood was smeared against the bricks all the way down the side of the building to the parking lot below. The intruder had come through the window of the third-story apartment after attaching rope to a ventilator on the roof. It had been relatively easy for the assailant to slide down to the window, open it, then swing into the bedroom. There was blood and a partial footprint on the window ledge where he had rappelled down to the parking lot below. The blood trail had led down to the street and stopped at the curb. Unless the assailant had stopped the bleeding or disappeared into thin air, he must have had a getaway car parked there, Detective Williams surmised. The only other evidence between the window and where the blood trail ended at the curb were a few more partial shoe prints made by the blood on the bottom of the assailant's shoes.

"Whoever was in your bedroom must have more holes in him than a pepper shaker," Detective Williams said. The Washington D.C. Detective was used to investigating bloody crime scenes and had long since stopped being affected by the carnage left behind.

The MPDC detective sat across from Stevie at her dining room table. A paramedic was taking a close look at her badly bruised left arm.

"Did you see this guy at all?"

"No, I never saw anything other than the door slamming." Starting to feel the shock of actually having to shoot another person, most of the agents she knew had never pulled their weapons in defense. By the looks of the blood trail that was left behind, she couldn't believe anyone could live after losing so much blood. Stevie had been told that agents from the D.C. area were on their way to the scene.

"Have you had any contact with anyone, say, in an official investigation that would want to do harm to you?" Detective Williams asked. The detective had concluded within minutes that this was a murder plot, a burglar wouldn't come down from the roof on a rope and try and steal a T.V. or stereo. He also knew there were probably a couple of hundred apartments in the area that would be easier to burglarize. No, this was someone attempting to kill or rape his victim, the senior detective concluded.

Williams was in his early forties; he had worked his way up the ladder from patrolman to detective over the last sixteen year with the Metro Police Department. His easygoing and jovial outward mannerism was in stark contrast to his deep understanding of the criminal mind. Williams had a reputation of solving homicides quickly with a conviction rate of over eighty percent, which was the highest in the MPDC.

"Agent Dillon what do you do for the FBI, if I can ask?"

"I can't share that information at the moment, Detective."

"Oh, now I'm starting to sense some possible motive here," Williams said. He sensed that her job with the FBI might be the reason she had been targeted.

"Do you ever carry anything home from the Bureau that someone might want to gain access to or maybe some organization that might want you dead?" It wasn't that Williams was expecting an answer to his question, because he wasn't; what he was looking for was some type of non-verbal response that would answer the question.

"I really can't talk about anything until I'm cleared to do that, sir."

"I'll take that as a yes."

"Well, take it anyway you want!" Stevie snapped back.

"So the answer is no?"

"The answer is I am not at liberty to say at the moment," she said, knowing she had inadvertently answered the detective's question.

Stevie knew this was going to be a serious problem. She had to level with her superiors about bringing classified materials home. She knew investigators would take her computer. She had stored part of the code on her hard drive, something she knew would be deemed a security breach. To erase files now would be considered a crime and a cover-up, so she would just have to admit she brought classified materials home. There was no sense in turning a possible reprimand into a crime, she thought.

Detective Williams' cell phone rang.

"Williams...Yes, I'll be right over," he said, as he folded the flip phone.

"We found the guy you shot! He is an Arab male, dead from multiple gunshot wounds."

"Where did they find him?"

"They found him over on Highway One near Crystal City. He had apparently pulled over to the side of the road and bled out slumped over the steering wheel. The cause of death looks like massive blood loss from multiple gunshot wounds. Now, if I got this right, what we have here is a dead Arab male, who was in the apartment of an FBI agent, and the agent who apparently killed the Arab male, who really can't talk about it. Is that about right?" The Detective asked as he pushed away from the dining room table and put a small notebook back in his pocket knowing he wasn't going to get anywhere with the young Agent.

"I've told you all I can, Detective."

"I understand. I've called the FBI and told them this could be a terrorist related crime. They're sending agents over to take a look around and interface between us."

"Okay, thanks," Stevie said as she sat back into her chair.

"Listen, I have to go over to the other crime scene. I'll leave one of the officers here until your Bureau guys get here. There's a Starbucks down the street. You want me to get you something?"

"No, I'm fine, but thanks anyway." Stevie was sitting at the table wondering how to feel. She had killed another human being, someone she had never seen! Now, with the information that her assailant was an Arab male, pretty much confirmed that she had been targeted! It was clear the assassin had tried to kill her because she worked for the FBI, but why?

Soon after Detective Williams left, two FBI agents arrived on the scene. Stevie informed them that the man she had shot had just been found dead. One of the agents, Lee Marshall, immediately left to go to the other crime scene leaving Ed Tripp at the apartment alone with Stevie. She had seen Tripp before and had been introduced to him a year earlier during a briefing. He was in charge of the Terrorism Task Force, and Stevie knew he would be handling this case, which meant every detail would be scrutinized.

"Are you okay?"

"Yeah, fine, sir."

"Tell me exactly what happened here." Tripp said, taking a chair across from her. She noticed he was wearing a Kaki suit, something most agents wouldn't dream of wearing. A small man, Tripp looked like an actor rather than a senior supervisor. His salt and pepper hair was thick and resembled a younger Robert Redford.

Stevie went through the events of the early evening leading up to the shooting. However, while describing what had happened to Tripp, she wondered how to break the news that she had defied regulations bringing classified documents home.

"Do you have anything here in your apartment a terrorist organization would like to get their hands on?"

"Nothing they wouldn't already have," she said cautiously. *There it is*, Stevie thought. There would be no going back now! Tripp, an experienced interrogator, picked up on her comment immediately.

"What is that suppose to mean?" Tripp pressed.

"I have been working on some code here at home," she said. *There it was*, she thought. *Now I'm going to have to deal with breaking the rules.*

"Were you authorized to bring that information out of Quantico?"

"Actually, no." Stevie was aware this was a serious security breach and there would be serious repercussions. "I really didn't bring actual classified documents out."

Stevie explained that she committed to memory certain passages for further study and coded other information on paper.

"Where is the secure information now?"

"On my computer."

"Is it on the hard drive or a DVD?"

"Both."

"Is there code on any other computers or DVD's?"

"No." She knew that was enough of an admission to lose her job with the Bureau.

"I'm going to have to take the computer and all your notes," Tripp said almost apologetically.

"I know." Stevie's mind was reeling, she knew that this could jeopardize her career and might result in her termination.

"I'm going to have to put you into protective custody until we can sort things out. Sorry, but that's policy," Tripp said.

He understood, this was a case of a young agent trying to do her job, but nevertheless, it was still a serious security breach and would have to be handled that way.

Tripp's phone suddenly rang. After answering the phone, he said nothing, only listening to the caller on the other end, then hung up.

"Dillon, they identified the dead man. He's a known terrorist suspect wanted for masterminding a suicide attack in Los Angeles last year that killed twenty-seven people."

"Mustafa Radiz?" Stevie asked.

"So you read my posting about the possibility of Radiz being in the D.C. area."

"I did," She said.

"You might get a medal for this one, that is, if you can get out of the mess you are in for this violation of FBI policy," Tripp said as he smiled. "You don't know him personally do you?

"You mean Radiz?" She said shocked. "No..."

"Good," Tripp said, smiling.

"I have seen his picture, but never had the pleasure until tonight."

"Well, he's dead, and it looks like you're the agent who's going to get the credit for bringing him in! If you want to call killing the man bringing him in!"

Stevie understood what Tripp was saying. The Bureau would have preferred to capture Radiz alive to get information; now he was dead and dead men didn't talk, another strike against her, she thought.

Stevie wondered what Mark Latham would think? How would he react when he found out what she had done? She didn't want him to be reprimanded for her actions. She had made a terrible mistake, a lapse in judgment. She knew she was the only one responsible. She would make that clear to the Disciplinary Review Board. What would actually happen after all of this she didn't know, but Stevie desperately wanted to continue her career with the FBI. Her future was now in someone else's hands, and she would have to resign herself to that fate. Ironic as it seems, she has assassinated an assassin and may have inadvertently killed her career. But one thing was for sure, she thought.

14

May 1st 2012
Southern California

"It looks like a smog-free day in Southern California!" Doug said, looking out over the left wing of the plane toward the Santa Ana Mountains.

"That's rare!" Tony replied as he leaned over to take a better look outside. The sky was deep blue with a hint of brown tinge hanging just above the mountains.

"Yeah, it really is," Doug added.

The sleek blue Cessna Citation X banked over the mountainous terrain bordering *John Wayne Airport.* Doug sat in a tan leather seat just in front of a navy blue sofa on the port side of the airplane. As he viewed the mountains in the distance, the jet went into a steep bank then started descending and, after a few minutes, made a final turn to line up with the runway. After a few more minutes, Doug felt the wheels touched down softly on the tarmac with a sharp screech. The big blue jet rolled down the runway and decelerated quickly, turning on the first taxiway that led back to the executive jet terminal. The corporate jet made its way slowly with the jet engines whining toward a group of hangers and then lurched to a complete stop. The plane parked in front of a modern, glassed front building, which was the private terminal. The engines whined down as his new co-pilot Jim Archer made his way back into the main cabin and unlocked and lowered the plane's pressurized door.

"Beautiful day, Governor. I hope the flight was smooth enough." Ferguson Industries had just hired Archer, a blond-headed young pilot in his late twenties, as co-pilot, to replace Tom Miller, the chief pilot who was nearing retirement. At six-foot, four-inches, Archer looked a little tall to be a fighter pilot who flew F-16 Falcon jets on the weekends with the Air National Guard.

As the pressurized door opened, air, with the unmistakable scent of jet exhaust, rushed into the cabin. Tony was the first to exit the jet and for good reason; he was the only protection Doug had now. Everything seemed to be secure down on the ground as he scanned the tarmac for anything unusual. He didn't see anyone loitering around, so he radioed back to Archer that everything looked fine. Archer gave the okay to Doug and Senator Atchison that they were cleared to leave the jet. Both men exited the aircraft and began descending the stairs to the tarmac. As soon as Doug stepped onto the ground, he heard the unmistakable crack of automatic weapons fire, which he instantly recognized as a Kalashnikov. Then hot lead started impacting the aircraft all around him! Some whizzing just over his head. He heard loud thumping sounds as the bullets impacted the airplane just behind him. Doug instantly grabbed a frightened and stunned Ben and slung him to the ground; both men scrambled to the nose wheel of the aircraft and tried to disappear behind it for cover, but it was too small to shadow both men! Bullets ricocheted off of the ground all around them as the gunmen continued firing in their direction.

Doug didn't have time to spot Tony since the shooting started. He instantly knew there wasn't enough cover behind the small wheel and decided to make a break for one of the larger rear wheels.

"Stay put, Ben!"

"I'm not going anywhere trust me!" He screamed back.

As he scampered to the left rear wheel of the aircraft, Doug looked across the tarmac just in time to see Tony running, bobbing and weaving, directly at the two gunmen with his Glock up in the firing position. One of the two gunmen was firing short bursts at Tony who now was running a wide looping half circle towards the hangar where the two men were crouched in firing positions. As soon as Doug reached the tire, it exploded into black shards of rubber all around his face as a hail of automatic weapon fire hit around him. One small piece of the tire struck him in the right cheek stinging with the impact. It was obvious that one of the attackers had tried to lead him with the AK-47, but luckily, Doug got to the tire first. He desperately tried to move his head closer to the metal wheel for protection. The tire which, by now, was shredded rubber made that extremely difficult. Doug was pinned down with no weapon and no way to help defend himself against the two gunmen. All he could hope for was that Tony could stop them.

The man firing spurts of automatic gunfire at Tony suddenly stopped firing. He had emptied the magazine. Tony, realizing instinctively what had happened, stopped running and put the man in the gun sites of his Glock 31. He fired off one round hitting the man square in the center of his chest. The .357 slug exploded deep in his chest, and the attacker died instantly. The other gunman continued to fire wildly towards the airplane not realizing his partner was mortally wounded. Tony quickly directed his next deadly shot at the other gunman still firing towards the jet. The slug hit the man in the left arm tearing it away from the AK he was furiously firing; the weapon went flying into the air, before it landed on the tarmac, and another slug from Tony's pistol slammed into the side of the gunman's neck which sent him to the ground screaming. Tony rushed forward with his pistol in firing position. The first man Tony hit was sprawled on the ground and not moving; the second man laid screaming and holding his neck. But he was still alive and possibly dangerous! Tony only wounded the second man because he wanted to know who was responsible for the attack.

"Stay down, stay down!" Tony screamed at the man with the neck wound while pointing the Glock directly at his head.

Tony quickly kicked the AK-47 farther away from the man making it impossible for him to reach it. Blood was pouring from the wound in the man's neck, and the tarmac was flowing with the bright red blood from both attackers. Several men came running out of the jet terminal. Tony screamed at them to call the police. He knelt on one knee and scanned the area, thinking there might be a second wave of attackers.

"Doug, are you hit?" He screamed over his shoulder.

"No, we are both okay!"

"Get back on the plane and close the door!"

After they had struggled to their feet, however, Doug sent Ben up into the plane alone as Jim Archer made his way down to the ground, and then both Doug and Jim sprinted over to Tony's side. Both men picked up the AK-47s lying on the ground and knelt on one knee with their backs to each other in a defensive firing position.

"The police are on the way!" Doug said, as all three men scanned the area.

"That magazine is empty Jim! Get another one off the guy with the head wound," Tony yelled above the screams of the attacker that was still alive.

Jim quickly slammed the magazine into the AK-47 and loaded a round into the chamber. "I'm loaded and ready!" he said, as he turned an aimed in the direction of the hangar.

"You guys stay put. I'm going to check the hangar," Tony said, getting up and moving cautiously towards the building just thirty yards away. This was something he didn't plan on doing, but with both Doug and Jim out in the open, and easy targets, he needed to find out if any more gunmen where around.

He sprinted into the hangar and disappeared from view. Both men expected to hear gunshots, but there was no gunfire. Suddenly, Tony reappeared, running back over to where they were crouching.

"They killed three in there; looks like they were all mechanics," Tony shouted.

In a matter of minutes, the men began to hear the police car sirens as they watched four squad cars turn through a nearby gate and came screaming in their direction.

"We better put these weapons down," Doug said.

All three men laid their weapons down and stood up. The police cars came roaring up and screeched to a halt surrounding them. They put their hands up in the air and waited.

After a tense two or three minutes, the police finally gained enough confidence to lower their weapons too. People from the executive jet terminal were running out to see what happened. The Orange County Sheriff's department officers recognized the Presidential Candidate and the Senator and escorted them into the terminal and then to a private room.

One of the officers gave Tony his Glock back, just in case there was more trouble. Within ten minutes, the SWAT team was on the premises searching the airport, but no more terrorists were found. The pilot, Jimmy Miller, had been escorted off the plane and reunited with the group in the airport terminal. Within an hour, the FBI sent a bullet-proof Chevy Suburban to pick up all five men and take them to a remote location for questioning. The FBI was treating this incident as an assassination attempt, and the local police were making every effort to protect Doug and Ben from further attacks. Paramedics were treating the one attacker that was still alive; he was being rushed to the hospital in an attempt to save his life.

The telephone rang in Doug's room.

"Doug, turn on your television and go to channel 72," Cliff said excitedly on the other end.

The FBI had taken the men in for questioning but since both were considered highly visible targets they were taken to Laguna Niguel and checked into the Ritz Carlton Hotel and were now under Federal protection.

Doug quickly turned on the television. The image that immediately came up was a still picture of him with an AK-47 kneeling on one knee looking as if he was scanning the tarmac.

"Where did that come from?" Doug asked, as he raced back to the phone.

"Apparently one of the people in the terminal had a video camera and filmed the whole attack. The still photo of you is being shown on all the major networks, and our phones at election headquarters haven't stopped ringing." Cliff said excitedly. "Looks like you're a hero, Governor!

"I'm not the hero, let's get that straight; if there's a hero, it's Tony," Doug said, half embarrassed. "Cliff, I don't like seeing this kind of thing on television."

"Tony is getting great coverage too. His picture has been all over the media, and he's not running for President, is he?"

"What are the other candidates saying?" Doug asked. He hadn't been able to catch up on the news.

"The usual things. They're happy that you are okay and are appalled at what happened to you and Ben."

"Has any terrorist group taken credit for the attack?"

"Not yet, but there is speculation that it's an Arab group."

"I have a feeling that it's a Malaysian group, not Arab," Doug said, watching recorded images of Tony moving cautiously to the hangar area.

"Are you okay?" Cliff asked.

"Yeah, I'm fine, but I guess we're going to have to tighten our security; it's pretty clear there are people out there that want me dead!"

"It looks like you will be getting secret service protection now."

"Really, the President's press spokesman, Jean Mathews, said the president has ordered the Secret Service to protect you."

"Well, I guess that would help, but I'm not sure I need the secret service…" Doug wanted to call the shots and didn't want to argue with the Secret Service about it.

"I don't agree. I think you need all the protection you can get. We're damn lucky we still have Tony; he took some big chances and could have been killed!"

"That's exactly why Tony is at my side! He's fearless and drop-dead accurate, even if he is a bit reckless, like he was today."

After Doug hung the phone up it rang again almost immediately.

"They almost got you!" The caller said.

Doug recognized the voice on the other end of the line as the same person who had called him in Michigan.

"Looks like the terrorists are focused on you now. I guess they've figured out you're working against them."

"How did you get this number?"

"I'm smart I guess?"

Doug hit the speed dialer on his cell phone. The phone quickly dialed the number that agent Nelson had given him to trace phone calls.

"Well, I have done a number of things, lately. Why don't you just tell me who you are, and we can speak more intelligently about things."

"I can't do that or I won't be able to speak at all…"

"So you saw the attack," Doug said, stalling for time.

"Yeah, your bodyguard didn't seem to have much of a problem taking care of things. He's good, very good with that Glock. It even looks like you're going to get secret-service protection.

"I'm still thinking about that one. What do you think?" Doug asked, trying to keep the caller on the phone.

"Listen, Governor, you're going to have to be more careful. This attack wasn't that well planed, but you might not be so lucky next time! Also, don't let them try and convince you that this was an Arab attack, it wasn't!"

"How would you know that?" Doug said, stalling.

"I can't prove it yet, but I know I'm right! It just makes sense… Listen to me. There's going to be a massive attack supported by a group in Malaysia against the United States. The new President down there, this guy Putra, is the new kid on the block and desperately wants to make a strong statement in the Muslim world. Governor, it looks to me like you're my only chance; the two other candidates aren't set up to do anything, if you know what I mean. Keep this in mind, you won't be able to help anyone dead, Governor."

"You've talked about all this attack stuff before. Can you give me some specifics? Maybe I can help you?" Doug asked, but the phone went dead in his ear.

Doug was confident the caller was an insider. He must be with some government organization, probably the CIA or maybe FBI, Doug reasoned. For some reason, the man was convinced the next large scale attack would come from Malaysia. Doug suspected the caller wasn't going to give himself away by giving specific classified information that could be tracked back to him. He was too smart for that, but the story made sense to him. The new radical leaders of Malaysia had asked repeatedly for Muslims to rise up against the Great Satan. To kill Americans at home and abroad was clearly their intention. Whoever this guy was, he was convinced that a large-scale attack was about to take place. The only thing that didn't make sense was if someone in the Government knew and had conclusive evidence to what was about to happen, why were they not acting? The government regularly acted on the kind of information that the caller seemed to posses.

The phone then rang again and Doug quickly picked it up.

"Not enough time, we couldn't trace it," Agent Nelson said.

"I tried. He's too smart to stay on the line."

Doug then went over the entire conversation with the agent.

"Listen, let's keep trying. If he slips up we'll get him."

"He's pretty convincing; the guy seems like he knows what he's talking about…"

"Well, maybe and maybe not. Hey, tell your bodyguard that was some deadly marksmanship. The guy saved your life with some damn fine shooting."

"I'll do that, he's a good man," Doug said.

"I don't think there's any doubt about that," Nelson said.

"Have you guys made any progress cracking the code?"

"No word so far," Nelson said. "The code breakers are working on it. You'll know when I know."

"I'd like to know."

"I'll do what I can," Nelson said, knowing that some of that information might end up being classified.

Doug hung the phone up. The seriousness of what had happened was starting to sink in. He had always understood that he would become a target for assassination if he won in the election or even if he didn't. He had accepted the risk as one worth taking, but he never thought it would happen so quickly. The people supposedly in the know still had him losing the election. *Why kill me now?* he thought. Why in the hell did they want him dead, now? His mind was racing. How could a terrorist organization know he would be flying into Orange County? Now he was now more concerned about the safety of his family. One of the first calls he had made, after the attack, was to John

Bennett to get some security people together to protect Liz and the kids. It would only be necessary temporarily, just long enough to get the secret service in place. He might not need their protection, but his family certainly did, and he was going to make sure that happened. Everything has changed now, he thought.

15

May 4th 2012
Sandy Hook, New Jersey

"We're too late," Ali said angrily as he emerged from his cabin glancing at his watch.

"It's the tide," Tan said. "We've lost speed…" He wasn't surprised that Ali was agitated.

"When will the tide change?" He demanded angrily.

"In two hours," Tan answered obediently, watching Ali while making a course correction at the same time.

"We've come all this way and you didn't plan for this, you imbecile!"

"Allah will provide for us my brother, trust him," Tan said slowly.

"You better trust Allah and hope he smiles down on you. Nothing is going to get in my way, not even your stupidity!" Ali said, as he left the wheelhouse leaving Tan to ponder if he might be the next to die.

The trawler made a wide circle as it cleared Sandy Hook from the blue expanse of the North Atlantic. The sun was bright in the sky, causing a glare in the wheelhouse. Tan pulled out a pair of wrap-around sunglasses and put them on to improve his vision. They were entering the most dangerous leg of the trip. Although Newark Bay wasn't as heavily patrolled as New York Harbor, it was still home to the sprawling Port of Newark Marine Terminal. The bustling traffic area was randomly patrolled by the United States Coast Guard. After skirting the edge of the New York's City harbor, the old fishing trawler chugged against the strong, out-going tide, but making steady progress.

"Why now?" Tan said angrily.

Tan had thoroughly planned their approach to provide protection to smuggle the nuclear core into New Jersey, but now he realized he should have waited for the tide change, moving this slowly would expose them to more scrutiny. The New Jersey side of the waterway would offer a better line of entry for them, less traffic, less exposure, but still dangerous. The harbor area was always at a state of heightened alert. With the new strategy of smaller attacks coming weekly on American streets, the authorities were like angry hornets stirred from their nest. Tan prayed they could avoid being boarded today. One boarding had been enough; they might not be so lucky the next time. As he scanned the area, he could see New York Harbor in the distance loosely formed at the confluence of the Passaic and Hackensack Rivers. Having such a large expanse of water to navigate would increase their luck. There was enough sea room to avoid the patrol boats and enough traffic to blend into the regular traffic patterns. Tan smiled slightly, as the thought occurred to him, about how much lethal destructive power he was smuggling into the United States. When he thought about the magnitude of destruction they would bring to the infidels, his heart soared. Nothing Ali could say could make him feel bad about what they had accomplished so far. By the will of Allah, they would succeed.

The Tuesday afternoon traffic in the harbor area was busy with tug boats and barges everywhere. Tan avoided a large, red-hulled container ship as it steamed east. "Good," Tan whispered as he continued to scan the area. "Lots of traffic..." To his surprise, so far, they hadn't spotted any Coast Guard Patrol boats, a testament to the power and greatness of Allah. Without being challenged, his vessel was now steaming past the Newark Marine Terminal. "Thank you, Allah, for your benevolence. I promise you with my life, I will kill many infidels in your holy name." The heavy smell of industrial fumes invaded his sensitive nostrils as he guided the boat northward towards the river. This foul air was a signal from God that this evil place should be burned to the sweet, untainted earth that lay just beneath the surface. The thermal nuclear device will cleanse this area, he thought. Something that should have been done long ago.

"How much further?" Ali's sullen voice echoed from the cabin below.

"About four kilometers."

Ali continued to hide out, away from the prying eyes of the authorities. It would be easy to be spotted with powerful binoculars. His Arab features could be easily recognized and would surely arouse suspicion. This was a dangerous passage, and he wouldn't take any unnecessary chances of being discovered and compromising the mission. Any sign of a suspicious Arab male aboard a boat would be a red flag that would result in being stopped and boarded. The plan was to steam up the Passaic River to their warehouse facility. Then, under the cover of darkness, unload their lethal cargo and conceal it inside the warehouse.

The trawler chugged steady along northward, toward the entrance of the river, picking up speed as the tide slackened. Tan could see the entrance clearly now. He turned the boat slightly to starboard, correcting for the set of the ebbing tide and aimed the bow for the center of the river's entrance. The pressure was beginning to mount, and the tension was being translated into pain, causing Tan's shoulders to stiffen and ache. He realized that he was now grasping the wheel too tightly, so he slowly loosened his iron-like grip and felt some relief in his shoulders. The entrance of the river represented safety to Tan. In his excitement, he pushed the boat's red throttle handle a little farther forward to increase the shaft speed against the surging tide. "If we can just make the river, we'll be safe..."

he whispered under his breath as the boat plowed ahead through the dirty waters. But, as Tan's mind wondered, and the tiny trawler sped towards the entrance of the river, he couldn't help but imagine they were being tracked by the Coast Guard. He knew they could be closing in on them right now. His nerves were shot; he was aware they could be tracking him at a distance by radar. Now, the closer he got to the entrance, the more nervous and rattled he became. Beads of perspiration formed around his temples as the boat continued to plow through the water towards the safety of the river, which now was just seventy meters away. Knowing that safety was finally close at hand, Tan scanned in all directions and didn't see any patrol boats. He then began to relax. "Please, Allah, allow our journey to be safe." He again reached for the single-throttle lever with the familiar red ball on the end, pulling the lever backwards to decrease the engine's RPMs. "No use in blowing the engine now, we're almost there." The day remained clear with beautiful blue skies that seemed to signal a fitting end to their perilous trip. Seagulls were flying along parallel with the boat soaring and dipping their beaks into the water, squawking as if they were escorting the vessel to safe harbor. Tan was sleep deprived and overwhelmed by the cumulative effects of the voyage. His muscles were now going limp from the flush of adrenalin that had flooded his blood stream earlier, and his brain demanded sleep. Tan's dream of killing hundreds of thousands of hated infidels was now closer to being realized. It was soon to be transformed from a brilliant plan to a destined reality, willed by Allah himself. He wasn't sure how he would feel at that glorious moment when the great weapon was detonated. He knew he would then ascend to Paradise and to his virgins. Now, calm again and looking forward to that glorious day, he thought, "Nothing will stop me now," as the boat entered the lower reaches of the Passaic River. Tan, again changed his focus from anticipation and fear, to the moral rectitude of Islam, which made Paradise possible only for the true believers. "Nothing will stop me now," he promised again and again, "Nothing at all!" The JI would teach these filthy dogs a lesson, not with the sharp blade of a sword, but with a deadly weapon of mass destruction invented by the infidel enemy himself. What perfect symmetry that was, Tan thought.

Sheriff Joe Lombardo spotted the fishing trawler entering the Passaic river channel. As it moved northward up the channel, he quickly made a decision to board the vessel. Lombardo was responsible for patrolling the upper and lower reaches of the river down to the bay. As a father of two young boys, he had achieved two objectives: he was able to provide a respectable living to his family and work on the water, which was something he had always wanted to do.

Lombardo eased the throttles forward to the twin, Yamaha, two-hundred-horsepower outboard motors, and the twenty-five-foot patrol boat quickly shot out of the water and planed off in pursuit of the trawler that was now about a quarter of a mile in front of him. The water was smooth, and the patrol boat felt like it was flying over glass as he approached the trawler from the stern. The wind threatened to blow his baseball hat off so he reached up and took it off and threw it just under the windshield. As he came alongside, he saw a lone Asian man at the helm of the fishing boat. He flipped his loud speaker on and ordered the trawler to stop. The man at the helm then slowed the boat to an idle speed. Sheriff Lombardo came alongside the trawler, handing the line to the man as he came out of the wheelhouse.

"What is your destination this morning, sir?" Joe said, as he glanced up and down the boat from bow to stern.

"Up the river for repairs," Tan said, smiling, attempting to look passive.

"Not many fishing trawlers up that way," Lombardo said as he stepped up over the rail and onto the deck of the fishing boat.

"I've been told there are services up the river."

"Let's take a look at your registration papers," Lombardo said. He instinctively felt something was wrong. Lombardo didn't know exactly what the problem was but things just didn't seem right. He had never seen this boat in any of the harbors or in the river before and something in his gut told him there was more to this than met the eye.

Tan had gone back into the wheelhouse and returned with the documentation papers for the boat.

"Who owns the boat?" Lombardo asked with a piercing stare.

"I do, sir."

"Well, let me see some identification that proves you're the owner.

"I just buy this boat. I have not transferred ownership," Tan said, attempting to be cool.

"Coast Guard already looked at papers, say okay!"

Lombardo could have been a New York City detective with his instincts. Things weren't adding up. Although the Asian man didn't show any signs of panic, there was something going on, something the man was trying to hide.

"Let's have your driver's license."

Tan handed him a passport and a driver's license for New York State; the sheriff, closely examined both documents and decided they were in order.

"Let's take a look below," Lombardo said.

Joe stepped into the wheelhouse and then down into the cabin. He could see that there were two bunks and both had been slept in. He could also smell the unmistakable remnants of someone being seasick. He then stepped back up into the wheel house.

"Where's your buddy?" The Sheriff surprised Tan with the question.

Tan could feel the panic set in, and he struggled to stay calm, but he didn't know what the Sheriff had seen to make him suddenly ask the question.

"No one else on board," Tan said, trying to control his anxiety.

"Where have you been?"

"I fished all night."

"By yourself?" Lombardo asked as he scanned the wheelhouse.

"Yes, by myself."

"Catch anything?"

"No, I was unlucky, I guess." Tan was losing confidence in his ability to answer the questions.

"So you fish by yourself a lot? How do you handle the nets single handed?"

"It's difficult, but I good fisherman," Tan said doing his best to be convincing, but he sensed the Sheriff didn't believe him.

The boat slowly idled up stream with the Sheriff's boat tied alongside. Lombardo knew the man was hiding something, he just didn't know what at the moment, but he intended to find out.

"You just keep the boat heading up the river. I want to take a look around in the engine room." The sheriff again disappeared below deck into the small cabin to the hatch that led to the engine room.

Tan noticed that he was unconsciously gripping the wheel again with more pressure than was needed, his stomach was tightening, and he began to notice beads of sweat forming on his forehead; he wiped the sweat away quickly with his shirt sleeve. "Relax," he told himself, "nothing is going to happen. It is Allah's will that our dreams come true."

The Sheriff had grown up on boats and knew the workings of most marine power systems. Lombardo's father had been a fisherman and, together, they had worked on dozens of fishing boats while growing up in New Jersey. He noticed the large cylinder attached to the boat's engine with black hoses. It appeared to be a heat exchanger, but he had never seen one connected externally from an engine like this. Lombardo also noticed that heat exchanger looked newer than the engine itself. He knocked on the outside of the large container with the butt of his service revolver and the cylinder seemed to be empty when it should have been full of water.

The trawler made its way under a bridge and then through a bend in the river with the Sheriff's boat gliding alongside. Tan looked up at the bridge as a couple of cars crossed at the same time the boat passed under. He was nearing the point of panic when the small hatch that led forward opened slightly, he could see Ali's dark face looking up at him. Tan made a quick gesture with his head to indicate to him that the Sheriff was aft in the engine room. He seemed to understand and didn't say anything; he then slowly closed the hatch back.

"What's the large cylinder for in the engine room for?" The Sheriff asked.

"To cool engine, it's new." Tan said with a reticent smile not wanting to utter another word if he didn't have to.

"There is no water in it, and the engine seems to be running fine, how could that be?"

"I don't know. It worked fine when I put in," Tan said.

"It can't work fine! There's no raw water in it to cool the engine," Lombardo said now looking confused.

Tan knew that Ali could hear every word being said.

"I think we need to take this boat back to the Sheriff's department, dock down river, and take a closer look around, sir." Lombardo was watching closely to see Tan's reaction.

The words barely left the Sheriff's mouth before he felt a red hot pain in his chest just below his left nipple, the force of the impact threw him backwards and he stumbled and fell down into the aft cabin landing flat on his back. The loud sound of a gunshot had only become audible as his body was being violently thrown backwards. Sheriff Lombardo knew instantly he had been shot. He often had nightmares about being fatally wounded in an exchange of gunfire. Now it was real! He desperately tried to get his radio off his belt and up to his mouth so he could radio for assistance, but his left hand wouldn't respond; he tried to get to his feet but the strength and coordination had suddenly left him. He was utterly helpless and dying. He felt heavy lying on his back and could feel the warm, red blood pulsating from under his back. The pain in his chest was excruciating and he knew he was losing consciousness. He thought about his wife who was working in town at the bank and wished he could see her once more, to tell her how much he loved her. For a moment, an overwhelming sadness came over him, then a sort of floating sensation before the cabin surroundings faded to black as he lost consciousness.

"Help me move him into the engine room," Ali said, as he emerged from below deck. He had been watching and listening to the Sheriff and had decided to shoot him rather than to have the boat searched again. They were too close to their goal to let a fat cop stop them now. Both men struggled with the body as they pulled it through the door that led into the engine room. They rolled the Sheriff over against the hull and put a sheet over his body.

"Untie the boat and let it drift," Ali ordered "I'll clean up the blood."

Tan looked out of the wheelhouse before leaving; the boat was in a part of the river where every building was abandoned. Farther up river there were more rust-stained buildings that lined the shoreline with no visible activity that he could see. He untied the Sheriff's boat and it began to fall behind the trawler as Tan added more power. Finally, the empty boat was rocking back and forth in their wake as they motored up river.

"There're won't be any evidence in his boat leading the authorities to us, so don't worry!" Ali said, as he wiped the blood off the floor. "Maybe they will think he just fell overboard and drowned."

"What about our boat?" Tan said as he swung the wheel slowly to port to round a bend in the river.

"We'll sink it at the warehouse dock. If anyone saw us towing the Sheriff's, boat the authorities could track us down. We can't take that chance. We've got to get rid of the boat."

Tan's nerves were shattered and he was tense again. The gunshot had come unexpectedly and had passed just inches from his right leg. At first he didn't know who had fired the shot; only when the Sheriff fell backwards and he saw the blood on his uniform did he realize that Ali had shot him.

Ali was still agitated from the killing. "We will slaughter these infidels like sheep! They will never stop the will of Allah with fat stupid sheriffs like him!"

Tan said nothing. He guided the boat the last five miles to the abandoned warehouse. It was now dark and the boat pulled along the bulkhead under the cover of darkness. Ever since the sheriff had been shot, Tan couldn't get his mind off how easily Ali could take a life, even the life of Muslims. Tan knew he wasn't as angry as Ali, but he was different; he was committed to Islam and only doing his duty; killing was just an unfortunate aspect of that duty. But without Ali's cold and deliberate actions, fueled by anger and discontent, they would probably have been in jail by now, but Ali was dedicated to the cause. If he was in jail, Tan thought, his plans to ascend to Paradise would be over. He should thank God for Ali, but at the moment he couldn't do that. Not without knowing if he was next to be murdered by Ali for some unknown reason. Tan made no excuses about being expendable. Everything was subordinate to the ultimate goal, and of course the great will of Allah himself.

The two worked feverishly during the night to transfer the U-233 core and its container to the warehouse. Just as the skies began to turn gray with the light of the approaching dawn, they finished. After the core had been safely moved, they went back to the boat to cut the rigging away. The water at the bulkhead was over twenty feet, and Ali was afraid that some of the trawler's rigging would protrude above water after it was scuttled. Ali had taken rope and tied the sheriff's lifeless body to the engine mounts so it wouldn't float to the surface.

By the time the sun had fully risen in the eastern sky, the trawler was resting in the greasy black mud on the bottom of the Passaic river, without a trace of her ever being there.

16

June 14th 2012
Quantico, Virginia

Agent Dillon had been sworn to secrecy about the attack on her life. The Washington Metro Police and the FBI had worked to keep the true identity of the attacker, Mustafa Radiz, out of the newspaper. Although Stevie's breach of security was deemed a serious matter, it was apparently not serious enough to terminate her. The Disciplinary Review Board took into account that she had no other violations on her record, and they acted unanimously. Even though her computer had been compromised online, the members of the investigating board decided that placing a reprimand in her file concerning the breach would be sufficient. No other action would be taken. Stevie had become emotional and cried when she learned that the panel wasn't going to boot her out of the Bureau. Of course, she had eliminated a dangerous terrorist, too; that must have helped, she thought. Members of the board had been positive about her contributions to the overall mission of the FBI and were clearly giving her a second chance.

She had learned that Mark had also supported her the entire time. Stevie hadn't gotten a chance to speak with him yet. He was a pretty special guy, she thought. Days before she had been forced to admit to herself, that she had fallen in love with him, something she knew would never work out.

In the week since the investigation, Stevie hadn't been able to work officially on the code, but having part of the code still in her memory she had continued to work, anyway. She was determined to redeem herself and break the code. Deciphering any part of the code would be significant. The whole incident had been unbelievable, like a horrible nightmare, but it was real; now she felt that she had to redeem herself. She had gone over the sequence of events over and over. It always ended the same way, splattered blood all over the hardwood floors of her bedroom like a slaughter house. Stevie could still hear the deafening explosion of her pistol and the smell of gunpowder burning. Then she saw lifeless bullet-ridden body of the terrorist in the car; she had seen the crime photos.

Agent Dillon was sure that the code the terrorists were using changed periodically, which meant that the code she was working on probably wasn't being used any longer, but the message buried in the code might be important. However, it was all they had at the moment. Now, because of her mistake, the bad guys knew the FBI had some of their code! *How stupid could I have been*? She thought. Surely Mustafa had let his organization know about the breach.

They had probably changed the codes already. Again, this would make the codes in her possession obsolete.

It was a bright and beautiful June day outside, and she was once again working with added security assigned to her. For now, she was working in her office, but there were plans to move her to an "undisclosed" location for her own protection.

It was starting to become apparent to her that the words the SX 10 had deciphered weren't usable. It meant nothing because the syntax was all wrong. The super computer had placed the words in sequences seeking to find the proper order to make sentences or phrases. She had been scanning page after page of sentences that had been produced by the SX 10, but none of it made any sense. Stevie had worked on each word, even attempting to coordinate each single word with an opposite meaning in Arabic, but this had also proved futile. She had changed all the words to the opposite meanings and had the computer run possible syntax variations, but still nothing could be gleaned from the code. For the time being, she had ruled out any rearrangement of letters based on number patterns. The computer had already done that. Stevie suspected there was a second layer of coding, and this would mean that certain words, those that were now in front of her, would have to coordinate with other words with exactly the right number of Arabic letters. This was highly unlikely, unless there were only a few meaningful words, just a few which were actually used in each transmission to communicate. For example, in English, God is also dog spelled backwards, but there weren't enough words in Arabic to have any meaningful conversation, she thought. It was much more likely that each word had a different meaning that was predetermined based on a particular date. If that were true, the multiples were almost endless, but not quite. To code all Arabic words with other words would be too lengthy and difficult. To make it simple, only a hundred or so words would be used, just enough to communicate effectively, and no more. Also, word streams could be coded by use. Just a few words that might only be used when speaking about a certain subject. So words like "book" would not be coded with an opposite word, because it would probably not play a role in a terrorist attack, only those words that dealt with action would be used. Words to designate time would also have to be part of their vocabulary and coded from prying eyes.

As she sat looking at her computer screen, she heard someone come up behind her. For a moment, fear temporarily took over, and she didn't want to turn around. Even though she was in a secure building, the idea of someone wanting to kill her still permeated her senses.

"Aren't you going to say hello?"

Stevie recognized Mark's voice and swung her chair around, instantly relieved. She hadn't been able to talk to Mark since the investigation.

She was excited he had come by to say hello. She had desperately wanted to talk to him and apologize for what she had done. She never meant to put him in such an awkward position. It had made Mark look as if he didn't know what was going on in his department, but he couldn't have known!

"Hello," She said, innocently, after a moment of wondering what to say. She could feel her face blush.

"Are you okay?"

"I'm sorry, Mark, I really am…"

"Hey, no harm done, everything turned out okay. You were just trying to do your job, that's all…"

"I know, but if I hadn't been so stupid, we wouldn't have had to go through all of this."

"You were just trying to do your job, don't worry, you made a mistake. We've all done that before," He said, reassuring her.

It was really too bad Mark was married, Stevie thought. If circumstances were different, she would have let him know how she felt. But she knew she couldn't do that. She could never do that. She had already complicated his life with her negligence. To get involved with him would only do more harm. Still, she couldn't help but imagine some scenario where the two of them could somehow get closer.

"Mark, I know I blew it. These murderers are probably onto us, now, because of me.

"Maybe not," Mark said, as he sat in a chair next to her. "Tripp is investigating this Mustafa guy. They're trying to find out where he called home. Who knows what they'll find? The reason the agency didn't come down on you any harder is because you took this guy out. That's not all bad, you know? We would have probably exchanged the code for him given the opportunity!"

"I guess so, but I still feel bad about everything. I didn't do things by the book, the way I should have!"

"Put it out of you mind, and let's just try and decipher the code; there is so much we need to know."

Stevie wanted to embrace him and tell him how much she appreciated his support, but she just didn't.

"So what have you come up with so far? I'm not trying to pressure you, but it's important we know what's going on."

"Not too much I'm afraid. It's got me and the SX-10 baffled. The code is extremely complex; after going through every layer of it, including the numeric coding, I believe it's some kind of word-association code. I think we're going to need some help, probably from the CIA.

Agents had recovered and processed the vehicle that Radiz had died in. It was towed to the FBI crime lab where technicians went over every inch of the vehicle. The registration information found in the car was forged and by checking the VIN number, the investigators had discovered that it had been reported stolen months earlier. The license plates on the car were stolen as too. Further investigation revealed that other than Radiz's fingerprints, no other prints could be found in the car. During a closer inspection a small piece of paper with a phone number was found under the driver's seat. The number was written in Arabic and agents believed it was Mustafa's handwriting.

The phone number was given to Tripp to track down. The number turned out to be a phone in an apartment in Newark, and local agents were ordered to put the apartment under twenty-four-hour surveillance. After checking with the apartment manager, agents learned that the small flat was leased to an Arab man named Abdullah Amid. However, when pictures of Mustafa Radiz were shown to the apartment manager, she instantly identified him as Abdullah. The man had been a recluse of sorts, and the apartment manager couldn't really say what he did for a living. The perception by other tenants around the complex was that he was a quiet type who didn't associate with his neighbors.

Tripp had flown to Newark, arriving before the warrants were issued to search the apartment. He was a twenty-six year veteran investigator who knew how to investigate a crime scene, and that's why he wanted to do this one personally. He was also the FBI's head supervisor working with the JTTFS and NIS. He had been assigned to the case because he was part of the new group of investigators within the Bureau who worked exclusively in terror-related investigations. The unit called Terror Threat Task Force was put into place to investigate only terror-related crimes and provide intelligence to the FBI director. Information was then shared with the CIA and other intelligence agencies through SCION. Since the September 11th attack on the World Trade Center, FBI directors had been committed to concentrating effort and talent exclusively against terrorist organizations. However, with hundreds of thousands of young militants graduating from the insidious Quran Schools in countries like Pakistan and Saudi Arabia and transforming themselves into terrorists, the CIA and the FBI were straining to keep up with where these people were located.

As soon as Tripp arrived at the apartment complex, he decided to immediately gain entry. He and a local Agent named Tom Mitchell entered the apartment at 9:50 a.m. Inside the apartment they found it dark with the windows covered with aluminum foil taped to the inside. Both Agents had their service pistols drawn and checked the bathroom, bedroom, and closets for any occupants, but none were found.

"This place is filthy," Mitchell said looking around the living room.

"Yeah, a real shit hole!" Tripp said as he moved about, looking around to get some idea of who lived in the apartment.

Both men stopped to put on latex gloves and continued to look around. As Mitchell opened the drawer to a small table next to the sofa, he noticed it stopped about halfway out. That struck him as odd since there seemed to be nothing in the drawer at all. His instincts stopped him from pulling it out any further.

"Don't move. I think we might have a booby trap here," Mitchell's said as he moved slowly back away from the table, instinctively, then stopped.

"What makes you think that?"

"Because the drawer slid out real easy and then stopped and there is nothing in the drawer."

Tripp looked under the drawer and, with a flashlight, saw two wires hanging down in the back.

"Let's get the hell out of here!"

Both men scrambled back to the front door and instructed the police to evacuate everyone from the apartment complex. The Newark bomb squad was called out to disarm the booby trap.

"If it's a bomb, I think this guy is trying to hide something by destroying the apartment if someone started to poke around in there, like we were doing," Tripp said.

"What makes you think that?" Mitchell asked. "Why wouldn't he just rig the door with explosives?"

"Too risky, someone else could have gotten killed that didn't need to be killed. An innocent person being blown to pieces would certainly draw attention to him, something he obviously didn't want. No, he was trying to kill anyone that was searching that area of the apartment.

"Yeah, you're right there, I guess. But why booby-trap it in the first place?"

"Two reasons. We just need to figure out which one. He might just want to kill anyone nosing around his personal things, or he is attempting to destroy something in his apartment he doesn't want anyone to find."

"Which one do you think is?" Up to now Mitchell hadn't realized searching a terrorist's apartment could be dangerous, but this was more than he expected, pulling the drawer out one more inch could had ended his life.

"I think there's something there he doesn't want anyone to see, probably near the sofa or in the table."

Mitchell was impressed with Tripp's assessment.

Both men were standings fifty yards from the apartment still waiting for the bomb squad to arrive.

The bomb squad finally arrived and evacuated the entire apartment complex. Within minutes, the explosive device had been disarmed. The device had been removed from the apartment then secured in a bomb proof vessel on wheels. The rest of the apartment had been searched by the bomb squad but nothing else had been found.

"Let's go look around some more," Tripp said as he started walking across the parking lot.

The news media had set-up their trucks and were already asking questions. The Newark Police Department had a spokesman available for the press and was answering questions. The presence of two FBI agents brought on even more questions. Tripp had spoken to the Chief of Police and asked him to keep things quiet for at least twenty-four hours since this was an ongoing terror investigation, even longer if that was possible.

The dirty sofa had been moved away from the wall and the table with the drawer was still standing.

"Help me turn the sofa over," Tripp said.

The two men grabbed the sofa on opposite ends and turned it over on its backside so they could take a closer look. Behind the sofa were a couple of dirty drinking glasses covered with dust and some cigarette butts.

"Bag those cigarette butts," Tripp said. He noticed that one corner of the sofa had upholstery tacks instead of staples holding up the lining.

"What have we got here?" Tripp said, as he pulled his pocketknife out. Being careful not to touch the tops of the large upholstery tacks where a fingerprint might be located, he cut the black lining material and took his small flashlight and looked into the space under the springs. The light illuminated a small, red spiral notebook that was placed between the springs and the back of the covering.

"Mitchell, I've got something here," Tripp said, as he reached in and pulled the small notebook free.

Tripp opened the book and saw two columned lines separated by a pencil mark drawn down the middle of each page.

"Can you read Arabic?" Mitchell asked.

"No, can you?"

"No, but we need to get this copied and sent to Washington to someone who does!" Tripp resumed his search of the sofa and found nothing else of interest. He then secured the apartment and called the crime scene investigators so they could finish their investigation. He then called the Chief of Police on his cell phone and asked him to hold off telling the media anything, because he had found something of importance in the apartment. The Chief agreed and put orders out to everyone at the site to shut information down completely, until he said to do otherwise.

By late evening, Tripp was back at the Bureau, Mustafa's notebook in hand.

17

June 25th 2012
Passaic, New Jersey

It was hot and dusty in the warehouse building. Ali was killing time by playing *Kabah.* The board game was designed for two players but Ali always played alone. Competition angered him, so he preferred to play only against himself. But even playing the game alone didn't always guarantee he wouldn't become angry. In fact, he got angry every time he played the popular Muslim game. If one of his fictitious players got behind in the scoring he would become angry with himself for not concentrating hard enough on the imaginary player's behalf. Tan firmly believed that Ali's eccentric behavior proved his partner was slightly unhinged emotionally but there was nothing he could do about that. All he could do was concentrate on his job, the task of making a working bomb.

Ali's behavior had begun to bother Tan, but he didn't ask questions because this type of effrontery directed at Ali, even about a simple game, could lead to a quick and harsh reaction. Ali was sitting in one of the dingy office areas by himself studying a worn game card and trying to think of the answer as sweat trickled down his already perspiration-soaked T-shirt. The vacant warehouse, although dirty and hot, provided a perfect refuge for their bomb making operation. This particular warehouse was indistinguishable from rows of others just like it along the river. It was located in a deserted area so neglected that it didn't even warrant a guard to protect it. The facility had been leased as a possible overload warehouse to be used sparingly by the Jefferson Coffee Company, or at least that is what the landlord was told. The company supposedly had offices in Costa Rica but was a front for an Islamic terrorist cell in Central America.

Ali was keenly aware that he had been followed by the authorities coming out of the mosque a couple of days before. He had been fortunate enough to elude his pursuers and had gotten away without being questioned, a blessing for which he had given Allah credit. His divine intervention had saved him, Ali believed. For safety he had stayed away from the warehouse for two days just in case the authorities were able pick up his trail again. The last thing he wanted to do was lead the FBI back to their hideout and the bomb. He had made the decision to stay under a railroad bridge before returning to the warehouse. Once he was sure that he had not been followed, he returned to the warehouse under the cover of darkness. Even though he felt safe at the moment, he knew that if he were spotted again it would put an end to their plot. From this point on, he wouldn't be able to leave the safety of their hideout. He had escaped from the FBI's prying eyes once, but he knew he might not be so lucky next time. Allah might just consider him a fool under those circumstances and unworthy of his intervention. His training told him the authorities probably had his photograph by now. In fact, the FBI had probably photographed everyone entering and leaving the Mosque for months.

It would have been just a matter of a few hours before every law enforcement officer on the east coast would have a photo of him. Going back to the Mosque wouldn't be possible now. To go back there would be suicide. He and Tan were on their own, no more messages, no more information from their handlers. Any knowledge the FBI would have gained by having his photograph would be useless if he just stayed inside and away from their surveillance. There wasn't much the authorities could do now. The weapon was near completion, and all they had to do was deliver it to the target, Ali thought. Since all the components were in place there was no reason for him to have to go back out on the streets again. He wouldn't show his face until he and his partner were ready to burn New York City to the ground.

Tan walked into the office and stood silently while Ali continued to play the board game. He didn't want to interrupt him so he remained silent, careful not to interfere while he concentrated. Finally, Ali became aware that Tan was standing there.

"What do you want?" He said, without looking at his partner as he broke the rules of the game and read the answer on the back of the card.

"I wonder if we should move the date of the attack forward," Tan said as he made, what he considered a bold move and sat down on a nearby chair.

"I've been considering it. But our orders are clear about the timing."

"But after what has happened, I'm not sure that we have that much time."

"They were aware this might happen, but no one ever instructed us to change the dates under any circumstances, do you remember anyone saying that?"

"It was never mentioned…"

"Then we have to wait," Ali said, as he picked up another card and tried to think of the answer before he turned it over and simply read it, again.

Tan decided to drop the idea. He stood up and left the office before Ali became upset over the game. It was never a good time to discuss anything when he was playing *Kabah,* but at least he had brought the subject up. There might be a chance that Ali would think about it and eventually change his mind, Tan thought.

Both men had labored hard to dig perfectly camouflaged spider holes under the concrete floor of the warehouse. The holes were square and just large enough to slide through. Pieces of junk were in easy reach to pull over the holes to conceal the openings. Within minutes, both men could easily hide from any intruders who might want to get into the locked building. Tan was certain that an investigation had already begun and the FBI was probably looking for Ali at this very moment. He had acted guilty and he was Arab, that's all it took these days. There were enough pieces out there now for the FBI to start putting the puzzle together and zeroing in on their location if they worked hard enough. Tan feared that was exactly what they would do. Now with the fat Sheriff dead, there had to be people looking for him as well. Their careful planning had not taken into consideration the killing of a police officer, but it had happened and it certainly complicated their mission even if Ali didn't think so. Tan was nervous, but not nervous enough to confront him again. Confronting his volatile partner could be a serious mistake if the message was misconstrued in some way. Ali had said no, and for now Tan would have to leave it that way. So they would just have to hide out for awhile and take their chances that the FBI would not find them. Tan, over time, had begun to worry about his partner. The planners couldn't have chosen a more brave and dedicated warrior than Ali. But it had been increasingly more difficult to work with him over the months. For now, however, there was nothing that could be done. Their plan would have to go on. He would have to accept that Ali might not be the best leader for this operation, but that was out of his hands, Tan thought.

Part of the master plan had been to slow down the terror attacks in the United States, to get the FBI and CIA to relax, but the planners knew this would only be effective for so long. With a pause in suicide bombings, sooner or later the authorities would sense that something was wrong and would certainly start speculating about what was really going on. Everyone involved in the initial planning knew it was a delicate balance in guerilla warfare that had to be timed perfectly to be completely effective. There was very little room for error. Just hold off the attacks long enough to keep the authorities off guard, but not so long as to draw attention to other possibilities. Now the attack on the United Nations building was on and he would have to rely on Ali to make the right decisions! Because of the surveillance at the Mosque, all lines of communication had been forcibly severed with handlers in Malaysia. Their plans called for them to lay low, call no attention to themselves, and then deliver the bomb on time. Yes, they were on their own, but that didn't intimidate Tan. Nonetheless, he did have to admit to himself that it was going to be a long and difficult hibernation period fraught with anticipation, anxiety, and danger.

Ali Al-Rubaie had been educated in Syria; he had considered himself fortunate that he had been educated by a religious boarding school and still was intelligent enough to get into the University. The religious schools taught very little other than the *Quran,* and this fact alone made it difficult for Ali to get into a University where more was expected intellectually. Ali was smart and, through hard work and study, was able to graduate with a degree in law. However, soon after his graduation, both his mother and father had been killed by Israeli attacks in Palestine. The same attack that had taken his parents' lives had also horribly disfigured his little sister. Ali believed that this madness was caused by bombs made by the great Satan and used by the Israeli military. At the University, he had studied modern Arab history and had learned how and why the Arab world lost two wars against the Zionists! The existence of the state of Israel was unacceptable to him, and the personal loss of his family had to be avenged. Ali had decided that revenge would have to be carried out against the American people who had supported Israel with their advanced killing technology, murderous weaponry that had been directed towards innocent Muslims for decades. The great Satan of the West had made it possible to defeat the entire Arab world with lasers and smart bombs, to effortlessly kill innocent people and cowardly destroy their way of life without ever being seen. To Ali, the great Satan was mostly to blame for these two horrible defeats at the hands of the Zionists. He and many others believed that the only way to defeat Israel was to make the cost too high for Americans to continue to be allied with the Jews. The one way to break the will of the Americans was to kill as many of them and their Allies as possible.

18

June 26th 2012
Quantico, Virginia

The building was being pelted by sheets of wind-driven rain as Stevie ducked through the double glass doors. The shock of the dry, cool air inside made her shiver.

"You'd think they would turn the air conditioning down and save the tax payers a little money!" She said softly to herself, still shivering from the cold, dry air.

Lately, when she walked into the building, she felt lucky to still have her job with the Bureau. It would have been easy for her superiors to pull the plug on her career, but they hadn't. Stevie knew she had broken some serious FBI regulations; usually this kind of security breach would cost an Agent his or her job, but this time it hadn't. She had been lucky and she knew it. The bad news was that she hadn't been able to work on the code for weeks. Stevie ran to catch the elevator after clearing security. She was in the familiar confines of her office by seven thirty. "There, I'm thirty minutes early." She said to herself as she stuffed her things under her work station. After a few minutes more, she had started the process of coding new information into the computer. "Come on!" She pleaded as the first error message of the day came up.

Even though the supercomputer was capable of processing nearly at the speed of light, it was slow to accept new coding information. Stevie carefully reentered the information under the soft-blue lighting of her office. The information found in New Jersey had been cleared and turned over to her for decoding. The information had already been shared, via SCION, with the Central Intelligence Agency.

This just might be the break we needed, she thought, as she continued to wait for the computer to process the information. She had to admit it was nice to be back at her desk working. As she continued to wait, she took a moment to glance at a photograph of her mother in a frame next to her computer terminal, a mistake. The supercomputer continued to churn away, processing the information she had just entered into its vast memory. As she sat waiting, Stevie thought about how proud her mom would have been if she had only lived long enough to see what she had accomplished in her life. She still felt an enormous amount of regret about what had happened back then. The circumstances surrounding her mother's passing had been extremely difficult, *but I guess that is the way it is for everyone*, Stevie thought.

At the moment, she didn't want to think about her mother. Not now, not today at least! So many bad things had happened to her lately, going back over the last month of her mother's illness would be too much right now. Emotionally, she was still trying to recover from so much, like the fact she had brought classified materials home, which had nearly resulted in her being fired. As if that wasn't enough, she had shot and killed another human being, something she thought she would never have to do. So thinking about her mom right now certainly wasn't going to help her emotional state, she decided. *Just leave it alone for now…you need to get this done…* she thought as she continued to enter information into the computer. She was excited about the possibility of finally breaking the code. But no matter how much she tried not to, she couldn't stop thinking about her mother. She was optimistic that the list of words in the code book would be critical to breaking the code. As she worked, her exhilaration slowly turned to sadness, sadness she couldn't stop from overwhelming her, again, like so many times before. Her mind raced back to her mother and her prolonged and tortuous bout with cancer. As she sat at her desk, starting another terribly important day, she hoped that her mom was in a better place and that she didn't feel the same pain of separation she herself felt at this very moment. What was done was done, and she knew her mother would want her to be happy and move on, but it was difficult. Stevie had learned to push unhappy thoughts to the back of her mind, to compartmentalize her sadness without shedding a tear and then move forward with her life.

The first time through, the computer had, in a matter of minutes, sorted through billions of possible combinations. The numbers and the Arabic letters assigned to them had been arranged and rearranged millions of times but, again, with no discernible syntax. The SX-10 was still attempting to put the words into meaningful order in different dialects that were already programmed into its massive memory. But Stevie was beginning to think the difficulty might lie in some little known Arab dialect that was causing the computer problems, some weird, obscure *Bedouin* dialect not in the program. What agent Ferguson was able to discern from the list of words supplied by Tripp seemed to be relatively simple at first glance.

Each word on the left side of the page was the definition of the word on the right. So it was now clear the Arabic words the computer had found originally really didn't have their normal meanings, as she had thought. They were simply words that meant something else; that "something else" was probably the key to the code. As she went down the columned list, she could see word associations, which were confusing. The words were a mixture of only verbs and nouns, words she clearly understood. They appeared to be arranged in a simple code like kids would make up. The odd thing was there were no adjectives. The fact that they were nouns and verbs only was important, but why? The unlikely verb "*emancipate*" was written opposite to the noun "*deluge.*" So it appeared at first that nouns were being substituted for verbs, but farther down the list, other nouns were coupled with other nouns, so that theory went out the window immediately. There was the possibility that the columns of words might somehow be coded as well.

The simplest way would be to invert the columns of words periodically to complicate things further. It would be easy to reverse the columns of words one week and change it back the next. Simple but effective! Just another complication thrown into the process by the people who created the code. However, for now, she would proceed on the assumption that they weren't reversed. The SX-10 was the fastest supercomputer in the world, with the ability to sort through possible combinations at a peak rate higher than any other known supercomputer. It gave code breakers the ability to sort through vast quantities of data at an incredible rate of speed. The decoding operations that were done in a matter of seconds, would take an army of human decoders months to complete. But the speed and the rate at which a computer could tumble numbers was in no way equal to the human brain and its ability to out think a computer. Stevie thought the hardest part was already done; the computer had been able to change the random numbers and Arabic letters into words. Now, all she had to do was figure out how to put them in order.

"It looks like we might finally have what we need to get this job completed." Mark said as he came into Stevie's work station.

"I hope so. We need a break. The computer is starting to smoke a little like my old Audi!" Stevie said, as she smiled at him.

"If you have a minute I'll catch you up on some things! First, that guy you shot was traced back to a low-rent apartment in New Jersey."

"Yeah, I heard that." Stevie was shocked that he lived so far away from where the attack had taken place. She had just assumed the terrorist was from the D.C. area. To her the fact that he actually lived in New Jersey led her to believe the plot to kill her was more widespread than she had originally believed.

"Yeah, and he went by the name of Abdullah Amid, not Mustafa Radiz, which you already knew, but he also had rigged the apartment with explosives to kill anyone snooping around."

"What?"

"Yeah, Tripp almost bought the farm!"

"At least he got the code book." Stevie said. The idea of this guy knowing how to make bombs added a whole new dimension to the situation. She realized that her apartment could have been bombed as well. Rigged to explode just to stop her from breaking the code!

"Yeah, Tripp and a local agent just barely avoided setting the explosives off. I've spoken to our bomb squad here and they want to check our cars before we leave today. Also, the director has ordered you and me to be moved to safe houses as soon as possible."

"Safe Houses?" She said slowly. "No kidding? Are we going to be allowed to continue our work?" Stevie didn't want to be taken off the project now, not after all the work she had put into it.

Mark knew this would be her reaction. He was impressed with this young agent's tenacity. She was tough! Even with the pressure of knowing that someone might want her dead, she was fighting back and was committed to doing her job.

"You're one tough young lady. Are you sure you want to continue? You know I can get you reassigned?" Mark asked, even though he already knew the answer.

Stevie didn't hesitate. "Of course I want to continue!" It wasn't hard to see Mark respected her. Suddenly, it became almost impossible for her to suppress her emotions for him, but she did.

"Thanks…" Was the only word she allowed to escape her lips.

"I knew you would want to do this!" His remark was easily discernible as praise by Stevie.

"Is your wife going with you?" Stevie knew it was wrong thing to ask. But she wanted to be alone with him if only as good friends.

"Yes," Mark said, not really comprehending the personal nature of the question.

Where are we going, do you know yet?"

"They're not saying. But we aren't going to the same locations."

Stevie's hopes were suddenly dashed; she had wanted to be close to Mark. She wanted to be near him if only because they worked together. She knew it was wrong, but she needed someone to talk to right now even if they were just friends.

"You mean I'm going to be by myself?" she asked.

"Not exactly, you will have a couple of agents for bodyguards." Mark could see that Stevie wasn't happy about the prospects of working by herself. Her expression said it all.

"I don't need a bodyguard. I can take care of myself!" Stevie said.

"I don't think anyone would argue that, but just look at it as backup, so you can work without looking over your shoulder."

"I guess there is no way to change all this so we can work together at the same place?"

"No, I'm sorry, that's not how it is done," he answered softly.

"So, when do we leave?" Stevie said trying to sound brave.

"Tomorrow. You will go with agents this evening and get whatever you need from your apartment. Then we will both stay at separate secure locations tonight and leave for our safe houses early tomorrow morning."

June 27th 2012
Key West

The trip on the government owned Gulfstream III had only taken a couple of hours. Stevie had been told, once on board, that the plane was in route to Key West. After the light blue jet parked on the scorching hot tarmac and the engines whined down, a white Dodge SUV rolled to a stop next to the plane. Stevie and two other agents made their way down the aluminum steps and got into the SUV. After the luggage was loaded, the white Dodge pulled away from the airplane and drove to a nearby secured gate with a guard. After stopping momentarily the vehicle left the airport and sped off along the tropical coast that was lined with beautiful palms. It was an exceptionally nice day in the tropics of South Florida but to Stevie it didn't seem like much of a holiday. As the SUV headed back Northeast she noticed they were being escorted by two other plain-white, unmarked vehicles, one ahead and one behind.

"Are those guys with us?" Stevie asked casually.

"That's correct," the driver said.

The vehicles were traveling at the posted speed limit and looked normal enough. But inside things weren't quite so normal. Both agents carried loaded AR-15 automatic assault rifles in their laps. Stevie assumed that somewhere in the United States at this very moment Mark was being taken to some undisclosed location in the same manner. The whole idea of an FBI agent being moved away from Washington to be protected from terrorist assassins seemed surreal. The country had become so dangerous that, now, even FBI agents had to be protected. It all seemed so crazy she thought. The "War on Terror" hadn't gone very well over the past several years; even the code they were trying to break was probably only a small, insignificant contribution that was more defensive than offensive in nature. She didn't have the answers, but she knew something was going to have to change in the United States' willingness to deal with terrorists, something more than what was being done now.

The SUV and the escort vehicles picked up speed as they moved out onto the open highway leaving Key West behind. Stevie could hear the eerie sound of the big, off-road tires humming as they spun on the hot pavement outside. The vehicles crossed numerous bridges that spanned the beautiful turquoise waters where the Gulf of Mexico and the Atlantic Ocean merged gently under the tropical sun. Stevie had always wanted to travel down to the Florida Keys but had never had the chance. It was more beautiful than she had imagined it would be. Like so many other people who throughout the years had fled to the Keys to get away from the law or a business deal that had gone sour she was there to hide out too, something she found amusing since she was a federal law enforcement officer. As the SUV crossed a bridge, Stevie watched a flock of pelicans flying next to the guard rail just outside of her window. The beautiful white birds flew in a V-shaped line, each one flapping its wings just long enough to keep up with the bird that slightly staggered in front of him. After flapping effortlessly for a minute, all the birds would then stop and glide for awhile, changing their altitude to better find the drafts they depended on for flight. The pelicans were beautiful and Stevie wished she could be vacationing in this charming tropical paradise. But the two other agents that were setting next to her with AR-15s in their laps was a quick reality check that reminded her she was here on business not pleasure.

"So how long before you get this mysterious code broken?" Agent Tom Walker asked. Walker was a big man, maybe the largest FBI agent she had ever seen. He looked to be about six-feet, four-inches tall and probably weighed more than two hundred and sixty pounds. His blond hair and fair complexion gave away his obvious Scandinavian decent.

"I'm not sure," Stevie responded.

Walker would be one of her assigned bodyguards during the time she would be in Florida.

"Now I've got a question for you," Stevie said, "have you been told how long we are going to be down here?"

"Not really, just that we should plan to be here for long while." Walker's massive upper arms bulged under the suit coat as he repositioned his assault rifle between his tree-trunk size legs.

"Can you kindly tell me where we are going?"

"Yeah, we are going to a private island."

"Where?" Stevie felt a little annoyed that no one had told her exactly where she was going before now.

"Marathon."

I guess if you have to be in a safe house, a private island in Marathon was about as good a place as a person could wish for, Stevie thought. She was sorry she hadn't thought to pack her swim suit.

All three vehicles made a right-hand turn onto a gravel road at a high rate of speed, causing a plume of white dust to envelope all the vehicles. They came to a big metal gate and, as they approached, it automatically started to swing open. The vehicles slowed down enough to time the opening and then accelerated through quickly, Stevie looked back and, through the white dust, saw the gates closing again after the tail vehicle passed through. The SUV's drove straight down toward the water and turned in unison like fighter aircraft and then stopped suddenly in front of a set of docks.

"Don't open the doors until the damn dust settles," Agent Walker said to the other men in the vehicle.

At the docks, several boats were tied up, one large sport fishing boat and two smaller center-console fishing boats; the smaller boats were marked as county sheriff boats and each had officers sitting at the controls. For a moment, Stevie lost sight of all the boats as the dust drifted over them obscuring her view.

"Man, we really dusted those poor bastards," Walker said peering out the window towards the boats and smiling like a kid after some mischievous act.

Walker finally opened the door and stepped out of the SUV with the AR-15 leveled at his side with the safety off. He knew if someone were going to attack them, this would be the perfect place. The other special agent, a smaller man name Mike Ridder, opened the other door and stepped out with his AR-15 readied for any type of assault.

"Okay, Agent Dillon, let's move to the big boat there!" Walker said.

Stevie slid out of the vehicle with her briefcase, looking more like a political prisoner than an FBI Agent. As they walked towards the largest of the three boats, a man came out of the cabin door leading out to the cockpit of the fishing boat.

As Stevie moved towards the boat, she could hear the big diesel engines idling in a low rumbling sound, and she could smell the odor of diesel exhaust permeating around the stern of the boat.

"Good Morning," the Captain said, as the three agents approached.

The plain-clothed officers in the other vehicles had spread out along the dock taking defensive positions, with their service pistols drawn. All the agents had dark sunglasses protecting their eyes from the bright sunlight reflecting off the clear green water. Just as they stepped onto the dock, Stevie heard the two smaller sheriff's boats start their outboard engines, and pale blue smoke drifted up into the air as the engines caught and started to idle stubbornly.

"Are you Captain Bosworth?" Walker asked.

"Yes, Sir, I'm with the Monroe County Sheriff's Department.

"Sorry as hell we dusted you like that. I guess we came in a little too hot!"

"Hey, no problem. We're used to it down here," the sheriff said.

"Can I see some identification?" Walker asked getting back to business.

"Sure." The man pulled his picture I.D. out of his back pocket. He had been advised by the FBI to be in plain clothes and not to wear his badge while they transferred people to the island. Walker had already been shown pictures of all the men who would be in the boats and the men who would be escorting them down to Marathon.

The special agent studied the picture on the ID for a moment then gave it back to the Captain.

"You ready to get underway?"

"Yes, whenever you are." Captain Bosworth had offered to use his own fishing boat "*Creola*" to take the agents twenty nautical miles northeast to a small unnamed Key; locals called it "*Lost Key.*" It really had no name on the charts. Captain Bosworth hadn't been told where the FBI group had come from, but he assumed they had come from Key West, even though Marathon had its own airport.

"How long to our destination?" Walker asked.

"About forty-five minutes."

"Listen, I want you to make sure no one knows we've been here, understood?"

"As far as me and my men are concerned we never saw you."

"Will your men cooperate?"

"Sure, they're good men; they won't say a word. You can count on that." Captain Bosworth was more than happy to work with the FBI and had looked forward to this day from the time he had first been contacted. It would be something different from pushing paper in the office about bad checks and wife beating. He had been told that he would be escorting a visitor to "*Lost Key*" and he had been more than happy to help out. He knew that using his boat along with some of the Sheriffs boats trailing way behind was a good way to take their passenger to their safe house without causing suspicion. If a Coast Guard patrol boat or cutter were brought down from Key West, it wouldn't be hard to spot in these waters.

Bosworth never spoke to the young lady who stepped onto his boat, nor was he introduced, but he was sure this was the person they were protecting. She was FBI too, he guessed, because he could see that she was armed. He didn't know the Bureau hired such beautiful women. She was about five-feet, seven-inches tall and looked like a fashion model you might see on the cover of one of those female magazines like *Cosmopolitan*. She had blonde hair with a reddish tint cut short and stuck up on the top a little. He noticed she didn't seem to be wearing much make-up, if any, but it didn't hurt her looks. No, she was a damn nice looking gal, he thought.

Walker motioned to the young lady to move from the cockpit into the salon area. He opened the door and she walked in and sat down on the starboard side settee. The cushions were a floral design in blues and greens with a background color that was pale yellow. They must pay these Sheriffs pretty well, she thought.

"If you guys would, cast off our bow and stern lines and we'll get underway." Bosworth said.

The Captain climbed a stainless-steel ladder up to the bridge and immediately picked up the VFH radio handheld microphone and keyed it.

"Creola to Unit 4 and Unit 11, we are getting underway."

The radio immediately crackled back "Roger 4," and then a second response followed quickly, "Roger 11."

The sun beat down on the white deck of "*Creola*" as Walker and the other agents on board squinted behind the lenses of their dark sunglasses.

Ridder was the only other agent that would make the trip to the safe house at *Lost Key*. Special Agent Ridder was a seasoned veteran with six years in the Bureau and was trained in terror tactics. He was a smart, tough agent with an exceptional reputation in the Miami office. He was an average sized man at five-foot, eleven inches and one-hundred and ninety pounds, but he looked small next to his partner. Ridder was one of the best pistol marksmen in the FBI, which was one of the reasons he had been assigned this special duty. Both men were pretty formidable and highly trained special agents who could take care of themselves in just about any situation.

"Did you bring any sun block?" Walker asked Agent Ridder.

"Yeah, it's in my bag."

"Good I'm going to burn like hell out here if I don't do something." Agent Walker hadn't been exposed to the sun in months and his face was pale-white, almost pink. As Ridder stood watch with his automatic weapon Walker went over to the bag that was lying next to the bulkhead in the cockpit, zipped it open, and start rummaging around inside.

"Where is it?"

"The outside zipper pouch on your left."

"Okay, shit, I was in the wrong compartment!" Walker said as he zipped the other compartment open.

By now the big man was sweating profusely and it was dripping down on to Ridder's black leather bag. He finally saw the tube of sun block and pulled it out. After applying a generous amount to his face and neck he handed the tube over to Agent Ridder who did the same. Both men kept a careful eye around the boat and out onto the water surrounding the boat as it idled out of the small harbor. Some of the sun block crème wasn't fully massaged into the skin and Walker looked like he was wearing some kind of lady's moisturizing crème on his cheeks and forehead. The offshore fishing boat idled away from the dock then spun on her props to line up directly with the channel that was unmarked just ahead.

One of the smaller sheriff's boats was leading the way down the crystal clear channel with the other two boats following. As the boats pulled away from the dock, Agent Walker watched as the vehicles they had just arrived in a few minutes earlier now drove out of the parking area in a boiling plume of dust. The rumble of the big diesel engines below their feet sounded powerful as they turned the large, four-bladed props just under the stern.

"Pretty nice boat," Ridder said.

"Hell, yeah it is." Walker's white shirt was soaking wet by now. The big man wished that he could remove his suit coat, but that would reveal his shoulder harness and pistol to anyone who happened to be spying on them, so he decided to keep it on. The AR-15s held by their sides blended into the background of the dark suits they were wearing.

The boats cleared the harbor and started down the unmarked channel that would take them out into the main channel that ran up the coast.

"We'll be in the Hawk Channel in a few minutes," Ridder said looking back at the sheriff's boat that followed at about fifty yards.

"It doesn't look like a channel out there; it looks like the ocean."

"Yeah, but the reef is just about four miles out and it usually stays calm in here." Ridder said as he pointed straight in front of the boat.

The fishing boat started to pick-up speed as the diesel engines below came to life with increased RPMs. The boat started to squat down on in the stern, and she started to thunder forward up and out of the water. This caught the smaller boat ahead by surprise, so the sheriff, who was at the controls, quickly advanced his throttles as well, planning out ahead of the now charging Sport Fishing boat.

"This thing will go," Walker shouted as he leaned forward to offset his weight in the direction in which the boat was moving so he could keep his footing.

"Yeah, these guys want to get out to the fish in a hurry," Ridder shouted back over the sounds of the twin-diesel engines.

Inside the salon, Stevie sat as the big fishing boat moved out into the middle of Hawk Channel and turned northeast up the Atlantic side of the Keys under clear skies. It was hard to believe that all this had been planned just to protect her, a junior agent, from a potential terrorist attack. The air-conditioning inside the boat made the interior nice and cool. She was comfortable watching the low-lying islands now on the port side of the boat become small, dark-green smudges that seemed to float on the surface of the turquoise waters rolling by just outside. The cockpit door opened and Walker stepped inside; the noise of the engine's exhaust was loud but was quickly muffled again as the door was closed.

"How you doing?" Stevie could see Walker was out of his element; he appeared to be hot and sweating with pink splotches starting to develop around his ears.

"Better than you it looks like," she said, smiling at him.

"It's hotter than blue blazes out there!" The big man said as he wiped his forehead with his hand.

"Well, maybe we can get into some shorts when we get there?"

"Yeah, I brought some light clothes," Walker said as he continued to scan the water in all directions.

"You need any help from me?" she asked.

"Not right now; just stay down here where it is cool and nobody can take a shot at you."

"That's fine with me," she said, as she crossed her legs and put her hands on top of her knees and smiled cutely.

The boat was now moving at top speed, the smaller lead boat was jumping from wave top to wave top staying two hundred yards in front of the larger boat. The trailing boat ran relatively smoothly in the expanding wake of the Sport Fisherman. To anyone on shore, it would appear like normal marine traffic moving up the Channel towards Miami.

The door opened again and Bosworth walked into the salon closing the door behind him.

"Don't worry, she's on auto-pilot." Bosworth could see his presence had startled his two guests. "I just came down to show you where the refreshments are located." He walked forward to a teak bulkhead with a cabinet built into it; he released a latch and the door opened to a small refrigerator.

"There are soft drinks and plenty of water in here. Be my guest and make yourself comfortable," he said, as he closed the door to the refrigerator and moved back towards the door leading out onto the aft deck and disappeared.

"You want some water or something?" Walker asked as he moved forward toward the bulkhead refrigerator.

"No, I'm fine."

He pulled two bottles out and walked back towards the door trying to keep his weight balanced with the rolling floor beneath his feet.

"Hey, if anybody does start shooting out here, go below, and I'll come and get you if we need some additional firepower."

Walker opened the door and again the sounds of the engine exhaust came rushing into the salon. The Agent stepped back down into the cockpit closing the door behind him. He made his way over to Ridder who was scanning the water in all directions and handed him a cold bottle of water.

"Drink this, it'll cool you down." The two men drank their cold, bottled water as the fishing boat continued to power northeast through Hawk channel in the direction of *Lost Key.*

19

June 29th 2012
Quantico, Virginia

Ed Tripp sat in his office. It was Friday afternoon, but he knew going home this weekend would be out of the question. After returning from Newark with the codebook, he was determined to find what it had to do with the assassination plot against Doug Ferguson. He had just learned that the information he had uncovered in Radiz's apartment might be critical in breaking another code the FBI was already working on. Tripp didn't believe in coincidences. The fact the Radiz had attempted to kill an FBI code breaker couldn't be overlooked. The problem was that, until today, he had never been informed about the code, a real problem since he was the supervisor of the Counterterrorism group. His instincts told him that the existence of a secret terrorist code, coupled with the fact that a known terrorist suspect had attempted to assassinate a federal agent, meant that someone knew they were working on the code. That someone, Mustafa Radiz, had orders to assassinate the code breaker. Tripp was sure of it.

The very idea that Radiz had attempted to kill a junior FBI code breaker was enough to whet his investigative appetite. The ominous fact that an Arab cell was attempting to protect coded documents from Malaysia, was unprecedented and nothing less than chilling! Tripp recognized that this was a sign of cooperation between two groups who had never cooperated before, another fact that could not be overlooked. With a new Malay government and its radical Islamic leader, President Putra, making threats daily against the United States, this was something he hoped the CIA would know about.

After a few phone calls, Tripp was able to get two local agents assigned to the case. Special Agents Jim Freeman and Marty Valetta were both new members of the FBI Counterterrorism group. Both agents were assisting in the investigation. The Director wanted this case to be put on the fast track. The central question was, why were two terrorist groups so diverse and different cooperating on US soil?

Agent Valetta walked up to the doorway of Tripp's office and knocked, even though he was halfway through the door, more than anything, an afterthought.

"Get your butt in here, we've got problems!" Tripp had known Marty every since he came to the Bureau as a rookie in New York. They had worked together on another case a couple of months earlier when officially assigned to Counter Terrorism. Valetta had uncovered information about a truck bomb that was going to be detonated by elements of the *Saddam Martyrs Brigade* on the New Jersey Turn Pike in the afternoon traffic. He had had put heavy pressure on a local mob boss in Brooklyn to find out if any fuel trucks were missing, meaning stolen by the mob, and if so who they had been sold to. With solid investigative skills, he had tracked the terrorists who were in possession of the trucks and that had averted the disaster. It was a great piece of detective work and that was the primary reason he was now assigned to the FBI's Counterterrorism group.

"Something tells me I'm not going home this weekend," Valetta said with a Brooklyn accent. He knew Tripp well enough to know he was about to be assigned to a new case, and things would start sooner rather than later.

But Tripp didn't respond immediately.

Finally, he said, "I need you and Freeman to start checking some things for me."

"I knew it," Valetta said, as he sat down in one of the chairs in front of Tripp's desk. "A new case?"

"Yeah, you want some coffee before we get started?"

"Yeah, why not?"

Tripp turned around to a small, white coffee maker next to his desk. He pulled a white Styrofoam cup and filled it with black coffee.

"Drink this, Marty, and working the weekend won't be a problem," Tripp said, smiling, handing the cup across his desk to Valetta.

"I just want you to know I've got plans for the weekend."

"Sorry bubba, you know the drill…" Tripp said, as he turned and filled his cup.

A second knock at the door came as Agent Freeman came in looking at both men innocently.

"Oh, shit, I see it coming. We're not going home this weekend are we?" Jim Freeman said with a frown fraught with disappointment.

"You got that right, Jimmy boy!" Marty said, grinning at Freeman.

"Tripp, I was going to go sailing this weekend. I've got everything lined up!"

"You just need a cup of my coffee…" Tripp said, smiling too.

"No thanks."

"You know I make the best, come on, let me pour you a cup." Tripp said.

Jim Freeman could see a partially opened bag of some off-brand coffee next to the coffee maker. Now Valetta could see a twinkle in Jim's eyes even though he was disappointed; he wasn't so disappointed he couldn't have some fun with Tripp.

"I've never heard of *Latin Mist*, Tripp; have you, Marty?" Freeman said sarcastically.

Ed turned to look as the crumpled coffee bag sitting next to the coffee maker. "What…this?"

"Coffee is coffee. I can't tell the difference. What do you think, Valetta, pretty good, right?" he said, looking for support.

"Oh yeah, this is some good stuff, really" he said, smiling at Jim, then sticking his tongue out in disgust.

"Oh, okay I guess you guys have turned into some of those limp-wristed phu-phu coffee drinkers, paying five dollars a cup! Sorry I'm out of fat-free mocha, girls!"

Freeman winks at Valetta. "How can we do our best work with inferior products like this? I'm out of here!" Freeman stood up as if he was leaving.

"Sit your ass down…" Tripp said, smiling. Freeman was known as a lighthearted fun-loving guy, but he was also known as a determined and tenacious investigator. Freeman had made a name for himself with successful indictments against the notorious leaders of the Russian mob.

"Okay, you guys win! Maybe I'll start buying hotsy-totsy brand if you two come up with some useful Intel."

Freeman was in his mid thirties with bushy blond hair and a tan complexion from sailing on the Chesapeake. His powder-blue eyes were disarming in a way and didn't give away his true nature as a hard-nosed federal officer. He had been a member of the Michigan State wrestling team and still looked like he was in pretty good shape. He was addicted to running, even though his body looked like he would be better suited to weight lifting. He had come out of school with a double major in accounting and engineering. Finishing at the top of his class at Quantico, Freeman had quickly worked his way through several important investigations; one had resulted in jail time for a Congressman. Both he and Valetta were strong additions to Tripp's anti-terrorism team.

"What are we looking for, Tripp?" Valetta asked, wanting to get back to business.

"Okay this is what we're doing…" He paused for a minute, leaned back in his chair, and continued. His demeanor changed. Friday afternoon or not, everyone was going to be on this case. Having a moment to reflect as Tripp ordered his mind, Valetta thought, *that's classic Tripp able to be funny but in the same sentence become deadly serious again without ever missing a beat.* Now that he was serious again they would have to wait until the wheels quit turning.

Finally, Tripp said, "You guys heard about the assassination attempt on Stevie Dillon, right?"

"Yeah, from what I heard, she filled that son of bitch Radiz with lead. I wouldn't want her pissed off at me!" Valetta said, smiling and quickly returning some laughter to the discussion.

"Do you know her?" Tripp asked Freeman quickly.

"Yeah, I used to work with her when she was right out of Quantico."

"She must be a pretty serious shot, just ask the guys at the morgue, plucking the lead out of Mustafa's chest," Freeman added. "I never had the pleasure of shooting anybody with her so I wouldn't have known about that until now."

"I think I know what's going on here with the attempt on her life; we'll just have to prove it. Dillon is working on a breaking a code used by Radiz's group of murderers. The information is coded on a DVD sent to the FBI by Doug Ferguson. I guess you've heard of him too?" Tripp plunged on, hoping he was right about what he thought was happening in this case; otherwise, they were going to burn a lot of time for nothing.

"Yeah, he's the billionaire who's running for President, right?" Freeman said.

"That's correct, and a pretty good guy by all accounts." Tripp said.

"Where did he get the DVD?" Valetta asked, his inquisitive mind now racing ahead.

"At the moment, I'm not sure, but you can bet I'm about to find out. Here's the deal. We have an Arab terrorist, Radiz, trying to assassinate one of our agents. This particular agent happens to be a code breaker. That tells me the code is important to these guys, so we need to get to the bottom of this quick, because these guys are not going to stop just because one of them failed; in fact, I think they will be turning up the heat," Tripp said.

"Sounds pretty serious! You know, Ed, this new Malaysian President has been shooting his mouth off over the past few weeks now; in fact, I'm surprised our friends at the CIA haven't capped his ass yet, but maybe he has something to do with all this." Valetta said, as he searched Tripp's eyes for a reaction.

Tripp took another a sip of coffee. "Maybe, but here's the facts of what happen with Dillon," he said. "Someone got into her computer's hard drive at home and took classified code information she was working on."

"What was she doing with classified documents at home?" Freeman asked, shocked.

"She's young and overzealous and just made a mistake," Tripp said.

"Somebody must have been watching her pretty closely to know she had that at home," Freeman added.

"That's right, but that's not the end of the story, boys. I went to Newark to track this Radiz guy down and almost got blown to hell in the process!"

"How did that happen?" Freeman asked, looking shocked.

"The guy had a bomb waiting for us in his apartment, a booby-trap!"

"Wow!" Freeman said. "This guy was pretty deadly, until he ran into Dillon, at least!"

"Wait, I'm not finished yet." Tripp said.

"Yeah, but you're the lead counterterrorism guy around here, right, and you nearly got blown up by a dead man. That's serious," Freeman said.

"That's right. Let me tell you what happened. Tetrocelli, the guy I was working with from the Newark office, almost pulled a drawer out too far, just a little farther and I wouldn't be setting here making coffee for you boys."

Tripp didn't laugh this time about the coffee; this was a serious situation, and they needed to treat it that way. Freeman was good at being humorous in a macabre sort of way at times, but that had its limits.

"Listen up, this is what we need to do. Let's start looking into any unusual disappearances, unsolved murders, or break-ins that might seem out of the ordinary over the last three or four weeks in New Jersey, New York, Washington," Tripp said.

"What are we looking for?" Freeman was the first to ask.

"I'm not sure, but we know we have a terrorist who tried to kill one of our agents here in D.C., and we also know that he lived in New Jersey, so we have one dead guy who broke a lot of laws. Maybe he's done more. Let's find out. You know, trying to get his hands on explosives or something even worse."

"Christ, that doesn't give us much to go on. That's it?" Valetta asked.

"I know, but use your instincts. You guys are good at this open-ended stuff; that's why you guys work for me. Listen, get on Radiz's trail and see where it leads, but remember these guys are using bombs now against law enforcement, so be careful. He might have a few more set and waiting for us!"

"That's pretty encouraging!" Valetta added, frowning.

"So we are now assisting on the Radiz case?" Freeman asked.

"That's right..."

"Where do you want me to start?" Valetta asked.

"You to go to Newark and find out more about Radiz. You know, get everything the Bureau has on him. Also look into any unexplained deaths, especially law enforcement officers. I think this guy will have left a trail of bodies behind him. I'm convinced he was strictly an assassin, and assassins kill people, right, so find out who he's been killing."

"When do you want me to leave?"

"Right now."

"So I guess I'm going to the Big Apple?" Freeman said.

"Yeah, I have already called our people there. They're waiting for you."

"Do the same as Valetta?"

"Yeah," Tripp said

"Where can we find you if we need you?" Freeman asked.

"Like I said, I'm going down south to meet with Ferguson and find out how he got the DVD."

"So we don't know where it came from other than Malaysia?" Agent Valetta asked.

"That's right. It seems like this whole Malaysian connection might have fallen through the cracks. This kind of information is supposed to be disseminated through the Counterterrorism group and JTTF, but it wasn't."

"You mean you didn't know anything about any of this?" Freeman asked, shocked.

"Nothing, not a thing!"

"Holy Christ!" Valetta said, shaking his head. "How could that happen?"

"I don't know, but we need information as quick as possible!"

Leaving Tripp's office and walking down the corridor, they stopped to talk.

"What the hell is going on here?" Valetta asked.

"The director must think Tripp's on to something. You know Tripp's reputation. Who else would they get to clean this mess up?" Freeman said.

"Yeah, but we're not usually part of this high-level stuff."

"We are now, my man, we're moving up, Marty, get used to it!"

20

July 3rd 2012
Florida Keys

Stevie watched as the three boats motored slowly away from the dock; then they began to gather speed making their way between another low-lying island just North of *No Name Key.* The wooden dock extended off the water and through a thick, tangled mass of mangroves trees. The safe house looked to be about a hundred yards from the water's edge and was located in the center of the small island.

"Well, we're on our own now, Dillon!" Walker said. He was looking back over his shoulder at the three boats now speeding away from the island. The Sheriff's boats had just turned on to a more southerly course that would take them back to Marathon. To the east over the ocean, the clouds hung like huge white fluffy cotton balls over the Gulf Stream. The wind had dropped and the surface of the water around *No Name Key* looked like a watery mirror. Suddenly, Stevie could hear the lonely sound of screeching birds in the trees just above her head that startled her.

“Do we have any way off this island?” Stevie asked her handler. “I mean if we need to leave in a hurry?”

“Yeah, there is another dock on the north side of the island with a fishing boat all fueled up and ready to go. We can also call a chopper and a fire support team from Miami too. If we feel we need back-up, they can be out here quicker than a cat can lick his ass and we have more personnel coming in tomorrow.”

“That’s comforting to know,” Stevie said, looking down the dock towards the house while carefully walking to avoid getting her heels caught between the boards on the dock. “So I guess this is how the rich and famous live?” She blurted out after looking at the house. She was really thinking how trapped they were if an attack came; the isolation was good, she thought, but only if no one found them.

“Yeah, it looks real nice doesn’t it?” Walker had already gathered up some of their bags and started down the long dock through the low-slung trees while the putrid smell of the water around Mangrove roots permeated the air.

The pastel pink house was simple but elegant, she thought. It was well shaded from the tropical sun by trees, which allowed only shafts of light to penetrate to the island below, and the air was cool. The lawn was neatly manicured and everything, including the lime trees, had been landscaped with tropical plants and flowers. The entire house was surrounded by a beautiful porch painted in a pale turquoise color. Stevie noticed there were multiple ceiling fans over the porch to circulate air. She thought about how pleasant it would be just to sit leisurely under the porch and enjoy the cool air coming off the Ocean. She walked across the grass to the front porch, carrying only her computer case. She hadn't allowed anyone to touch it since leaving Washington, D.C. Locked inside was the only copy of the code book she would be using during her stay on the island. Even out here in the middle of nowhere, thanks to modern satellite communication, she would have direct access to the FBI computers back in Washington.

Walker was already familiar with the layout of the house, since he had visited the day before. He had made the strategic decision to place Stevie in a large bedroom that was farthest from the two entry points. Isolating her deep within the structure would ensure that anyone attempting to get into the house to do her harm would have to get through both him and Ridder first.

The house was totally self-contained with a complete system of both AC and DC electrical systems. The DC systems were powered by storage batteries that were constantly being charged by solar cells and which could also be charged by a diesel-powered generator if necessary. For fresh water, the house had reverse osmosis technology to desalinate the seawater. At a rate of 250 gallons per hour, they wouldn't have to be concerned about a water shortage on the island, unless of course the ocean went dry.

"I wouldn't mind having a place like this when I retire." Ridder said. He had just set some bags down by the front door."

"I guess you plan on winning the Lottery, then?" Walker had dropped his two large cargo bags too. He had even more sweat now pouring down his arms and down to his fingertips.

"How much do you think a place like this would cost?" Ridder asked as he picked up his AR-15 and started walking around looking out the windows that seemed to surround the entire room.

"I bet the island alone is a couple of million dollars." Walker had found some paper towels on the counter and was wiping his sweaty arms and hands off with a wad of them.

"That much?" Ridder said sounding surprised.

"Yeah, man! Don't look now but we're part of the rich and famous!" He said as he blotted his heavy brow with the paper.

"If you guys don't mind, I need to get to work," Stevie said. She had followed the two men into the house but didn't know what room to take.

"No, not at all. Let me show you your room," Walker said, as he picked up both of her bags and led her down a hallway towards the center of the house. Stevie noticed that all the walls were painted a soft white and the paintings on the walls all seemed to be in a seashell theme in more soft pastel colors. The floors were white pine and were polished to a high gloss. Stevie stepped into one of the largest bedrooms she had ever seen. It seemed to take up the entire rear portion of the house. The large room was strangely missing windows of any kind. It was well decorated with very nice furniture in a Caribbean theme like an old Humphrey Bogart movie.

"Where are the windows?" She asked Walker.

"As I understand, the owners wanted at least one room where the sun couldn't penetrate."

"Someone must have a sleeping disorder!" Stevie said, sarcastically, after placing her computer bag down on the bed.

"Well, it's kind of strange but certainly looks secure enough," Stevie added.

"Can I get you anything else?"

"No, I'm fine. I need to get started working as soon as possible."

"No, rest, huh?"

"No, I need to get some work done if you guys don't mind?"

"Okay then, here is the connection to the satellite system that was installed for you." Tom Walker pointed to the top of the desk where a single, black, insulated cable had been installed on top of the desk.

"Okay, thanks. I can take care of everything from here.

Walker was starting to cool down, but his white shirt was still soaked, Stevie noticed as he left the room. She opened her computer case and pulled out a bound copy of the code book that had been prepared for her back in Washington. She barely had time to look at it before she had been hustled out of town. She had always been a curious type, and now her curiosity was getting the best of her. Even though she was in this beautiful tropical paradise, she wanted to do nothing but dig into the code book and get started. Time was critical, and she wanted to make up for all her past mistakes by getting the job done as quickly as she could.

Stevie suspected the code would not be useful for any future code breaking, except for maybe analyzing the concepts that were being used. She only hoped the existing documents might be in sync with the codes on the DVD. There was a slight chance that Mustafa Radiz hadn't received his new code book yet. If that were true, the code on the DVD would match up with the code book. Then she might be able to break the code fairly quickly. If the timing was wrong, then the code book would be useless. She pulled her laptop from the case and set it onto the wooden desk. She then pulled a black rectangular box out of the same computer case. After that, she connected the black box into the wall plug for power and then attached the cable that ran from the satellite antenna to the box. After she finished, she plugged her computer into the box and turned it on. The laptop came to life. As soon as it had loaded all the programs she clicked on a small icon on the left side of the screen. The icon had the letters "SX" over a background color of scarlet red. After that, a series of green lights began to light up slowly from left to right across the front of the box. After all the green lights were illuminated a soft-green glow, the familiar logo of the FBI then appeared on the monitor. Stevie was then satisfied that her satellite connection was up and running. She laid the code book on the desk, opened it, and started to familiarize herself again with the Arabic words written in both columns. Everything seemed simple enough at first glance. The Arabic words were arranged in two separate columns. There was a third column of numbers on the border also separated by a line drawn vertically on the right side of the paper. It appeared to be a simple numbering system starting with the Arabic number one. The first word was "today" and opposite to that word was "destroy." As she scanned down the page, all of the Arabic words seemed straightforward. They were just common words opposite to each other and numbered. Her experience told her that only a few words in those thousands of words copied on the DVD would have real meaning. Finding the right words was like sifting through a landfill full of jigsaw puzzle pieces. A better analogy would have that entire landfill loaded with tons of puzzle pieces, not garbage. Of course, this would make the imaginary job even more difficult, since every puzzle piece would have to be examined individually, just like the coded message! In general, the words in the book seemed to be random and unrelated to each other. After she entered all the columns of words and numbers, maybe the computer could quickly make some sense out of it all.

The next thing she noticed was that several of the numbers on the numbered columns had a bracket that was connected to two other bracketed numbers and tied them together with a single connecting line. Mustafa had apparently highlighted in his own hand, with brackets, three numbers. In this case the numbers four, five, and six were bracketed together. Stevie thought if she took the four, five, and six numbered words and entered that into the SX-10 that would certainly narrow things down a bit. She knew, however there was more software being used by the terrorists to decode their communications. The coded words were probably "triggers" for their software. The words in the book were the key words that directed the software to go search in the right place to retrieve the data. Without that software, it would be difficult but not impossible to break the code. She also wondered how the terrorists received the numbers. The four, five, and six had to come from somewhere, but that was the beauty of this coding system; they could get three numbers in thousands of different ways from their handlers.

"Ah, the human brain…So complex and so clever," She sighed.

"How's it going in here?" Stevie was startled and instantly reached for her pistol that was strategically placed next to the terminal.

"Whoa...whoa... don't pick that up!" Walker said standing in the doorway with his hands out in front of him. Stevie was a little embarrassed and pulled her right hand back from over the pistol.

"Sorry about that, Walker! I'm a little jumpy I guess." For a moment, all she could think of was all that horrible blood in her apartment, then the memory of that horrible evening came rushing back uncontrollably, like so many times before.

"Yeah, I can see that. Just relax. We have everything covered out here. Stevie noticed that he had changed clothes and was wearing a pair of khaki shorts and a FBI T-shirt with sandals.

"I wanted to know if you wanted some lunch. We're about to make some sandwiches," he said, as he inched further into the room.

"Yeah, that would be great. I'll be there in a few minutes." She noticed that Walker was no longer sweating, other than a few left over sweat beads now clinging to his forehead. She picked up a slight scent of after shave lotion mingled with a touch of body odor as he turned to go.

Stevie brought up her secure e-mail connection from the satellite link, and she was surprised to find an e-mail from Mark. She quickly opened it and read the message: "WHAT DO YOU MAKE OF THE 456 CONNECTION?" MARK.

A flood of emotions ran through Stevie. She was looking for any small sign that might indicate to her that he might be interested in more than just discussing the code. He must have sent the e-mail to her as soon as he got to the safe house. Did that mean he missed her, already? After all they had been working very closely together for awhile now, she thought. Maybe he did…it was a possibility. What was she thinking? She tried to force the thought from her mind, suddenly realizing she was being irrational. In fact, she was being downright desperate!

She began typing an answer to his e-mail immediately:

> "456 IS PROBABLY THE CODE FOR THE PAGE OR JUST WORDS, NOT SURE YET. WORD ASSOICATIONS ARE UNCLEAR. HOPE YOU ARE FINE." STEVIE.

She now felt better and waited for a response. Maybe he was still at his computer, she thought. That would be great, because they could chat for awhile.

As Stevie waited, she thought about how clever these people who devised the code really were. With so many layers of code. Some of it was off-the-shelf electronic encryption, some numerical association, and then finally word association codes. Then, if all that wasn't enough, the codes simply expired after awhile. Whatever these guys were communicating about must be really important to go through all this trouble and complexity. Most coded messages passed by terrorists were nothing more than simple messages scribbled in Arabic on bits of paper and passed along by courier, or simply logged away in their memory. However, Stevie felt confident that they were close to breaking the code. She had one chance, and one chance only, to get it right. The code would then transform again and all the work she had done would have to start all over. "Keep your mind on your work, Stevie!" she reminded herself.

Mark Latham sat in a cool room, overlooking a field that eventually led to a stand of trees. Through the window, he could see the haze of the warm afternoon starting to obscure his view of the hills that lay to the west of the FBI safe house. The farmhouse was deep in the Virginia countryside. It was a place that was often used by the FBI to protect witnesses from those who might want to harm them. A lot of Russian defectors had probably slept in this house during the cold war, he thought. It had been a surprise to Mark that he wasn't moved farther away from his home in Arlington, Virginia. But from here, he and his wife would be safe enough. He sat in the leather chair knowing he had done much more to break this case than anyone would ever know. The problem with being here was that now he could no longer make anonymous phone calls to help speed things up. Mark Latham hadn't been able to say anything to Tripp about the codes on the DVD without taking the chance that Tripp would start to connect his interest with Malaysia to insider phone calls. If only the Michigan agents had followed up, he thought. If they had done their job, this investigation would be further along by now. No, for the time being, he would have to bow out or be found out. Anyway, any calls coming or going from the farmhouse would be monitored so he had no choice. Now he was locked in and couldn't place phone calls to the one man who seemed to react quickly, and that was Doug Ferguson. Mark didn't view himself as a maverick, but only as a person who would do what it took to help keep his country safe. In his mind, he had been forced to because the bureaucracy inside the intelligence community was going backwards not forward. The system was always getting in the way. He didn't consider himself some kind of vigilante or anything like that, he just saw how powerless the government had been in stopping the rise of violence. He didn't necessarily see Doug Ferguson as a political savior; he was just someone outside of the system that Mark thought might help, and he had been right in that assumption. The code the FBI had in their hands now was proof of that. He was reasonably sure that he wasn't the only one in the Bureau going beyond his responsibilities to try to change what was happening. But nobody talked about it. There were agents out there doing all kinds of unlawful things trying to curb the violence that was out of control. But Ferguson was someone that Mark was convinced could help the country, and he had decided to help him if he could. His assumptions had been proven right after the attack at the Orange County Airport where Doug and his crew gave out more than they took! The Governor could make a difference, and it appeared the terrorists were getting that message loud and clear. They couldn't afford a guy like him in office because he would wipe away all the bullshit and expose those who harbored them. The whole idea had come out of frustration with the system. Even though sweeping changes had been made, Mark still saw that there was a lack of cooperation between agencies. Of course, the politicians liked to paint a rosy picture for the American people, but it was all implied distortion. The reality was a little different. The same old problems existed and new leadership would be needed to really change what was going on. The need to do something just became an urge, an urge that had to be acted upon, so he started making anonymous phone calls, to get the word out. Not just to Governor Ferguson but too many people in and out of government. Everyone but Ferguson, however, had tried to catch him and send him to jail. But so far he had been lucky. Of course, he knew if he continued, he probably would get caught one day, but he hoped that if that happened it would be long after the country was safe again. Mark wasn't placing all his bets on Ferguson becoming the next President of the United States, but he did feel he could make a difference. Mark understood this was a serious game, but he had very little apprehension about playing it, none whatsoever, the stakes were too high.

As Mark read the response on his computer screen, he heard strange muffled sounds coming from downstairs. He had stopped typing just long enough to listen. His wife hadn't arrived yet, so he thought it might be her coming up the stairs to surprise him. She loved to surprise him and he liked being surprised by her. So Mark acted as if he had heard nothing and started to type a response to Stevie when, at that moment, a bullet was fired from a distance of only ten feet. Mark never heard the shot as it emerged from the silencer attached to the end of the pistol, not due to the muffled shot but rather the speed of the bullet. The 9mm slug entered his head from the left side just above his ear. The only sensation Mark felt was his head being pushed to the left by what felt like a hot burning piece of metal. For just a moment he felt like someone was standing next to him pushing sharply with their hand against his left temple region. There was no pain now, just a mild stinging sensation and then instant blackness that covered his eyes from the inside! He relaxed and felt himself slowly falling forward, but he couldn't move his arms off the table. He took his last breath and slumped over the computer desk not really knowing what had just happened to him. His body jerked a few times from involuntary muscle reactions, just left over impulses coming from his dying brain traveling the pathways of his nerves down his body.

On the computer screen the words

"GET COMFORTABLE AND WE WILL WORK LATER." MARK

still flickered on the computer display as the assailant pushed the round power button to turn it off, before the message could be sent.

21

July 6th 2012
Florida Keys

Agent Mike Ridder patrolled along the moonlit pathway that led around the island looking for anything unusual, something that might key his senses to a possible threat. It was a warm and humid night in the Florida Keys and his skin felt clammy. The leaves on the mangrove trees dripped with moisture as insects incessantly buzzed around Ridder's head. The moon was bright and full with its glowing reflection dancing across the surface of the water like a shimmering highway leaving the island. The full moon was good, it made his task of patrolling the area much easier. But Ridder was aware the same moon light could also betray his presence just as easily to attackers. Unless he was careful, he would be easy to spot by anyone trying to attack the island. At least on the island he could blend into the surrounding brush and trees unlike anyone who would be exposed trying to come ashore, Ridder thought, as he cautiously moved along the trail. There was no doubt in his mind he would feel a hell of lot better once back-up arrived in the morning. No assignment had ever been clearer than this one, he thought. He and Walker would have to protect Stevie with their own skins! No matter how tough it was, that was their job. Tonight, that's what they were being paid to do. Ridder was now growing more confident the bad guys couldn't possibly have the balls to attack them tonight.

Two men clad in black wet suits slid over the side of a black zodiac into the warm waters just off the low squatting silhouette of *No Name Key.* A single loan figure stayed in the inflatable boat. In Arabic, the man in the boat gave last minute instructions to the two men in the water. Later, he slid a large, black, waterproof bag over the side to each man.

"Allah is with you…" The man in the boat whispered just over the ripples of water that were lapping at the sides of the zodiac.

"And with you..." Each man in the water whispered as they began to swim away under the light of the full moon.

Stevie sat in front of the computer terminal squinting into the glow of the plasma display. The SX-10 was still processing a new request Stevie had entered a few minutes earlier. She knew the computer had a slim chance of deciphering the code since it practically had to reinvent the software that the terrorists were using. If this was the correct code for the DVD, the computer might just be able to hit the "right tumblers" and pick the lock, she thought. It was just a matter of sorting through the coded words and cross referencing them against the words in the code book; the computer could then employ some of its logic circuits to find the trigger words that would result in meaningful syntax. During her training on the SX-10, she had been informed that programmers had placed "hyper logic" programs into the computer that made the supercomputer extremely intuitive. So the SX-10 could then take what it had previously learned to project logical methods of solving the puzzle. Again, the nagging problem was that she might not have the correct code book; in fact, the chances were pretty remote that it was. Stevie went to the coding section of the software and entered the last few dozen words into the boxes provided by the program. It was tedious work. Each word had to be typed manually into the corresponding box. In less than an hour, all the remaining words had been entered into the computer. In her office in Quantico, all of this information could be easily scanned in, but now she was down to entering everything by hand. Just to ensure all the words had been entered correctly, she started to recheck each word. Any spelling errors manually made in processing the words could potentially cause the computer to fail in its attempt to break the encryption.

Suddenly, she was interrupted by the muffled sounds of automatic gunfire somewhere outside the house. As a reflex more than anything else, she typed in the last two words needed to complete her task. Then she grabbed her pistol and started towards the door. She was met by Agent Walker before she could get there. The big man was armed with an AR-15 and had a FBI-issued Kevlar vest on. He handed another Kevlar Vest to Stevie.

"Put this on and get back into the room!" Walker shoved another AR-15 at her and then said, "Take this and kill anyone who comes through this door!"

Stevie took the fully-loaded assault rifle, put on the Kevlar vest and, without saying a word, backed into the room as instructed. She told herself to be calm, they had all talked about the defensive plan and all they had to do now was execute it. She would be protected inside the house as two separate perimeters were now being set up by the other two agents. Ridder would defend the house from outside. Walker would defend from the inside of the house against any intruders. The last line of defense was in her hands, a .223 caliber fully automatic AR-15. She attempted to reassure herself that would be enough until help arrived. It was strangely silent outside, since she heard gun fire the first time. Maybe it was over, Ridder might have killed the intruders. Not likely, she thought.

As Stevie moved back into the room, she was glad there were no windows. The only line of fire that she would have to be concerned with at the moment would be the door.

She had the presence of mind to pick-up the code book that she had shoved into the waistline of her shorts with great haste. Then she checked the last two set of words for errors and pressed "enter." The computer now had everything it needed to break the code. She felt perspiration breaking out all over her skin, the most noticeable was just above her forehead. She first decided to sit in the corner near the computer. But she quickly changed her mind. This wasn't a good place, the glow of the screen would be the first focal point of anyone entering the room. That would mean they would be looking directly at her. Not a good place to be, she thought. The opposite corner would be much better, so she started to crawl on the floor in that direction. From her new position, she would have a split second advantage to fire first. The intruder would be drawn to the light of the plasma screen and that would be the last thing he would ever see. Since the first shots had been fired, it had been eerily quiet outside. Her mind raced trying to figure out what might be going on out there. She knew Walker must have already called in for reinforcements. Now all they had to do was hold on.

Suddenly, the floor shook violently under her, with an ear-splitting concussion of an explosion. The light fixture above her head shook violently with the shock wave. Dust was raining down in the room all around her, some getting into her eyes. She knew that the explosion had been set off by the enemy because none of the agents had brought any explosive devices to the island. She pulled the bolt back far enough to make sure there was a live round in the AR-15's chamber. After she saw the brass casing, she let it go. It slid back into place, locked and loaded. Then she turned another lever on the side to fully "automatic" then released the safety mechanism. Even though the room was cool and dry, her sweat was now starting to soak through the collar of the white T-Shirt. Whether it was the chill of the moisture or something else, she felt cold and shivered for a second. As she sat waiting, alone, in the bedroom, she made up her mind she wasn't going to die on this island; she would survive this somehow. She didn't like the idea of having to hide while other agents were trying to protect her. She got the urge to just run outside and back them up, but she didn't. Stevie knew that would be a serious mistake and wisely stayed right where she was. She was confident she could kill anyone that dared come through the door. These fucking terrorists obviously wanted her dead, she thought. Back in her apartment the night she was forced to defend herself, it wasn't personal, it was just training and a simple reaction to a threat. However, this was different, she thought. If these assholes were coming after her, she was determined that they were damn well going to die in the process. The difference now was she wasn't afraid like the night in her apartment. She didn't want to think too much, but she was aware some thinking would be critical in surviving this time. She would like to kill these bastards right now, but she knew she had to stay within the plan, a simple plan of survival that she had agreed to. As she sat in a defensive position in the corner of the room, thoughts of her mother came streaming back to her. She was glad her mom wouldn't know about any of this. She had suffered enough in her life. Stevie realized, slowly at first, that her source of strength back at the apartment against Mustafa Radiz must have come from her mother. Even now, sitting here facing an unseen enemy, she could almost see her mother's stern face looking down on her, saying, "Fight Stevie, fight as hard as you can! Don't let them kill my only daughter." She had seen that same kind of strength before. She had witnessed it as her mother fought the killer inside of her. The real strength she now understood was just being brave, just fighting back as hard as you could. That is what her mother had done. And the whole time she suffered, her mother had remained brave for Stevie! She had chosen to stay calm for her daughter and face the reality of it all with strength and character. Now, Stevie recognized the cruel and sustained illness had somehow strengthened her mom's resolve in those final months and weeks! Now, her mother's strength was making her stronger too; she realized that now, as she took aim on the door. Her mother had faced death bravely right to the end, and Stevie decided she would do the same thing. There would be no backing down, no whimpering, no tears, no pleading. If it's a fight they wanted, then that is what they would get! Nothing was more important than killing whoever walked through that door with evil intent! In fact, the sooner the better, she thought with defiant resignation!

Walker was now crouched behind a large stuffed chair he had pulled close to one of the windows that overlooked the front porch. He couldn't see anything out in the yard under the single flood light. Like Stevie, he had heard the explosion that had rocked the house but hadn't seen the flash or anything else. He didn't know where it had come from, but it sounded like it came from the eastern side of the island. He just hoped Mike was okay but, instinctively, he knew he probably wasn't. For now, all he could do was execute the plan and wait until help arrived. He knew it would take a while to assemble everyone back in Miami but then the team would come fast and furious by chopper. He had made the call for help as soon as he had heard the explosion, so things were underway back in Miami. The flight time would only be about twenty minutes after everyone was rounded up. So they were probably looking at an hour or more before help would be on the scene. Walker sensed it would probably be all over by then one way or another! An hour and a half would be too long, he thought.

With a thud, a large black pack came flying onto the porch and skidded to a stop just next to the front door of the house.

"Holy Shit!" Walker said as he ducked behind the chair for cover.

A deafening concussion was followed by a rush of fire and debris that came flying in his direction. The pressure wave immediately flattened the front of his face causing massive bruising as the skin and blood vessels in his face suffered trauma. Walker felt like his head was in a vice being squeezed as the concussion caused a drastic pressure change. He felt his eyes bulge out of his head then snap back quickly leaving behind a shocking numbing pain behind his eyes. He felt pieces of wood and glass slice his flesh as it passed across and into his body. Suddenly, he got the sense that he was watching all this unfold on a movie screen. He felt as if he was watching everything in super slow motion. The satchel charge had blown away over two- thirds of the front of the house. Luckily, most of it blew outward! He knew from his training that in a matter of seconds, attackers would come rushing in with automatic weapons ablaze to suppress returning fire in the killing zone. Walker realized he still had a firm grasp on his AR-15 with his now bloodied right hand. He instinctively brought it up into a firing position. Then he saw Stevie open the door and start to come into the living room.

"Get back, Get back! He screamed just as the automatic gun fire came ripping into the room splintering wood all around him. As Walker started spraying fire into the wide open gap that had been blown into the front of the house, he lost sight of Stevie and, when he looked back, she was gone.

Stevie had taken Walker's advice and had dove back into the bedroom as bullets exploded all around her. Bullets were now bursting through the walls, taking big chunks of the wall with it. Some of the bullets were passing straight through the room and out of the back of the house! Stevie found cover on the floor behind the bed near the corner where she had been seconds earlier. The force of the second explosion had momentarily shocked her into thinking that the house was being blown apart and that she needed to get out. She had attempted to run for cover before being driven back into the room by the automatic gun fire. Now she could only wait to kill or be killed, there were no other options available at the moment. At the same time, all sorts of thoughts passed rapidly through her mind, mostly ways to try to stay alive. Her mind raced, but the only solution was to stay put and kill anyone coming through that door! For now, that was all she could do. If they threw a bomb in the room, then she would probably die right here, she thought.

Tom Walker looked for the enemy but still saw nothing! He had seen some muzzle flashes just off to the right of the gaping hole in the front of the house. But, he didn't want to return fire until he saw someone to shoot at! Walker wasn't a particularly religious man, but he had already spoken to God right after the second explosion. All he had asked for was a little help and assistance against these evil doers. Like most men facing death, he had made a few quick promises. They were promises he intended to keep, too, if he got out of this mess. His legs were becoming numb and he couldn't move either his left or right. He realized that his only option at the moment was to stay put and try to cut down anyone that might try to infiltrate the house.

Then another satchel charge came flying into the living room and skidded up to the base of the bar and stopped. Walker saw the charge come flying in and, with superhuman effort, he pulled the large stuffed chair over onto his head and shoulders as the blast came rushing at him again. He didn't see the flash but felt the floor lift underneath him! The next thing he felt was the searing unbearable heat in the room. It hit his legs first, since they were fully exposed. Then there was a horrible burning pain he had never felt before, which began running up his lower legs into his thighs. "That's good!" He said in agony. "I can at least feel my legs again." Miraculously, his head and shoulders had been protected from the blast and the fire, and Walker still had his senses about him. He still clutched the AR-15 in his right hand with a death grip. I'm not letting go of the gun, he thought. At that moment, all he could see was smoke and fire around him. The pain was now easing as shock started to set in and block his senses. But he forced himself not to let go; letting go now would mean certain death. Walker made the personal decision that he wasn't going to die today! He was still in tremendous pain and wanted to kill whoever it was that had caused it. Walker could feel his strength coming back through his body, and he shoved the burning chair off of him. Just as the chair tumbled away he saw a short, thin man enter the burning room dressed in black, he had a mini Uzi raised and ready to fire. Rage took over as he saw his attacker only a few feet away and without hesitation both men fired at each other. The man in black quickly darted to his right to avoid the fire coming from the AR-15 but he was too late! One round from the AR-15 caught the attacker under the chin and blew his lower jaw away leaving an ugly gaping hole. His automatic pistol sprayed bullets wildly into the air and all around the room, but they didn't hit their mark as he fell onto the burning floor screaming in an inhuman shrill tone. Walker fired another burst into the man as he lay on the floor just in front of him silencing his shrieking screams. The death of the attacker seemed to clear Walker's head for a moment. He felt like he was ready to take on anyone else attempting to enter the house. "I can do this," He whispered. "Just stay awake."

From what little Agent Walker could see, the house wasn't going up in flames, at least not for the moment. Instead, both large and small pieces of wood lay scattered around the room smoldering. He tore a piece of his shirt off and wrapped it around his face covering his nose and mouth in case more smoke accumulated in the room. He realized, even in his present state of mind, that he couldn't continue to fight if he passed out from smoke inhalation. He needed to stay awake no matter what, he thought.

He had laid down his automatic rifle for a minute and, as he reached to pick it up again, he instantly felt something cold and hard pressing against his left temple.

"Don't move or I'll kill you!" The voice came from above and behind him. Tom had barely heard it above the ringing in his ears.

Agent Walker froze. He knew if he didn't he would die right now, right here! He wouldn't have chance, he thought.

"Where's the girl?" Tom recognized the Middle Eastern accent instantly. He again started to lose consciousness. "Fight it, Tom," he said under his breath. If he passed out now, the assassin would probably put a bullet in his head to make sure he was dead.

"She's not here!" He groaned.

"I'll give you one last chance then you will die, Zionist!"

Walker braced for the shot that would kill him in a matter of seconds. So this is how he was going to die! Damn, he thought, I would never have imagined it happening this way. Over the buzzing in his head he heard someone say, "I'm right here." Then gun fire rang out! For a moment he thought they were the shots that would end his life. But even in his muddled pain-filled mind, he knew he would never hear the shots that would actually kill him. He then reached for his weapon in a desperate attempt to protect himself. As he turned to aim his weapon, he saw the intruder lying on the ground beside him dead, bleeding profusely from the head and the side of the neck.

"Are you okay?" He heard Stevie's voice coming from across the room.

"Yeah, get down. There might be more," he moaned, still trying to protect her.

She cautiously made her way across the smoky room and tried to pull the heavy man across the floor to the kitchen and out of harm's way. But it was useless. She couldn't move him more than a foot. Stevie noticed the whole front of the house was destroyed. It was now open to the yard outside, and that was covered with smoking debris. It was strangely quiet. The smoke in the room was starting to clear, and she could feel the cool, moist air entering the exposed front room. Her body remained coiled and ready to shoot at anyone attempting to approach the house. But now there was only silence in the darkness. If anyone else was out there, they didn't seem too eager to jump into the fight at the moment. As she scanned the yard, she saw nothing and sensed it was over. She then heard the sound of the insects starting to make their normal night noises again. She considered that a good sign, a return to some sense of normalcy.

She didn't know how much time had passed as she sat there with Walker, but after awhile she started to pick-up the unmistakable sound of a helicopter's blades beating against the air. Help was coming!

"Thank God," she said, feeling for the first time that it was finally over.

"Tom if you can hear me, hold on. We'll have you out of here pretty quick," she whispered into the man's ear. He squeezed her hand to let her know he understood as he lay motionless on the floor.

After Walker was evacuated, Stevie went back into the bedroom to retrieve her computer, which hadn't been turned off. It was now the message flashing "Code Deciphered." With relief, she folded the computer and placed it in her bag and then left the debris-strewn room. Maybe these guys will pay now, she thought.

22

July 8th 2012
Washington D.C.

Tripp was speeding from Dulles towards FBI headquarters. Just minutes earlier he had received a call from the office of the director, Michael Foster, who had asked him to attend an urgent meeting with him and his staff within the hour. Tripp was informed that several agents had been murdered in one of the FBI's most secure safe houses by terrorists. He learned the suspected attack on Agent Dillon was part of a much larger, more sophisticated plot to kill other federal agents. Foster wanted to be briefed personally on the Dillon case, immediately. As he pulled into the special parking area, his cell phone went off again. Answering it, he heard the familiar voice of Agent Valetta on the other end.

"Ed, there is a county sheriff missing in Newark. He was a county water cop and his boat was found, without him."

"Any leads on what happened?"

"No, and there's no body either, and from what I hear, there were no useable forensics in the boat."

"What about Nelson up in Flint?"

"You're a mind reader. That's the next thing I wanted to talk to you about. I hate to talk about our own, but that guy is a real dead head! Nelson and his partner covered their asses by claiming they sent the DVD to headquarters. Now they're saying that Latham should have notified the task force, not them. They also let me know they have a strong suspicion that this whole thing could be nothing more than a political stunt with Ferguson's name written all over it. I get the impression they just blew the whole thing off." Valetta said.

"Even after the attack in Orange County?" Tripp said surprised.

"No, not exactly. They're saying now that they were about to get back on the investigation and were in the process of letting us know!"

"How convenient. I've heard all that shit before…son of a bitch!" Ed said angrily into the cell phone.

"Well, we got three agents dead and lord knows how many more are in the cross hairs."

"What do you mean?" Valetta said slowly as he absorbed the information.

"I'll let you know more when I find out more about what happened," Tripp said, as he closed the cell phone ending the call.

Tripp began to think about what had gone wrong in Detroit. It was the same old problem, the human problem. The problem of people working with people and ignoring procedure. "Shit!" he whispered to himself. Here were two highly trained FBI Agents speaking to a serious guy, the former Governor of the state of Alabama, about a terrorist plot and they decide the incident didn't need to be investigated! The more he thought about it the angrier he became. The cold, hard reality was that the encrypted information had been at headquarters for quite awhile and he knew nothing about it until after the attack on Dillon's life! Tripp tried to calm himself down because, in a matter of minutes, he would be meeting with the Director of the FBI. His mission now was to be cool and credible about what he knew about the plot; unfortunately, he didn't know all that much at the moment, which he knew wouldn't go over very well with the political types he was about to meet with.

J. Edgar Hoover Building
Conference Room

The conference room was generic enough, like the hundreds of conference rooms in government buildings all over the city. The walls were covered with a beige vinyl and an indiscernible raised design. The ceiling was the standard white acoustic tile with cold fluorescent lighting. A clear plastic pitcher of ice water was in the middle of the table on a tray with several classes turned upside down. After traveling all the way from Montgomery, he was apparently the only one able to make it on time! That was typical, he thought. He took the extra time to get a little better organized. His mind sped through all the details of the case, but horrific new events seemed to complicate the picture in his mind. He was sure that all the attacks were related, but he was not sure exactly why they were occurring right at this moment. People were dying and others being targeted and no one had any clues as to what group was involved. He really didn't know all that much about Mustafa Radiz yet, other than that his name was on a terrorist watch list! So far, the only people that had drawn blood from the enemy happened to be the bodyguard of an Ex-Governor of Alabama and a junior FBI agent in her pajamas! They were going to have to do better than that or more deadly events would overtake them. They needed to get to these people and start arresting them or killing them off; either way would be an improvement over the present situation! His mind raced back to the missing Sheriff in New Jersey. There was nothing that even remotely connected his disappearance to this case. However, he had a strong feeling about this incident. For now, he would keep that bit of information to himself. Somehow, he knew there would be a critical connection. How he knew he couldn't say, but he knew in his gut this disappearance had something to do with the case. At least for now, most of the activity was located in the New York, New Jersey, and Washington D.C. areas, geographically large but manageable. The plotters were probably living in this area; the only other attack had been in California, but the dead assailants had fake IDs from New Jersey. Yes, they were close, Ed thought. Tripp picked up his cell phone and called Valetta back. The phone rang once and Valetta answered.

"Yeah, boss, what's up?"

"I want you to work this missing sheriff case as fast as you can. I got a hunch on this one. Find out what they do on their patrols, and find out who they stop and why. This is all we have right now, and I want you to work it. I know this has something to do with the case."

"Done. I'll get back to you." The phone went dead. Ed was like Valetta, you didn't have to argue with him once he was motivated.

The private door in the back of the conference room opened and FBI director Michael Foster quickly entered the room with his two assistants. Director Foster was in his mid fifties and a political appointee of the current administration. He was a rather smallish man, with coarse, gray hair and a prominent, narrow nose that dominated his long, slender face. His navy blue wool pinstripe suit was probably made by one of the more popular tailors in the Washington D.C. area. It was obviously expensive but did very little to improve his overall looks, Tripp thought. Foster was one of those men who could make a high-dollar, tailor-made suit look cheap. However, Foster was one tough man who was trying desperately to stop the flow of violence that was engulfing the country, but he was also very political; the job required it.

"Good Afternoon, Ed, how was your interview with the Governor?" Foster asked as he reached out to shake hands.

"Everything went fine; he is quite a guy, extremely independent and quite intelligent…"

"Ed, do you think he has a chance to be President? I mean you met him, right, is he the kind of guy that could pull off the upset in this race?"

"Based on political history, I'll take the safe answer and say no. I really don't think it matters what kind of guy you are in his situation," Ed said.

"Well, I'm not so sure. The governor seems to be connecting with the people, and this incident at the airport has done nothing but help him," the Director said, as he sat down, flanked on either side by his two assistants.

"You know Jerry Barnes and Lester Knowles, don't you?"

"Yeah, we know each other." All three men acknowledged each other's presence without saying anything, just nodding slowly and making eye contact.

Both men were Washington bureaucratic types, professional administrators who were trusted party people put in positions to help the leadership. Lester Knowles was a short man in his later thirties, an ivy leaguer with a New England accent. His auburn hair was thick, and he wore it just a little longer than most men in his profession inside the belt. He handled all appointments and communication between the director and the rest of the world and derived some power from that. Jerry Barnes was a little older, probably forty-eight or nine, with an ever growing waistline and a fair amount of gray around his temples. He was an exceptional legal eagle type who interpreted the law for the director when he needed a second opinion. He was also schooled in United States Constitutional matters, as well, a real plus for any Director of the FBI these days. Barnes wore oval wire-rim glasses with gold frames and a prescription that enlarged his blue eyes ever so slightly. He rarely spoke unless spoken to but made constant eye contact with whoever was speaking. It was as if he was studying you for some reason, attempting to read your mind, get into your head.

"Let me fill you in on the attack at the Virginia safe house. An unknown number of assailants attacked and killed all three agents who were there. It's a really bad situation with a lot of family members left behind and all. Agent Latham was one of the agents lost. Whoever gunned them down took some classified information from the safe house during the attack. The good news is Latham's wife had not yet arrived, so at least she's safe, and no civilians were killed, thank God," Foster said.

"What kind of classified information did they get?" Tripp asked.

"Copies of the code book," Lester Knowles said, intervening for the first time.

"So they were probably aware the FBI was working on the code book even before the agents arrived at the safe house?"

"We must assume they did," Foster responded.

"I think we have to assume also that they were aware we had the code book all along. We believe the real reason they were there was to kill Agent Latham before he could break the code." Agent Tripp's mind was racing ahead trying desperately to stay ahead of Foster and trying to figure out where he was going with all of this. At the moment, he was just stating what must be obvious to everyone at the conference table.

"So you don't think they really came looking for the book then?" Tripp asked.

"No, I think they knew it was too late for that—they just wanted everyone working on their code, dead!" the director said coldly.

"But this kind of behavior is something new for these guys! To the best of my knowledge, terrorists have never plotted to kill FBI agents before. Why would they want to motivate us like that? They've got to know it is going to be personal now…" Ed said, as he held a yellow pencil in his right hand and twirled it between his fingers. He already knew the answer. He just wanted to know what the Director thought.

"I think we all agreed here that they're protecting something else. Something a little more serious than your average suicide attack. Obviously, they're trying to protect something very important, some kind of a large-scale operation. It looks like they're doing everything they can to keep us in the blind about what they are up to no matter what the consequences. It must be so important to them that they don't mind killing FBI agents," Knowles said, glancing at the director to confirm they were both in agreement.

"It appears they are shadowing our agents instead of the other way around," Knowles added.

"You know I hate to say this, but while we've been trailing them, they have probably been watching us and we didn't even know it!" the Director said. The way he said it led Tripp to think he was somehow being blamed.

"Agent Tripp, I'd have to say they have been watching us for awhile and we haven't been good enough to catch them at it or maybe they have someone inside?" Barnes said coolly, as he spoke for the first time in the meeting.

"Now we have three agents dead!" Foster added as if it was scripted.

"For the press, this is going to be like Christmas, New Years, and Thanksgiving all wrapped together when they find out about all of this! '**FBI Now Being Followed and Outgunned by Terrorists!**' the headlines are going to read. Can you imagine how that is going to sit with the President?" Knowles said, timing his remark to fall right after Barn's.

"Not that we are blaming you directly, Tripp," Foster said apologetically.

"Well that's comforting. It sure looked like that was where you were headed!" Tripp answered, wondering what Foster meant by "directly."

"No, not at all. We would just like to know what you have done so far, and how does this guy Mustafa Radiz fit into the picture?" Foster said following the script.

"Actually, we are still in the middle of the investigation, and we don't have a lot on Radiz yet. We do know that he was using the alias of Abdullah Amid. But both Amid and Radiz didn't come up in the INS computers. Of course, we have some information about him under Mustafa Radiz but it's sketchy, just that he was believed to be in the United States. Which, he obviously was!" Agent Tripp said.

Even though Tripp didn't want to bring up the mix-up in Detroit, or the lack of information he had on the encrypted DVDs, he knew it had to be done and the time was now. These guys were definitely covering their asses, he thought.

"Director, it just recently came to my attention that the code book I found was being used to break a code given to the FBI by Governor Ferguson. Did you know about the presence of a possible terrorist code being worked on at Quantico?" Ed said, deciding to go on the offensive.

"You know we just found out about that, too?" Knowles said answering for the Director.

"No, I mean did you guys know about this before I did?" Tripp persisted.

"Actually, we found out about the same time you did, if you're talking about where the DVD came from."

"Of course, that's what I'm talking about," Tripp said, knowing the political ramifications.

"That's the part we just found out about!"

"Is that for the record?" Tripp asked curtly.

"It is," Foster replied.

"Well, it seems we still haven't eliminated our communication problems, then," Ed said disgustedly.

"I think it may be more circumstantial than anything else. We received a call from Supervisor Stan Templeton in Detroit. It seems his boys thought this was some kind of political attention getter and just didn't want to waste a lot of time on it. But they did provide some assistance by providing wiretaps and forwarding the DVD," The Director shot back.

Tripp could see where this was all going now. It was all a bit of a cover-up, but only a minor one. Everyone would have to get on board with the idea that there really wasn't a communication problem in the FBI, just one person overlooking a minor detail. There's no doubt that's the way it was going to be explained. Tripp was no rookie. He could see where all of this was going. It was going to be blamed on a dead man, Mark Latham. The agent was about to be placed on an island by himself, posthumously, to take the blame for this small and inconsequential matter. Of course there would still be room on this island for him too if he wasn't careful, Ed thought.

"Yeah, since we just found out about all of this, I do think we might have to tighten some things up around here though. You know our internal communication within our own ranks, but nothing more than that," the director said casually, as if he was trying to sell the idea.

"So, Agent Latham was working on the code and using the code book I brought in to decipher what was on the DVD?" Tripp asked, just to make it a part of the official record.

"That is correct," Knowles said again, answering for the Director.

"Let's talk about Ferguson for a moment. How did the governor get his hands on these coded messages?" Foster asked.

"He's an international businessman and apparently asked for some help from some people he has a business relationship with in Malaysia."

"Just like that?" Knowles asked.

"Apparently, just like that!" Tripp answered curtly. "I haven't spoken to his guy down in Mobile who actually did the work yet, but I will."

"As I understand, he also has some kind of informer calling him about a potential plot as well? And that's why he decided to seek information on this in the first place?" The Director asked.

"That's correct. He says someone is attempting to work through him. But he doesn't know why. The Governor and his staff believe this caller is some insider. Someone that works for the State Department, CIA, or us," Tripp answered.

"Do we know anything about this informer yet? I mean could he be selling information to the other side?"

Tripp felt a little uncomfortable now having been asked a series of questions he could only speculate on. "Not yet, but I believe he is someone inside the Bureau and the rest I can't speculate on."

"Here in D.C. you mean?" Knowles asked.

"Yeah, it sounds like he is an insider. In my opinion a CIA guy would never do this."

"Why not?" Knowles asked.

"What is the CIA? Just a bunch of spies. They don't do this kind of thing. We are investigators and when people aren't listening it is tempting to tell someone."

"You really believe that?" Knowles asked.

"Yeah, I believe it, and I've got a couple of our guys working on it, right now," Tripp said.

"Good, then keep us informed. We want to know who it is if you're right!" The Director said.

"Where is Stevie Dillon?" Tripp asked knowing she would again be a target.

"She is in the Florida Keys in a safe house there," Knowles responded.

"Well, then I had better get down there as soon as possible," Tripp said, starting to get up from his chair.

"There's no need to do that. We have already sent additional protection down to secure the area!" Knowles said, quickly.

"We would prefer that you stay right here to coordinate the investigation," the Director said wanting to give that order himself.

"With no disrespect, sir, I think I need to be down there. If something happens there will be evidence that I'd like to get my hands on immediately. I don't want any mistakes made from this point on!" Tripp protested.

"Ed, if you aren't on their hit list, you probably will be soon. Because of that you need to stay right here where you will be a little safer. I have ordered you some additional protection as well," Michael Foster said.

"I think that is a mistake! I should be down there, but you're the boss."

Tripp decided he shouldn't complain again to the Director of the FBI and so he didn't. It was clear the director wasn't going to be persuaded otherwise so any additional complaining would be counterproductive.

"Gentlemen, I need to run to another meeting," the Director said. "Do we have secure links with the safe house?"

"We will within the hour," Knowles responded.

"Good! Tripp I want you to monitor the situation down there, Okay?" The Director said.

"I'll do that, Mr. Director."

"Thanks, let us know if you need anything," Foster said as he exited the room.

As Tripp walked back to the elevator he thought how stupid it was for him not to have the ability to go where he needed to go. He was an investigator for Christ Sakes! He was in charge of this investigation but he had just been handcuffed to his desk! He was on a short leash now, with the Director of the FBI holding tightly the other end.

23

July 9th 2012
FBI Field Office Miami

Stevie had been told it would be at least twenty-four hours before the debriefing. That meant that it would be at least twenty-four hours before she could speak to anyone about the code. She was aware that, if she disobeyed the guidelines of the debriefing procedure, she would again be breaking an FBI protocol, and this time she might lose her job. The only way to communicate with Mark was to do what she was doing now, cooperating. The protocol dictated that she could only confer with, and transfer information to, someone within the Bureau that was cleared to discuss code-breaking procedures. She desperately needed to tell someone, but there was a chance the computer could be wrong again. What if the code wasn't really broken, what then? The rules were the rules, she thought. She had barely kept her job by breaking protocol and ignoring policy, before. This wasn't like an action movie where the heroin could do whatever she wanted, no rules, just a script to follow. This was real life, real time. The policies of the FBI were too real to ignore! She didn't want to go to a Federal Prison either, and that's where you went when you didn't do things right. Hours after leaving *No Name Key*, she had developed a slight tremor in her hands. Every time she picked up a glass, her hand shook, which was probably unnoticeable to anyone but herself, but unnerving. She admitted to herself the attack had shattered her confidence in the FBI's ability to protect her, and now she was in fear for her life; that's what the terrorists probably wanted. For the past few hours, she had caught herself looking around every corner expecting to be attacked at any moment, expecting someone to jump out from the shadows and kill her. The memories of both attacks were intermingled and constantly played out in her mind. There wasn't a moment she wasn't plagued by the thought. The idea that terrorists could somehow penetrate the security of the FBI was mind numbing. Somehow, they seemed to know where she was at all times. But in reality how hard was that to figure out? she thought. *It's not like we are the only people on the planet that can track a person down. How long is this going to last*? she kept asking herself? The worst part was she had no control over her own situation; she felt a sense of undeniable helplessness. To her knowledge, assassinations of FBI Agents were all but unheard of, but she'd already had two attempts made against her life. She had survived two vicious attacks, and she was determined to survive the next one, with or without the FBI's help.

Time slowly passed. At the moment all she could do was be patient and sit in the fifth floor lounge, which might become her home for a few weeks. She needed to concentrate on her work and try to stop all of this. After what seemed to be an eternity, Supervisor Jack Patterson of counterintelligence arrived to conduct the preliminary debriefing and answerer some of the questions that Stevie had been asking. He had been notified of the fatal attack on the other safe house in Washington two hours earlier. At that time, he had been in New Orleans working with counterintelligence Agents on a cooperative sting operation that was underway in Louisiana. Two damaging attacks by terrorists on refinery facilities in Lake Charles had agents spreading out in the area and trying to get enough information to operate a sting that would ferret out the cells involved. The Bureau had gotten credible information that there was going to be a third somewhere in the state in August and Patterson was working against a deadly time bomb ticking away. Now he had been called back to assist on the debriefing group that was being assembled in Miami, since it might help with his work in Louisiana.

"Agent Dillon, how you doing?" He had shown the proper ID to the two guards outside that were dressed in black compact gear and armed with automatic rifles.

"I'm Jack Patterson, are you okay? Can I get you anything?"

"No I'm fine." Stevie said, biting her bottom lip without realizing it.

"Tell me how I can help… I was told that you wanted to speak to someone in counterintelligence, is that correct?"

"Yes, it is very important you get in touch with my supervisor. It is of the greatest urgency that this be done immediately."

Patterson was aware she could give this information to him directly without it being approved."

"Is Mark Latham your supervisor?"

"Yes."

"I'm afraid I have some bad news for you, Stevie, just sit back and relax for a minute!"

"Why do I need to relax?" she said objecting, but sensing why.

"Just relax, okay," Patterson said, trying to soothe her emotions.

There it was, Stevie thought. He hadn't said the exact words yet, but she already knew what he was going to say.

"He's dead isn't he?" she said, as she started to tremble, again uncontrollably.

"I'm afraid so. Same kind of attack you went through but, unfortunately, a great deal more lethal for our agents." Patterson said slowly.

Tears started to well up in her eyes, but she fought the urge to cry.

"How about his wife?" She heard herself say, still fighting back the tears.

"Apparently she's okay. She hadn't arrived yet. Mark was alone in the house with two other agents outside who were also killed in the attack."

Stevie felt weak, like she was going to collapse, but FBI Agents didn't collapse! Her emotions were temporarily overwhelming her, so she called on her inner strength to be strong. Stevie knew she needed to stay calm and keep a tight rein on her emotions. Mark was gone, but there was nothing she could do about that now. She decided to save her grieving for later; this wasn't the place or time. She needed to be strong and do her job. That was the most important thing right now, she reasoned. Once the debriefing was over she would request secured access to set up to the SX-10 so she could go back to work. In the meantime she wanted to be alone.

"Okay, I understand, may I be alone for a minute or two?"

"Sure, are you okay? Can I get you anything?"

"No, not right now, but thanks for asking."

"Are you sure?" Patterson said as he put his hand on top of hers.

"No, I'm fine—" She said as tears started to well up in her eyes. At that moment, it was as clear as anything had ever been in her mind that she did love Mark, as bad as it sounded to her, it was true. It was something she hadn't been able to avoid; it was just the way she felt. Sure, he had been married, but that hadn't stopped her from loving him, why she didn't know, and the sad thing was he never had a clue, she thought. Now he was gone and she'd never see him again. It was like her mother dying all over again. She wanted to run from the room and find the people who killed Mark and kill them herself, as she had done to Mustafa, but she knew that was a stupid thought, a thought manifested by anger and rage. That's exactly what they would want her to do, she thought. But she did want vengeance, she wanted to avenge his death, she couldn't deny that.

"Are you sure I can't get you something? Patterson offered as he started for the door.

"No, No, I'll be fine," she said as she wiped the tears from the corners of her eyes.

July 10th 2012

Stevie waited anxiously as the computer miles away came on line. After a few minutes, the FBI page popped up on the computer plasma display. A few more seconds later and she was into the SX-10 system via a secure government broadband line.

"Okay, what do you have for me? We need to catch these murders before they can do any more harm," she whispered.

There hadn't been any kind of response from Washington yet after her debriefing. As far as she knew, Mark had never had the time to check her progress and probably not been aware of the breakthrough. As the screen came up, she quickly scrolled through and completed all of the mandatory prompts. The computer finally came to the page where she had been working the night of the attack.

As she pulled up the "*Comprehension File*" there were four phrases, not sentences, immediately displayed. Stevie was excited because she saw phrases that the computer had deciphered that seemed to be relevant. Phrases that conveyed a message that now made some sense.

> **Attack without remorse. Use previous date.**
> **No change in target. Destroy UN.**
> **Beware authorities close.**

"God! That confirms it. There's going to be an attack on the United Nations building," she gasped. *But when?* she thought as her mind raced ahead with possibilities. She wondered if there were more lines in the code that the computer had just overlooked. She decided to work on that problem later. She knew she was on the verge of breaking the code wide open. But, right now, she needed to convey this information, although sketchy, to someone in Washington D.C. immediately.

24

August 17th 2012
Washington D.C.

Agent Valetta's investigation of the missing county sheriff had produced a few leads but nothing solid to go on. Tripp wasn't sure if his team was really getting anywhere with the investigation. He knew they were chasing a long shot, but he refused to redirect his agents away from following their instincts. Freeman had come up with several unexplained murders in New York that could potentially be linked to a terrorist group and was working hard to connect the investigative dots.

Unfortunately, after an exhaustive investigation, nothing of interest had turned up on Mustafa Radiz. Tripp was quickly running out of options and he knew it. It seemed as if Radiz had been beamed down to earth by Allah himself. No one could be found that actually knew him, other than his landlord, who only knew him by name. The most promising leads were coming out of New York. Out of the three murders that Freeman was investigating, one of the victims seemed to provide the most hope. He was an Asian-American male with connections to Malaysia. The case was still unsolved by the NYPD, but detectives had quickly learned he was an engineering student and a devout Muslim, which had peaked Freeman's interest.

"What are you reading Boss?" Freeman asked, as he walked unannounced into Tripp's corner office.

"Do you know how to knock?" Tripp asked sharply, but with a smile.

"Sure, but it didn't look like I was interrupting anything!" Freeman protested, knowing Ed Tripp was just yanking his chain. That was just Ed. He always liked to keep you off balance.

"To answer your question, I'm checking to see if any of these terrorist punks decided to blow anything up yesterday that we haven't heard about yet."

"What, you don't listen to CNN like the rest of the civilized world?"

"I prefer to interpret my own news if you don't mind! I don't need to watch a thirty minute news program when I can read the same information in two minutes, especially when most of so called experts don't know what the fuck they're talking about!" Ed said sarcastically. "It's a waste of my time!"

Jim Freeman decided to leave that one alone. Ed didn't seem to be in a good mood.

"Well, were there any attacks in the last twenty-four?"

"Nothing," Tripp said, carefully folding the paper and setting it on the corner of his desk. "The last thing was the attack on Dillon in Florida."

"I didn't think so. I watched all the news programs and I haven't heard about anything lately, I'd bet money that Agent Dillon would like to change career paths about now."

"I wouldn't blame her. The Bureau hasn't done a very good a job protecting her. Having said that, this whole thing is getting kind of weird! It's been months since a suicide bomber attack, I'm at a loss for what's going on." Tripp said. This thought of being confused wasn't something he would share with just anyone, but he was interested in Freeman's thoughts.

"Yeah, I think it's strange. I'm getting a little stressed, too, you know, like it's the calm before the storm. The whole thing is becoming a bit unnerving. Of course, that's what these guys are aiming for, isn't it? Maybe they are singling us out and going after only law enforcement types, you know like Stevie and the water cop, Lombardo? Hell, they almost got you and Tetrocelli, too."

While scratching the top of his head with the eraser of his pencil, Ed said, "Maybe just changing their focus for awhile. You know, declare open season on FBI agents to make the evening news. Just use that for their propaganda on *Aljazeera.*"

"Sure why not? We now have three agents murdered, two badly wounded, and one so traumatized that she may not want to be a Special Agent for the FBI much longer. I'm only speculating on that of course! So we certainly can't say they haven't been busy lately, because they have!" Jim could sense Ed was frustrated from being stuck in headquarters, something he had no control over, but it was eating away at him.

"So, why the big change all of a sudden?" Jim asked.

"I still think they are planning something spectacular, something bigger than even killing law enforcement, but they know we're looking at them; maybe they are just trying to get us to look the other way, you know, like a feint in boxing."

"After what happened in Florida and with Latham right here, they would have to know we're all watching our asses, right?" Jim answered.

"Yeah, no doubt! We just have to figure out what their next move is and stop them before they do it, and watch our backsides at the same time!"

"Sounds real easy, boss," Jim said sarcastically.

"Fuck you Freeman! We need to get this right—and quick—or I think a lot of innocent people might die!"

Freeman had flown in from New York to meet with Tripp about his investigation. He was at a stopping point and wanted a face-to-face with Ed. Further investigation had revealed the kid had frequented a New York City Mosque known for its radical Islamic rhetoric. The victim had been found with his throat unceremoniously slashed from ear to ear and his computer missing. If that wasn't enough, he had just returned to the city from a one-day, hurry-up trip to Boston, which had further piqued the Agent's curiosity in the young student's activities, so Freeman felt like he needed some direction.

"Here are some photographs…his name is Syed Badawi," Freeman said, as he pulled a set of photos out of a large brown envelope and handed it across the desk to Ed. "These are the before and after shots!" Freeman said in his Brooklyn accent.

"Nasty way to die! So you're sure his name is Badawi?"

"Yeah, his family confirmed that," Freeman said, studying Tripp as he studied the photographs.

"What else do you have on this kid?"

"Well, he was an engineering student at Polytechnic University in Brooklyn and just recently returned from Malaysia after a long sabbatical."

"Religious trip?" Tripp asked with interest.

"Not according to his family."

"Well he fits the profile," Tripp said, obviously energized by what he had just heard.

"That's why I brought it to you. Seems like he took a one-day trip to Boston and his laptop is missing too! That also fits the profile!"

"This is our man. He's going to be a part of this string of dead terrorists…I just feel it!" Tripp said, as he motioned to Freeman to hand over the folder to him.

Tripp now sat silently reviewing the information in the folder.

"Yeah, I'd bet the farm this guy had something to do with all of this shit! I want you back in New York City as soon as possible; find out everything you can about our deceased engineering student. I want to know who he went to school with all the way back to kindergarten. Make sure you interview as many members of the family as you can, and anyone else he's connected to!" Tripp handed the file back to Freeman. "I'd help out but, as you know I can't."

"Anything else?"

"Yeah, go to Malaysia if you have to! Just work this thing hard so we can start tracking people down and put an end to this— Now get out of here." Tripp said, smiling at Freeman.

"Don't worry about that, Boss. I'm all over this!" Freeman said, smiling back.

"Yeah, I know but I'm really worried about this one—I almost went up in smoke in New Jersey awhile back, and now we have three FBI agents dead and two more critically wounded. It might be quiet on the streets, but around here people are dropping left and right! If they're trying to make a point, they sure as hell are succeeding!"

Tripp was now convinced that this young engineer was somehow connected to the terrorist cell in New Jersey. The problem was that he was now lying in a New York City morgue. Tripp had a hunch that Mustafa Radiz knew Syed Badawi. There was a good chance they were connected because they lived in such close proximity to each other. Another thing was clear, Badawi must have been killed by a member of a terrorist group, if only his computer was missing. Maybe terrorists were killing each other now, Tripp thought. That would certainly be a nice development, wouldn't it, he thought.

Attempting to develop a lead with the aid of some great investigative work Valetta had been able to convince the local T.V. networks to show a picture of the missing water Cop on their news programs at five O'clock. The pleas went out to the public for any information concerning his disappearance. It was just one of the leads he was working but probably the most important. A potential witness had called the eight-hundred number set up by the FBI. The trail was growing colder by the minute on the Sheriff's disappearance. Valetta knew something would have to be done quickly to find out if there was fowl play involved. He brought the caller in for questioning the next morning. He had then learned that the witness had spotted the Sheriff's patrol boat from a bridge the same day he had gone missing. The man had been a passenger in a friend's car that just happened to be crossing the I-280 Bridge over the Passaic River. The time of the sighting checked out, although the driver of the car hadn't seen anything unusual. The witness remembered that he had seen the patrol boat alongside a motionless, rust-stained fishing vessel in the center of the river. The Sheriff's boat's blue flashing lights had caught his eye as they crossed the bridge. The man admitted that he couldn't see much from where he was seated in the vehicle. However, he gave a good description of both boats and their approximate position in the river. According to the radio logs at the Sheriff's department's dispatch office, Sheriff Joe Lombardo hadn't reported stopping any river traffic up to the time of his disappearance. The Sheriff was to be relieved from his patrol duty at four-thirty p.m., but he never showed up at the dock. There were only two plausible answers for his disappearance. The Sheriff either fell overboard and drowned, which was extremely difficult to do with a personal flotation device on, or he stopped someone and they killed him, Valetta concluded. So far, the description of the fishing trawler was pretty good, but the witness said he could only see silhouettes of two individuals in the wheel house. Thus, no positive IDs were possible.

The Interstate 280 Bridge is one of the most traveled bridges in the United States with over ninety-three thousand vehicles crossing it daily, Valetta had looked it up. He knew there had to be other witnesses that could have seen the two boats stopped near the bridge. He then decided to ask the television stations to air another "request for information" concerning the disappearance of the officer.

Agent Valetta, unlike Tripp, wanted to be careful and let the evidence direct his investigation not his gut feel. He wasn't good at working hunches, as Tripp liked to do. Tripp was good at it, he wasn't. Tripp was a legend when it came to hunches! Valetta, however, recalled earlier in his career with the FBI that he had gotten into trouble following his intuition and not the facts. He had followed what seemed to be an obvious lead in an important investigation without relying on credible evidence to support what had occurred. And that had turned out to be a serious mistake. The murder case he was working looked like an average, everyday Mafia hit in New York. The deceased was a known mobster that had been found with his head beat in with a pipe and then, for good measure, strangled by a garrote. Valetta thought it was just another mob murder by a couple of overzealous hit men to even some score. However, the case later took a surprising turn when the wife of the slain mobster confessed to murdering him over another woman. Out of rage, she had hit him thirty-five times in the head with a lead pipe. She then had fashioned a garrote from a roll of wire she purchased for hanging pictures and just about took the poor slob's head off out of rage. She admitted later that she wanted it to look like a mob hit. Back then, Valetta had followed his hunches and had got it all wrong! He had vowed to never let that happen again. That incident hadn't been a career-ending mistake, but a lot of people in New York still gave him a lot of grief about it, even today. But the important thing was that he had learned from his mistake. What else could a kid from Brooklyn do! Whenever it came up in his mind, he would just tell himself "Forget about it!" but he never could. It was a constant reminder to him to stick to the facts.

The Coast Guard Group located in the city of New York had given Valetta total access to all of the official Coast Guard US documentation numbers of fishing vessels that had been stopped on routine patrols over the past year. After finding several boats that fit the general description, he had been able to eliminate them one by one, leading ultimately to a dead end. The Coast Guard Chief Operations Specialist in New York City suggested that he should expand his search to the Coast Guard Groups North and South, perhaps by a hundred miles in both directions. Valetta took his advice and had searched the Coast Guard records for days and was able to find some similar vessels while locating all the owners, but again came up with nothing. However, one thing was suspicious. After speaking to over thirty boat owners, he learned that no one could understand why a fishing trawler would be traveling up the Passaic River into a highly industrialized area. Valetta had decided one more time to expand this part of his investigation. If this didn't provide any additional leads, he would drop it. So again he expanded the search from Maine to South Carolina in a final attempt to see if a vessel was stopped that might fit the description of the vessel that the witness saw from the bridge. It wasn't much but it was all that he could do at the moment.

With the assistance of the Chief Operations specialist, information from the entire Atlantic seaboard started to pour in concerning fishing vessels that had been routinely stopped by the Coast Guard. The most promising lead was from a Coast Guard Group near Cape Hatteras located in Buxton, North Carolina. A vessel that fit the general description of the fishing boat had been stopped in the Intracoastal Waterway in May. One member of the boarding party had a good recollection of the fishing vessel and the man that claimed to be the skipper. The skipper, according to Mike Johnson, the Boatswains Mate who was aboard that day, was a thin Asian male in his late twenties or early thirties. Agent Valetta thought the lead was promising enough to fly down with an FBI artist. He wanted two sketches made: one of the fishing boat and one of the skipper.

"Things just might start to connect here if I'm lucky," Valetta had said after receiving the information from the Coast Guard down in Buxton.

Valetta had called Mike Johnson after arriving at the local airport. Valetta and his artist Tim Wilson then rented a car and drove down to take the ferry out to Hatteras Island. The outer banks were beautiful, and Valetta made a mental note to go by and see the famous Hatteras lighthouse if he had time after the interview.

"I wish I could spend some time down here sketching the area," Tim Wilson said as he looked out the car windows at the countryside racing by in a blur. Tim worked out of FBI headquarters in D.C. and was considered one of the best sketch artists the FBI had. His drawings had been featured several times on TV crime programs. Jim had the uncanny knack of being able to merely listen to the description of a person and then draw a near perfect photo- like comparison. Most people who had worked with him thought he was akin to a psychic with artistic abilities.

"Yeah, it is a beautiful place. It looks like things are a little slow around here, right now though…" Agent Valetta said, as he drove along the highway into Buxton under a deep blue sky.

"Tourist season is ending," Tim said, still staring out of the window at some of the colorful homes built along the road.

The car pulled up at the United States Coast Guard Group building. It was on the water with patrol boats lined up behind the building.

"This looks like a nice place to work," Valetta said as he looked around.

"Except when you're in the middle of a hurricane trying to rescue some poor unfortunate souls off Cape Hatteras!" Tim said.

"You got a point there!"

The two men went in the building and were soon face to face with Boatswain's Mate Mike Johnson, a short, heavy-set young man in his late twenties.

The three men went to a quiet office on the first floor of the brick building for the interview. The office was the usual nondescript government office. The solid walls were painted with gray enamel that perfectly matched the unassuming gray metal desk and chairs. The room was lit by the cold blue rays of fluorescent tubes mounted on the ceilings.

"Have a seat," the young coastguardsman said. "Do you want me to close the door?"

"Yes, please," Valetta said. Tim Wilson walked behind the desk and pulled his sketch pads out and put them on top of the desk along with pencils he would be using. He didn't like using composite drawings made from the photos of various facial parts. He was too good for that. He only used composites pictures when the witness couldn't accurately verbalize to him what someone looked like from memory.

Agent Valetta took out a small digital recorder to record the interview.

"So tell me about the guy you stopped," Valetta said, as he turned the recorder on.

"Not much to tell, really. We saw this old fishing trawler moving north in the waterway. It looked as if it might not be safe to operate so we stopped it," the young coastguardsman said as he rubbed his hands together nervously.

"What kind of condition was the boat in?" Valetta asked.

"Pretty bad. It was an old boat with bad wiring and generally in bad condition."

"Who owned the boat?"

"The boat was newly purchased and he had the proper papers and a passport."

"What was the name on the passport?"

"Kong Tian Nai"

"Are you sure?"

"Yeah, I wrote it down in my notebook." He handed the notebook over to the Agent Valetta so he could copy the spelling.

"Do many people use a passport aboard fishing boats when you stop them?"

"No, I thought that was odd too," The guardsman said.

"Yeah, I think it's odd. So it was a US Passport, right?"

"Yes, it was."

Listen, I need to check this passport out. While I'm gone, why don't you guys get started and let's get a drawing of the boat and the man you spoke to?"

This might be the first real break in the case! Valetta thought as he left the room. Again, he didn't like hunches but, for some reason, he knew there was going to be a problem with the passport. If the guy was a United States citizen, what reason would he have to use a passport for identification? It didn't seem to add up, he thought, as he dialed the phone number to FBI headquarters so they could check the passport for authenticity. After a short wait, Agent Valetta learned that there was a valid passport issued to Kong Tian Nai. Valetta was surprised but not devastated by the results of the search. He still believed it was a fake passport. Valetta then asked headquarters to send by e-mail a copy of the passport documents, including the photograph, to him immediately.

"We have a valid passport. They're sending over the documents now!" Valetta said, as he entered the small room where the artist was busy sketching.

Valetta walked around the back of the desk behind Tim and looked at the sketch he was working on. It was of a thin-faced young man with a New York Yankee baseball hat on his head.

"So this is him?"

"Yes. I never forget a face. Maybe the name but never the face, that's why I write the names down," Johnson said.

"So he was wearing a New York Yankee cap?"

"Yeah, I couldn't forget that!" he said, obviously bothered by the fact for some reason.

"Why's that? Because he was Chinese? You don't think the Chinese don't like the New York Yankees," Tim asked, as he continued to add more shading to the face of the man he was drawing.

"No, because I'm a Red Sox fan! No offense, but I hate the Yankees!"

"Hey, watch out there! I'm a native New Yorker and I love the Yankees!" Valetta said pouring on the accent for effect.

"How's this look?" The artist asked.

"Looks exactly like the guy. That's pretty good," Mike Johnson said, impressed with what he saw.

"I'm going to pull up that passport data. Can you get me on a computer?" Valetta asked.

"Sure thing," both men left the room and left Tim to finish up.

As the picture emerged from the file and became visible on the flat screen display Valetta asked.

"Is this the guy?"

The Coast Guardsman took one look and said. "That's not the person on the boat that I saw," he replied.

"I knew it!" Valetta said. He knew it was a fake passport and that the person on the boat was probably illegally in the country.

Valetta printed a copy of the information and slid it into his brief case. He then interviewed Mike Johnson for another hour and a half recording the conversation.

"Let's get finished up here. I want to get back to New Jersey as soon as possible and get these drawings to our only other witness. Let's find out if this is the vessel he saw," Valetta said.

He had forgotten all about the Hatteras lighthouse as he drove on to the ferry for the mainland thinking about his next move.

25

October 19th 2012 7:33 a.m.
New Jersey

"Be careful, Allah wills it—" Ali said as both men retrieved the small nuclear device from its hiding place under the floor. Tan had successfully installed the U-233 core. Now he was confident it was ready to detonate and that everything had been installed correctly. Tan had meticulously checked and rechecked the circuits that would explode the external charges that would begin the deadly nuclear reaction. The core would supply enough thermal nuclear force to destroy the United Nations building and most of New York City that stood around it.

The white Ford delivery van had been disguised as a plumbing truck. The name on the side was one of the larger companies that served New York City. A decal had been made, and the two men had carefully applied it to the side of the truck. The bomb was now loaded with 12 kilograms of Plutonium and, minutes before, had been attached to the metal floor of the van. Tan had carefully constructed a plywood cover with covey holes for parts that hid the nuclear device completely from prying eyes. Tool boxes had been placed on top of the cover along with cardboard boxes labeled with the names of various plumbing supplies. To someone looking inside the truck, it looked like a normal work truck loaded for a day's work, just like the thousands of other commercial trucks that drove the streets of the city of New York. The idea was to blend in and not be scrutinized by the authorities or even a casual observer.

An electronic detonator was carefully wired with the commonly used brown, green, and yellow wire used to wire trailer lights for cars and trucks. The wire ran under the van and up through the floor to a switch that was mounted on the inside of the passenger seat. If anyone were to look under the truck for any signs of a bomb, the wire would appear like any other truck that was wired to pull a trailer.

Tan Gaddam had felt serene for the past few days. But now he recognized that his time on earth could be measured in only hours. Earlier, he had prayed to Allah during the assembly to ensure that his work was done correctly and that he would be martyred by the detonation of the bomb. So many of his Muslim brothers had died at the hands of the Americans, and this would be his measure of revenge against the Great Satan. His own death would be a personal message to those infidels who would not submit to the will of Allah. None of this was his fault. The enemy had asked for this. It was their fault instead for supporting blood-thirsty leaders. The strategy was to kill the innocent, because that was the only strategy that would work against America's strong military. The people had to die, not the soldiers in their strategy. The message was death and destruction to the non believers! This would now be clearer than it ever had been.

"Are you ready to travel to Paradise, my brother?" Ali asked, as he emerged from under the van.

Tan didn't answer; he just shook his head in agreement. It was strange to see Ali so relaxed, because he had never been relaxed. He even seemed to be happy, maybe for the first time in his life. It had taken enormous patience over the last two months to work closely with this Arab who always seemed to be agitated, demanding and, at times, violent. His strange and volatile behavior seemed to put their mission in danger, but in the end it hadn't. His relentless pursuit of delivering destruction to America and his determination had made the real difference. Tan could see all that now. Ali was the most dedicated one, but he was dedicated too.

Tan said nothing, but nodded his head that he was indeed ready. He suddenly felt deeply emotional. He felt like he was going to lose control and become weak in Ali's eyes. In his mind, he knew it was a matter of faith and that faith would have to sustain him today, because it was the will of Allah that he should die. Tan desperately wanted to be serene again, but that feeling had left him. It was Ali that had made him suddenly sad because, in a different time, they might have been friends. To Tan it would seem only right that if they were going to die at the same moment in time, in complete agreement with their actions, that they should have become friends, but they had not. To Tan, this was sad but unavoidable.

Tan got into the truck behind the wheel as Ali walked to the two, tall, rusty doors. With all his weight, he pushed the left door on its over head track, out of the way. The old door with its metal wheels creaked and groaned in defiance but slowly opened to the bright sunlight. Outside it was a beautiful autumn morning. The sun was blinding. Tan had not ventured outside in days, and the sun felt good on his face. After so many nerve-racking days and hours they were finally close to reaching their goal. For months, they had hidden their activities well, and now it was time to take the drive to East 42nd street in New York. Being caught now was unimaginable. Over three years of planning was now going to finally payoff. There would be no room for failure, only success and Martyrdom, Tan believed.

Tan started the engine. At first it sounded like it wasn't going to start, then it finally coughed to life. Tan pressed the accelerator pedal down to increase the RPMs and warm it up. After a moment it was idling just fine. He put the truck in gear and drove it outside of the warehouse in plain view for the first time. Tan could smell the gasoline exhaust as it wafted through the driver-side window. It was the smell of success, the delivery of the nuclear device was assured! We will do this, he thought confidently. No one can stop us.

The Newark area had been the perfect place to complete the bomb. Even with traffic, the drive time would be a little more than hour. It wouldn't be enough time for the authorities to stop their plan. They would make their way carefully to the New Jersey Turnpike, take the Rt-3 exit toward the Lincoln Tunnel, and get on to I-495 East. Their objective was East 42nd street and First Avenue. If they made it to within fifty yards of the building, it had been calculated that the blast would blow the bottom of the building away or vaporize it completely. All of this was dependent on the core being depressed by the two explosive charges that were positioned on either side of the enriched U-233. This rapid compression would start the nuclear reaction that would create the massive explosion.

"What a beautiful day Allah has given us to become blessed martyrs," Ali said, as he sat down in the passenger seat and pulled a dark, wool skullcap over his head. The cap would help disguise him from the authorities. Even to Tan Ali now looked Latino, not Arab.

Tan pressed the accelerator, and the utility van picked up speed and moved out of the yard onto the pavement. As Tan drove the van, he took time to glance down at a small photograph he had taped to the dashboard. In the photo stood a small, frail man and a woman whose smile was locked in time. It was a picture of his father and mother, proud parents of their son whom they loved. Would they still be proud of their son? Would they understand? He began to feel emotional again, but again he fought back his feelings. This is not the time, he told himself.

The Jersey Turnpike traffic was moving well. The Ford panel van sped toward the City of New York at sixty miles an hour.

For Ali, this moment was a time of exhilaration and pride. If he was afraid, Tan couldn't see it in his demeanor. Tan knew Ali was proud of their accomplishment and wanted to personally deliver a tragedy of unequaled proportions to the crusaders of the United States. Something that they could never forget. A blow so horrendous, so devastating that, for generations to come, his name would be remembered by his Muslim brothers around the world. If God was willing, the American people would turn against their leaders, and anarchy would lead to outright insurrection. America would be permanently weakened, and its citizens would know true fear, the kind of fear that would paralyze every man and woman and make them flee the major cities that their government could no longer protect. Cities like Los Angeles, Philadelphia, and Boston would be considered too dangerous to live in by its own citizens. This fear would do more damage to the American way of life than the bomb blast itself. The fear of another nuclear attack would turn large cities into vast ghost towns of economic destruction.

The van slowed to a stop in a line of traffic waiting to pass through the toll booth. Ali leaned back in his seat keeping his face from being seen clearly from the outside. At any moment, a person with a cell phone could make a call to the authorities reporting an Arab man in a van. That would be enough to have them stopped. Within minutes, it would be over. If that happened, the plan was to go ahead and detonate the bomb right on the spot. Although a bomb blast of this magnitude would be terrifying anywhere in the world, in the heart of Manhattan it was going to be devastating. From the Hudson River, clear across to the East River, death and destruction would shake America to its core. Only eighteen blocks from Central Park, the terrorists hoped that the radioactive fallout would render the park useless to the citizens of New York for many years to come.

Tan dropped the tokens into the basket, and they sped on their way toward his martyrdom. The two men had driven the route several times and knew exactly what lanes to be in to have the minimum exposure to the authorities. Great care had been taken to ensure that their delivery vehicle would blend in with the regular traffic that flowed into the city every day. From the side of the highway or from anyone in a passing car looking at the van, they would never suspect that its lethal cargo was about to change the course of American history, that it carried a bomb that was about to bring a Hiroshima-like attack to the shores of the United States.

9:48 a.m.
New York City

Tan turned the Van on to 42ND street and slowly drove towards the United Nations buildings. The street was like a canyon between the high rise buildings that lined the Hudson River. As the van moved closer to the concrete barricades that funneled traffic to the guard enclosure, Tan could feel the blood rushing into his head. His heart felt like it was going to pound out of his chest. This was the moment he had planned for. Now he could clearly see the target in front of him. Was this what he really wanted? Did he want to go through with it? He glanced over at Ali. The serene look was now gone and had been replaced again by a strange, maniacal look on his face. To Tan, Ali didn't seem to be afraid but, instead, angry again, just as he had always been. It didn't matter now, Tan thought. Nothing matters but Paradise. All that mattered now was to set the device off as close to the building as they could. However, it was still clear to Tan that anger was still the driving factor for Ali. Tan knew Ali would have carried out this horrible attack even without the promise of Paradise!

Tan continued to edge the van forward within a long line of traffic waiting to enter the main entrance. The closer the better, he thought as he sat waiting. He wanted to get it over with now. The pressure was becoming unbearable.

Tan didn't know how much longer he could endure the wait. The serenity that he had enjoyed earlier was gone. He wanted to jump from the truck and run, but it was too late. Ali had his fingers on the switch, and he would detonate the bomb if anything unusual happened. Tan now fully resigned himself to his destiny. As the moment grew closer, his mind raced with thoughts of how painful it might be to die this way. Or would it be painful at all? He had convinced himself that it wouldn't! Other thoughts flooded his mind as he sat waiting. How long would it be before he received his just rewards as martyr? Would it come instantly, or would he have to wait in some purgatory existence for awhile before he entered eternal Paradise. Stay calm, he told himself, it will all be over soon. This is your destiny. Nothing can change that now.

The white panel van continued to inch forward in the line of traffic. Tan could see the security officers looking vehicles over before waving them through the iron gates. An entry document sat folded on the dashboard of the truck. It was a copy of the security notice that had been sent to the security desk at the United Nations to allow the plumbing truck to enter the premises for routine repairs. It had been issued by the director of maintenance services to the *Atworth Plumbing* Company. In fact, the order for plumbing work had been a carefully orchestrated ruse by a secretary of the Sudanese delegation to the director of maintenance. The request for plumbing repairs had originated in her office.

Once the appointment was set to do the repairs, she called and secretly cancelled the appointment directly with the plumbing company without notifying anyone at the UN. She knew the critical security clearance would still be in effect at the gate for the plumbing truck. The secretary was a member of a radical Muslim group based in Sudan. She had conveniently called in sick for work this morning and was already boarding a flight to Jakarta as the truck loaded with a thermal nuclear device sat idling near the gate of the United Nations building.

Tan tried to calm himself even more as he put the truck in gear to inch forward again in the traffic. Any hesitation or outward sign of emotion, once they were at the gate, could alarm the guards. He looked again at Ali and his demeanor hadn't changed. He was the same angry, determined man Tan had known from the beginning, but he was hiding it well now.

Tan suddenly felt an overwhelming sense of loss. If he was going to die with Ali, it was a tragedy that they had never really been friends he reminded himself. They had lived together and been through such danger together, but he felt no closer to this man than he had the first day they had met. To commit such a holy act in the name of Allah with someone whom you could never really talk to, or get close to, left a hollow feeling deep inside him. He was about to die with someone for a cause that he believed in, but with a person he didn't even respect as a human being. That part of it seemed wrong. Tan had seen Ali kill an innocent Muslim just to achieve his own martyrdom. Would Allah accept this? He now seriously doubted that Ali would become a martyr after death. It seemed to Tan that too many decent tenants of his faith had been violently pushed aside just so that Ali could selfishly establish himself as the greatest of all soldiers for Islam. Tan now worried that his association with Ali would keep him from reaching Paradise as well. *Foolish thoughts, be calm*, he told himself again. Paradise is waiting!

"Identification please," the guard said, as Tan pulled the truck up to the barricade.

Both men handed their forged drivers' licenses over to the guard. Both licenses had been obtained by both men earlier in the year. The guard was of Middle-Eastern decent, Tan was not sure the country of his origin, but they had been briefed that the guards would be multinational.

The guard studied the New York driver's license then gazed at the men. He briefly glanced into the back of the truck but didn't take the time to call maintenance or look any further into the contents of the truck as he waved them through an opening barricade.

"We're in. Allah is great!" Ali said softly as if strangely mesmerized by his own success.

"We are one step closer to God!" Tan answered, his voice now quivering with unmistakable fear, which didn't go unnoticed by Ali.

"Calm yourself," he ordered angrily under his breath. "This is for Allah!"

26

October 19th 2012 9:50 a.m.
FBI Building Miami, Florida

The phone next to Stevie's desk rang. Instinctively, she knew it was Quantico because she hadn't had any personal calls from programmers there in awhile. Stevie picked up a yellow legal pad in anticipation of taking notes. As she expected, it was a software engineer, a young MIT graduate she happened to know, who gave her the official go ahead to run the updated program once again. She had been convinced it would take a few more days, but apparently someone was cracking the whip back in D.C. to get the program working. After hanging up, she started running the codes again. Based on her advice to Tripp, alert levels across the country had been raised because of the high probability the computer may have gotten some of the code right. But the American people didn't pay a lot of attention to government warnings anymore, because they had learned, the hard way, that terror attacks were totally random.

Stevie had also been contacted several times by Tripp concerning her progress. His investigative group had come up with some promising leads but still needed the information from the encrypted DVD to help with the investigation. He desperately needed information and was as frustrated as she was with the delays. Both of them sensed time was running out, but there was nothing they could do to speed things up.

Finally, everything was set, and she typed in the passwords for access to the computer located over eleven hundred miles away. Working through the prompts, she again entered the code words exactly as she had done every time before. There was a bit of delay as the computer ran the sequence of words once again. The supercomputer was capable of running at over twenty-billion floating–point operations per second, and it wouldn't take long to get an *evaluation*, a term that Stevie liked to use when the computer indicated it had series of decryptions.

Instantly, the computer came back with the "*Code Broken*" message! But all this really meant was that the computer had syntax that needed to be reviewed by a human code breaker. Scrolling through the pages that displayed the actual decoded data, she found that there were six hundred and eighty syntax models to review. The words were arranged in sequence from the simplest to the most complex. Stevie took a deep breath and began to review each grouping of words that were written in Arabic. Syntax, as understood by the computer, was not much different from the way a linguistic expert would look at critical word-linking. Experts used "*linguistic elements,*" which are words that are put together to form "*constituents*" or phrases. These elements had to be in groupings that connected into the orderly properties of language. It was important to keep the words and phrases in Arabic, so meanings wouldn't be confused by being intermingled with the properties of another language.

The third through fifth phrases read in Arabic:

> **"Nations under One House Erase from Memory God Wills"**
> **"God Wills Nations under One House Erase From Memory"**
> **"Erase from Memory Nations under One House God Wills"**

As Stevie continued to scan other possible syntax, the computer had come up with another thirteen phrases that were similar to the third, fourth, and fifth. She wasn't quite sure how the computer had come up with these associations, but they had repeated themselves over and over with the syntax only changed slightly. This was it! Stevie was sure, because the same phases had come up so many times with such slight variations. "Okay, what do these phrases really mean?" It came to Stevie instantly! It was so obvious. It was an inescapable conclusion; terrorists were planning to destroy the only place in the United States where nations met, the United Nations Building! The attack would be in New York but she still didn't have any idea of a specific date!

She then dialed Tripp's office number. Unfortunately, she received a voice message. She left an urgent message about what she had found and then hung up. Next, she called his cell phone and again reached a voice message and left the same message on that phone too.

She had time to run the same word groupings over one more time. She again entered the information and waited. The room seemed cooler than it had just minutes before. As she waited, she pulled a sweatshirt over her head. The SX-10 again ran the data quickly. As she waited, she began to have doubts about the programming and its reliability. Could she really tell someone with any certainty that these short phrases really meant what she thought they meant? Certainly, a group of people would have to verify this. She knew they wouldn't take her analysis at this point, or would they? "I'm about to find out," she said to herself.

She was certain the coding was correct; the computer again verified the same data, so it had to be correct. Stevie desperately wanted to pick up the phone and call security at the United Nations Building herself to warn them. But she couldn't do that. Something of this magnitude would have to be vetted by the Director of the FBI and then released as a serious credible threat.

There were still parts of the code that needed to be broken. The CIA would want to know the country of origin of the coded message. They would also want to know what groups were responsible and that would involve a lot more investigation, since no terrorist group was going to put their signature, coded or not, on something like this. For the time being, Stevie needed a confirmation from someone above her pay grade that the new data were in fact reliable, even though she was convinced the computer had finally broken the coded messages. Just a little more work and she would be out of here, she hoped.

27

October 19th 2012 9:58 a.m.
New York City

"Keep driving. We must get closer." Ali said, as Tan slowly maneuvered the panel van around the circular drive. They were now inside the security perimeter adjacent to the plaza just west of the United Nations Building. Tan caught a glimpse of New York City's famous glass canyon. For Tan, the reflections of the buildings were odd because they perfectly framed what was going to be destroyed in a matter of minutes.

"Park there!" Ali said quietly. Tan could see from his demeanor there wasn't going to be any hesitation, no indecisiveness, when the final moment came. No manifestations of self-doubt or leniency for the innocent, just the determination to kill with impunity. So Tan rightfully believed that their lives would end in just a few moments, but this was their destiny and nothing could change that now.

There were several vacant parking spots just before the last turn of the circle drive. This would give them an opportunity to park closer to the entrance. But with two armed guards standing in front of the glass doors it would be too dangerous to get any closer. Ali had ordered him to stop and park in the first vacant spot, which was only about forty meters away from the front of the building.

Tan knew that his life was now in the hands of Allah, his God. There was nothing else to say or do but sit quietly and think his last thoughts here on earth. He had planned, when the time came, to concentrate on his beautiful Malaysian home. He began to think of the beautiful lands where he had been born. As time began to run out, he focused, not on his fear, but on the alluring jade-colored sea and the misty mountains where the surf pounded the white sand beaches. A place so different and so far from this cold and indifferent place full of concrete and glass he came to destroy. This Godless city had no right to exist and, in a moment it wouldn't, he thought, with a new, heightened sense of self.

Ali, at that same moment was thinking about how perfect this place was as a killing ground. No one could have chosen a better place. He knew Allah's great hand had guided them here safely to stop the Great Satan of the west. The water in the river nearby would help spread the radioactive waste for miles, exposing and ultimately killing tens of thousands. Yes, this was the best place, Ali thought. The destruction of the United Nations Building, a puppet organization, had sponsored so much of what Ali hated about the Western World. The whole world would now understand that no organization could get in the way of the will of God! He was now convinced that God had put him into this place to begin a series of extraordinary events that would start to cleanse the world of infidels. Those who had for centuries wanted to exterminate Muslims had created the ultimate destructive power that would destroy their own will to resist, he reasoned as he readied himself to push the button that would end his own life. The infidels had created this destructive force that would now be the beginning of their own end. Ali had never believed that a superior western society had developed such treacherous weapons on their own, but instead, he believed it was the hand of Allah guiding the infidels to build them. It had been part of his great plan to let the non-believers punish themselves, to be responsible for their own extermination. Ali didn't believe he was guilty of any crime; he was merely carrying out the will of his God. It was his sacred will; it was Allah at work leading his faithful against Satan. It was his will to protect Muslims worldwide through the actions of two of his devoted followers. It took an evil society to develop such a weapon, and it was fitting they would feel the wrath and destruction of their own military might. This demonic, secular civilization was in fact decadent enough to place their safety and security in weapons rather than looking to the real God for their protection. That would be their colossal mistake. These were Ali's final thoughts as he slowly depressed the chrome button mounted next to his left hand. At that moment, the electrical circuit was completed and a rush of energy ran through the wiring and into the primary detonator!

Tan had just begun to relax in his visions of home when he felt, only for a split second, a horrible burning pain that seemed to engulf his entire body. For only a brief instant, did Tan realize that the device had worked properly and he had carried out his mission successfully. But not enough time to feel happiness or sadness, just enough time to feel the intense heat for a fleeting instant and then nothing but emptiness.

The enormous compressive energy supplied by the explosive charges on each end of the device rammed the two metal plates quickly towards each other, compressing the spheroid center of the nuclear device that contained the U-233 core. The fissile mass immediately started the fission process and this, in turn, detonated the second more devastating nuclear explosion. The vaporizing effect of the incredible heat, which by now was over nine hundred and eighty thousand degrees centigrade had, in an instant, created a 1,200-foot crater that was over eighty feet deep with edges of molten rock. Just as quickly, the United Nations buildings had been blown apart and they were instantly vaporized. The entire destructive force set against the building took less than a sixteenth of a second once the core exploded. As the building was becoming part of the plume streaming up into the atmosphere, the Hudson River became a boiling cauldron of hell. In each direction for over a half mile the water spewed out and up as a part of the immense cloud traveling upward. The harbor tug *Sampson* was smartly making its way down river at the instant of the detonation just a mile below the UN building. The Captain, Jonathan Kilroy, wasn't at the helm but was eating a sandwich in the galley below when the impact of the blast hit his vessel. He felt the sudden surge in power followed by the stunning impact just as the boat was blown tumbling into the air and skipping across the surface of the water. The impact of the bulkhead slamming into the Captain's cranium killed him instantly. The side of the vessel facing the blast melted into molten steel instantly, then the smoking hulk, now partially melted, was thrown on the bank of the river where it finally came to rest, screeching and howling to a stop. No one on board survived. How could they? By now, the hellish plume was racing even higher into the atmosphere with more radioactive steam that would ultimately rain down ash and debris while transforming most of the buildings within a four-mile radius of ground zero into radioactive ovens. This invisible and painless ash of fallout would begin to kill hundreds of thousands of New Yorkers in a matter of hours. Buildings on both sides of the river were nothing but smoldering foundations as the second shock wave from the explosion blew the fires out instantly. The Jacob Javits Center and the Port Authority were now part of the plume rising over the city at a rate of six thousand feet per second skyward as were the remains of the people who had been walking through the area at that moment. Madison Square

Garden was now gone, too, now only an indiscernible depression among a few tangled I-beams that were twisted and reaching into the air like a macabre sculpture. The whole area was still super heated, with vapors and gases escaping in great, belching gasps from the underground sewer systems. Everything, as far as the eye could see, was smoldering from the intense heat that had just blasted through the city, melting everything in its path as if it were merely made of wax.

The heated blast of radioactive air raced out towards Central Park, igniting the trees into a flaming inferno, then instantly, the fires were blown out by the following shock wave. The force of the blast blew what was left of the trees out of the ground by their roots. What now remained of the park was nothing more than a huge, barren landscape—black, charred, and lifeless. The metal benches where people had been sitting seconds earlier were now melted and lying flat across the ground distorted by the intense blast of heat. There was no visible evidence of the people who had been sitting there reading their morning papers moments earlier.

The rogue scientist who had developed the nuclear device had been pleased during the planning phase when they learned that a detonation near the United Nations building would cause even more deaths than a detonation in the center of the City. With the Hudson River so close to the building, it had become the perfect target. Not only was it a worthy target because of the significance, but for two other reasons as well. First, the location was one of the most densely populated areas in North America and, second, the river would help spew the deadly radioactive ash farther around the city. This would, in turn, kill more people than any other detonation point that could have been targeted. The founders of the United Nations could not have constructed the building in a better location for such a killing field. Of course, that had been the will of Allah.

The lead renegade scientist, Butrus Al-Rahiim, was from Pakistan. He had read carefully the reports of the nuclear devices that had been detonated by the American military in both Bikini Atoll and the blast in Rongelap Atoll in the South Pacific. He was aware that the effects of the blast at Rongelap, which was detonated at ground level surrounded by water from the Pacific ocean, had increased the size of the plume that mushroomed over sixty thousand feet in the air. This plume could be as deadly as the blast itself and he had convinced the terrorists funding the attack of that very fact. There had been a series of intense discussions by Al-Rahiim and members of the JI about how to deliver the bomb for maximum impact. Some in the JI group wanted to fly the bomb over the area with a stolen airplane and then detonate it while still in mid air. But because of the synergy involved in exploding the nuclear device at ground level they had chosen instead to drive it into the west plaza. Since there were so many buildings in such close proximity of the blast the delivery van would cause almost complete destruction of all the structures within a two and a half mile radius of ground zero. The immediate destruction to buildings and the effects of a larger radioactive plume made the ground detonation a better choice in their planned massacre.

Immediately after the blast, the city of New York was turned into a burning, hellish inferno of fire and smoke as combustible materials were now reigniting. The fires were being furiously fanned by north winds that were now blowing across the city with gale force. People that were more than six miles from the blast were pouring into the streets to escape the fire that was now spreading rapidly in their direction. The daily commuters who were speeding towards the city moments earlier had now pulled over to look at the fiery mushroom cloud that was rising above the city. A deep, rumbling sound moved outward in all directions followed by the shockwave, which broke windows and created glass projectiles screaming through buildings and shredding everything in its path. Those not killed in the initial blast and those who had been protected by solid walls of concrete wouldn't be spared the effects of radiation. In a matter of hours, they would start to see radiation burns appear on their arms, legs, and faces. Some who had been looking in the direction of the blast were now starting to feel the symptoms of severe retina burns. Some were screaming as they began running away, only to trip and fall to the ground moaning, crying, and rubbing their eyes. Some unfortunate souls had just laid down right where they were and were now writhing with pain.

The explosion and intense heat had spared few, but in the next twenty-four hours, radiation would kill most of the rest. Those affected would be in a life and death struggle for weeks to come with thousands more who would die from developing cancer from exposure to deadly radiation.

Pia Garcia, a thirty-two-year-old cleaning lady had been working all morning on the first floor of the Museum of Natural History at Central Park. After the blast, she was miraculously still alive. The moment she entered the closet area, she was protected by solid concrete walls that saved her life. Being below ground level, most of the blast swept harmlessly over her head. She had stepped into a basement closet only seconds before the nuclear detonation as she looked for cleaning supplies. The blast had completely annihilated the building above her, but she was alive and relatively unhurt except for her eardrums, which were now ruptured and bleeding. The pain was excruciating, but she had somehow survived. She was face down on the floor, a floor that should be cool to the touch but was, instead, hot and uncomfortable.

The initial blast created pressures of up to twenty psi at ground zero, which had generated a wind velocity of over four-hundred and seventy miles per hour within a one-mile circle—extending out from the blast site. Somewhere near the museum, the air pressure had only reached ten psi, which had allowed Pia to live. Pia had no idea what levels of pressure the human body could take, but she was still alive. She was lucky because, above her, in the museum all one-hundred and twenty-two people who had been in the building were gone. Pia fought through the pain and thought of her precious daughter Juanita who was with her grandmother in the Bronx. Stunned, she lay on the floor as her tears dropped to the hot concrete under her head. In her confused state of mind, lying in the dark hot space, she wondered if she would see her baby again. Surely her daughter was okay, she thought. This was only a local explosion that she had somehow been trapped in, some accident in the building maybe? For a moment she thought about her friend Mary who she had seen moments earlier. Was she alive or dead? She continued to weep and, now, she began to sob uncontrollably; the horrible thought of dying and not being able to see her mother and daughter again suddenly occurred to her. For now, she would have to wait for help not knowing that her fate was already sealed as a consequence of radiation exposure.

Gary Melcher stopped his sleek Seven Series BMW to look at the huge mushroom cloud rising rapidly up into the air. He had been rocked by the blast, and his car had been blown across two entire lanes of traffic and up against the inside railing of the highway. He sat in the seat checking himself for injuries. He then sat motionless and tried to gather his thoughts. Things had happened too quickly. Cars were blown into each other, and he could see at least five or six accidents from where he was. Obviously, there had been an explosion, but that hadn't yet registered in his brain. He thought he had seen a flash of white light but, since he had been looking to change lanes before the explosion, his eyes had been spared. Some drivers had pulled their cars off the highway and now seemed to be wandering around as if drunk. Some were rubbing their eyes and looking about wildly. The whole scene was surreal. Several people were stumbling around with arms outstretched as if they were extras in some cheap horror film. Gary slid out of the front seat and ran to a young lady who was staggering down the middle of the highway.

"Hold on there, lady," he said, as he grabbed her and pulled her out of the roadway.

"I can't see," she said softly, as if it didn't surprise her. Her demeanor seemed odd to Gary, but he knew she was probably suffering from the effects of shock.

"Come with me. You can't walk right here," he said, as he helped her out of the road, helping her sit down next to the guardrail.

"What's wrong with my eyes? They're starting to burn." She said as she began to moan.

"I don't know," he said. "Just stay here and I'll be back."

"Don't leave me," she pleaded softly between moans.

"Just sit here and I'll be back."

Gary then ran across the road to get a man who was now blindly walking off in the direction of an overpass.

"Sir, stop right there. I'll help you!" Gary yelled while closing the remaining few yards between them.

"I can't see!" the man exclaimed, looking about wildly.

"Yeah, I know. Let me help you," Gary said, as he grabbed the man's arm just under the shoulder and began to lead him back to the center of the highway.

"What happened to me?" He said with a trembling voice.

"I don't know, but you're going to be okay," Gary reassured him, not knowing what else to say.

"I was looking at the city and saw a white flash and after that I couldn't see anything."

He walked the man over to the center guardrail and sat him down next to the young woman who was now crying and moaning.

"You two are sitting right next to each other. Don't move, and I'll be back in a second."

Gary stopped dead in his tracks in shocked disbelief. He saw a wave of smoke and fire moving toward him at an alarming rate. All he could think of was to find cover. Just in front of him to his left was a small retaining wall with a drainage pipe. He instinctively ran and dove in behind the wall and crawled into the pipe saving himself from the firestorm that engulfed the area a split second later. The roar of the blast was deafening! It had been muffled somewhat in the enclosed concrete pipe but the pressure of the air had come from somewhere on the other side and it now forcefully rushed into Gary's face almost blowing him back out of the pipe. Feeling the pressure, he dug the heel of his shoes into the sides of the rough concrete and held on. He felt the pain as the skin blistered on his face and he began to smell his own hair burning.

"Gary, hold, on!" He screamed to himself while the blast of air buffeted his body. "You'll live, just hold on!" He screamed again. He was attempting, by shear human will, to live through the firestorm that was blowing by just above him.

Then it was over as quickly as it had started! Gary Melcher opened his eyes. He could see the inside of the pipe clearly; there was pain coming from his face and hands. He folded his arm and brought his hand back to where he could see it. Both hands were red and blistered. Large, oval, water blisters had already started to form on the top of his hands that were exposed to the superheated air, but he was alive!

Gary decided to stay in the drainpipe for a while longer in case there was another wave of fire. He knew there was no reason to hurry. He was okay for the moment, and he knew anyone above him was likely dead. He closed his eyes and tried to relax for a while.

28

October 19th 2012 3:45 a.m.
Washington D.C.

"We've finally got something concrete to go on. I think we finally have a sketch of this little guy!" Valetta said, as he handed a file folder over to Tripp.

Tripp opened the file and stared at the drawing for a moment.

"He tried to use a New York Yankee cap to blend in, didn't he?" Tripp said without looking up, still staring at the sketch as if he was trying to divine knowledge about the man from the sketch.

"Yeah, but it definitely worked against him! One of the Coast Guard guys was a Boston fan and he didn't forget that hat."

"See Marty, the Boston fans aren't really that bad, are they?"

"Yeah, right!"

Tripp stood up with the sketch in his left hand and walked around the office scratching his head.

"This guy was smuggling something on this boat. I know he wasn't a fisherman!" Valetta said.

"What makes you think that?"

"Well, my witness in Newark believes this is the boat he saw in the river. There is no reason for a fishing trawler to be in the Passaic, and fishermen don't operate fishing trawlers by themselves, either. The Coast Guardsman said the man was alone on the boat. My guess he is a terrorist smuggling something to New Jersey."

"I'd be willing to wager he wasn't alone on the boat, either. We've got to find this guy quick!"

"I think they murdered the Sheriff too," Valetta speculated.

"Yeah, looks like he could have stopped the wrong person that day and got whacked!" Tripp answered.

"We have Agents combing the Hackensack and Passaic rivers for the fishing trawler right now. If there's anything there, we'll find it!"

"I'd be surprised if you find the boat, Marty. Whatever was smuggled aboard is probably hidden by now, along with the vessel! We need to find this guy right here with the hat; maybe he can answer some of our questions! I want this sketch posted on our most-wanted list and use the name that the coastguard gave you, Kong Tian Nai. Maybe he's used the name before and someone will remember him."

Valetta's cell phone started ringing in his inside suit pocket.

He pulled it out, "Valetta."

"Right, we'll be there as soon as possible!" He said, as he snapped the phone shut.

"We found the fucking boat behind a warehouse pretty close to Newark, it was sunk at the dock."

"I'll get a plane ready to fly us to New Jersey! You get the sketch online now before we leave!" Tripp said as he picked up his phone to call for a plane.

"But you're not supposed to leave, Tripp, remember?" Valetta said smiling.

"Get your Italian ass out of here and let me worry about that!"

October 19th 2012 10:00 a.m.
Greater New York and New Jersey Airspace

The jet was flying over five hundred miles per hour, but it seemed to Tripp as if they were hardly moving at all. He wanted to get to the crime scene as soon as possible and, at this moment, the jet wasn't flying fast enough for him. He knew they were in a race against time, to stop whatever was planned by the crazed bastards. The pieces of the puzzle were finally starting to fall into place. He knew they were onto something big, but exactly what, he wasn't sure. Ed Tripp had ignored the orders of the Director of the FBI by leaving Washington D.C., but he felt he had no other option but to get on location and find out what was going on.

"What do we have so far?" He asked, while sitting in a leather seat adjacent to Valetta.

"It looks like whoever these guys are, they just left a few hours ago." He then pulled out a small notebook where he had scribbled some notes.

"Fresh tracks were found coming out of the warehouse and foot prints of at least one man, maybe two. The vehicle was a truck of some kind, probably a utility van."

"So they left in a truck?" Tripp asked.

"It looks that way. We'll be getting more information shortly. Our agents are checking around right now to see if anyone saw anything."

"Good, we need a description of the vehicle."

Without warning, the plane shook violently just for a split second. At that very same moment, a flash flooded the cabin with an eerie white light. Then a shockwave hit the plane rotating it about eighty-five degrees on its side. Both men held on tightly to the arm rest as the pilot righted the aircraft.

"What the hell was that?" Valetta said has he looked around the cabin.

"It was an explosion!" Tripp said without hesitation.

Ed's first thought was that the source of the explosion could have been a mid-air collision near their aircraft, but he didn't say anything.

After a few minutes, the co-pilot opened the cockpit door and quickly made his way back into the cabin.

"Take a look out of the window on the left side," he said, as he pointed at one of the large oval ports.

As both men moved forward in the cabin to get a better look, Ed was momentarily confused at what he was actually seeing. Then after another second it registered. "Oh my God! That looks like a nuclear blast!" He could now see a huge orange and reddish mushroom cloud of fire and smoke belching skyward. Everything looked as if it was happening in slow motion. Within a minute, an ominous churning cloud had reached their altitude and was still climbing higher into the blue sky above. The plane's flight path had taken it fifteen miles from the City of New York passing through JFK air space in route to Newark.

"Oh my God, that's some blast!" Valetta said not really hearing what Ed had just said.

Smoke was still rising rapidly from a large area bordered by the river. What looked like a tidal wave of fire and destruction was racing away from the base of the cloud outward in all directions. In a flash, smoke and orange flames erupted, as the shockwave continued to move outward across the city. Within a quarter of a second, almost quicker than the brain could comprehend, the area was engulfed in smoke. The shockwave of the blast had traveled so quickly away from ground zero that the two men couldn't really tell if the blast caused the eruption of fire or if it had been the result of the destruction of the city. It was a strange effect that neither man had ever experienced before.

"Incredible!" Valetta blurted out. The full scope of death and destruction hadn't really crossed his mind yet.

Tripp reached for a satellite phone mounted on the bulkhead just in front of him.

"Get on the radio and see if you can find anyone else who knows what's happened," Tripp said to the co-pilot.

He then punched in the numbers to FBI headquarters.

"Everything is burning down there!" Valetta said. Ed was on hold and stretched the phone cord to look out the window; then the phone went dead.

"These fucking guys have finally done it!" Tripp said in horror.

"Gentlemen, have a seat! We have been ordered out of the area by air traffic control!

"What?" Tripp said as he stood stunned. "Out of the Area?"

"We just received confirmation that was a nuclear attack, sir!" The co-pilot said slowly, still looking in the direction of the ominous mushroom cloud still climbing high into the sky above the airplane.

"Holy Mother of God!" Tripp said, as he took his seat, still holding the phone receiver in his hand.

The jet banked sharply to the right, and he heard the engines moan as the pilot went to full thrust. As the jet banked south, he sat unable to say anything now. But he knew hundreds of thousands of people were burning in agony on the ground below. They were too late! What kind of world was this where evil could prevail so easily over good? He placed the satellite phone back on the hook, unable to talk to anyone at the moment. He just sat, stunned…they were too late, he kept thinking, over and over again!

29

October 19th 2012 10:59 a.m.
Montgomery, Alabama
Ferguson House

Doug hung up the phone in his kitchen. He was standing near the window gazing out over his green pastures in total disbelief. He had just spoken to Jim Starke, a political backer from Montgomery, who had called and told him to turn on the television. As soon as the image on the TV appeared, he saw a video feed out of New York of an ominous mushroom cloud that now stood over the city. Anger quickly followed by disgust began to well up from inside, and he immediately turned away in an attempt to calm himself, but the images were just too disturbing. He stood motionless in the kitchen, now looking out at the tranquil countryside, wondering how the world could have evolved into its present state. This was now a world where women and children were slaughtered without remorse under the guise of a religion. A world that had become so evil, so horribly vile, that hundreds of thousands of innocent lives could be taken without even a hint of concern. In fact, in some parts of the world, Doug knew there would be celebrating, even dancing in the streets, as people were suffering and dying in New York. There would be those who believed that this was a justified action by legitimate Freedom Fighters! Many of the world's poor and exploited people would celebrate the terror being inflicted on his people. What a disgusting world it had become, Doug thought. He didn't need to watch T.V. to understand the magnitude of what had just occurred! This had all been predicted by experts, but no one really believed it would happen, not here at home. Many of these same experts had testified in endless and boring sessions before Congress predicting that terrorists would someday secure nuclear weapons with the horrible intent of using them. There had been speculation that WMDs might eventually come from Iran or North Korea, but nothing had been done to stop it. Now the question was, what could be done, to retaliate for this act of mass murder? What could the government do to those who carried out this horrendous act of violence? What could the country really do? Doug knew the answer—probably nothing! No one had ever given this scenario a lot of thought. Sure there was plenty of ideas about how to prepare for such an event, how to save people in the disaster, how to find their bodies in the ruble, but not much about what could be done to ensure it didn't happen.

In Washington, there had been endless debates about the viability of such threats, but nothing about retaliation. Therefore, the consequences, for whoever did this, would be more of the same, chasing terrorists around countries that would give the United States the free reign to do so. Places where tribesman, in some out-of-the-way, lawless shit hole, could defy our military by refusing to turn these murderers over for justice. There had never been any real deterrence for such an act, and that was problem. Doug knew there would be no one to blame, just shadows fleeing and disappearing in the mountains somewhere to continue their evil plans of death and destruction! Middle Eastern governments were funneling millions of dollars into terrorist causes, and so were their businessmen, all out of the reach of American justice in an undeclared war of attrition. There was no real deterrence at all, and there never had been, Doug was convinced.

The phone rang again. Doug picked it up.

"Have you heard?"

"Yes." Doug said as he recognized Leonce's voice.

"They've finally done it. Who knows how many have been killed."

"We knew this could happen. What are they saying about damages?"

"From what we're being told, those who are alive are attempting to get out as fast as they can! New York is going to be a ghost town by nightfall except for the disaster groups that are moving in. Doug, the damages are horrendous, mind boggling!"

"When is the President going to speak?"

"Any minute now. As I understand it, he has flown to a secure location; they think Washington may be next!"

"Okay, let's listen and see what he has to say!"

"I'll do that, but this country is now in a shitload of trouble, partner! We've never been to the brink before, but we are sure as hell there now!" Leonce said.

"Where are you right now?"

"I just got back home!"

"Okay. Listen, call everyone. We need to meet." Doug said, decisively.

"Right now?" Leonce asked.

"As soon as we can!" Doug repeated.

"Okay, where?"

"Let's meet in Biloxi. No one is going to bomb Mississippi. We'll all be safe there."

"You heard that ground zero was the United Nations Building, didn't you?"

"No!" Doug quickly thought of all the international ramifications from a direct attack on the nations of the world."

"Yeah, if we win the election, I don't think we will have to worry too much about international approval for whatever we have to do!"

"We need to come up with statements condemning this action as quickly as possible."

"Okay, I'll get back with you."

All of the major news broadcasts were now originating out of affiliates. All feeds from the networks in New York were strangely silent. Doug knew a lot about the effects of a nuclear blast. Even if the buildings were still standing, the powerful electromagnetic pulse or *EMP* from the nuclear device would have fried every transmitter within miles. He was familiar with military plans to use *EMP* to destroy enemy communications with tactical nukes. This was the reason most of the network "feeds" were now apparently being directed to stations in Washington D.C. Doug quickly concluded that either the buildings were gone or the transmitters were inoperative.

It was obvious to all that the terrorists chose the U.N. as ground zero to show the world that nothing could stop them, not even the United Nations. But there was something else, Doug thought. They probably wanted to disrupt the electoral process in the United States as well. As he thought about the up-coming Presidential elections, he was convinced that this was one of their major objectives. It was simple. The terrorists believed they could neutralize the political power of the U.S, government with one, well-timed catastrophic attack.

Politics being politics, the party holding the White House was going to have to take responsibility for failing to prevent this attack. That pretty much left the President's Party as the big loser in the presidential elections, since they held the executive branch! It was clear it would now come down to either the other major party or the Freedom party, Doug politically calculated. The American people were not likely, under such dire circumstances, to re-elect the party whose leaders let this disaster occur.

He hoped this wasn't the results of the plan that he had stumbled onto in Malaysia. If that was true, he knew the government had prior knowledge and enough viable information and still could not or did not take the measures to prevent this catastrophic loss of life! This was a bad omen for the future, because the intelligence community wasn't able to stop this type of attack. Doug's mind raced ahead, first thinking of his family. The kids were safer where they were in Europe for the moment, and Liz in California. He was scheduled to meet her in Los Angeles later in the week after speaking in Tucson and Phoenix.

The phone rang again.

"Hello."

"Doug I don't want you to run for President any more. They're going to kill you; look what they've done in New York!" He recognized Liz's trembling voice.

"Don't worry. The kids are okay; we'll be okay too," he reassured her.

"No, you don't understand! You've done your duty. It's over, enough is enough! They'll kill all of us, Doug! Think about all those poor people suffering in New York right now. They did nothing to these murderers and they don't deserve to die like this!"

"Liz, I understand. Listen, I'm going to cancel my next two speeches, but I have to attend an important meeting in a few hours. I need you to fly to Biloxi as soon as possible, and I'll meet you there. Call the kids and have them stay where they are for now. I know that they'll want to come home, but just tell them to be patient. This isn't the end of the world; it's just another horrible event in this war, but we'll make it through this!"

It was a beautiful autumn day in coastal Mississippi. The entire state was experiencing clear skies and cool fall temperatures. However, Biloxi now seemed deserted. The normal casino traffic was strangely absent. Usually, the drive down along Casino Row would be crowded with cars and pedestrians, but the streets were strangely quiet with almost no traffic. A few cars were entering the Casino parking lots. The state had struggled since *Katrina*, but things were on the move again and people were finally coming back to the gambling tables.

"Looks like everyone has left town!" Tony said as he looked out the window of the black Chevy Suburban. The secret service agent setting next to Doug said nothing but continued to scan the streets under his dark, metal-rimmed sunglasses.

"Yeah, every city seems to think they are next." Doug said, looking at some notes he had on his lap without looking up.

"No one would try to blow Biloxi off the map. That wouldn't be good enough for these crazed bastards," Tony said, as he gazed out over the water toward Horn Island. The water had a calming effect on him. "My Dad took me out there fishing one time and it was great. We caught redfish out on the western tip of the island. I think it might've been the best day I ever spent with my father. I guess we won't be fishing for awhile though, not after all of this?"

"We're going to solve this problem, maybe quicker than anybody thinks." Doug said, as he continued to make notes on a small yellow pad.

"You mean if we win the election, right?"

"We're going to win the election; then we'll solve this crisis, and then we'll take some time off and go fishing," Doug said.

"I'd like that…"

"My Dad used to take me fishing out there too. We camped on the island and then fished all night. To keep the mosquitoes away, we'd build a fire on the beach."

The SUV sped along the waterfront to their hotel. Doug knew the caller had been right, and he had a good idea who was responsible. He also knew that for months the government had information that could have led to action against the terrorists that attacked New York, but that hadn't happened. It didn't happen because the government had no clear policy to do so. Of course, up on the Hill, there would be harsh words on both sides of the isle. After a short grace period, the finger-pointing would begin among the members of Congress and the administration, but finger-pointing wouldn't help anyone now. Then investigations would be set into motion and the guilty nation would reject any connection to the "individuals" who committed this criminal act. Same old shell game. How could you blame an entire country for the actions of a few crazed unknown terrorist, Doug thought. The CIA and FBI would put the broken pieces of the puzzle together, and anyone who was found to be supporting the group would have their likenesses plastered on various websites and federal buildings. Rewards would be offered for information and convictions of those responsible. When the President spoke in defiance of such attacks, it was broadcast to the Muslim world and more effigies would be burned along with the flag, and nothing would really happen. The government was still fighting terrorists in Iraq, even though a free Iraqi government had been elected. The war was unpopular at home and only the strong resolve of a few top leaders in the government continued to prop-up the Iraq government. Precious American blood was being spilled daily on the dull brown sands of Iraq while, simultaneously at home, terrorist attacks had increased. It was clear to Doug that there might not be peace in his lifetime.

The Suburban turned quickly into the hotel drive and stopped. Tony and the two secret service agents got out first looking in all directions for threats. After the all clear, Doug then got out of the vehicle and made his way into the Hotel, walking directly to the elevator. A suite with an adjoining conference room had been reserved and all discussions would take place there. After checking in, Doug turned on the television to get the latest news. The reporter was saying FEMA was on the site with disaster crews trained in nuclear catastrophes. Very few electronic images were being allowed out of the city because of the horrible carnage and devastation. The latest estimates of human loss was projected to be at least four hundred thousand, although no one could be sure. World leaders were standing in line to offer their expressions of sadness to the American people. There would be expressions of condolences as long as the United States did nothing to retaliate. Doug knew the condolences were tied directly to the US not taking direct military action against other nations, no matter how guilty they were. The US would have to agree to leave adjudication to the World Court or be condemned by its Allies. Doug was disgusted, because he had seen all of this before. He knew, now more than ever, that powerful and unrelenting forces were being directed at America. The powerful men who bankrolled the attack would have to be held responsible, even if war broke out in the process. The responsible countries that supported these attacks, even unofficially, would have to be held responsible. Doug waited for the President's speech like every other citizen wanting to know what would be the next step, after this unprecedented attack.

30

October 20th 2012
New York

The City of New York was under Martial Law. As expected, nations from around the world had been shocked by this remorseless act of terror. The outpouring of sorrow was just beginning to flood into the White House as the world woke up to learn that the city of New York had all but been destroyed by a terrorist attack. However, as suspected, there had been spontaneous and ghoulish celebrations that had broken out in the Middle East. In Syria, the authorities had cracked down immediately to quell these provocative displays of hate in their country. Even leaders of terrorist groups, like Hamas, were making conciliatory statements attempting to mask their real feelings about the attack. After all, it was clear to their leaders to make bold statements at the moment could result in awful consequences for them personally. Better to take the heat off by lying low and being largely conciliatory. Strangely silent was President Putra of Malaysia and his supporters in the JI who had issued no statements to the world.

Out of control fires caused by the nuclear blast were still burning in a six mile radius of the site of detonation. Flames from the nuclear device had spread outward to Jersey City to the west and within miles of Bayonne to the South. West New York and the surrounding area had disappeared into the flames as well as parts of Long Island closest to the East River. The breathtaking beauty of Manhattan's high rise edifices were gone now, having become part of the plume.

Powerful US military satellite imaging was being used to record the effects of the blast site. The space-based *Radar System* was pulsing fifteen hundred pulses per second in frequencies between 300 MHz to 30 GHz. As these pulses hit earth and reflected back to the waiting antennas far above, a three dimensional relief map was being developed of the charred, radioactive landscape far below. After the images were downloaded from the imaging system, the entire surface area appeared to be concaved like a gigantic bowl.

At first, the technicians were puzzled by the strange bowl-like images being relayed from space. But as they analyzed the images in more detail, they could see more clearly the effects of a nuclear blast in a large metropolitan area like New York. This effect had been caused by the outward destruction of the blast. In the center, where the UN building had been located along the river, nothing was left standing, but as technicians zoomed in closer and then panned out on the landscape, the sloping effects of the blast could be seen. As the explosion moved outward, it had lost energy, thus decreasing its destructive effects. So parts of the buildings, mostly the bottom halves, were left in place with just the top portions of the buildings being blown away. Of course, the farther away the buildings were from ground zero, less of the top structures were destroyed. As the Radar imaging recorded more and more images and then moved out away from the center, the effect was a gradual sloping. At a point, approximately five miles out, most buildings although charred and radioactive, were still standing, fully intact but severely damaged.

October 21st 2012 7:50 a.m.
Miami, Florida

The unidentified white G-2 Gulfstream lifted off the runway and then banked slowly to the Northeast from Homestead Air Base. From her seat near the window, Stevie could see the beginnings of the Everglades below reaching out to the west toward the Gulf of Mexico. That was another place she had wanted to visit, which would just have to wait for another time, she thought. At least she was free of the confines of the Miami FBI building and apparently on her way to another secure location. Even though she had very little information about where she was going, she was positive she would still be on the case. She knew the government would want to know who was responsible for the attack in New York and quickly. One fact still bothered here, though. Why hadn't more security been placed around the UN Building before the attack? The only explanation she could come up with was that other experts at the CIA hadn't concurred with her assessment.

The cock-pit door opened, allowing a stream of sunlight to flood into the main cabin. The co-pilot causally walked back to where she was sitting.

"We have an urgent call for you, Agent Dillon. You can use the phone on the bulkhead."

"Agent Dillon, this is Ed Tripp. How are you doing?"

"Under the circumstances, I guess fine!"

"Yeah, I bet." Ed said empathetically.

"I'm sorry that I wasn't able to break all the code in time." She offered apologetically.

"Well, I think you did a great job under the circumstances. If the rest of us had done as well as you, we might not be having this conversation."

"I'm sorry I couldn't tell you where you are going until now, but it was for your protection."

"I understand, Sir."

"You're coming back Washington to work with a special group of people." *I'm finally going home*, she thought, now elated at the prospects.

"That's fine with me, Sir," she said, attempting to sound calm.

"What we need at this point is pretty simple. We want to know who is responsible for the attack. We're going to have a new President in a few weeks and we want to be able to tell him who was responsible."

"I understand. I've already been doing that and we are getting close…"

"That's good, I'm counting on you."

"I know that, Sir."

"I'll meet with you when you get home." Ed said.

"Ed, can I ask you a question? You don't have to answer if you don't want to."

"Sure, go ahead."

"Why wasn't there more security at the UN Building?" she asked.

"From what I have learned from the Director, the U.N. security people refused to add additional security personnel and did nothing to strengthen their perimeter against an attack..."

"Even after the information I found on the DVD?" she said.

"That's right. I guess they didn't believe it. If we would have had a specific time and date, things might have been different. Who knows?"

"I guess I understand," she said, wishing she could have decoded more information.

"Okay, I'll see you when you get in," Tripp said as he hung up.

She sensed Tripp was under a lot of pressure by the sound of his voice. She was aware he might not survive the political backlash that was sure to come. She hadn't ruled out the possibility that she might even be in the middle of another investigation, this time a Congressional investigation. If it came to that, and if one of these showboating politicians wanted her job, then they could damn well have it, now!

31

October 22nd 2012 8:30 a.m.
Biloxi, Mississippi

The drapes were pulled back in the hotel suite that faced the Mississippi Sound. Doug had already prepped for his meeting and was now waiting, with great anticipation for everyone to arrive. His suite offered an excellent view of the marina just across the street from the hotel. As he gazed out across the expanse of water, he could see a lone shrimp boat moving out of the harbor. The boat was draped with its usual free loading collection of hungry pelicans.

"What an uncomplicated life those guys have," John said as he walked up.

"Yeah, that's what I was looking forward to in my retirement, you know, something a little less stressful than this," Doug said.

"This whole world's gone crazy and now it's starting to look like we might be right in the middle of things."

"That's why we signed up, John, remember? We wanted to make a difference!"

"Hell yeah, but that was before we had a chance to win the election!" John said, still staring out the window. "I just never thought we'd have a chance at winning—"

"So you're having second thoughts, huh?" Doug asked, already knowing the answer, John would never back down from a challenge.

"No, not at all! It's just that the job just got more problematic, for a couple of good ole boys from Alabama!"

"I wouldn't argue that; however, I think this country is in a lot more trouble than most people can imagine!"

"You mean, even after the massive and unprecedented attack in New York," John said looking confused by Doug's statement. "How could any person not understand the seriousness of the threat out there, after all this—"

"No, I'm not saying that people don't understand the threat, and where it's coming from. Sure they understand that. What I'm saying is this whole situation has now seriously spiraled out of control. We've let it get this way. It's this way because, as a nation, we are way too tolerant. I think our tolerance has emboldened these sons of bitches to a point of no return. We've been too tolerant for the times we live in. Things have changed, and most people still can't see it that way. This reminds me of another conflict

I read about in military history class back in college. You remember your military history at the Citadel, right?"

"Yeah, I think so, but that was a hell of long time ago. I don't remember all that much. I've always been more concerned about the judiciary in Alabama than the military history of the world," John said, smiling.

"Do you remember studying the Goths and how they finally defeated the Romans?"

"The only Goths I know anything about are the kids I see in the court room dressed in black and sporting some really bad hair," John scoffed.

"Then let me refresh your memory, councilor. The Goths were barbarians who fought the Roman Empire and even though they didn't have a modern army, they eventually defeated the much superior Roman legions anyway. The main reason the Romans were defeated was because over time they lost their edge in weapons technology. But as it turned out, that wasn't the most important reason they lost."

"Okay, I'll take the bait. What was the most important reason?"

"It was Goth's hatred for the Romans that finally gave the advantage to them. Are you starting to see any similarities here? I mean their hatred was so real, so palpable, they would do anything to win and they finally did! "

"Yeah, I see the similarities. Every radical Muslims in the world seems to have a hard on for the United States. It's part of their creed, but I wouldn't agree these bastards have a technological advantage or any other advantage."

"What makes you think that? They just destroyed the largest city in the US with a nuclear weapon."

"Okay, Okay, I see your point!" John said abruptly.

"The way I view it, we are in a dead heat on weapons technology, and I have to give our enemy the advantage in this war against modern civilization!"

"But how could they have an advantage? Without question, we have more weapons and a larger and more capable military."

"Because they have a thousand years of revenge as a motivating factor. We don't have that, John. Simply put, they're more motivated than we are, so the weapons really don't matter."

"If you remember the Emperors of China constructed a wall for thousands of miles to keep out the intruders who attacked and terrorized their nation. We can't do that, can we? The attack in New York is only the beginning of our troubles! Our enemies come in ones and twos and either die in the attack or disappear out of our reach. Don't make the mistake of thinking these ruthless assholes can't win a war of attrition, because they can. History is full of technologically advanced nations being defeated by armies with a lot less technology! Hell, the Viet Cong drove us right out of the jungles of Viet Nam. I was lucky enough to live through that one.

Biloxi 9:33 a.m.

Finally, all the members of the election committee were accounted for and Cliff had just finished with the pressing financial issues of the party. Doug had allowed Cliff to finish up before finally taking charge of the meeting.

Outside, it was a brilliant, sunny day, but inside the room, no one seemed to notice. Emotions were running high with each member feeling a tremendous sense of loss.

"I know that we're all deeply saddened by what has happened in New York," Doug said. "But I think we need to use this attack on our nation to harden our resolve against our enemies. I'm confident our people will now see this struggle more clearly. This will help us and the party! They will want retribution against those who would wipe us off the face of the earth! This new realization will give our party tremendous advantages in the election. In fact, I'll be shocked if we don't win!" Doug proclaimed.

Cliff was the first to follow up on Doug's prediction.

"As everyone knows, we consistently poll in five major regions to measure the effectiveness of our platform's message. What we find over and over again is that every time we experience a terrorist attack, our candidate picks up more support. As unfortunate as it sounds, it appears the worse things get, the more people seem to support our party."

"That doesn't surprise me! I think the people have been negative for a long time about the political environment they see in Washington," Leonce added. "Sure they want change!"

"The other two parties aren't providing answers, just promises!" Ben said, "It only makes sense that if they can't supply answers, then the people will quickly turn their backs to them, and that's precisely what's happening at the moment. Both parties have lost the trust of the American people, and Doug's right. We do have a good chance at winning all the marbles here!"

"I couldn't agree more. We have an excellent chance of winning this thing!" Bart said. "We need to start making decisions about what we're going to do, when and if that happens. We need to plan our strategies carefully for the victory. We'll have more political capital than any administration in history, so we'll need to put pressure on Congress immediately. But we have to understand that we will be a lame-duck administration from the outset, if we don't exercise our power decisively. The only way we're going to get congressional support is by having some successes against our nation's enemies. Without those successes, we lose the support of the people, and without the people on our side, Congress will defeat anything we propose!"

"I'm not as confident as Bart, but I know he's right about their cooperation level. I can tell you, with one-hundred-percent certainty, both parties believe that we are intruding into what they think is rightfully theirs," Ben said. "So I believe we'll have precious little time to make some progress, before they start to undermine our efforts here at home. Don't think for a minute that this attack will stop the political divisiveness in this country. It won't! If we win, things will get worse long before they get better, I believe."

"So you guys believe Congress will be against us, no matter what we decide to do?" Doug asked.

"I agree with that assessment. There'll be a short honeymoon, but after that, lookout!" Bart said. Doug looked at Ben and Leonce and they both nodded in agreement.

"That's the reality of the situation," Leonce added.

"Okay, what about our European Allies? How about their military plan to punish the responsible parties?" Doug asked.

"They're not going to help us in any significant way!" Bart replied dryly. "Not anymore—"

"After a terrorist attack of this magnitude against us?" Doug asked. The question had been directed at Bart Foster because he trusted his educated assessment of the Europeans, especially the Brits.

"I don't think they will—" Bart said.

"You'll have to explain that one to me," Doug said.

"Different realities," Bart replied coolly.

"What do you mean by that?"

"You're education and experiences are a perfect example of the differences we have with the European's. You happen to be educated at a prestigious military college and served in the strongest military in the world, right?"

"Yes, I'm proud of both, by the way."

"So, it's very simple to understand. You have never lived in a country that didn't have the kind of military power this country has. Because of that, you don't understand the European mind. Most of them don't view the world in the same way we do, so they don't evaluate threats in the same way you do. During the cold war, their way of existing was primarily not to confront the Soviets because they couldn't. So they let us do it. So what makes you believe, now, that anything is going to be different?" Bart asked contentiously.

"So even after an attack of this magnitude you don't believe they would help us militarily?"

"Not likely, just a couple of thousand troops here and there, no more, and we shouldn't expect any financial support either. The Europeans just don't feel secure in our Hobbesian view of the world, but they are also confident that we'll take care of everything. And if we don't, it will be our dead soldiers, not theirs."

"Yeah, he's right!" Ben said. "Token assistance and nothing more."

"Then I don't think we're going to worry about what they have to say about foreign policy!" Doug said after a moment of pondering what he had just heard.

"The thing we need to do is find out who did this, and find out soon. Then we can deal with them in a way that will make our enemies and their supporters take pause!" Bart said. "If we don't, we can expect another attack maybe sooner than later."

"Take a look at this!" Leonce walked over to the TV, which had been muted during the meeting. He clicked the "mute" button for sound.

The images on the screen were being broadcasted from Kuala Lumpur. Men, women, and children were dancing in the street and burning the American flag. It was clear from the actions that they were jubilant about the death and destruction in New York.

"Well, you talk about hate. There it is," Bart said, pointing at the television.

"What have we ever done to Malaysia?" Doug asked.

"Nothing!" Ben responded instantly. "Nothing at all!"

"Since when did the deaths of innocent people become a reason for celebration?" Leonce said in an angry voice.

"It's a natural phenomenon for people that are disenfranchised to blame someone else," Bart said. "That's what they're doing. They've been told that we are the reason they struggle to exist and they believe it."

"Of course Putra is whipping up the flames of dissent!" Leonce added.

"Exactly! Right out of their play book. First, they create hate and frustration among the people, then second, they recruit the disenfranchised young men and women and turn them against their enemy—us!"

Ben stood up looking at the television with anger. "Turn that off! I've seen enough!"

Ben continued, "the biggest problem we face is using the same kind of failed foreign policy against terrorists. If we do that, we will have every Muslim extremist in the world knocking at our door. We must find a way to make the Muslim world turn against these extremists! They can do a better job of killing them than we can. If we can do that, we can begin to solve the problem. We can't win a war against two billion Muslims. We need to find a way to separate the terrorists from their supporters. "

As the most senior statesman of the Party, Ben's words were sobering for everyone in the room.

"So you don't think we can win a war against Malaysia or some other third rate Muslim nation?" Leonce said, with concern.

"I'm not saying we can't win these battles. Hell, we've done that. What I'm saying is, we can't win the ideological war. As long as hundreds of millions of people support these terrorists, I not sure we'll ever win. We can't fight the entire world, Leonce, that's just not possible!"

"So we need a way to change the minds of the Muslim people who support these militants!" Doug said, now looking out the hotel window at the expanse of water before him.

"Oh, like radio free Europe or radio free Iran or radio free Malaysia? Hell, that shit doesn't work!" Leonce grumbled. "It is a waste of time and money. I've never voted to fund those programs and never will!"

"No, something a little less subtle. Some way to isolate the extremists from those who just want to live and raise their children in peace. Well, I've got an idea. Do any of you remember the *Farewell Dossier* back in the cold war days?" Doug asked.

"I do," Bart said. "It was a campaign of computer sabotage perpetrated on the Soviets by the CIA."

"Yeah, it came about because President Mitterrand of France took Ronald Reagan aside during a conference in Canada back in the 80s and told them they had recruited a K.G.B. agent in Russia who was telling the French how the Russians were stealing and buying technology from the west. The agent spilled his guts and told the French everything."

"Yeah, I remember that," Ben said.

"What happened?" Leonce asked. "I guess I haven't heard about this one."

"Well, what happened was, the CIA set up a number of computer geeks in the CIA to offer up engineering data and plans to the Soviets that were seriously flawed." Doug said.

"What do you mean by flawed?" Leonce asked.

"The engineering data was severely altered and then given to operatives to sell to technology smugglers, who then sold it to the soviets. My company even helped on the project!" Doug said.

"You mean your company worked with the CIA?" Leonce asked surprised.

"Yeah, we did."

"Then what happened?" Leonce asked, intrigued.

"In this disinformation mission, the CIA was able to convince the Soviets, through brokers who sold stolen technology, that they had the latest western power-plant control software. The soviets then used the stolen software to build a system to run powerful pumps and turbines on the Siberian pipeline. Of course, the software was bogus, leading to excessive pressures that happened to be above the operating limits of the machinery."

"So something blew up?" Leonce said.

"Yeah, I'd say so. Our NORAD monitors heard the explosions and feared there had been a nuclear detonation in Russia; however, after a few satellites passes, the images came in and the CIA learned that it was the largest non-nuclear explosion in history at an estimated three kilotons!"

"Holy, Shit! Set off because a bunch of computer nerds at the CIA!"

"Exactly!" Doug said.

"So I'm assuming that, since the Soviets had been tricked into purchasing this bogus technology, they probably slowed down on their technology theft after that."

"You bet! From that point on, their engineers had to check everything out. It turned out that it was faster to let Soviet engineers design their own technology, rather than spend years attempting to understand ours. The real problem is they had to go back and check everything they had stolen over the years, and that cost them billions of Rubles."

"The real success of this program was not that one of the Soviet pipeline facilities was blown to oblivion, but that they no longer trusted their suppliers of bagged technology. They were fearful of another mistake, another explosion. So the problem was solved without a war!" Doug said.

"If you are saying that we are going to start blowing innocent people up to make them fearful, I want to tell you I'll never be a party to such a thing! I can't envision our country being transformed into the same type of monsters who kill innocent people," Ben said.

"Ben, I'd never suggest that, but there might be something like that might prove to be effective."

"What are you thinking?" Ben asked.

"The nuclear genie has been taken out of the bottle, so why not capitalize on that threat to work against these people?"

"If you have a plan let's hear it Doug!" Bart said

32

Tuesday October 22nd 2012
Quantico, Virginia

Stevie walked into the dark office and flipped on the overhead lights. The first thing she noticed was a fresh, white shirt hanging on Mark's credenza. The hook on the wire hanger was bent ninety degrees so that it could hang properly on the end of a flat surface. She walked over and picked the shirt up and held it close to her nose hoping to smell some fleeting scent of the man she still loved, but there wasn't. She slowly made her way across the office to his familiar desk where she saw a color photo of his wife Susan. She was a pretty blonde, the soccer-mom type, with blue eyes and that classy face looking back at her with a posed smile.

"I'm sorry I fell in love with your husband," she said softly to the woman in the photograph, but then she felt resentment towards her for having been so close to Mark, a closeness she would never find with him.

Stevie had volunteered to clear Mark's personal items, nothing that was FBI property, of course, but everything that belonged to him and needed to be sent to his family. She felt it was something that she could do for him even though he was gone, something that Mark probably would have trusted to her if he had known he was going to die.

As Stevie sat there, she pulled open the top desk drawer. There she found the usual collection of office items. A cork covered metal ruler, a couple of boxes of paper clips, a small calculator, and many other small items. Everything in the drawer seemed to be minor property of the FBI, so she left it in place. She knew it would all have to be moved out later but, for now, she felt good about leaving everything exactly the way Mark had left it. She didn't want to move anything, because it was the way Mark had left it before his death.

She then pulled open the top drawer on the left side of the desk. She took out some loose papers lying on top and partially obscuring a clear plastic tube. She pulled the tube out and set it on top of the desk. She checked deeper into the drawer for any other items that might be hidden there, but there was nothing else. She pulled the red cap off the top of the plastic tube, then emptied the contents onto the desk. It was a single piece of paper coiled tightly.

"What do we have here?" she said to herself, softly. As she unrolled the paper, it appeared to be some kind of artwork. It had been drawn with a fine tip pen like Mark always used. The drawing was an intricate drawing of the world, a flat map like a *Mercator* projection of all the continents. The North American continent was in the middle with Asia to the left and Europe and Africa to the right with the expanse of oceans between them. Each country was neatly drawn in by hand. Each border was done in letters and numbers instead of solid drawn lines, which immediately caught her attention. It must have taken countless hours to draw the letters curving each one to the contour that was necessary to make the border between countries. The numbers and letters looked like an electronic ticker tape that display stock quotes, except with no motion. It was obvious that it was something that had been drawn by hand. What it was, she really didn't know at the moment. Her first thought was that it might have been some kind of hobby; drawing artistic maps might have been one of his pass times for all she knew.

As she studied the map, she was interrupted by a soft knock on the door.

"Can I come in?" Came a male voice from outside.

"Yeah, sure…"

She was relieved to see it was Tripp.

"Everything okay in here?"

"Yeah, I'm trying to separate Mark's personal items from all the FBI stuff." She felt a little irritated that Ed Tripp had chosen this exact moment to come by and chat.

"What do you have there?" Ed saw the paper, even though Stevie had let the map roll back up on its own.

"Just some kind of drawing. One of Mark's hobbies, I guess."

"Oh, yeah I never knew he was an artist?" Ed said, with an inquisitive expression.

"Yeah, me either. It looks to me like something he might have been working on before he died."

"I guess we should give it to his family; they'll probably want it."

Stevie was relieved, he hadn't asked to see it. There was something about it that wasn't quite right. It just didn't seem like artwork to her. But whatever it was, she was going to study the drawing a little closer before she gave it back to anyone. Mark was a highly intelligent and clever guy. If he left this in his office, there might have been a reason to do so.

"Listen, I know you have been through a lot and you might be blaming yourself, but you really shouldn't. We all just came up a little short on this thing," Tripp said, as he pulled a chair from beside the door and moved it closer to the desk.

"Yeah, I know, but the whole thing is so horrible, so many innocent people have died. It's so disturbing, it's unbelievable!"

"Well, there is plenty of blame to go around, believe me," Ed said. "But we need to find out who these people are and quick…I know you have uncovered several names, but make sure you get everything that's on that DVD decoded, Okay?"

"I will. Sir."

"Don't blame yourself for any of this, okay?

"I won't," Stevie promised.

Stevie appreciated Tripp. She could see that he truly cared about her.

The term "Old School" came to mind as Ed stood up to leave the room. He had made the basic assumption that she needed to be consoled, but in this case he was right. She did.

"If I can help you let me know. Everyone's sad and shaken but we have to keep going, now more than ever," Tripp said, as he walked out of the door leaving her alone again.

After he left, she unrolled the drawing. As she studied it more closely, Stevie still felt that it was an odd drawing, something she had never seen done before. Even though it looked like a piece of art, she knew instinctively that it wasn't. It was something else, but exactly what, she didn't know. She made a quick decision to take it with her and have a closer look. The thought of keeping it for herself even crossed her mind. "Just something to remember Mark by," she said to herself softly. Stevie knew it probably wouldn't be right, but she didn't care about that now. She wanted something that was Mark's, something she could keep for herself.

Thursday October 23rd

Stevie continued to work on the code, by secure communications, through secure links with the CIA. Both organizations met via these links three times per day to discuss their findings. Progress had been made, and most of the code was now broken. The esoteric Arabic phases were still difficult to comprehend, but Stevie knew the language well enough to feel secure in what it all meant.

It was becoming clear that this attack was probably a joint operation between groups located in the Middle East and Malaysia. The names supplied by decoding had helped, and now CIA field operatives were starting to find more information, most of it supplied by informants. It was clear from the beginning that this attack was state-sponsored because of the high-grade nuclear materials needed and the overall logistics needed to pull off something as complicated at this. In addition, the nuclear material left a residue at ground zero, and it had been tracked back to Iran and possibly China.

The warehouse where the nuclear device had been assembled was in New Jersey, and the sunken fishing trawler had been raised at the same place. It was confirmed that the boat had in fact carried the nuclear weapon detonated in New York, which led to the confirmation that the nuclear device must have been picked up off shore, probably off Cape Hatteras.

Stevie was desperately trying to find more code names to help identify who was actually involved in this catastrophic attack. Numerous undercover code names had been collected by the CIA through the years and could be cross referenced to identify who was involved in the attack. A code name could be cross referenced with fresh intelligence to confirm a connection between the attackers and their handlers. If this could be done, then the case against the perpetrators of this violent attack could be blown wide open. Usually, even though dangerous, code names were often used to authenticate a message between terrorists. This ensured that it was valid and should be followed exactly as the coded message was written. So confident were the terrorists that their code couldn't be broken by the West that they continued to use the same code names. For the most part, the terrorists had been correct, simply because the codes changed so often they were almost unbreakable. But the SX-10 wasn't just an everyday, run-of-the-mill, code-breaking computer. It was a hundred-million-dollar piece of equipment the terrorists knew nothing about. This state-of-the-art leviathan was going to be instrumental in changing the course of terrorism, Stevie thought. If they could precisely pinpoint who was responsible quickly enough, the inviolable air of superiority would come tumbling down among those who were involved in the attack. For several nights in a row, Stevie had avoided watching the news. She felt it was so depressing that it might negatively affect her work, so she hadn't watched. The devastation in New York had been unimaginable. The destruction and carnage was nothing less than unbelievable. But it was also undeniable that the terrorists could claim a great victory against America. The death toll was expected to be over four hundred and fifty thousand. It was the single worst attack in the history of mankind that had stricken fear in virtually every person in the United States.

Stevie was afraid too. There had been so many rumors that Washington was next. As she worked, hour after hour, her mind would drift and she would suddenly catch herself thinking about it. It was this same psychotic thought process that was negatively affecting people all around the country. But it wasn't some type of human psychosis, it was real. It could happen! It had already happened.

33

January 28th 2013
Washington D.C.
White House

Doug had risen at dawn and had already finished the breakfast that had been prepared for him by the White House kitchen staff. He had finished the *Washington Post* and his first cup of coffee, as well. Liz was awake but still lying in their bed reading.

"So, Mr. President, what are you thinking about?" she asked as she put her book down beside the bed.

"I'm just thinking about all the problems we need to solve."

"Can any of this really be solved?"

"I believe it can, but it won't be easy." Doug said, smiling at Liz and thinking about how beautiful she was in the morning.

It was hard to believe that they were living in the White House and that, in minutes, he would meet with advisors in one of the most important meetings of his Presidency.

"I was thinking about the inauguration too. I wish it could have taken place under better circumstances," he said, as he adjusted his silk tie in the mirror pulling the knot close to the cotton neck of his shirt.

"Forgive me for saying this, but we probably wouldn't be here if we lived in better times," Liz said.

"Yeah, I know, but all that counts now is that we are here and people are depending on us."

As Doug recalled, it had been a beautiful winter day in Washington D.C., seasonably cold, but with a brilliant sun bathing the Capitol steps with a golden hue under a canopy of a deep blue sky. Standing by his side had been Liz and, in the gallery, their son Jeff and daughter Amanda had watched as their father had been sworn in by the Chief Justice of the Supreme Court. It had probably been the single-most gratifying moment in his life, but he experienced it with a mixture of pride tempered with humility. This Presidential inauguration had been accompanied by a harrowing cloud of despair that hung over this great event, even though the sun had shown brightly all day, as if welcoming him to office. Doug knew the country and its people didn't deserve what had happened in New York, and he was determined to do something about it.

"How do I look?" Doug said, as he walked over to Liz, who wore nothing but a sheer, silk night gown.

"Very Presidential," She whispered in his ear.

Doug leaned down and kissed her before leaving.

"Good Luck," she whispered.

January 28th 2013
West Wing

It had come as a total surprise to the political experts, but most believed they should have seen it coming. All the signs had been there with the country fed up with their government, and for not stopping the biggest disaster in American history. There was no doubt in Doug's mind why he had been elected! It was a clear and unmistakable mandate to fight back. He was there to protect the American people at all costs to stop the madness that had enveloped their country. His security initiative had already been written, revised, and sent to lawmakers. He wanted to be ready when the intelligence community came to an agreement on who had perpetrated this horror on his people. It would be his job to find answers and develop new global policies to deal with international terrorism and the countries that clandestinely supported it. No more double talk, no more hiding behind those in the security council of the United Nations who were willing accomplices in their protection of the enemies of the United States.

Doug's Cabinet members sat in the Cabinet room waiting to begin their first official meeting in the White House.

"Good morning, gentlemen, welcome," Doug said.

"Good morning, Mr. President."

The members of his Cabinet had not yet been approved by Congress but were helping to make decisions along with other party members under what was considered war-time conditions. They consisted primarily of the same people who had recruited Doug to run for office: Ben Atchison, Leonce Collins, and Bart Foster. John Tolbert had been elected to office with Doug and was now the Vice President of the United States.

President Ferguson now looked at the man who would become his Secretary of State.

"Ben, what's first on our agenda?" The President asked as he made himself comfortable at the middle of the oval table in the Cabinet room of the White House. The sunflower yellow walls of the room stood in contrast to the serious nature of the problems at hand.

"I think your speech to the Nation would be a nice place to start."

"So it's completed already?"

"Yes, Mr. President, and I have copies available for everyone.

"Great, then let's get into it right now," Doug said.

"He had ordered his first Presidential address to be prepared right after his inauguration. He had made the conscious decision to avoid threats or negative statements about America's enemies during his inaugural address, out of respect for the Republic and the office of the Presidency. The inaugural address was one of vision, not of idle threats. His speech was a call to action directed to the American people to believe in the Republic that had lasted for over two hundred years. He had spoken about hope, and he had gone to great lengths to reassure a broken and fearful country that a more promising future was "Just over the horizon for all Americans..."

Ben passed copies of the speech to each member of the Cabinet.

"Gentleman, what you have in front of you is a bound copy of the President's first speech that he will make to the nation and to the world tomorrow night," Ben said, then he opened his booklet and began reading aloud.

"The latest death toll is estimated to be over four hundred and twenty-two thousand innocent Americans from this cowardly attack on the innocent people of New York. Our enemies and those who support them have made a grave mistake in carrying out this attack against the people of this nation. This single attack has already surpassed the total number of combatants lost by the United States in World War II. Since the world is no longer a safe place for peace-loving people, then there will be no peace for those who want to throw the world into a state of chaos. We will be forced now to use all weapons and methods against those who have attacked us."

Ben stopped for a moment and looked at the President.

"So far so good. Very strong and clear in its intent!" Doug said approvingly.

"Mr. President, the whole world will hear this speech, so it was written to convey the ominous potential destruction to the enemy and their supporters. We're looking for impact, here," Ben Added.

"Senator, before we go on, will our allies be briefed about our policy changes before the President's speech?" asked Army General Bill Miller, a tall and imposing figure at six-feet, four-inches tall. His gray and receding hair, along with his immaculate uniform decorated with ribbons won in battle gave him the appearance of strength and competence. He was the acting Chairman of the

Joint Chiefs of Staff. He was a veteran of both Gulf Wars and knew the Middle East better than any other Military commander currently serving in the arm forces.

"No, General, the President has made a decision not to do that! I'm sure he would be willing to share with us the reasons why later. But there isn't enough time. Who knows where terrorists will strike at us next? We need for our enemies to take pause concerning their future actions. We think this statement by the President will accomplish that!

"I hope you are aware, Mr. President, that this is going to make the United States extremely unpopular around the world, especially with our allies," General Miller added.

"General, you mean unpopular enough to have someone murder four hundred thousand of our nation's people? You don't think they could get that upset do you?" The President said quickly, in response to the General's negative remark.

"I guess we are pretty unpopular at the moment, but the whole world isn't our enemy either, Mr. President," General Miller countered, challenging the President.

"General, I seem to view things a little differently than most. It seems to me that, when you fight wars as we have done in the past, and our allies have to be pressured and blackmailed to come to our aid, then perhaps they aren't our allies after all. When the United States commits hundreds of thousands of men and women in uniform and our allies don't send enough troops and materials to fight Haiti, for Christ's sake, then I'm not sure we can call these countries our allies! General, it's time for the United States to put some pressure on these people, pressure that no one else can relieve but us. Those governments who will not conduct themselves peacefully will decide their own fate, not I. The world is too dangerous and too small not to do everything in our power to clean this mess up. We don't have the next ten years to accomplish this. Hell, if we wait that long, we won't even have a country to protect! I mean to change the game we've been playing. Furthermore, I'm not going to allow Congress, or those allies you referred to earlier, to water down our efforts to solve this crisis."

The points covered thus far in the President's speech were simple, but they also represented sweeping changes in our foreign policy. The first item proposed was to cut off foreign aid to any country that didn't have a freely elected democracy. This meant that countries like Egypt would no longer get the three billion dollars in foreign aid that they received annually from the United States. The second proposal a more sweeping change that proposed the United States develop a Terrorist Control Center or TCC. The primary objective of this new command and control center was to address specific threats quickly and simultaneously on political and military fronts with those countries involved. The TCC would monitor countries that represented a threat to the United States on a minute-to-minute basis.

This organization would operate twenty-four hours a day, seven days a week, and represent the entire government. The TCC would have the full responsibility to direct a response to those who would threaten the homeland. Any immediate threat identified by the TCC against our country could result in a wide range of responses from economic isolation to the total and complete destruction of the enemy without respect for international boundaries. Our Navy would be put on constant alert and move to implement blockades the TCC ordered. Also, the Air Force would blockade these countries from the air. Our aircraft carriers like the nuclear-powered Ronald Reagan would be sent into the Mediterranean to be on station and ready to act against any Middle Eastern nation that was perceived by the TCC to be a threat.

After reading more of the text of the speech, General Miller was the first to speak.

"So, what we are proposing here is to strike the enemy anywhere anytime politically, economically, and militarily, if I'm reading this correctly," General Miller said after reading a few more paragraphs.

"That's correct, General," Ben said.

"Will the opposing country be warned before such an attack?"

"Yes, always. We want to minimize civilian causalities and negotiate from a position of power," Ben said.

"General Miller, let me assure you, we are not going kill innocent people. It's not our objective to emulate our enemies; instead, we want to defeat them on their own turf. We want to apply so much pressure on the leaders of these nations that they will no longer tolerate these radicals within their borders. What they do to these terrorists is their business not ours! Our objective is to match our military strength against the nations that support terrorists. The second objective is to hold those responsible who commit crimes against humanity and make them pay for their deeds. The TCC, if run correctly, will force leaders of foreign governments to deal with the problems they have inside their own borders quickly before we move against them. I believe they can do this more effectively than we could ever do it," Doug said.

"What about countries who will never cooperate?" General Miller asked.

"We will first give them the choice of turning over the terrorists that operate in their country; if they refuse, we will isolate them from the rest of the world until they comply. If that doesn't work, then we will have our military strike capabilities as a second option. If a strike is made against the United States by a terrorist group located in a country like Syria, they will suffer as we do, and we have to make that clear to them through the TCC. Of course, we will then warn the leaders of the country to evacuate all women and children from major cities. We will not invade these countries, but simple destroy each city until the government complies with our demands. We are not going to put our soldiers in harm's way to secure territory that we don't want and is impossible for us to hold."

"Do you gentlemen really think this can be effective? Do you know the chaos this type of foreign policy will touch off around the world?" General Miller said.

"General Miller, it is not our country that is creating chaos, it is the terrorists," Ben said.

"What if this touches off a war or the Middle East shuts off the oil supply to the world?"

"Then I think the world would have to get involved in solving these problems too."

"How do you know this won't create a world war directed against our nation?"

"General, I believe there is already a world war against our nation!" Ben said angrily.

"General Miller, what we want to accomplish here is relatively simple. We want the governments of countries that secretly support terrorists to stop that activity. We mean to do that by making them pay for their subversive activities. I suspect the first priority for these leaders will be to remain in control and in power! With the exception of a few, most of these leaders are dictators and despots who really don't care about their people in the first place. If they get the message that we are serious, then I believe they will clean up their problems," Doug argued.

"I guess it does, but this type of behavior could touch off a world war, against the United States," the General repeated.

"General, I have to agree with Ben. We are already in an undeclared world war," Doug said.

"Economically, Europe and the rest of the world wouldn't mind seeing America taken down a notch or two. The trick here is to deal with one terrorist nation at a time. Our objective is to make terrorists unwelcome, wherever they go," Ben added.

"General Miller, this is really our only choice if you think about it. We must match our military force to the problem where it makes sense. We can't have high performance jet fighters chasing terrorists in Toyota pickups. We can't have United States troops being shot at every day, while being outnumbered in the field and looking behind every rock for this guy or that guy! That hasn't worked and never will. We can't have our treasury drained by long and protracted wars against insurgents around the globe. Nor do we want to fight a long and deadly guerilla war of attrition in Southeast or Central Asia. It is too costly to our nation. I'm not going to have our servicemen brought back in body bags as the world tricks us into believing they are our friends and, believe me, that's what they're doing at the moment!" Doug responded coolly.

Ben waited for the President to finish before he began speaking again.

"General, the idea here is to bring psychological fear to these leaders that they have never known before. We want to hold them and the governments accountable for supporting terrorism. Until the attack in New York, our people would never have supported this type of policy, but they have to now!"

"I won't argue that. The American people are afraid, and I'm sure they want retribution of some kind. I just want to keep my commanders from facing War Crime Trials in the future."

"I'm pretty certain of one thing; the terrorists who destroyed New York won't be brought to justice, and there won't be any war crime tribunals held for the supporters of these maniacs either, and you can count on that—Nor will any of those associated with these psychopaths be brought to justice by the world court or anybody else. Except for the terrorists who died in the crime, the rest will go free and unnamed, free to commit other crimes because there is no one out there to stop them, General," Ben said.

"That's why the Freedom Party was founded in the first place. No one could see this coming. Now, we are more worried about what the courts will say, courts run by people who are at best ambivalent about our existence and our survival!" Ben added vehemently.

Bart had been listening closely to the exchanges and wanted to take the time to frame the world as he saw it and also attempt to convince General Miller of the seriousness of the situation.

"General Miller, here is another serious problem," Bart said, speaking for the first time. "Our friends in Europe really don't care about stopping terrorism, except on their own soil, of course. They can say whatever they want, but I agree with Doug, I don't believe them for a minute. Since the twelve Europeans members organized, they have wanted to find a way to make the world's monetary system hinge on the Euro. At the very same time, they want our government to spend itself into oblivion fighting terrorism. They know our government and system is weakening, the longer this war goes on. Who do you think will be there to pick up the pieces once our economy fails? They will of course. France, Germany, and all the others see nothing wrong with letting us fight this war alone. After all, after World War II, we were left unharmed and then we were able to pick up the pieces. Our manufacturing was not devastated, our country did not lie in ruins as theirs did, and we were ready to take over the world economically. And because of our strong manufacturing base already in place, we did. So they won't feel guilty in the least for doing the same thing if it should happen to us! As a result, they are not going to help in any meaningful way, nor will they be with us when we reach out to troubled spots in the world to protect ourselves. We have all seen this over and over; they send a few troops here and few troops there, provided we put enough pressure on them. This is a totally different situation now. Our enemies have gone nuclear, and there is no way of knowing how many more nuclear devices they have. Hell, we may not be here in the next thirty seconds. They may be driving into Washington right now as we speak. The equation has changed, and now we have to ponder committing to a new option, the nuclear option. We really don't have much of a choice. I hate to come across as an alarmist, but I'm only hoping that we aren't too late already!"

"As long as OPEC countries only accept our dollars for oil shipments, the EU will never really want to help us," Leonce said. He continued, "the only reason the dollar is used is because it is deemed to be the most stable currency in the world. When we lose that advantage, the damage to our economy will be as catastrophic as the attack in New York."

"You mean the OPEC countries only take dollars?" Cliff asked in disbelief.

"That's correct, except for Iran. Right now, the whole world has to have huge inventories of our currency to buy oil from the Middle East. This inventory goes a long way in financing our government. It is a good deal for us; they have the oil wells and we have the printing presses." Bart said jumping back into the conversation.

"Nice deal! How come I didn't know that?" Cliff said, baffled by what he had just heard.

"Not many people do. But that is precisely why we dominate the world economically," Bart argued. "If that stops anytime soon, we could never afford our spiraling trade deficits. Believe me, nothing would make European leaders happier than finding a way to make that happen. If we can't stop terrorists from disrupting our economy, we will be ruined economically. Our people will not work and live in the cities if they don't feel safe!"

"That's why the stakes are so high," Doug added. "It isn't that the past administrations didn't know this, they did. In the past, we could sit around appeasing the Middle East and the rest of the world from a position of strength. Things were stable enough at home and our cities were relatively safe. Our citizens were protected. Some would even say isolated, from the problems of the world. But I think everyone agrees that's all over now. If our citizens can't feel safe to work in our manufacturing and banking centers, our democracy is in grave danger just as Bart said."

"If OPEC ever changes this policy, or if the International Monetary Fund decides not to use US dollars, then our economy will probably collapse!" Bart said, as he closed his papers and leaned back in his leather chair directing his attention to the President.

The TCC would streamline the response time under the full authority of the President, leaving absolutely no wiggle room for offending countries. "Directives" would be made by the TCC, and they would monitor the offending country's progress to ensure the directives were being followed or further action would be taken.

The most critical problem at the moment was finding out who was responsible for the attack in New York. The second problem was much more demanding, and that was how to convince the OPEC Nations to continue to use our currency exclusively for oil shipments around the world. Saudi Arabia might now be thinking in the short term that Euros might be a more stable currency. Doug couldn't let that happen. It might come down to brute force to convince these oil rich nations to continue to use the dollar as their trade currency. The threat would be simple enough: use US dollars or spend billions building new facilities! Doug knew the gloves had to come off! This was going to be the ultimate bluff, and Doug and his administration would have to stare down the world to make it happen. He knew oil prices might go higher and the economy could absorb that, but the country couldn't survive the paralyzing fear people were now experiencing, fear about living in the largest and most important financial centers in America. Doug needed to protect the nation economically, as well as militarily, that much was clear. This was a desperate, dangerous, high-stakes game of brinksmanship, and he knew it. But as far as Doug was concerned, he was backed into a corner and there were no other options but survival. The country had just experienced a devastating nuclear attack, and no one knew how many more might be planned. This was the most viable solution. He knew nothing else would work, no other strategy that would fix these problems quickly, before it was too late. The next nuclear attack would not happen on his watch, even if he had to take on the entire world. His country's survival wasn't negotiable and wasn't going to be decided in some capital in a faraway land. This policy would have to work and he, as Commander in Chief, had to save his country at any cost. In his mind, it was much different than the dilemma that Harry Truman faced when he bombed Hiroshima and Nagasaki. Then, it was a choice on how to end a war that was basically already won, while losing the fewest American lives as possible. We are faced today with the same challenge Truman was faced with, Doug thought, with one exception; we have been attacked here at home with a nuclear weapon. We are going to move forward with our plans.

34

January 28th 2013
Washington D.C.

Stevie had just taken a small bite off of her chocolate-chip cookie. Her decoding work was grueling, and she had just exceeded thirteen hours straight in front of the computer. She knew the cookie was going to be her only meal this evening, since she was nearing the end of the code. Stevie had counted the number of times she had started the program over in an attempt to finish the job; that number had just gone over one-hundred and fifty-six. The end of a coded message was usually the most important section of code since key names of operatives were usually found there. With the capabilities of the SX-10, she felt the computer had probably completed enough computations to build a Mars space probe by now, complete with rover. She had immersed herself in decoding since returning to Washington. But this hard work had paid substantial dividends because she had uncovered several suspect names from the code. Her work had been corroborated by code breakers at Langley and deemed totally reliable. Stevie had assumed that the names she had found had been turned over to field operatives to verify. But she also suspected that death warrants were being issued against these individuals by the CIA. If that was happening, it was a result of her skill, but she was okay with that. Of course, she didn't know how helpful her work had been. It was just like the CIA to keep people at the FBI completely out of the loop when it came to the success or failures of cloak-and dagger intelligence operatives.

The nation was still in a state of shock since the attack. In many cities, the shock had manifested itself into outrage, which had then boiled over into riots demanding something be done. In Washington, mobs had turned out to demand change in government policies towards terrorism in hopes that America could be more protected from the scourge of Middle Eastern radicals. Things were getting worse on the streets of America by the minute, and the new President was probably feeling the heat, Stevie thought.

As bits of code churned away deep in the SX-10, Stevie had time to take another look at the map she had found in Mark's office. She discovered the Arab countries seemed to have the most numbers and letters written in. She had to scan the small, barely legible, hand-written numbers with a magnifying glass. For whatever reason, Mark had taken an enormous amount of time to define the borders of each country with tiny script. To the untrained eye, it appeared to be nothing more than a stylistic drawing. Something clever and different, maybe even eccentric. The problem was Mark never seemed to be eccentric to her. But she couldn't even be sure that he had drawn the map at this point.

"What is this?" She whispered. Then she saw a single word that seemed to explain everything. Just at the northern border between Iraq and Syria, she saw the name *Damon* in a stream of letters. That was a code name that she and Mark had used for a terrorist named Abu Sabir. To her knowledge, no one in FBI Foreign Counterintelligence used that particular code name for Sabir. If it was code, it must have been written by Mark Latham she was now convinced. If it was coded information, then it was obviously coded information about intelligence matters, she quickly assumed, but why? And why had he left one code name in the clear? That didn't make any sense unless it was a "*marker*" to give the examiner a clue. It finally became clear to her; Mark had meant for her to find it, but why? Why would he do something like that, she thought?

The small letters and numbers seemed to her to be a classic coding process. Mark had found a way to hide information right in the middle of FBI headquarters. Maybe he had secretly hidden classified information in the drawing, Stevie thought. This wasn't a new way to hide information; it had been done in medieval times. If this was a code, it was a clever way to hide information. She suspected he had left a single decoded word known only to them that would tip her off to the type of contents within the code.

"What are you trying to tell me, Mark?" She whispered. "Why would you write a code name of a terrorist just for me to find?" she said aloud, thinking as she spoke. The whole idea didn't make a lot of sense, she was forced to admit. But she had sensed more than once that Mark was frustrated in his position. Maybe that was it, she thought. She made a quick decision to stay silent about the document until she knew exactly what it was.

She redirected her attention back to the SX-10. The computer needed her to review a document. Across her flat screen, the words *"Attention needed"* was flashing repeatedly. When she clicked on a small oval icon at the bottom left side of the screen, a new page popped up. The computer program had found the name Abdul-Hamid. The name meant "*servant of the praised one,*" and he happened to be a notorious terrorist who was a lieutenant of Abu-Sabir. Both men were wanted for planning and funding suicide bombers in America, and they were believed to be living in Malaysia since the JI had taken over there. The name Abdul-Hamid had been found on the document, which seemed to be a brazen attempt to say, "This is who I am. Come and get me." Either the computer was wrong or this crazed maniac wanted someone to know he was connected to the bombing.

Stevie immediately called Tripp about what she had discovered. She decided to remain silent on the encoded map she had found in Mark's office.

"We got another name!" Stevie said excitedly.

"Who is it?"

"Abdul-Hamid."

"Yeah, I've heard of him. He works with Sabir; he's someone I'd like to have a shot at killing some day; he was involved in the bombing of our Embassy in the Philippines!" Tripp said.

"Let me guess. We could never prove it!"

"That's Right. He's a pretty slippery terrorist."

"They all are! Do you think we will ever be able to nail this asshole?"

"I think I hear some frustration in your voice."

"Yeah, you do. These guys kill hundreds of people and, as far as our government is concerned, it's business as usual. We know they are terrorists, we know they are killing and planning to kill more, and we just sit on our hands and do nothing until we get enough evidence to go after them, I mean after the lawyers say we can of course!"

"I think those days are rapidly coming to an end, sister. This guy Ferguson is going to be a different kind of President!"

"I just hope Sabir doesn't have any plans in the cooker right now or people are going to die!"

"Are you sure this is the same Abdul-Hamid we know? There are probably thousands of people with that name!

What was the code name that matched up with his in the computer?"

"There wasn't another name. When the code was broken, his name came up as one of our existing code names, nothing new," she said.

"No new code name?" Tripp asked

"No, the name was in the clear except for the usual code names we already have linked to him."

"Sounds like he wants to be famous!" Okay, let's give the information to the CIA and see what they think. They have a file on this guy, too."

"Hamid must have a death wish or something."

"Or he knows something we don't," Stevie said, as she closed her file.

"I'd bet the farm these guys played a role in all of this. We've intercepted communications from them before, and we know they've been in Jakarta for at least a year. Agent Latham worked on all of this. He even tried to convince the Director to bring these guys in, but our legal eagles wouldn't agree! I'll find out what else the CIA knows and try and confirm their whereabouts. Then we will notify the White House, through the director, of course," Tripp said.

There it was, she thought. Mark was on to these bastards, and no one would do anything! It was late and she needed to get some rest, but, before that, she wanted to take another look at Mark's map. She again pulled it out and placed it on her desk. The hand-drawn document was about eleven inches wide and about twenty inches long. She didn't know the type of paper, but it had apparently come off some kind of roll. She carefully unrolled it, laying it across her desk, and then she placed large metal paper clips on each end. Stevie began to copy the letters and numbers from the area where the name "*Damon*" was embedded in the border. The waving motion of the letters made it too difficult to concentrate on the letters and manipulate them in her mind. Why had he done all this? She thought. This must be coded information, probably about specific intelligence that Mark knew and wanted to record. But why did he code the information? The dilemma for Stevie was who to tell about this and when. She knew as time passed it would become more difficult for her to inform the Bureau, and delaying on something like this wasn't a good career move, Stevie knew. The map, no matter how unostentatious it may seem on the surface, could be considered an important FBI document. She decided to hold on to it for a while longer anyway. Mark had been her friend, he had supported her, and now she was going to protect him and his reputation, no matter how difficult it was for her.

35

February 4th 2013
Cabinet Room West Wing

Bart now held the powerful position of Secretary of Defense, a job that he would have never imagined himself being appointed to, but the inscrutable fact remained he was now in charge of the most powerful military force in the world. However, he was keenly aware that this same military force couldn't stop two lone terrorists from destroying America's largest city, and that was the problem wasn't it? The action of a single person could kill millions; this was a new time with new threats, he thought. Before his appointment, he believed he could be more effective by remaining in the House of Representatives. But the new President had disagreed and made it clear that he would never accept "no" for an answer. Bart wasn't convinced his background and experience fit this high-ranking political position in the government. After all, he was a short, studious, non-military type, by his own admission, and a man with very little experience in military matters. But now, fully confirmed, he was committed to doing the job as intelligently as he could do it. He knew his strongest and most tenable attribute was his scholarship and command of World History, which he now vowed to use in making decisions.

"Good morning, Mr. President, if you're ready, we've been tweaking our next round of proposals for Congress and the briefs are ready for your review," Ben said, getting the early morning meeting started in the White House situation room.

"Tweaking, that scares me, gentleman. I thought we already knew what we were doing?" Doug said, as he smiled and then opened a leather binder with the gold Presidential seal embossed on the front.

"There shouldn't be any surprises. We've just cleaned up the initiatives; you know, make them more impactful." Ben said, as he carefully adjusted his small, steel-rimmed glasses so his bifocals were in the right position, then he began reading from the lengthy document, "Number one, cancel foreign aid programs to countries that will not arrest terrorists and jail them." After reading, he waited for a moment to see if the President had any questions; he apparently didn't, so he continued reading. "Number two, cut military aid to countries that we suspect are supporting terrorism. Number three, no more sales of grain products to countries that support terrorism, either directly or indirectly. We also will change our foreign troop deployments worldwide by pulling our forces out of places like South Korea and Germany. We are suggesting an immediate and complete removal of US troops around the world, except for those bases where we must maintain a nuclear strike capability."

"Are we still suggesting that we pull our forces from the Middle East?" Doug asked.

"Yes, Mr. President, our initiative is based on intimidation, not a policing action. We don't want our troops anywhere near a nuclear detonation, either," Bart responded.

"This is risky. Our actions could turn the whole damn place into a terrorist haven. You know that, right!" Doug said.

"Mr. President, we can't continue to fight the whole world in a conventional manor, but even if we could, it's pretty safe to assume we wouldn't win. More importantly, the polls indicate the American people have had enough of this kind of warfare. I'm afraid the "Genie" is out of the bottle, sir," Bart said.

"Are we sure about this, I mean absolutely sure?"

Both men shook their heads in agreement. Then Bart said, "If we could guarantee that these guys would never attack us with a nuclear weapon again, we'd probably try something else, but there are no guarantees of that. Unfortunately, this is a new and different kind of war now, Mr. President."

"It's the only way that I can see to solve the problem..." Ben assured the President.

"Sir, the normally brave and heroic nature of the American people has been shattered. This war has escalated to a new level without us having much to say about it," Bart added.

Two additional addendums were proposed and agreed to by the President during this meeting.

"Mr. President, we must also issue a stern warning to the OPEC nations that policies towards them are fundamentally going to change now. The United States will now pass bills through Congress to approve drilling for oil wherever it can be found within the borders of the United States."

"So we're now going to take on the environmentalists as well, as if we don't have enough enemies?" The President chuckled.

"I don't see any way around it!" Bart answered.

"The terrorists have made life difficult for all of us including environmentalists," Ben said, innocently.

"These policies will appreciably cut the United States' dependency on foreign oil; then we'll present a bill to Congress to restart expansions of safer nuclear power plants in the United States as a part of the oil-reduction initiative. Our next proposal will ask Congress to provide unprecedented funding for the development of hydrogen fuel-cell technology with the end product to be subsidized by the federal government," Ben continued.

"Gentleman, let's make sure we get Congress to support the use of soy and grain fuels to make up for the loss of exports and lessen the economic impact on the US grain producers. I want to visit with the major US automobile manufactures, too. We need to convince them to begin producing ethanol fuel cars along with more hybrids and electric vehicles," Doug said.

"Mr. President, if we can get these initiatives agreed to, we can cause short term disruption in the Mid-Eastern oil markets and send some fear their way for a change! Just the rhetoric alone will upset the world oil markets, but our bark is meant to be as effective as our eventual bite," Bart added.

"I hope you guys don't own any oil stocks, because your portfolio is going to take a major hit." The President said, signing off on the final policy initiatives.

"Yeah, we're going to get OPEC's attention immediately, but again this is their worst nightmare! Oil futures are going to go right down the tubes," Bart said, knowing that the big multinational oil companies would now target their legislation immediately to try to nullify their policy proposals.

"I hope we drown these sons of bitches in their own oil! Before this is all over I'm hoping their oil reserves will be about as worthless as the sand these Arabs live on." Ben added.

Doug took another a deep breath. "Okay, now let's talk about the JI in Malaysia."

"Mr. President, the CIA has confirmed the JI was directly involved in the attack; there's no mistake about that. We've also confirmed the terrorists who carried out the attack in New York were supported financially by President Putra and his government. We've all heard his tyrannical rants over the past few months; now we know he was serious!" Bart said, as he read from the contents of his intelligence folder.

"From what I understand, a single terrorist from the Middle East was involved in the bombing too. If we all agree with the CIA's assessment, then Putra and his gang will become our first targets," Doug said coldly.

"They're the responsible parties," Bart answered.

"So if we are all in agreement, this is the first group of bad guys that need our full and undivided attention?"

"I think you're right, Mr. President," Ben said.

"For the record, what are your recommendations?" Doug asked.

Ben Atchison was the first to speak. "We must isolate them from the rest of the world by cutting off all international commerce to them. Their trade partners are mostly friendly nations like Great Britain, so it's not likely a blockade will lead to any kind of military confrontation."

"What else?" The President asked.

"We must motivate the people of Malaysia to rebel, so they will be able to hand over JI members to us. The CIA has the names and will supply them to whoever steps forward and takes control."

"Are we certain they will rise up against their government?" Doug asked.

"I think their military will be the first to make a move," Ben said.

"What if they don't?" Doug asked.

"Then we will threaten them with a nuclear response at the time of our choosing, and we'll offer no quarter to their military. Our threat will be viable enough and we'll make sure everyone in the country understands what's about to happen. We'll destroy one major city after another until they comply. Of course, we will give them plenty of warning so innocent people can evacuate the area. We don't want this to be another attack like the ones in Japan; nothing can be gained by that. Mr. President," Bart emphasized.

"Since Thailand is on their northern border, and just happens to be eighty percent Buddhist, they're no friend of this Islamic Republic. We must convince them to close their border with Malaysia. We'll have to make it clear to them that any other neighboring countries that harbor these terrorists will be next," Bart added.

"I would suggest giving Putra the chance to stay in power, but he must agree to rid his country of terrorist organizations or risk ending up in a prison in Guantanamo Bay for the rest of his damn life. If we do this, we could prevent the chaos that's going to follow if this guy suddenly disappears," Ben said, hoping to make a strong point to the President.

"With all due respect, Ben, I can't agree to that!" Doug said coldly. "Every person that's had anything to do with the attack in New York must be handed over to us, no exceptions. I'm really not concerned about the chaos they might have to experience. No one over there gives a good Goddamn about our country, or our chaos, do they?"

Both men could see this wasn't going to be a negotiable point with the President. It was time to agree, argue, or resign. But before Ben could respond, the President said, "Gentlemen, I want to make one thing very clear to both of you. I don't want any of our ground troops in Malaysia, none! Is that understood?" Both men again acknowledged that they understood. "Our objective here to instill enough fear in the population to get a full-blown insurrection going, not to get any of our people killed!"

Since the nation was on a war footing, the Terrorist Control Center had been rushed through Congress with minimal opposition. Any congressman opposing this legislation would have found going home extremely dangerous politically. People wanted action, they wanted policies that would be effective against terrorism, and they wanted to extract revenge for those who were responsible for this grizzly act of terror.

The TCC was now fully operational, and all communications were now being fed to operatives on a minute-to-minute basis. Data about the actions of governments all over the world were now being monitored. Top secret spy satellite data were also being fed directly to the TCC for evaluation and consideration. Communication had been streamlined, and representatives of the new organization could be reached twenty-four hours a day by the President. Even before his speech, information was being fed to the heads of states of all countries that the United States was planning "*Serious and Immediate Action*" against those responsible for the attack in New York. Shockwaves rippled around the world! Words of caution and restraint were starting to filter back through the State Department, which was simply directing the information to the TCC, and of course to the President himself. As world leaders sensed that the words of the government were being supported by the American people, they became more and more uneasy. The politically-correct and opinion-sensitive United States that had been so paralytic in the past in the face of terrorism was now transformed into the lethal agent of retribution as the world's only true unchallenged superpower. These incredible changes were now threatening their own foreign policies abroad and at home. It was obvious that massive changes in US foreign policy were about to take place that would drastically affect their economies and have profound security implications.

The President's third broadcast to the world broke into all communication mediums so that virtually every country in the world had to listen. His speech outlined quickly, and without parsing words, that "The government of Malaysia had been wholly responsible for the October attack on New York City." He made a plea to the people of Malaysia "To hand over all leaders and members of the JI party to American authorities or suffer grave and catastrophic consequences..." He warned, "any other nation who might harbor these individuals will suffer the same consequence…" Although he didn't use the words "nuclear attack," it was certainly understood that this was a possibility. He also spoke about the act of destroying the United Nations as an act against humanity, which every world leader should "Consider as a threat to their government and people at home…"

Immediately after the speech, the TCC contacted the office of President Putra who couldn't be reached. So all communications were being directed to the Malay minister of State, Ali Syed Balani, who had no immediate response. The TCC had already ordered the nuclear submarines *USS*

Jimmy Carter and *USS Connecticut* to the South China Sea and would be there in less than forty-eight hours. Each attack submarine carried a lethal inventory of Tomahawk Missiles, Harpoon anti-ship missiles, and Mark 48 torpedoes. The Tomahawk Missiles were armed with nuclear warheads to provide the ultimate punch in a war that might start in a matter of hours. The submarines were capable of mining operations if needed to isolate ports in both Malaysian land masses. The USS *Connecticut* SSN-22 and the USS *Jimmy Carter* SSN-23 were two of the three existing submarines in the fleet of Seawolf class of the cold war. Even though these three subs were the last of the group designed for use in a US versus Soviet type war, all three subs, including the USS *Seawolf* SSN 21, still carried a hefty arsenal of nukes.

Information had been pouring into the TCC from the CIA concerning the individuals that would be needed to be turned over by the Malaysian government. No one in the CIA could ever remember a leader of a country being sought by the US Government other than President Noriega of Panama. Now, the Malaysian President was at the top of the list of 855 known terrorists believed to be in that country. This list had been transmitted to every government across the globe to be turned in immediately to the United States government. The TCC had been in touch with the government of Thailand concerning their southern border with Malaysia. The United States had made a formal request to block the border with their neighbor to the south and reassured the government that the United States had no interested in doing harm to their country. However, if Thailand knowingly allowed members of the JI party to infiltrate their country, they would be required to arrest them and turn them over immediately. If they didn't, then the US would consider this to be a grave act that would eventually lead to war. The leadership of the TCC also informed Thailand's government that two nuclear attack subs were heading for the South China Sea, and the United States government was also directing US war ships into the Straits of Malacca to blockade trade. The Terrorist Control Center now had thirty-two state department officials fielding calls that were pouring in from various countries, attempting to understand what the intentions were of the United States government. Since the United Nations as an organization had been crippled by the attack, this was now the only direct line of communication with the United States, other than the State Department, which had for all practical purposes been circumvented by the Administration's new policies.

36

February 11th 2013
West Wing

"Have we heard anything yet?" Doug asked, with a tenor of impatience in his voice. He had just returned from a briefing with a key group of Congressman.

"So far nothing but deafening defiance!" Ben replied. "It appears that Putra is going to attempt to ride this thing out to the end, same old game."

"Well that's what we expected, right, so it's time to change our strategy and try something else," Doug said impatiently, hoping to find a quick consensus.

"I agree that we need to begin the next level of initiatives," Bart said, with his usual lack of emotion. "I don't think we have any choice at this point. We're running out of options here."

"I couldn't agree more! We've backed these bastards into a corner that they don't know how to get out of," Ben said, agreeing with Bart's assessment.

The next step, which had simply been named *Level Two Reprisals* were intended to give visible evidence that the resolve of the United States was unwavering. The US military would strike with the most lethal force in its arsenal, a nuclear weapon. The use of nukes against an uninhabited region of Malaysia was meant to be a deadly harbinger of things to come if the regime didn't step down. Doug hoped, against all hope, that this awesome show of military force would create insurrection in the streets and accomplish his objectives.

The TCC had been busy for days explaining to heads of state, worldwide, what "*Level Two*" and "*Level Three*" reprisals would mean for the people of Malaysia. The President had made the decision to make the people of Malaysia fight their own wars of survival. His decision not to allow US ground troops to fight as "proxies" for Malaysians to overthrow their own regime meant that the people would have to spill their own blood to accomplish that objective. The new President wasn't interested in fighting the war of his enemies, a guerilla war of attrition. That wasn't going to happen!

The president's strategy, which was the ultimate show of force, was simple enough. He had anticipated that some of the foreign powers who still had diplomatic ties with the Malaysian regime would explain to President Putra the severity of their situation. Doug's hope was that Putra and his terrorist associates would attempt to flee the country, but that hadn't happened yet, which was troubling. The TCC had made an official request to Thailand to seal their borders. The CIA had provided a "most wanted list" to their security forces for those individuals to be extradited back to the US. Thailand's government, without hesitation, had agreed.

To the south, Singapore cooperated and had received an extradition list, as well. This was done quickly by their government because of the real fear of having their ports mined. The United States, in each case, was getting full cooperation because of the risk of a nuclear response, a new wrinkle in American foreign policy. The *Level Two* option was beginning to produce dividends and respect, but as anticipated, very few friends around the world. For those who still might have their doubts about America's resolve, a less than subtle reminder was about to unfold to change their opinions. Doug had made a new kind of foreign policy decision. The United States wouldn't rely solely on the friendships of other nations any longer; instead, the US would rely on respect as well.

"General Miller have you and your staff decided on a target?" The President asked.

"We have, Mr. President. We've chosen a small island that is twelve kilometers from the mainland called *Sibu;* it also has a smaller sister island that will be destroyed by the same detonation."

"How many people live on these islands?"

"Just a small resort community and some tourists; maybe ten to fifteen, according to our latest intelligence," he said, pointing to the small islands with a red laser pointer on a map of Malaysia.

"How are we going to ensure there will be no one left on the islands when we detonate?"

"The plan is to send e-mails directly to the resorts and, of course, notify Putra's government to get everyone off the island. We'll also covertly land a group of Navy Seals on the island twelve hours before the scheduled detonation just to make sure."

"What about the smaller island?"

"Same procedure, Mr. President."

"General, if we destroy those islands, I don't want any innocent people left on them, are we clear on that?" Also, let's make sure we send a sufficient ground force to ensure we have the upper hand. I don't want any body bags coming back home."

"I understand, Sir. The force that goes ashore will be more than adequate."

General Miller and his staff had been working furiously to develop an assault plan. The *Level Two* initiative would use a small, tactical nuclear weapon dropped by air onto the island. At this point, no one in the administration wanted to think about going to the *Level Three* initiatives, because then a major city would be targeted for total destruction. The attack on these smaller, outlying islands was intended to be a sobering introduction to the overwhelming power of the United States' military and to reintroduce the nuclear option, that had always been off the table.

This was no longer considered a war of attrition by the administration, per se; it was much more than that. It was now a systematic plan to destroy the infrastructure of Malaysia. The American President no longer had the luxury of viewing this country as a population of just guilty and innocent people. Instead, it was a nation that had gone totally wrong. It was a government that had decided to change the power arrangement in the world by attempting to destroy the United States. Doug now believed this was a war of civilizations that had to be won at any cost. This was the same conclusion that had forced another US President, Harry Truman, to strike with nuclear force, although this time around, it was going to be a bluff. If all went as planned, Doug would force regime change without spilling a drop of blood on either side. He was going to use the threat of using a nuclear weapon as a catalyst for change. *Sibu* Island was close enough in proximity to the mainland for the people of the southern provinces to see and hear this frightening power of a thermal nuclear blast.

Bart had carefully studied the sixty-six year old plans from the second World War to destroy the ice-capped summit of Mt. Fuji with a nuclear weapon. A plan that had been immediately scrapped by President Harry S. Truman believing that Mt. Fuji's religious significance would only harden the enemy's resolve to keep fighting. *Sibu* Island had no religious significance. But attacking Mt Fuji would have, in turn, made it even more difficult to invade and defeat Japan. Truman had chosen instead to bomb the cities of Hiroshima and Nagasaki, a much more lethal attack on the infrastructure and civilians to make a point, which Japan's leaders quickly understood. The memory of those two attacks from World War II gave legitimacy to the idea that the United States might repeat this same horrible action in Malaysia. Like a calculating high-stakes poker player, Doug was now using this piece of brutal history to up the stakes for the enemy and attempt to break their will.

Doug had inherited a newly completed and tested United States "Missile Defense Shield" that would protect American soil from conventional nuclear attacks. It was widely believed by other military powers that the new President would feel confident enough to use nukes against any country who miscalculated his determination to punish those who sought to destroy his country. But that had been a benign point until now, because it was thought that no nation would attack the United States with a nuclear weapon. This new strategy of reprisals was something different, and world leaders were desperately trying to catch up. How could the United States use such weapons to punish just a few?

Cameras would be placed near tiny *Sibu* Island to record the explosive force of the blast. Later, these same images would be fed to the Malaysian people, to create chaos and fear.

"General, let's do everything we can to ensure that no innocent life is lost."

"We will, Sir."

"How soon can we strike?"

"I think we need to give the people on the island a week to clear out then—"

"General, that isn't what I asked." Doug said, interrupting the General in mid sentence.

"Everything is in place. We can be operational by tomorrow if you like," Miller responded.

"Okay, give the orders in three days, and then take anyone else off forcibly, if necessary!"

"Yes, Sir."

"If we get this right, it will all be over in a couple of weeks or even sooner." The president said confidently.

"Mr. President, may I suggest we officially warn Putra what we are about to do?" Ben asked.

"I'm not sure how much good that will do, Ben. He probably already knows what's about to happen. Do any of you have problems putting together a communiqué informing their government of our intentions?" Doug asked the other cabinet members in the room.

Everyone was silent for a moment with no objection being made to a warning being issued. "Okay, Mr. Secretary, by all means, let the man know what's about to happen," the President ordered. Within minutes, the message had been transmitted to the Putra regime via Pakistan. President Ferguson didn't expect any of these blood-thirsty tyrants to give themselves up. He instead believed Putra would stick to his same old strategy, which was to bang on his deck with outrage as the cameras rolled pleading for help and claiming total innocence.

The TCC was deluged by frantic communications from countries worldwide wanting a diplomatic explanation. The American President had spoken directly to the Prime Minister of Great Britain, the President of Russia, and the Chairman of the People's Republic of China. He had kept to a closely worded statement asking for these governments to help immediately in getting Najib Putra to turn himself in. The President had made it clear this was the only way to avoid reprisals. All three heads of state had attempted, although in vain, to lengthen the scope of their talks. But President Ferguson had held fast to his plans and rejected any further discussions. The Chairman of the People's Republic of China had threatened that these actions could put his country on a war footing with the United States." Doug had chosen not to respond to the threat, he really couldn't.

37

February 13th 2013 1:00 a.m.
Southern Tip of Sibu Island South China Sea

The two black zodiacs were being inflated on the rolling deck of the submarine. The sub was dead in the water in the South China Sea just off the southern tip of *Sibu* Island. The Seawolf class *Jimmy Carter* had surfaced to deploy two Seal teams ashore. The humidity was oppressive and perspiration wasn't evaporating making it seem even warmer to the seaman working on deck. The teams would only have four hours to go ashore, complete their mission, and be back to the submarine by 0500. More Seals swarmed on deck, dressed in black with smears of gray, black, and green paint on their faces. Every man was carrying a variety of attack weapons, and they expected action tonight.

"It won't be long now, Seals!" Petty Officer Jim Carlota said to one of his squad members. The members of the teams were nervously making final equipment checks. After a few more minutes, both inflatable boats were shoved into the ink-black waters alongside the sub.

"Good Luck, Sir," one of the submarine's enlisted men whispered to platoon leader Lt. Mike Patterson.

"Thanks, Sailor, we'll be back soon so keep the air conditioning on extra cold for me!"

"Aye, Aye, Sir." The young seaman said, as he pushed the inflatable away from the steel hull.

The Seals began to paddle in short, powerful strokes in the direction of shore while another member of the team cranked the camouflaged outboard motor. The motor sputtered to life and began to power the boat forward into the inky-black night. Then the motor on the second inflatable fired up, and both were out of sight in seconds.

"Let's get in there and get this done!" Platoon leader Mike Patterson said to his squad over the sound of the motor and splashing waves. "Magic" Mike, as his men called him, was a pretty typical Seal officer, lean but bulky in the right places. He was one of the few officers that could actually out swim and outrun literally every man in his sixteen-man platoon. He wasn't quick to anger and stayed calm even under extreme pressure, which was an attribute that hadn't gone unnoticed by his superiors. The men called him "Magic," but not to his face, of course, but Lt. Patterson was keenly aware of the nickname he had been tagged with. The men had given him the name because he always seemed to win at whatever he did and always made it look easy, like "magic." He wouldn't be an 0-3 for long, most of his men believed. A few more missions, and the scuttlebutt was he was going to be promoted. During a training exercise in Florida a year before, Magic Mike had incapacitated another Navy Seal officer under simulated recon conditions. The "accident" as it was later termed "was caused by a breakdown in communications that led to the injury of a Seal Officer." The facts greatly differed from the reality of what had happened during the simulation. Recon rules called for immediate submission when taken by surprise by a member of a competing team. The unfortunate "accident" had happened during the training exercise. The other officer, a former football player at the Naval Academy, apparently didn't get the briefing memo about being submissive! During the mission, the young officer had chosen to go hand-to-hand with Magic Mike instead of surrendering as he was required to. The officer, a relatively new 0-2 named Matt Ryan, who was fresh out of Coronado, was big and strong but apparently not quick enough for Lieutenant Mike Patterson. After Magic had forcefully subdued the junior officer, Ryan had to be hospitalized for a strained neck and mild a concussion.

Petty Officer First Class Jim Carlota was in command of second squad. Jimmy's mission was to search the smaller southern island off *Sibu.* His orders were to search the island and to ensure non combatants hadn't been left there. He had been ordered to evade all military forces he encountered; he was told the Seals were not looking for a fight. However, if his squad met resistance, then they had orders to engage and terminate all resistance.

Both squads were carrying a full complement of combat arms, but were still lightly equipped so they could move quickly. They still had enough fire power to subdue any military force likely to be encountered on the island. Both Seal team leaders were carrying 9mm *Sig P226* handguns and *MP-5* submachine guns. One Seal in each inflatable carried the *N-91 RH* sniper rifles. All the remaining men had a combination of automatic weapons and grenades and two *M-79* grenade launchers just in case resistance was greater than expected.

Because the *Jimmy Carter* had submerged just over two miles off the southern tip of the island, there hadn't been a silhouette of the large, three-hundred and fifty-three foot submarine in the black of the night. The submarine would stay submerged and then reappear in four hours to pick up the returning Seals. If for some reason, the Seals didn't show up on time, the sub commander had strict orders to leave at full speed to a safe distance away from the island and remain submerged.

Lt. Patterson held his left closed fist in the air as a signal to cut the engine. All the men then started paddling towards shore just fifty yards away. Mike could see the shoreline clearly with his night vision gear. The waves crashing on the beach had muffled any sounds of the motor. The boat was caught by a wave and surfed the last distance remaining on to the beach. The black inflatable slowly stopped as the hull ground on the sandy bottom. Magic Mike didn't have to issue an order; every man hopped out into the foaming surf and picked up the zodiac, hauling it to the edge of the beach. Again, only using hand signals, Mike reconfirmed that one of the Seals would stay with the inflatable until the main force returned. All the Seals had studied the maps of the island memorizing where the small resorts were located.

Patterson gave the order to move out. Silently, they moved into the palms and underbrush bordering the sandy beach. The plan was to move carefully under the cover of darkness and toward the first resort, code named *Alpha One*. It was located on the extreme southern tip of the island. Then the team would proceed northward to *Alpha Two*, followed by *Alpha three*. Their camouflage faces were invisible in the darkness, and the team moved with stealth into the jungle.

After reaching *Alpha One* and observing the small resort for a few minutes, two Seals moved in under the protective fire support of the five remaining squad members concealed at the edge of the clearing. Quietly, they made their way to the entrance of the first of the two buildings. The lights were off, and it didn't appear as if anyone was there. One of the Seals moved into the lobby while he was being covered by his buddy kneeling in the doorway. He quickly moved toward the front desk and saw no one.

After further checks, the two Seals emerged from both buildings and moved quickly to the opposite side of the clearing where they were joined by Lt. Patterson and the rest of the squad. Not breaking their silence, the first Seal to enter the building pointed at his eyes and twisted his head side to side. Lt. Patterson nodded that he understood no one was in the building. Magic Mike then gave the hand signal to move out, making the signal with sign language "*Alpha-2.*"

The second building was evacuated as well. Magic Mike was convinced the islanders had heeded the warning to get off the island. He also believed that the third resort hotel would be empty as well.

By 1:45 a.m., they had reached *Alpha three.* This time things were different. The lights were on in the hotel. Mike signaled to the squad to move in two at a time to the southern perimeter of the building on his signal. Two Seals moved forward, pairing up naturally without being ordered. Mike watched the house for a good five minutes and saw no movement. He wondered if guards were on the perimeter, hidden in the jungle, waiting for someone to approach the building, ready to fire on his team as they moved out. Without further recon he wouldn't know. He had to make a snap decision: more recon or go now. Time was running out; they had very little time to make it back to the Zodiac and then back to the sub. His gut told him no one was covering the perimeter. He gave the hand signal to go. Both men moved out of the thick jungle and quickly and silently made their way to the edge of the building. Two more followed, then finally everyone was at the edge of the resort except for Mike, who was sweating profusely in the jungle heat at the edge of the clearing, alone. He wiped the sweat off his brow and then stood up and ran with his weapon across the clearing. One Seal signaled that he could hear voices inside. Mike signaled back to take a look. The man rose up and looked into a window next to the front door of the small hotel, then ducked back. He quickly signaled Mike. "Four people… all civilians, tied up!" Mike asked again to make sure he understood. The Seal again, agitated a bit, quickly made the same series of signals with his hands.

Mike thought for a minute, then gave the signal for two men to go to the back of the building and take a look and then report. He instructed the next two Navy Seals to proceed around the front of the building to the other side and take a look. When both men came back, he would have five Seals assault the building with two in position to defend against any resistance that might come out of the jungle.

After a couple of minutes, the men came back and signaled to Mike that they saw no one. Mike then gave the order to move into the building. Bursting through the front door the men first encountered the small group of two men and two women tied up in the center of the room. One of the women screamed!

"Don't kill us please!"

"Shut up! Don't make a sound…" Mike said in a low whisper.

"Who are you?" Another woman asked her voice trembling.

"Navy Seals, shut the fuck up; we'll do the talking! Are there any guards?"

"No, they left about an hour ago to get off the island!"

"Cut them loose." Mike said to one of the Seals who pulled a large Seal commando knife out of its scabbard attached to his right leg.

"How many guards were here?" Mike asked the same lady who couldn't seem to keep her mouth shut.

"Six," she said, as her hands were being freed. She stood up and rubbed her wrists, which were red and bruised.

"Which direction did they go?"

"I couldn't see, but I overheard them saying they were leaving the island. If they did that, they would have to leave on the western side of the island, that's where the boat dock is."

"How were they armed?"

"I don't know. They just had some rifles."

"They had AK-47s, Sir," a man said. He was still tied up on the floor; he looked to be in his early twenties.

"Did they say where they were going?"

"I heard them saying they were going to Little Sibu Island before they left for the mainland." The young man said.

"Break radio silence and give Carlota the heads up!" Mike said to one of the Seals…

Turning back to the people still on the floor, he said, "listen, we've got to get out of here and quick!"

"I need to get my things from my room before we leave!" one of the women still tied up on the floor said.

"There's no time for that. We've got to get off the island now and we don't have room for luggage!

"Tiger two, you got six bad guys headed your way," The young Seal said.

"Roger, Tiger one, understood. How are they armed?"

"AKs, over!"

"Roger, Tiger one!" He whispered.

The radio went dead. Both men wanted to keep the chatter down to a minimum. They couldn't be sure who might be scanning the radio waves.

2:25 a.m.
Little Sibu Island

Carlota had just reached the edge of the jungle where their zodiac was waiting. Just as the squad was about to pick up the boat and carry it down to the water, the sounds of another motor filled the air. Jimmy searched the waters offshore with his night-vision gear and saw a large power launch heading to a pier that extended several hundred yards to the water.

"Hold up, we got company." Carlota whispered. All the men melted back into the jungle. He motioned to his men that they would go to hand signals again. They took up positions along the edge of the beach. They would now wait until these soldiers made their way into the interior of the island before they made their escape.

Jimmy was now watching as the men tied their boat up. As he observed them, he hoped they would simply cross the beach to the west rather than walking in his direction. After a moment, his hopes were quelled when the men started to march diagonally, which would bring them fairly close to their own position in the brush. He immediately gave the signal that the bad guys were headed their way and to be ready to fire on his order. Everyone nodded.

The enemy soldiers continued to walk in their direction, although not turning up the beach towards where the Seals were hiding. There was still time for them to turn and walk into jungle before they came to the exact spot where the Seals were positioned. Sweat was dripping off of the squad leader's nose. The tension was building; every muscle in Jimmy's body was tight, and the hair on his neck was starting to tingle. *Fuck, wouldn't you know it these guys are going to walk right on top of us,* he thought. Then all six men made a slight turn in their direction and started walking right at them.

He slowly signaled to his squad to begin firing when he fired. The soldiers making their way towards them didn't have night-vision capability so they were blind to what was about to happen. Damn, Jimmy thought, too bad we couldn't have left a little sooner. These guys wouldn't have to die.

All but one Seal was in a position to fire. During their training, lines of fire were pretty much agreed on in these situations. The men farther down the tree line would fire at the targets farther to their right. The men closest to approaching soldiers would take out the guys on the left and center. This would keep the lines of fire clear.

Suddenly, the sound of a single shot shattered the silence of the night. Then the other Seals opened up with their automatic weapons. In a matter of a couple of seconds, all six men lay bleeding out on the beach. Jimmy sprang up and ran the twenty yards to where the men had fallen. Two other Seals had followed and, together, they cautiously removed all the weapons from the dead men.

"Get the boat in the water." He said.

The Seals then launched the boat into the surf and cranked the motor before their squad leader and his companions made it back and climbed aboard.

"Lets' get the fuck out of here!" Jimmy said as he took his place in the inflatable boat. There was silence in the boat as it sped back to the exact latitude and longitude where they would be picked up. Every man knew the importance of finding the *Jimmy Carter.*

38

February 14th 2013 7:30 a.m.
Quantico, Virginia

Stevie sat staring at the small, hand-written letters and numbers on the map. The artfully drawn images didn't look like art to her, more like doodling on paper. She was convinced, however, that this was something Mark had created to hide confidential information. This was nothing new. Maps throughout history had been used to conceal information, she knew. This drawing, if viewed from a short distance, was prosaic enough to go virtually unnoticed by the casual observer. Trying to conceal personal information within FBI headquarters wasn't a good idea, but to conceal it like this was pretty clever, Stevie had to admit. But why had he left it behind right out in the open where it could be found? That didn't make sense.

After his death, Stevie had begun to suspect that not all was right in Mark's world. If this map contained confidential information about the FBI, then that might confirm her suspicions. She recalled he had told her that working as an analyst was disappointing at times. He had said not being able to physically go out and be part of an investigation had taken its toll on his psyche. This lack of hands-on investigative work and having to work through others in the field to pursue facts was nerve racking sometimes. He had also confessed, in idle talk, that he eventually intended to get back into the field, but his attempts thus far had been thwarted by the Director of the FBI. She had always believed there was more to Mark's personality than he was willing to let on. Although he was supportive and helpful most of the time, she had noticed he could be distant and distracted too. Even though he carried on as a happy-go-lucky guy, she had sensed there was something that wasn't right. *Maybe that's why I found him so interesting*, she thought. Later, his admissions about his discontent confirmed some of her suspicions.

In between electronic conferencing with the CIA team working on the code at Langley, Stevie had been busy with her own special project. She was attempting to unravel the mysteries of the map she had found in Mark's office. The margins outlined in letters and numbers were artistic enough, but conspicuously odd, she thought. Her fear was that Mark Latham might have been selling classified information, even though she sensed that wasn't the case. To find out what was going on, she would just have to break the code. The terrorists who had made two attempts on her life and then murdered Mark obviously had some accurate intelligence. But they wouldn't have killed Mark if he was giving them vital information, or would they? Maybe they would if they were finished with him. Stevie was aware that other high-level FBI and CIA agents had gone bad before, so her thoughts about Mark couldn't be easily dismissed.

She had deciphered a few words, but without context, she couldn't be sure what they meant. The code apparently used multiple codes for each line of letters and numbers. That meant the "discernable" content could only be known when the last code was broken. The number of codes was not restricted to a sentence but only to the line of letters running along the border. The borders had clear starting and stopping points along the edges. It appeared that, when a line ended, a new code was begun. Stevie had calculated that the document probably contained at least three separate coding processes. So she would have to break all three in each line, one by one, without the help of the SX-10. She couldn't take the chance of using the Bureau's computers for fear of being found out. Once again, Stevie found herself not adhering to protocol by not reporting what she had discovered to her superiors.

As she worked on the code, it was only a matter of minutes before Stevie unraveled the first three sentences using a well-known coding system called *Gray Code.* For whatever reason, Mark had made the first layer of code easy to decipher! She was familiar with *Gray Code*, which was based on the binary system. It was an antiquated coding system that wasn't used anymore. This code was slightly different, though. It had some interesting anomalies thrown in to confuse. The change in the normal *Gray* process was the binary code for each letter of the alphabet had unusual scrambling done by using letters instead of zero or digit one. In this case, Mark had used the letters E and R. The repetitive use of the letters made her immediately think of a binary-type code. However, unlike the usual binary codes that had just eight unit places, this code appeared to have ten. She quickly figured out that the two extra places were also substitutions for zero and one; she just had to know which one was which. After breaking all three relatively simple codes, she stared at the message that she had written down on a legal pad:

> "THE BUREAU HAD REFUSED TO TRACK ABU SABIR OR FOLLOW-UP WITH CIA."
>
> "CHINESE APPEAR TO BE PROVIDING SUPPORT."

It was the last decoded sentence that really shocked her! "I have notified DF, hope he wins!" Stevie sat back in her chair trying to make sense of what she had just read. This represented the direct linkage! "So that's it!" She said to herself. She worked on the code components over and over, but this was the only way the letters would work in unison to make syntax. Mark was leaking information, classified information, to Doug Ferguson. But why? What was even more difficult to figure out was why he used such an easy code to decipher. Mark was certainly capable of writing a code that would take months to decipher, but he had made it easy for someone to break. To her, it appeared he had written the code so that it could be decoded easily by someone who did this kind of thing for a living. "So he wanted this thing decoded" She said to herself. It all made perfect sense now! Mark had planned to leave something behind just in case something happened to him. Mark was trying to play his trump card even from the grave. He must have thought that secretly calling a Presidential candidate and leaking classified information would put the Bureau under investigation. That had to be it. He had probably been trying to get someone inside the FBI to look at the information he had found about Abu Sabir and the Chinese. Of course, no one wanted to think of this kind of an alliance, did they? It was crazy, but was it really, she wondered. It was time to let someone know about what she had uncovered. Now she was certain Mark wanted this message to get out if anything happened to him. She was sure of that. She was convinced his frustrations had forced him to become an informant. If all this was true, then if someone had listened to him earlier, the attack might have been averted. If it had been suspected, by the United States, that China was involved, they could they have been confronted diplomatically. If the Chinese had known that their connection with terrorists had been discovered, then this knowledge alone would have been enough for them to pull the plug on the operation rather than confront America militarily. But apparently, someone hadn't wanted to report something like this. Maybe it was just as simple as a lack of confidence in the Intel. Suggesting that the United States confront another Super Power and being wrong could be a career ending move. Mark had still come close to stopping the attack in New York, anyway, by contacting Doug Ferguson!

In retrospect, any communication between Abu Sabir, a known Middle Eastern terrorist, and the JI should have thrown up red flags over at Langley. Why hadn't the FBI investigated further, Stevie wondered.

After an hour, she had deciphered more information and found out Mark had gotten this information from NSA cell-phone intercepts, none of the intelligence was all that revealing, except that some suspected low-level Al-Qaida members were talking to Chinese agents and the Pakistanis at the same time. "So that's it!" She then decoded the next several entries. As she read the information, it appeared that Mark had come to the conclusion that Al Qaida and the JI in Malaysia were planning a joint operation. With Putra beating the war drum, Mark had come to believe an attack was coming and that the Malaysian regime was going to be behind it! With the possibility of China being connected would then explain why President Putra had been so emboldened to make worldwide death threats against the United States; he had one powerful ally for protection. How much of this information had been relayed to others inside the Bureau she wasn't sure, but the decoded transmission between these parties clearly pointed to a possible link among Al Qaida, China, and the JI. *This is as close to a "smoking gun" as we're going to get*, Stevie thought. She reached for the phone on her desk and called Tripp. It was time to let someone know what she had found.

39

February 15th 2013
Island of Diego Garcia, Indian Ocean

Lt. Colonel Donald Murphy applied power to the four General Electric-100 turbofan jet engines mounted deep in the wings of the B-2 Stealth Bomber. The black flying wing with its unmistakable double-W-shaped wings began to roll down the runway and pick up speed. Within a few minutes, both engines were powering the Black stealth bomber at liftoff speeds. Soon after that, the plane was airborne above the island runway and quickly climbing high above the cobalt blue Indian Ocean.

The Co-pilot Major Dan Gibson monitored the colored electronic EFIS system in front of him, which was now displaying vital flight, engine, and sensor data for the B-2. Dan was a graduate of the Air Force Academy and one of the few men in the world to pilot a B-2. At five-feet eleven-inches tall and weighing just under 190 pounds, he was fit and trim and looked like a fighter pilot, which he had been before going into the B-2 program. He was Colonel Don Murphy's best friend and wanted to learn everything he could from this veteran pilot who had flown twenty-two missions from Kosovo to cities in Iraq in this state-of-the-art bomber.

"All systems go!" Gibson said, through his voice oxygen mask sucking air after speaking.

"Roger!" The airplane shook a little while going through some mild turbulence as it continued to climb through the deep blue skies above the ocean below.

Flying the most sophisticated bomber ever made was a demanding job for any pilot. But piloting the stealth bomber was a real rush for even the most seasoned pilots. Even though the bomber had a one-hundred and seventy-foot wing span, it was a virtually invisible on radar. All of his life Don Murphy had wanted to fly high performance aircraft. As a student at the University of Michigan, he excelled in engineering to pave the way for getting into the Air Force Flight training program. It had all paid off when he got the chance to get into the B-2 program. No one could have been luckier than he was being able to fly the Air Force's most expensive and sophisticated aircraft at over two-billion dollars per copy.

The flight plan was to climb to an altitude of thirty-eight-thousand feet and fly a northeasterly course to the Northern tip of Sumatra, then turn and fly southeast down the Straits of Malacca, crossing over the mid section of the

Malaysian peninsula south of Kuala Lumpur. Once over the mainland, they were to descend out over the South China Sea and then make the final bombing run towards the tiny island that lay just south of Sibu Island. They would deliver one B83 strategic free-fall nuclear bomb and destroy two small islands owned by the government of Malaysia. The flight path would take the B-2 through no other nation's airspace to minimize controversy. However, Malaysian airspace would be violated. It was part of the game the President was playing. The American B-2 bomber would fly over Malaysia, strike their target, and then fly back over Malaysia without being seen. The message being sent would be hard to ignore. "We can kill you anytime we please and you'll never see it coming!"

"I knew this was going to happen sooner or later!" Col. Murphy said, as he relaxed behind the controls as the auto pilot took control of the aircraft.

"You mean using a nuclear weapon?"

"Yeah, the bad guys went too far this time. Who would ever believe what happened to New York could have happened? I still can't believe it did," Murphy said, as he scanned the flight instruments. The plane was now at twenty-four-thousand feet and climbing, buffeting slightly as it made its way through more turbulence.

"Do you think we'll have to come back and do the job right?" Dan asked turning his head to look at Murphy, really wanting to know what he thought.

"I'd hate to try and predict what's going to happen; the world is pretty screwed up right now, man!"

"As far as I'm concerned, they asked for it!" Dan said defiantly. I had two good friends die in New York that day.

"I think it has been coming to this for years, and things aren't going to get any better soon. Our military isn't set up to fight two-man terrorist teams operating secretly against us! If we don't stop them, they will keep picking us apart until someone gets their attention!" Murphy pulled his flight mask off, breathing in oxygen from the cabin.

"Yeah, it looks like the new Commander in Chief feels the same way!"

"The real question is how many innocent people are going to have to die in the process?"

"I think that will be up to the people who support the terrorists! It's apparently their choice now."

The B-2 continued to power through 38,000 feet. There was almost no cloud cover and the skies were clear. At their present speed, they would round the tip of Sumatra after darkness fell.

"Thank goodness the *Kitty Hawk* is in the South China Sea. Our fighters and AWACS will hopefully keep the skies clear over the target area if China decides to get involved."

"They're not going to get involved!" Murphy said confidently. "No way!"

"Are you sure?"

"I'm positive! It will be like a turkey shoot if they try to go against us, and all for a bunch of murdering terrorists. No, I don't think so. Now if you had asked me if they will ever try to test us militarily, I think that's a different story all together!"

"I hope you're right on the first and dead wrong on the second!" Dan said, as he bent to the right to look up through the canopy into the dark blue sky above the aircraft.

"Listen, tonight, nobody is going to see us coming, and if the Chinese try anything they will have about fifty F-18s to deal with! And besides, the AWACS will be up as well letting us know if any bogies are lurking about. In this fight, the night is ours, my man!"

The flight plan included a single-air refueling by a KC-10 tanker to top off the B-2's tanks just in case they had to fly around any concentrations of attack fighters after their strike.

"There he is!" Dan said as he got a visual on the KC-10. The stealthy B-2 quickly caught up with the much larger aircraft and slid silently under her in position for refueling.

This was one of B-2 pilots' most difficult jobs. The fuel fill was twenty-five feet behind the canopy of the bomber. He would have to rely on light signals from the boom operator to position the aircraft for fueling and then hold it there while fuel was pumped in.

"You guys have any money?" The boom operator's voice came squawking into both pilots' head sets.

"Yeah, we got money! Can't you tell by what we're driving here? Anybody that's got one of these babies must have plenty of money, right?" Col. Murphy shot back.

"Where you guys headed all alone tonight?" The operator was located in the rear of the aircraft and started to "Fly" the boom down to the sleek black B-2 bomber hanging just below the KC-10 tanker.

"No can say!" Col. Murphy said, holding the big bomber steady by concentrating on the red and green positioning lights above his head.

"Oh, secret huh?" The operator said, as he carefully maneuvered the extending white boom down towards the B-2. Lt. Mike Blake knew exactly where the bomber was going. In fact, he was certain the whole world knew what was about to take place. That was the whole point of their mission tonight, but he liked to banter about with these jet jockeys. It took the edge off of this complex and precision in-flight maneuver. He knew the pilot couldn't tell him where they were going; it was the way the military was, even if you knew the other guy knew, you couldn't talk about it.

The fueling lasted just over twelve minutes and the B-2's tanks were fully topped off.

"That should do it, KC! Tell Uncle Sam to put it on our tab!"

"Roger, Sir. Have a good evening and don't get into trouble out there."

"Did you hear this guy? Don't get into trouble? What the hell is that supposed to mean?" Murphy said.

"Yeah, that's funny. Here we are with a nuke that we're about to drop, and this guy says don't get into trouble? That's Classic, man," Dan said laughing.

The aircraft banked gently to the left and was instantly lost in the blackness of the night.

The Stealth Bomber was equipped with a single, three-way switch that the pilot could select from three different modes of aircraft operation. The three operation selections were "**Take off Mode**," "**Landing Mode**," and "**Go to War Mode**." It was time for Murphy to turn the switch to "**Go to War Mode**."

"Turning main mode switch to *Go-to-War*."

"Roger," Dan said, watching Murphy turning the switch.

As the bomber approached the northern tip of Sumatra, and before turning to run up the Straits of Malacca, the co-pilot then activated the exhaust temperature control system to minimize thermal signature. The GE-100 engines were internally mounted in the body of the wings and, with the cooling system for the exhaust working at its maximum range, the aircraft left almost no heat to be picked up by enemy thermal energy sensors. During the mission briefing, intelligence officers had said there would be no military ships in the Straits of Malacca tonight, but they would be prepared anyway.

The co-pilot was monitoring the countermeasures system, the Lockheed Tony AN/Apr-50 defensive Management System, to stay out of trouble. These defense systems would protect them from enemy missiles on the ground and in the air.

In less than an hour and a half, they would be ready to make the final bombing run on Malaysia's tiny Sibu Island. After the nuclear blast, the islands would cease to exist. The only thing left would be a huge underwater crater a half mile wide on the ocean floor.

To Col. Murphy, the payback didn't seem to equal out for the losses the United States had taken in New York, but all of that was way above his pay grade. Tonight, however, he was hoping to send a strong message to those who would want to harm America again.

40

Washington D.C. February 14th 2013
The White House Situation Room

Doug was busy reading a briefing warning that China had put their military on full alert. Satellite photos were streaming into TCC headquarters. The fuzzy images were showing signs of increased activity at Chinese military bases across the Asian continent. The President and his advisors, which now comprised his National Security Council, were meeting below ground level at the White House.

"Looks like China might jump into this!" Doug said, as he laid the report down on top of the oak table that ran the length of the room. *So this is what it's like to be President of the United States*, Doug thought. He had noticed that Ben had already smoked two cigarettes this morning, two over his limit. Bart had worked through the morning going over military assets with General Miller, double checking every detail just in case some other country didn't like what they were doing. For the past twenty-four hours, anxiety had grown to a near crescendo among the President's cabinet.

Using a nuclear weapon against another sovereign nation was taking its toll on every person in the room.

"What's your secret, you don't look worried?" Doug asked.

"Just payback time, that's all; nothing we can do now except dish it out!" Tony said without emotion.

"So you're comfortable with all this?"

"I'm not sure *comfortable* is the word, but we've got to do something, right?" Tony said shrugging his shoulders. "We can't just sit around and wait for the next time, right?" He couldn't understand why everyone was so afraid. Putra had been caught red-handed and now it was fucking payback time. It was that simple. If the rest of the world didn't like it, so what? There wasn't anything else that could be done.

"Mr. President, the TCC has just requested we come up on direct link with them, if that's okay?" The duty officer asked.

"Sure, go ahead."

"Suddenly, the plasma screen sparkled to life with images of the busy control room miles away at Ft. Mead. The amount of diplomatic data streaming through and being processed along with foreign intelligence was building by the hour, as the world waited for the United States' response to what the President was calling the "Last Action" against a terrorist the government of Malaysia."

Doug didn't recognize the face of the middle-aged man whose image came up via the fiber optic link.

"Mr. President, I'm Jim McCauley. I was appointed to represent the State Department here at the TCC, Sir. Can you hear me okay?"

"Yes, Jim, we can hear you just fine," Doug responded.

"Sir, we have some breaking information from the Bureau that is kind of unusual, but we thought you might like to hear about it."

"Go ahead."

"Well, one of our analysts over at FBI headquarters has information that might explain why the Chinese government is showing signs of getting involved. I thought, if it's okay with you, I'd just put her on and let her tell you in her own words."

Stepping in front of the camera was a very attractive young lady wearing an FBI T-shirt and jeans.

"Mr. President, my name is Stevie Dillon, and I'm employed as an analyst at Quantico. I worked with Mark Latham who was my superior. He was one of the agents who lost his life in the safe house attack in Virginia."

"Yes, I was briefed on that…the same thing almost happened to you, didn't it young lady?"

"Yes, Sir. I'm glad to be alive!" Stevie said excitedly, realizing she was really speaking to the President of the United States.

"I heard Mark was a real asset to the Bureau. We'll miss his service I'm sure, but go ahead with what you have found, Agent Dillon."

Stevie thought it was nice for the President to say what he had about Mark, and this made her feel more comfortable about what she was about to share with him.

"Mr. President, I recently discovered intelligence information collected by Mark Latham. I've been working on it because this information had been coded and hidden away to keep it confidential. All these raw data had been intercepted by NSA and handed over to him to decode, but I suspect after a while, that he began to keep much of this intelligence to himself because he was leaking it to you."

It took a second for Doug to digest what Stevie had just said.

"So what you're saying is that Latham, an FBI employee, was the informant?"

"Exactly, Mr. President. That's evident from what I have decoded, but actually, the leak isn't all that important at the moment!"

President Ferguson liked this young lady's spunk; here she was telling the President of the United States what was important and what wasn't!"

"Okay, then go on—"

"Well, Sir, over the past year, we have worked on a lot of codes intercepted by the FBI and of course we have been working with the CIA as well. Mark had apparently deciphered coded messages that were being transmitted between government leaders in Pakistan and ministers of government in The People's Republic of China. Apparently, no one was listening to him, because nothing had been done to move that information up the line, and of course, Sir, he was frustrated."

"Ms. Dillon, if I could break in for a second here, those communications wouldn't be out of the ordinary since China and Pakistan have a joint venture with *Chengdu Aircraft Industry*," Bart Foster said. He had been on the Armed Service Committee who had banned technology transfers to both countries. The result had been that China, Russia, and Pakistan had grouped together to develop a new fighter aircraft program.

"Yes, Sir, I believe that's common knowledge to everyone. Mr. Secretary, they did develop the FC-1 together, but I think they may have developed something else," she said, matter of factly.

Ferguson liked this girl; she was smart and tough. She had just slammed one of the most intelligent and powerful men in the United States government. By the look on Secretary Foster's face, she might need a little help from the President later on, Doug mused.

"To continue, Sir, my supervisor had found much more involvement by these parties than just working on the FC-1 project."

"The FC-1 is a replacement fighter used by the Pakistani Air Force, if my memory serves me correctly. It is based on the Mig-33 design," Bart said, explaining the aircraft more thoroughly to the Cabinet members in the Situation Room.

"That's correct, Sir, but it now appears that the FC-1 project connection might have led to something more sinister, like possibly conspiring with Muslim radicals inside the Pakistani government to build a nuclear device for terrorists. This may sound crazy, Mr. Secretary, but it seems that the Soviets and the Chinese wanted to exploit their connections in Pakistan to achieve some of their own objectives."

"Young lady, that's preposterous. China would never do such a thing, nor would the Russians!" Ben said. "We haven't heard anything like this from the CIA and certainly not from the FBI."

"Let the young lady speak!" The President interrupted. "Let's hear what she has to say."

"Well, I think that's part of the problem here. Mark was a good analyst, but no one was listening to what he had to say. Of course, I don't know that for a fact, because he never shared any of this information with me, but I think he purposely left this paper trail so that it would be found in case anything happened to him," Stevie said.

"That makes sense to me!" Doug said.

"Yes sir, it does. Russia has serious economic problems, and China is now emerging as a real economic force. As a result, they both have an interest in supporting any group that could economically destabilize the United States. Mark believed that large-scale attacks like the one in New York could speed the process up. I think we could all agree this is a possibility."

"Does the Director have this information?" Doug asked.

"I'm not sure, but Mark apparently tried to inform everyone of what he thought was happening, but it looks like they took the same attitude as the Secretary.

There goes another powerful politician, being put in his place by this young FBI analyst, Doug thought.

"Ms. Dillon, how did you get this information to the TCC so quickly?" Doug asked.

"I happen to know one of the FBI officials that's on duty today, so I called him, and he said I should come over right away."

"Who would that be, Ms. Dillon, for the record of course?"

"His name is Ed Tripp, Sir."

"Oh yes, I know Ed."

"Yeah, well he invited me over, so here I am."

"Ms. Dillon, I want you to get that information over to the White House as soon as possible. If you need help from any other agencies, I'm authorizing it right now. We want to know everything that Agent Latham knew or suspected as quickly as we can get it."

"Yes, Sir, Mr. President"

With the conversation over, the video link was terminated.

"It seems this whole affair has grown considerably more complicated if what this young lady is saying happens to be true." Doug said.

"If it's true, yeah, but I'm not convinced any of this is factual!" Ben said, indignantly. "There are some damn smart people over there and nobody did anything about this? That's hard to believe."

"It could be the reason why the Chinese are so interested in our actions in Malaysia." Bart offered studiously.

The new President leaned back in his leather chair then took a moment to look around the table at his team. He had to admit they looked a bit confused, if not bewildered by these new developments. "Definitely a good thing," Doug thought. Who wouldn't be bewildered by a conspiracy that could mean the end of modern civilization if it escalated to a nuclear exchange? Things had gotten more complicated very quickly!

"Gentlemen I'm beginning to believe the Cold War never really ended; it just went underground for awhile. Potentially, we could have the same old players involved now, co-allied with Muslim extremists." Doug said, calmly, not wanting to show his own discomfort in this development.

"So are we saying Russia might be involved here?" Ben asked.

"It's possible," Doug said.

"I don't think it is out of the realm of possibility," Bart said, "for Russia to go along with such a plan. Hell, in World War II it began with Russia and Germany on the same side and ended with Russia invading Berlin. Greed can be a powerful motivator. After all, we're talking about knocking off the only super power left in the world. Why wouldn't they want to do that? It's certainly in their best interest, or so they believe!" Bart was now starting to see how such a plan could have come together.

"I can't believe any of it! We need firm intelligence to confirm all of this. We can't be going off half-cocked with something this potentially dangerous going on if it is true. What if the Russians are involved?" Ben asked.

"Eventually, we can get the intelligence, but that's not going to help right now, Mr. Secretary. It's starting to look like we might have a showdown with the Chinese in a few hours!" Doug said, impatiently.

"I don't think we can back down now!" Bart said.

"We're not going to back down, gentlemen! One thing I do know for sure is that four-hundred-thousand innocent citizens have already died, and we couldn't do a damn thing to stop it from happening, so we're sticking to our plans, is that clear?" The President said.

"General Mitchell, do we have enough naval power to defeat the Chinese in the South China Sea?" The President asked.

"They'll have to try and stop us by air, and we have enough aircraft in the area to take care of them. We've estimated that we have a kill ratio of ten to one, and I'm comfortable with that assessment. So, to answer your question, yes we can. We also have three nuclear attack submarines in the area with missiles on board. The Navy will be able to destroy any Chinese naval vessels that may try to challenge our forces," the General said.

"What if they go nuclear and try to hit us here at home?" The President asked cautiously.

"They won't do that, Sir!"

"How do you know?"

"Since they only have the strike capability to hit the West Coast with their missile systems we have the advantage. I don't think they will give any consideration to that option. Conversely, we can hit every major city in China. We have the capacity to make the Chinese mainland a glass parking lot if we want to. And besides, it's doubtful that any of the Chinese missiles will get past our defensive missile shield. But as you know, there are no guarantees in war."

"Yeah, we all know that. Then, as I said before, we will continue with our plans. I don't think we have any other options."

"Yes, Sir, Mr. President."

"General, can we prevent foreign fighter aircraft from approaching from the east, west or north of the Malaysian coast lines, say up to four-hundred miles off shore?" Doug asked.

"We can do that."

"Then let's enforce a no fly zone in those areas. Let's make sure the Chinese and Russians are notified of our intentions in that regard. I want them to understand that, whatever we do in Malaysia is our business; we'll deal with them if we have to!"

"What are the rules of engagement, Sir?" General Miller asked.

"Use deadly force if necessary!"

"Yes, Sir." General Miller walked over and picked up a red phone at the end of the table to notify the staff at Ft. Mead.

No one in the room objected to the President's orders, nor were they shocked. Not since the Cuban Missile Crisis had such momentous decisions with such grave consequences been decided by a United States President.

Flash messages were transmitted to heads of state around the world within minutes of the President's warnings. Almost immediately, protests started coming in from around the world. This new foreign policy of the United States was shocking to the rest of the world and fear was running rampant in the streets of Europe and the Middle East.

Doug was hoping that his plan would work before things went too far and the United States found itself in another world war.

41

February 14th 2013 11:35 p.m.
South China Sea

The radio crackled inside Lt. Colonel Murphy's helmet, "Charlie Tango Alpha, Charlie Tango Alpha, this is Red Sky Leader." The Boeing E-3 AWAC was flying high above the South China Sea two hundred miles northeast of their position. Don Murphy was happy to hear from these Navy guys tonight. The AWAC aircraft would be his eyes in the sky in case some bad guys had plans to sneak up on them during the mission.

"Red Sky, Charlie Tango Alpha, go ahead."

"Yes, Sir, good evening. Thought you would like to know we have some bandits traveling at Mach I in your direction from North East; they're probably Chinese J-10s fighters. We've vectored our F-18 Super Hornet strike force to intercept, over."

"Roger, Red Sky, do you have a radar contact on Charlie Tango Alpha, over," Colonel Murphy asked wanting to know if the AWACS was able to track him, just a precaution to make sure everything was working aboard his B-2.

"Negative, Sir, we have no radar contact with your aircraft, you might as well be invisible!"

"Roger, then we are a 'Go' on our mission." Murphy knew if his aircraft wasn't visible to the AWACS, then the bandits wouldn't stand a chance of seeing them with their radar systems. The only hope the Chinese had was to blindly stumble onto them in the dead of night; that is, if they could make it past the Hornets that were being vectored in the inky darkness into their flight paths.

"Looks like the Chinese want to mix it up!" Major Gibson said.

"Yeah, looks like they're determined to go for a swim in the South China Sea tonight," Murphy said confidently. "Those Hornets are going to ruin their evening!"

"Have you been in anything like this before?"

"Yeah, one of our guys in an F-18 got a glimpse of me over Iraq one night. He got after us pretty good before the controllers told him who we were; we were flying with beacons off so the guy in the F-18 he didn't know we were there. He wouldn't have caught us, though! I went down on the deck using the J-band terrain avoidance mode and kicked it in. He would have had a difficult time putting anything up our pipes; we were so low, I had gold paint from several Mosques on our belly when we landed back home!"

Major Gibson wondered if Murphy was blowing smoke up his ass or if he was really that confident in the B-2 abilities.

"An F-15 Eagle couldn't get on your ass, huh?"

"Nope!" Colonel Murphy shifted his eyebrows up and down, obviously showing off. It was the only part of his face the co-pilot could see.

The Colonel is so cool under pressure, the young officer thought. Going down on the deck tonight over Malaysia wasn't something he wanted to think about right now.

"What about the Malaysian Air Force and their Mig 29s, do you think there's any chance they'll come up?" Both officers had been briefed about the Mig 29s, which had been purchased years earlier by the Malaysian Air Force and were possible combatants.

"Not a chance! They have been moth balled because of the lack of parts! If they get into the air, they'll be shot out of the sky in seconds. They probably know that, so I don't look for them to come up trying to start anything. If we have to come back in a couple of weeks, well, things might be different because they're going to be really agitated if you know what I mean.

"You got that right, Colonel!"

The F-18 Super Hornet under the Command of Captain Jimmy "Tight" Bolger activated and released the first of his four AIM-54C Phoenix missiles. Bolger was happy that the Phoenix missile had been put back into the armaments of the Navy. After briefly being discontinued as a weapon system, the missile system was brought back for special use by the F-18. The missile would again be retired from the fleet very soon, but not before it worked its deadly magic tonight. Tonight, tracking this bandit at just less than one-hundred miles and being able to knock him out of the sky was the way to go, Captain Bolger thought.

The missile released and, quickly, its fiery trail disappeared in the black night at twenty-six thousand feet. The pilot quickly acquired the next target and released the second Phoenix missile.

"Go get um *Spike*!" Captain Bolger whispered under his breath. He had two more bandits and two more missiles, then he would tackle getting his bird back on the deck of the carrier, no easy job on a dark night. His Radar Intercept officer Lt. Malcolm (Skip) Masters was wringing the air for more targets.

Directly off his right wing was Bolger's wingman Captain Mike Rogers and his Radar Officer Mackie Smith. Both men could see the missiles leaving the other F-18s as they flew West-North-West over the South China Sea. Captain Rogers would make sure they had plenty of armament left if any more bandits stumbled into the deadly circle of a hundred miles around the two aircraft.

The first Phoenix missile found its mark, hitting the J-10 Chinese fighter as its pilot desperately tried to climb up while turning sharply to avoid the missile. The Phoenix struck just aft of the left wing blowing the jet fighter in half. The other Chinese pilots heard the first victim of the American Phoenix missile and attempted to break formation and scatter to avoid being hit by the next missile that might find them.

Summarily, all but one of the Chinese J-10s was downed by the single F-18. The last remaining Chinese jet fighter had avoided being hit due to his wild maneuvering in the night sky, but he was moving southeast in the direction of the two F-18s that the Chinese pilot hadn't picked up on his radar yet.

"Hey, Tight, looks like one got away!" Mike Rogers radioed.

"Yeah, I see him. I guess I'll become an Ace next time out."

"Negative, Negative, we can get in closer and get him with a Sparrow!

"No, you get him with your Phoenix."

"Roger, Roger…"

In a matter of a few seconds, Captain Rogers fired his first missile in combat and downed the lone remaining Chinese aircraft high above the ocean.

The B-2 descended to bombing altitude and started the final bomb run towards the Malaysian island of Sibu.

"Charlie Tango Alpha, Red Sky Leader."

"Yeah, go ahead, Red Sky."

"Rest easy boys, the Navy is out to night, the bandits are out of the sky. I repeat, out of the sky!"

"Roger that! Tell those Fighter Jocks thanks for the cover," Murphy said.

"Roger, I will do that! This is Red Sky clear, good luck!"

"Roger Red Sky—"

The bomber was buffeted by slight turbulence as it continued to descend towards the target. The subdued color electronic flight instrumentation glowed in the cockpit. After the plane reached bombing altitude, Murphy would slow the aircraft down to drop the B83 free-fall nuclear device. With their exact position being calculated by satellite, finding the drop zone would be easy.

"Arm weapons systems," Murphy said, as the bomber neared the drop zone.

After several minutes all systems were armed.

"Dan, on your go you are free to release the weapon."

"Roger," he said, as he concentrated on his weapons console.

"Weapon Released! Let's get the hell out of here Colonel!"

The B83 began its free fall through the night as a forty-six Kevlar-nylon ribbon parachute, held by sixty Kevlar suspension lines were instantly deployed by three 4-ft diameter pilot chutes pulling the large chute open with a pop! The parachute system began to reduce the bomb's velocity from six hundred knots to just over forty knots within just a few seconds. Lt. Colonel Murphy advanced the throttles to full power. The B-1 quickly accelerated to get out of the blast zone as fast as the F-118-GE turbofan engines could push them.

"I sure hope there is no one down there," Murphy said cautiously.

"They were warned; that's more than the folks in New York got, and it sure made our job more difficult!"

"Yeah, you're right! Let's just get the hell out of Dodge."

As soon as the bomb was released, an electronic tactical message was relayed to air controllers. In a matter of minutes, the message would be relayed to TCC back at Ft. Meade, then to the White House Situation Room.

The flight path back to Diego Garcia and eventually back home to Whiteman Air Force Base in Missouri would be different, just in case they had been spotted on the way over. The new flight plan would take them up the coast just south of Kuantan on the South China Sea side of the peninsula, then west, passing just south of Lumut. This flight plan would be well north of Kuala Lumpur.

The reality of their mission started to sink in to Colonel Murphy, not that he hadn't thought about it before. He had. He and his co-pilot had just piloted a United States war plane that had released the horrors of a nuclear weapon on the territory of a foreign government. It was at that moment that it sunk in that this American President was going to be different from all his predecessors. Maybe it was going to take all out war to stop these terrorist organizations that were dead set on destroying America. Maybe a war with all the horrors involved would make the supporters of these terrorists turn against them, if the price to support them was perceived to be too high. The President had just upped the stakes in the war.

Lt. Colonel Mike Murphy didn't have to worry about all that; all he had to do was just make an ordinance delivery and that had just been accomplished. The rest, as they say, is history! He'd let this new President worry about the rest.

42

February 15th 2013 9:30 a.m.
White House West Wing

Now the two small tropical islands lying just off the eastern coast of Malaysia no longer existed. Sibu Island and her smaller sister, which had taken millions of years to evolve, had been destroyed in a less than a second. The magnificent powder white sand that had once formed the narrow beaches ringing the islands was gone. Except for a deep circular crater on the bottom of the ocean, there was no other evidence that the islands had ever existed. Now, strangely absent below the surface, were any signs of marine life. Where just a day before countless species of small, colorful tropical fish had darted along the reef, now only a blue void existed. The nuclear warhead weighing less than twenty-five-hundred pounds had, in an instant, displaced millions of tons of coral and rock. All around the globe, sensitive seismic instruments had recorded varying levels of vibration of the earth's crust generated by the powerful blast. The people of Malaysia were now experiencing the pangs of insufferable panic delivered by the United States military. Intelligence reports were now indicating that President Putra was under extreme pressure to step down. The United States had again issued statements to the regime to step down or pay the consequences. Millions of Malaysians were packing their belongings and were now part of a mad exodus to the borders clogging roads to the north and south. The airports were full of screaming people demanding flights out of the country. The Islamic régime had not responded to US demands and, instead, high-ranking individuals along with President Putra had gone into hiding. Numerous political groups immediately organized, and were demanding a change in the government. The President, in fear for his own life, had opted to go to a secure, undisclosed location surrounded by members of Malaysian military for safety.

Doug Ferguson was scheduled to address the American people at 11:00 a.m. eastern time. Prior to that, he would first meet with his closest advisors and then later with a high-level foreign delegation representing European heads of state. The delegation from France, Germany, and Great Britain intended to establish a joint line of communication with the new American President to prevent any further "aggression," as European newspapers were calling it. Without the organizational structure of the United Nations, the world no longer had a collective voice to address the United States. Doug had openly embraced the idea of meeting with the delegation to give Europe's leaders a better understanding of his actions. The President intended to make it clear that, from this point forward, he would offer no quarter to terrorists or to the governments that allowed them to exist within their borders. What had occurred politically, with the election of the Ferguson administration, had been difficult for the Europeans to understand; a victorious "third political party" was something new and different and not yet understood. This new development was fraught with suspicion and apprehension that was now aimed directly at the new President. However, his resolve would become clear enough to Europe after their discussions, Doug thought, as he made his way down to the White House situation room.

He had made the point with his own government, with perfect clarity, that he wouldn't hesitate using a nuclear weapon against any country that supported terrorists from this point forward to protect the American people. With those few words, Doug had ended all efforts by the United States military to win a "guerilla" type war. His focus now would be on those countries, which "*De Facto*" supported Islamic Terrorist groups.

At the moment, the President was much more concerned about the ultimatum that had been given to the Malaysian government less than twenty-four hours earlier.

President Putra had been communicating at length with the rest of the world but not with the United States. The NSC and the President thought this especially troubling since the destruction of Sibu Island had not forced an overthrow of the Putra government. It was becoming evident that the President might have no other choice but to strike again, this time against a Malaysian city! Everything would now hinge on the actions of the Malaysian people themselves if this plan was to work. Of course, ample warning would be given to prevent the deaths of innocent people. A comprehensive list of known terrorists had already been forwarded to the Malaysian government with the usual assurances that these people would get a fair trial.

The first name on the wanted list was Najib Putra. He had, on numerous occasions, urged Islamic terrorists groups to kill Americans anywhere in the world. Information supplied by Mark Latham, postmortem, had become the smoking gun that the President had needed to make the charges stick. There would be no negotiations or mincing of words. Doug had decided that hollow rhetoric was out of the question and immediate action was necessary! He would have to be steadfast in his threats or risk losing the initiative. Diplomacy alone would never solve the kind of problems America was facing; only action could do that now. Doug was resolute in that belief. The government of the United States was teetering on economic collapse, and experts believed it would only take one more catastrophic attack before America's economic foundation would begin to crumble.

For the last several hours, the world's media had been carrying broadcasts from President Putra who was now denouncing what he called, "A vicious act of terrorism against his country!" This hadn't surprised anyone in the President's Cabinet; in fact, this was exactly what they had expected. It was standard operating procedure by terrorist states like Putra's.

The President and the NSC were confident the solution was within their grasp. The use of a nuclear weapon as a catalyst to start a rebellion against a regime was a way to separate the people of Malaysia from its radicals. It was a threat so menacing, so unavoidable, that turning against their leaders was the only viable way to avoid the systematic destruction of their way of life. The regime, through vicious rhetoric, was attempting to whip up support around the world from their Muslim brotherhood. To convince more religious leaders to threatening yet another Jihad against the United States. The problem for President Putra was that over four-hundred-thousand Americans were already dead and more were dying painfully everyday! The American people had turned the page on "fair treatment" for terrorists and those who supported these bloody bastards. The word "negotiate" had been wiped away from America's lexicon for the moment.

The mood within the White House Situation room was tense. The conference table, where so many Presidents had taken council on foreign policy decisions would again be used to make, arguably, one of the most important decisions ever made by a sitting President other than Harry S. Truman.

"Gentleman, let's get started," Doug ordered. "In an hour, I'll be meeting with the European delegation concerning our military actions in Malaysia. Are we still in general agreement with our plan of action?" Events were getting serious fast and he wanted to know what his Cabinet members were thinking.

"Mr. President, I don't think any of us have changed our minds. We need to go forward no matter what the circumstances are! But the real wild card here is what the Europeans have up their sleeves to try and stop us," Ben Atchison said. He knew the Europeans well, and he expected the delegation to put pressure on the Untied States to agree not use another nuclear strike.

"What can they do?" Bart asked.

"I don't think a threat can be ruled out. They'll try anything to bring us around to their point of view. Of course they'll probably start with trade restrictions, but shit, we don't do enough existing business with them now because of all their other trade restrictions, so they must know that's not going to work! Of course, they can use their old standby and start to cover their own asses by whipping up hate against us among their own citizens. After that, it's anybody's guess," Ben said.

"So, you really think they will ask us to 'cease and desist' our actions in Malaysia?" The President asked. Doug knew European leaders were angry because his administration hadn't given them any input in the decision to use nuclear weapons.

"Without a doubt! These people are like the rest of the world; they will never accept unilateral action against another sovereign nation, and their position has always been the same. Ben responded dryly. "It's always been their way to neutralize our Super Power status." Ben was slumped in his chair fatigued by the crisis that was underway.

"So, after such a horrendous attack, they'll turn their backs on us, just like that," the President said. His expression was both aggravated and distant.

"Yes, unless we agree to do things their way. We all knew that before we started down this road, didn't we?" Ben said, looking a little confused about Doug's question.

"This wasn't some little kick in the ankle by these crazy bastards, Ben! I would think after something of this magnitude they would understand our actions! For God sakes they're trying to wipe us off the face of the earth. Don't the Europeans know that?"

"It's not in their best interest, Mr. President," Ben replied simply. "They don't want to get wiped off the face of the earth either, but better us than them!"

"So, in your view, what should we do here, just to confirm we are thinking the same thing?" The President asked.

"I think we need to stand our ground no matter what they say or do!" Bart Foster said interjecting himself into the discussion.

"What if they decide to go to war to stop us? That's a possibility isn't it?" Ben quipped, playing devil's advocate.

"Mr. President, we can't back down now. We are already in a war for our existence. How could we ever back down? That's what makes this action so completely necessary. We don't have a choice!" Bart said, becoming more animated than Doug had ever seen him.

"Mr. President, this whole thing could get pretty ugly if China decides to intervene and back us down by military force!" General Miller said, after Bart paused.

"General, you know I appreciate your concern, but I can't believe that China would consider military action. War games aside, let's focus on the military threat from China first and then, later, we can assess any threats made by the Europeans after my meeting with them."

"Our plan calls for taking out all China's major cities and military installations immediately with our I.C.B.M.s should they try to launch a preemptive strike."

"But can all of this be done with a reasonable expectation of success?" Doug asked, wanting to know General Miller's honest opinion.

"Absolutely, we have invested heavily in our missile defense system. Our defense shield can handle whatever China decides to throw at us. They won't have much of a chance of landing a nuclear warhead on United States soil. But I have to warn you, Mr. President, that millions on their side will die in an exchange like this. The world has never seen this kind of destructive force!"

"Does anyone have any questions about the assessment?" The President asked.

"Not on military action, but another problem just as important is starting to develop here at home."

"Let's hear it then!"

"We have some weak knees starting to develop in Congress. I'm not sure we can get them to go along," Leonce said.

"You mean against China?"

"Yes."

"It's too late. They have already given me that power!"

"I know, Sir, but there might be some serious politics at work here to get rid of us. I'm starting to hear the word impeachment coming up," Leonce said.

"Yeah, I've heard the same shit, but they're not serious. The American people would have their asses over something like this so soon after an election; it's just a threat, it will never happen!" John Tolbert said, confidently.

"That's something you guys will have to work on. I've got to do my job right now!" Doug said.

"Don't worry about it, Mr. President," John said, confidently.

The President welcomed his foreign visitors to the White House. Doug had never personally met any of the senior diplomats who sat in front of him. The President, although new to office, recognized the fact that this was an unusual meeting. It was a quick response by the European leaders to make their views known to the new President, a person the European delegation knew very little about. It hadn't been possible to hold direct meetings with leaders of Europe because of the attack in New York. Now, the European leaders had the opinion that world affairs were spiraling out of control and this new American President's unprecedented actions were the reasons why. This was one of the few times in American History that a sitting President had not held cordial meetings with European leaders prior to serious international policy decisions. After all, these leaders, together with the United States, felt that they controlled world events.

President Ferguson shook hands with each of the career diplomats representing Great Britain, France, and Germany.

"I welcome you to the White House, and I extend a warm welcome from our country to yours," Doug said, as he sat down in a large upholstered chair across from his three visitors.

"Mr. President, we would like to thank you for seeing us in such an unusual forum. Soon, you will be having formal meetings with the leaders of each of our countries, but due to the serious nature of the actions taken by the United States, our countries thought this meeting might better communicate our interests." Jack Tony was a senior diplomat assigned to the British Embassy in Washington D.C. a large, bulky man with strawberry colored cheeks. His gold rim glasses hung on the end of his nose as his blue eyes peered directly over the top of them at the President of the United States.

"I must apologize for not inviting you previously, but as you can imagine we have been very busy with the grievous and cowardly attack on our nation. We have suffered grave and unimaginable losses," Doug said gravely.

"That is quite alright. We certainly understand the situation you're faced with, Mr. President. Let me start by saying we would like to speak off the record because of the unusual nature of this meeting. We are here informally, on a fact-finding mission representing loosely all of Europe," Ambassador Tony said, with look of genuine seriousness that couldn't be dismissed.

"Explain how that is possible. I mean informally representing Europe and all? I don't quite understand what you are saying, Mr. Ambassador." Doug said.

"Let me explain, if I could. Our leaders met in Paris yesterday and because of the enormous stakes here, we as a group of diplomats were given a number of policy proposals that were to be informally presented to you, Mr. President," The Ambassador from Germany said. Ambassador Helmut Stein was a small man who looked more like an administrative assistant to the British Ambassador. "We are one of the United States' staunchest allies," he said, as if he was too new in his job too to know that tidbit of history.

The President had already begun to sense that he wasn't going to like what these diplomats had to say. Both Jack Tony and Helmut Stein oozed with European arrogance! Other than the simple greeting and a limp handshake from the French diplomat, he could only imagine what the professional French diplomat thought of him.

"Mr. Ambassador, the United State is fortunate to have such important allies, and of course, we want to do everything in our power to continue to cooperate with our NATO partners and with the EU in particular," Doug said earnestly.

"Well, Mr. President, there is a great deal of consternation among not only our leaders but our general population about what is happening in America," Jack Tony continued, cautiously attempting to feel out the President.

"You mean of course about our losses in New York?" The President hadn't lived such a lackluster, back-woods existence that he didn't see the opportunity to set the tone for the entire conversation to follow.

"No Mr. President, while all of us and our countryman are shocked and saddened by the events in New York, I'm speaking about your military's action in Malaysia, Sir."

Continuing to play the part of the somewhat slow dimwit from Alabama, the President said, with a perplexed expression, "You mean dropping a bomb on a small uninhabited island in the middle of the ocean, is that what you are referring too, sir?"

"Well, Mr. President, we think it is more than just that," Jack Tony said, somewhat timidly starting to sense that the conversation wasn't going in the direction he had intended.

"What he means, Mr. President, if I might speak," the French Ambassador spoke for the first time. Phillip Dupre' seemed to be a bit more arrogant than the other two men. His body language was stiff and unfriendly, unusual for a diplomat, the President thought. "We believe that this act perpetrated on another sovereign nation violates international law, and that the United States, as a well-meaning civilized country, should consult with its allies before risking war with other nations," he said, as if preaching to the President in a tone that bordered on arrogance.

The statement of the French Ambassador didn't surprise the President, nor did his attitude. In fact, the only thing that surprised him was his unfriendly attitude towards a man he had never met. Still, Doug knew personalities or personal friendships would not enter into this discussion.

"Mr. Ambassador, I respect your opinion. How could I not?" Doug said, as he bent forward at the waist seemingly to make a point. "After all, it is your opinion, and you certainly have a right to have it. But I see my opinion as every bit as important as you see your own. I'm sure you can understand that simple premise. Now having said that, let me explain the position of my government. The international law that you speak of so highly has never stopped one single attack that I know of by any country since its inception. And furthermore, the purpose the World Court serves is only to determine who is to blame after an action has taken place. I have always noticed, as a minor historian, that where war is involved, the rulings of the World Court seem to always agree with the victor not the vanquished. For the sake of argument, I will use as an example the end of World War I and World War II, where the court was useful in determining many things about the losers of that war. I hope you don't misunderstand me. I respect the international rule of law, but when it is violated, there doesn't seem to be an effective enforcement arm to bring justice to those who have been hurt. For months, the leader of Malaysia has stood in front of the world and has urged his followers to kill innocent Americans, and we have irrefutable evidence that they have done just that! Now, any reasonable person would be forced to ask what has the world court done to prevent that from happening. I am forced to say, nothing, Sir. So you must understand, Mr. Ambassador, that we, the United States of America, as a sovereign nation, have the right to protect ourselves. However, I'm a bit perplexed at the moment, because I have seen no statements or actions by the World Court in this affair," Doug said calmly, with a directness that was meant to intimidate.

"We can't do that at the moment! Malaysia is a sovereign nation and will need time to respond to these allegations," the French Ambassador said, arrogantly.

"So, even as we sit here under the threat of another nuclear attack on our soil, we will need months, maybe even years, to sort this whole thing out in the World Court, is that what you're saying?" Doug asked.

"We must respect the law, Mr. President, no matter how inconvenient it can be at times," the French Ambassador said, as a matter fact.

"Then it is settled, we will take care of our own security until the International Court decides to take a position!" Doug said, after the French Ambassador had responded.

"Mr. President, you simply don't understand our position in this matter! This situation is grave and dangerous and we are only attempting to help settle our differences here," Ambassador Dupré complained.

"Well, Sir, allow me to vigorously disagree with you once again. European leaders are not doing all that they can to help my country! Furthermore, I believe that your governments have sown the seeds of discontent with your citizens for years against the government of our country. Your politicians have done this for their own selfish political purposes. Now, you expect me to feel obliged to give in to yourself serving demands? That will not happen, Sir. If you have a population that is upset and angry with the United States, then you need to deal with that problem, since much of it was caused by your own politicians. Just because you have convinced your citizenry to believe in the rule of international law, doesn't mean that you will convince our nation to do so as well. If that system now fails you, I'm not sure what you expect us to do about that," The President said defiantly.

"With all due respect, Mr. President, that is an outrageous collective condemnation of all our countries," the French Ambassador complained losing his composure.

Doug remained calm as he leaned back in his chair again. He took a moment to look at all three men that sat across from him. The silence became deafening. After several minutes, the three career diplomats started to show signs of nervousness. It was obvious to Doug that they didn't know how to restart the conversation.

"Gentleman," Doug said, finally, breaking the protracted silence, "what you haven't been able to understand is that the people of this country have spoken! They fully understand what we are up against now, and they also understand that Europe isn't going to come to our rescue. We feel that we will either prevail or perish. We as a nation can no longer look at these attacks as isolated acts of violence perpetrated by just a few extremists. Our people and our economy cannot survive another attack like the one that took place in New York. The terrorists and those who support them have declared war on us! Certainly European nations understand that concept. Let me assure you that I'm going to do everything in my power to stop those who will make any further attempts to attack my country! Now, unless your governments can guarantee that we will not be attacked again, we need to move on to the next subject, if there is one," The President said softly and deliberately.

"Mr. President, you know that we can't guarantee another country's safety, but we can negotiate between your government and theirs until the United Nations is up and running again," Tony said, reentering the conversation, desperately attempting to lure the President back into negotiations.

"Mr. Ambassador, I don't think you quite understand what I've just said! The terrorists chose the United Nations building as ground zero. They have made a statement, a strong statement. That statement is extremely clear. They don't see the United Nations as useful to their cause, and frankly, Sir, nor does the United States at this moment—"

"With all due respect, Mr. President, we believe that with certain economic incentives, the Malaysian government can be brought around to our way of thinking and provide long-term security to the world," the British Ambassador said.

"Forgive me, Sir, for not agreeing. We have wasted enough time discussing our differing opinions. What the United States demands at this moment is the complete and uncompromised support of her allies. Unless your governments are ready to pledge their total support, then I suspect we are finished here," the President said, as he stood up to signal the meeting was over.

"Mr. President, you know your actions could start a war with the People's Republic of China and that could lead to a world war," the French Ambassador said in a grave voice.

"If that is what they want, then unfortunately, that is what they will get. The United States has no other viable options. We are bleeding to death here! We will not sit idly by and watch our country endure another nuclear attack, nor can we allow the People's Republic of China to decide the fate of our Nation."

The three men realized the meeting had just come to an abrupt end with nothing having been accomplished. They slowly rose from their seats and began to walk out of the room.

43

February 15th 2013
Peninsula of Malaysia

"I'll never leave this land!" President Putra uttered feebly to his defense minister, a senior member of his Guardian Council. Najib Putra, a thin. rather studious looking man in his mid sixties, wore large, square-framed glasses, which tended to magnify his dark brown, almost black, eyes. He was wearing a long black thobe of a Muslim religious leader with a wide, flat turban, accented with white piping rounding the top. His father, Almad, had studied under the Iranian Mullahs including the Ayatollah Khomeini, who had worked so hard to begin the revolution that finally overthrew the Western-controlled Shaw. So, as a young man in the 1970s, young Najib had witnessed firsthand the Islamic revolution that had swept across Iran like a Holy fire. After his family returned to their native Malaysia, his father began his final struggle, a revolution to overthrow the western-style democracy that ruled the country. Although his father hadn't lived long enough to see his dreams come true, his son Najib had. The oldest of three brothers, Najib had suffered side-by-side for years with his father to make this dream become a reality, but he had lost both of his brothers in the conflict. After coming to power, he issued a "Fatwa" against all Americans worldwide! After all, it had been the Americans who had tried to aid the government of Malaysia in stopping his father's revolution. Now, the Fatwa he had issued, coupled with his support in the bombing of New York, endangered his regime. But Najib felt no remorse for his actions, nor would he; it was God's work that he was to doing. He wondered quietly to himself if Allah would intervene or would he have to become a Martyr in this great struggle.

The once powerful President was now hiding from the forces that would attempt to break his grip from the government he had worked so hard to control. He was living in the only underground bunker complex in Malaysia that could withstand the effects of a nuclear blast. The complex had been built years earlier by the prior government for important government officials by a German company. The multi-layered tunnel system was built over three-hundred feet below the surface. The cool climate control room with thick concrete walls was in stark contrast to Najib Putra's sprawling mansion on the coast, a palace full of bright, sunlit rooms and verdant flowering flora that adorned the courtyards.

"Will we choose to die as Martyrs, Holy One?" The defense minister asked faithfully.

"Sadly, I think it may come to that if our friends in China do not come to our aid."

"What about the women and children your holiness, will they have to die as Martyrs as well, if the Americans decide to rain death down on our homeland?"

"They don't deserve to live. They have never been faithful Muslims and most have ignored the wishes of Allah! I hope you remember how we had to sacrifice ourselves for them during the revolution. It was us, the revolutionaries, who fought to overthrow the government, not them! Don't you remember?" Putra asked indignantly. "Has your memory faded?"

"But there are many innocents, Holy One!"

"They are unfit to meet Allah in the afterlife, so it's not a matter I will concern myself with, nor should you!" Putra was sitting in a large, luxurious, royal-blue chair rather than his usual cross-legged position on the ground as he always did in public, for the masses. The chair sat in stark contrast to the cold concrete walls and floors in the bunker.

"But there are innocent women and children who will die, Holy One, and the Koran says…"

"Silence! This isn't the time," Putra said, as he reached for a glass of orange juice sitting on a small mahogany table beside him. "We will not give in to the unjust infidels just to save the nonbelievers, never! They will have to suffer as we have to suffer!" he said, before he took a small sip of the juice and set it back on the table.

The Minster didn't respond. He now attempted to try to hide his despair from Putra. He was a deeply religious man who believed in the Islamic Republic but feared that he would now have the blood of millions on his hands if he didn't convince his supreme leader to become a Martyr on his own, without taking millions of innocent women and children with him.

"I want our military to kill as many American infidels as possible when they invade our land!" Putra said to the defense minister.

"Holy One, I don't believe they will send their soldiers this time. The American President has said…"

"It's a trick, a vile lie to keep us off guard! I know these Americans; they're soft! They'll never kill innocent people. They don't have the stomach for that. If we can draw enough blood from them, they will run. That this is their history. They always give up and run!" There was a moment of silence as the defense minister contemplated his order. He was positive that there would be no invasion. "I will get the message out to the military…Holy One," he said, in a submissive voice.

Panic was growing on the streets of every city on the Peninsula. In Kuala Lumpur, hundreds of thousands of people were frantically streaming from the city in a state of terror. Cars were backed up for hundreds of miles with horns blasting incessantly in a desperate attempt to get out of the target area. The nuclear blast at Sibu Island and the threat of another had undermined the stability of the country. The people were convinced it was partly the actions of their own government that had been responsible for provoking the attack by the United States. Now they believed the American President was enraged and was looking to revenge the losses of his people. The government had forcibly shut down every newspaper in the country to stop the growing panic, but this action had only heightened the fears of the people. They expected a nuclear attack at any second and feared their government was withholding information.

Doug Ferguson was getting regular briefings from the CIA from operatives on the ground. Things were going badly for the Putra Government. The religious dictator was unable to stop the growing panic that was sweeping across his country. The effects of the bomb dropped on Sibu had rattled windows all over the southern part of the peninsula, but feeding the panic were millions of e-mails that were being sent to private citizens from the United States government warning people to get out of Kuala Lumpur before the next detonation.

The NSC knew that a new upstart government, if one should be organized, would have very little time to round up, then turn over, members of the JI party. However, Doug had started broadcasting a message of hope via the CIA and TCC to operatives in Malaysia. The United States would work with the new government, should they be able to capture Putra and hand him over immediately to US authorities. A new government would then be formed and members of terrorist groups could be hunted down methodically. This would give the new government time to round up the rest of the terrorists on the most-wanted list. The majority of Malaysian citizens were convinced that Putra would never negotiate and would take the rest of the country into a nuclear holocaust before he would give in to the demands of the western infidels. This defiant attitude had resulted in even more hysteria among the citizens who were now convinced that Armageddon was at hand. The chaos had resulted in a complete breakdown in Malaysia's economy as banks refused to open. Most of the population was on the run, trying to avoid being killed in this war of wills between the American government and President Putra. They believed that America would strike again and soon! The internal systems of the government were starting to shut down as people fled for their lives, making things even more difficult for the regime. Anger was at a boiling point within Malaysia towards the United States for its actions, but there were no American troops to strike back against! But there was also rage and anger being directed at the Malaysian government by the people whose lives were now threatened. People on the street believed all of this was senseless, and the attack on the US had been a serious mistake, something that shouldn't have been done and that their supreme leader was culpable. Since the American President was making it clear that no ground troops would be used in this conflict, most Malaysians were convinced that they were right in the nuclear crosshairs of the United States military.

February 15th 7:30 am
West Wing

United States spy satellites had begun streaming back images of Southern bases in China, where the Chinese military was beginning to mass on their southern border. Most military analysts believed that this was the gathering of a military strike force to be used if the United States invaded the peninsula of Malaysia. Members of the TCC were in direct contact with Peking and tense dialogue was flashing back and forth between the two governments. Doug was monitoring all communications but not taking direct control of those negotiations yet. The Chinese were threatening war against the United States for shooting down four of their fighter aircraft in the South China Sea. The United States negotiators were making it clear that the President was acting out of self defense and wouldn't tolerate China's involvement in the dispute. The primary function of the TCC now was to feed carefully-chosen classified materials to the Chinese government as proof that President Putra was responsible for the attack in New York, of course something the Chinese already knew.

Doug had just walked into the situation room for an emergency meeting that he had called just an hour earlier.

"Good morning, Gentleman," Doug said, as he entered the room. The NSC members had been busy all morning preparing themselves for the meeting, a meeting that could usher in a nuclear nightmare.

"Is everyone ready?" All members nodded. "Then let's start with you, General."

General Miller moved his laptop slightly to view the screen better in the available lighting and said, "Gentlemen, the situation with the Chinese is becoming more serious by the minute. Our operation on the Peninsula has forced them into a war footing and they are beginning to make overt actions to confront a possible invasion of Malaysia. As you know, we have an ongoing dialogue with them via the TCC, but nothing has been worked out as of yet. The good news is that they are still talking to us! The real threat here is that they will attempt to invade the same areas that we are threatening. If that happens, we will be in a full blown war against China. Currently, we are letting the Chinese know that any military move towards Malaysia will constitute an act of war and that we will attack their military force as it advances. We are making it clear that our military we will engage their forces if necessary. We have additional aircraft carriers steaming to the area, and we have B-52s, B-1s, and B-2s on alert to engage the enemy should he decide to attack. Currently, we don't have enough air power in the area to fight the entire Chinese Air Force, but we will within a few hours. Let me assure you of this, we're in a very fluid situation here, and anything could happen."

"Mr. President, have we informed the Chinese that we know about their involvement in all of this?" Leonce asked. He considered the Chinese as a future enemy whether all this was resolved, or not. "They must know by now we are serious."

"Not yet. There's no reason at this point to ratchet up this confrontation. However, if they continue to press us, we will certainly let them know that we consider their involvement in the attack on New York as an act of war!" Doug answered.

"You know, Mr. President, that our Allies aren't going to back us in a war with the Chinese! They can't support us politically, because they have convinced their own people that we're the aggressors. To attempt to change things now would be impossible for them. The way it looks to me, we've got a serious problem. The Russians and the Chinese are going to become allies against us if war breaks out, and Europe being Europe, is just going to stand by and try and stay out of the whole thing. That pretty much leaves us all alone in this conflict! We're going to have to manage this war, if there is a war, very carefully. We need to string this confrontation out over time, solve one problem before we get into another. We can't fight the entire world at one time; we don't have the military assets to do that. In my opinion, we must do everything possible to keep the Chinese at bay until we settle this crisis in Malaysia and then start warning Russia not to get involved. We've got to isolate the Malaysian government from China. If we can't do that, we'll lose the initiative and none of this will work," Bart said. He had already, mentally, walked through every situation he could think of. He stared across the table at General Miller, hoping he was up to the fight if it came to it. He wasn't sold that the General could pull this off.

"I don't think we have any choice but to manage it that way! The problem with an all-out war is this, the aftermath of such a war would be untenable and leave the world in a situation where no one can survive. I know we can't survive the social or economic outcome of an all-out nuclear conflict," General Miller added. The General believed their strategy, if events got out of control, could end up becoming one of the largest military blunders of all time. But, like the President, he had agreed there were no other viable options.

Bart didn't like Miller's assessment, but he didn't comment.

"Mr. President, if I could break in here," John said.

"Go ahead."

"Mr. President, the news media has started to release stories about the incident with China, and there is speculation that we are about to go to war. Of course, members of Congress are shaken by these new developments, God, who wouldn't be! If things continue as they are now, our support in the House will start to deteriorate quickly. Doug, people are afraid. We need to start briefings as soon as possible. I'm aware that secrecy is important, but they are screaming over there for more information."

"I understand, but for the moment, we're not doing that. Too many leaks come out of there and, besides, I'm not going to get caught up in a political battle right now. The minute that happens, we will be involved in endless debates with Congress as one side maneuvers against the other for power, and we will be in the middle. If we need political help, I would prefer to take my case to the American people. If the politicians get upset with that, then so be it! We don't have time for politics as usual right now," Doug said defiantly.

The mood in the room had become gloomy over the past ten minutes. It seemed that the new administration had more problems than could be addressed. Time was running out for the Malaysian city of Kuala Lumpur and the President's plan. If the ultimatum was not met, then Doug would have to make a decision. He would either live up to his word or back down from his threats, both were undesirable options.

"Mr. President, we are ready to begin the blockade," General Miller said. "We are just waiting for your orders, Sir."

Bart hoped Miller's plan was up to the demands of the actions being taken against the United States.

"Have we already blocked the South China Sea and the Straits of Malacca?" The President asked.

"Yes, Mr. President, that's been done."

"Then that should do it for now! If anyone is thinking about sending ground troops into this operation, forget it. We will not send troops into harm's way!" No one had mentioned this contingency, yet, but the President wanted to end any thoughts of moving away from the plan.

"I agree! If we threaten to use weapons of mass destruction and then cave in to international pressure, everything will be lost!" Leonce said.

"But Leonce we're not going to kill innocent people!" Doug sensed Leonce would be willing to strike the cities regardless of who was occupying them. "We all agreed this was going to be nothing more than a bluff, but if necessary we would bomb evacuated cities making them uninhabitable as punishment."

"What if the people won't leave?" Leonce responded coldly. "What if they defy us, what then?"

"We will confront that problem when it happens, but not until then!" Doug said.

44

February 16th 2013 0:635 a.m.
USS Kitty Hawk South China Sea

Captain John Taylor scanned the horizon with his binoculars, more of a habit than anything else. The South China Sea was relatively calm as the *Kitty Hawk* made her way to the southeast, while the sun climbed above a yellow horizon and slightly overcast skies.

"Captain, we have just received a "FLASH" encrypted message for you, Sir." A young Ensign handed the messages over to the Captain.

"Have you read the message?" he said, looking up at the young officer."

"Negative, Sir!"

Captain Taylor held strict to the "need to know" rule concerning secret documents. He didn't want the whole crew to find out what might or might not be happening; they would have to wait for orders just like he did.

CINCPACFLT
Commanding Officer (CV-63)
Attack Imminent. China Threat
Level One. Proceed to 5N 103E.
Defend Maleast N/S. God Speed.

Captain Taylor read the message quickly and placed it in his trouser pocket. He had just been ordered to protect the Eastern Coast of the Malaysian Peninsula against an invasion force of the Army of the People's Republic of China, which was now considered "imminent" by CINCPACFLT! He then ducked back inside the gray metal hatchway leading to the bridge.

"Get Commander Olson up here, please." The Captain said to the Junior Grade officer.

Captain John Taylor was a forty-eight-year-old Commanding Officer of the nuclear powered USS Kitty Hawk. As a graduate of the Naval Academy, he had come up through the ranks serving USS FORRESTRAL (CV-59) as Operations Officer and, later on, the USS Theodore Roosevelt (CVN-71), before becoming the Commanding Officer of the USS Kitty Hawk. He was just under six-foot, two-inches tall and, at one-hundred and eighty-five pounds, he looked trim and fit. As with most Navy Captains, he wasn't overtly friendly with the enlisted men but was well respected and generally liked by everyone. He worked out daily and could still bench press over two -hundred and fifty pounds. Captain Taylor had taken part in both Iraq wars and was a seasoned Naval Officer. His short-cropped brown hair had started to turn gray around the temples. There was no flare to his command; he was a no-nonsense commander. He was a hard-nosed Naval Officer more out of the old navy rather than the new one. He still valued his commission as one of the most important milestones of his life.

"Captain." Tom Olson stepped up behind the Captain having just come on to the bridge.

He pulled the orders out of his trouser pocket, unfolded it, then handed it to his Executive Officer to read.

"Well, looks like the Chinese may want to get involved in this confrontation!" He said, looking at the Captain and handing the message back.

"Yeah, this whole damn thing could get ugly quick! Let's steam southwest to our assigned latitude and longitude and, Tom, let's get some eyes in the sky as well. We don't want any surprises."

"Aye, Aye, Sir"

Captain Taylor hoped that this new President knew what he was doing; a war with the Chinese, although winnable, would be messy as hell.

The battle group quickly received their orders and started moving at full speed farther southeast to protect the east coast of Malaysia from any invading force that might attempt to breach their position by sea or air. Satellite information was streaming into his ship's command center. Chinese War Ships had already put to sea and were steaming in their direction. The two Seawolf Class Submarines were being positioned between the Kitty Hawk and the Chinese Strike force to the Northeast. Any ship attempting to get near the Kitty Hawk or any of their strike force vessels would be sunk by one of the two nuclear attack submarines long before air cover would be needed.

Washington D.C.
The Pentagon

Admiral Peter McMurray, a thirty-year Naval Officer, was in charge of the force now steaming towards the Chinese. He had been promoted to "Fleet Admiral" just the day before and was now in charge of redeployment of United States naval forces around the world. He sat overseeing this deployment in the Pentagon War Room, now a frantic hub of desperate activity. Of critical importance to the Admiral was moving his forces out of naval bases in Rota, Spain, and Naples, Italy, as quickly as possible along with naval aircraft out the Naval Air Station located in Sigonella, Italy. It was critical that forces be evacuated from territory that might become hostile in a matter of hours. He had been warned that the Europeans might not side with the US actions against China. This evacuation was a critical part of the United States' war plan. If US forces were caught in port, they could be seized by European military should they make a military decision to neutralize United States Naval forces. The seventh fleet in the Pacific had already been ordered to put to sea for a possible confrontation with China. With sixty-two ships, it was the largest by far of all of the US fleets around the world. The Air Force was busy moving aircraft out of Europe as quickly as it could be accomplished, to bases in Keflakik, Iceland, Guam, and back to the United States, to keep them out of harm's way and in a more defensive deployment. The Untied States was mobilizing for war against any foe that might raise objections to operations in Malaysia. Rapid redeployment was underway with all American military assets around the world! The Admiral was in constant communications with his naval forces as they steamed out of the Mediterranean and into the Atlantic.

Admiral McMurray had also redeployed all eighteen trident submarines around the world. In effect, this force of Ohio Class boomers was being placed strategically to destroy any Nation that decided to oppose the United States' actions. Each submarine carried twenty-four missiles that could be rapidly launched in less than one minute. This massive nuclear deterrent was the "wild card" that had to be taken into consideration by any nation wishing to oppose the United States. In a matter of days, this deadly doomsday force would be silently waiting for the order to destroy any country that decided to make an attempt to stop the United States attacks worldwide. World leaders were being briefed by the TCC of the deployment for war. For the moment, world leaders were frozen in a state of disbelief.

Washington D.C.
White House President's Private Quarters

After watching the major news networks for hours, Doug turned the T.V. off. Tony was on his way up to see the President, sensing he might need company. Due to Doug's busy schedule, Tony hadn't really seen a lot of his boss and wondered if his services were really needed any longer. He didn't particularly like Washington D.C. and wanted to get back home as soon as possible. The prospect of staying in Washington for the next four years really didn't have a lot of appeal to him.

"How's it going, boss?" Tony said, casually as he entered.

"Hey, come on in, you Cajun cracker! Can I get you something to drink?" He stood up and walked over to the bar.

"Yeah, some Wild Turkey and water will do it!"

"I got some really great scotch if you like?"

"The Turkey will do, but don't drown the bird."

"You got it." The President pulled a crystal scotch glass out and looked back at Tony.

"I don't need crystal; plastic's fine if you got it!" Tony said, smiling.

"We don't have plastic around here, you redneck!"

The President handed Tony his drink then walked over and sat back down in a leather chair.

"Tony, I'm not sure that this was the best thing that I could have done. I knew having this job would be really difficult, but I never imagined it would be like this," the President said. He was lounging in a blue, button-down oxford shirt open at the collar and black suit pants.

"Yeah, I'm starting to feel the same way, and I'm not the President!"

"So this is getting to you too?"

"I'd be telling you a lie if I said it wasn't; sure it is. I liked it a hell of lot better when we were private citizens."

"I'm sure that's the way everybody feels when the weight of the job is placed on their shoulders; this is a hell of a big job."

"Well, I feel like a prisoner, here, if you want to know how I feel!" Tony moved to a chair directly across from Doug. "For the next four years, we're screwed, my friend, so we might as well finish the job while we're here."

Doug continued to sip scotch from his glass. It appeared to Tony that Doug had aged ten years. He was well dressed and shaved, but he still looked haggard. Tony had already seen the changes. Doug wasn't as happy. How could anyone be happy with the world so screwed up? Tony sorely missed seeing the happy-go-lucky Doug Ferguson he knew back in Montgomery. He missed the good times, too, the golf and riding down to New Orleans in the black Suburban on business trips. The banter between them that used to go on every day had all but stopped, now. But Tony knew Doug was committed to solving the problems of the American people, and like most people, he hoped he could.

"You know, Tony, I never knew how many enemies this country had around the world, and to tell you the truth, I never knew how many enemies I personally would have just taking the oath to this job. Right about now, I wish we could just go fishing and leave all this behind us. I sound like a quitter don't I?"

"No, no one should have to face what we're facing now, it's really tough."

"But, having a beer on Bourbon Street and listening to a good band with no worries seems appealing at the moment, remember that?"

"Yeah, that was before all the campaigning for President started!" Tony looked perturbed.

"You sound a little fired up." Doug said, as he took another sip of scotch.

"I guess I am, don't get me wrong, I know somebody's got to do this crazy job, but hell, I wish it was someone else doing it!"

Doug didn't respond. He couldn't. He had volunteered for all this.

Finally, he said, "maybe I've been too aggressive, maybe even reckless. You know what people are going to say! Maybe they'll think I'm doing all of this out of anger!" Doug moved his glass around and around in a circle while he stared down into the glass.

"I don't think so! These guys are responsible for slaughtering a lot of innocent people. Someone has to make these blood-thirsty bastards accountable. Our country hasn't had the strength and determination to do this before now, that's why you were elected. This is exactly what the country wants; they want you to protect them!"

"I wish I was as sure as you are, Tony."

"Well, you were a few months ago, remember?"

"Yeah, that was before I knew how dangerous this world is! I mean I knew it was dangerous, but a nuclear bomb set off by terrorist in New York? I'm just a small-time ex-governor from the South. Maybe I'm not equipped to handle all of this."

"You want to know what I think?" Tony asked.

"Yeah, sure let's hear it." Doug said.

"I know your instincts, and they are always good. I've watched you for years, and you always seem to know what is going on in the other guy's head. You're going to have to go with your instincts here, too. If you can get these terrorists in Malaysia and hold them responsible for supporting this attack, then we have a decent chance of winning this thing. We will win because these bloody bastards who run these shit-hole countries that support terrorism will want to stay in power above all things; they'll play ball; that's what you've been saying all along. We've just got to make sure the other side doesn't let them off the hook, like China or Russia. The trick is holding their feet to the fire! The world has to know you're serious, and that there's no one who can stop you."

"Yeah, I know you're right, but it is much more complicated than that. Right now, I have war ships steaming into harm's way, and China is rattling their sword and threatening us."

"Boss, someone has to figure a way out of this. This is a dangerous world and nobody is going to stand up for the interests of the American people except the American people themselves, that's why you were elected!"

"Tony, I know that, and I don't want to sound indecisive, but I am worried that I might be starting something we won't be able to finish."

"Anyone would feel like you do, but I say the hell with the rest of the world; they're certainly not worried about us!" Tony said. The President barely heard his words as he drifted back into his thoughts.

February 17th 2013 06:30 a.m.
West Wing of the Whitehouse

The President walked into the White House situation room.

"Good Morning, Mr. President," All the Cabinet members said in unison.

"Good Morning, Gentlemen. Let's get started. What's coming in from TCC?"

"Mr. President, we have some more troubling news from NSA." Bart said.

"Well, let's have it, what's going on?" Doug said, as he took his seat at the conference table, careful not to show his emotions.

"We've got total silence coming out of Malaysia at the moment. They're not communicating with anybody. We're not picking up communications from them at NSA."

"So they have stopped communicating with the outside world?" Doug asked, as he took a cube of sugar and dropped it into a dark blue cup, full of coffee, that had just been placed in front of him.

"Apparently."

"So has Putra left the country, or is he just waiting to become a Martyr?"

"We don't have intelligence on that, to be truthful. We really don't know what's going on," Bart said.

"So, there's just silence? We're telling them we might obliterate Kula Lumpur and they are ignoring us?" Doug asked.

"That's exactly what's happening. The lines are just dead," Bart said.

"Can this get any worse? We are trying to hold these sons of bitches responsible and they won't answer the damn phone! How is that possible?"

"I don't know, Sir. Maybe they are saying 'do what you want, we can't stop you,'" General Miller said.

"Well, I want our intelligence people to find out."

"There's more bad news. The Chinese war ships have put to sea and satellite photos show them moving southwest towards our task force," General Miller said.

"Do we have enough forces in place to prevent them from interfering militarily without using a nuclear strike?"

"We do, Sir, if our estimates are correct! You know, if our kill ratios are correct. We have a huge technological advantage, here. I'm sure we will prevail, Mr. President."

"Let's make sure that we are ready to take all their major cities out if they decide to go nuclear!" Doug said.

"Mr. President, with all due respect, I wouldn't put all my trust in the Nuclear Defense Shield, I'm confident it will work, but there aren't many half measures in war. I suggest we launch our nukes against them now and destroy the Chinese attack group at the same time, Mr. President," General Miller said. "We shouldn't wait. They're coming at us right now; they must know what that means; they know what can happen!"

"No, we're not going to do that, General, not yet anyway."

Doug tried to stay calm, but it was hard to believe what he was hearing.

"But Mr. President, they might get lucky and take out one of our major west coast cities. This lack of action could kill millions of Americans. We must act now in my opinion, with full force!" General Miller argued.

"No, let's wait. That's why we built the missile defense shield, to ensure we can protect ourselves. I think the Chinese would be suicidal to try to attack us with nukes. We've got time, General, so let's just stand down on firing missiles at China. Let's keep a steady hand here," Doug said calmly.

"Mr. President, do we have your permission to strike the Chinese forces in the South China Sea?" General Miller asked for clarification.

"General, your forces have their battle plan, and I am authorizing the use of that plan when our forces are ready."

"Thank You, Mr. President." The General motioned to a young Army officer and signed a document in front of him. After signing the paper, he gave it to the officer who left the situation room.

"Ben, what have our friends in Europe had to say about all of this?" Doug asked.

"Mr. President, TCC has informed our Allies in Europe about the situation with China and, of course, they are nervous and want us to halt our actions in both Malaysia and in the South China Sea."

"What else would you expect? What, they have some kind of financial deal for us?" Doug said sarcastically.

"No, just plenty of demands."

"General Miller have we detected any military activity on their part?"

"Not yet, Mr. President."

"Well, see there's some good news!" The President said, with a wry smile.

"Mr. President, I think the General is right. We need to be wary of the capabilities of our MDS. I wouldn't count on it to defend our country. After all, it hasn't been adequately tested, and no one knows if it even works!" Leonce protested.

"We're going to have to wait, Leonce. We need to see if we can bluff the Chinese down, not destroy them!"

"Long-term, I don't think it matters much. Sooner or later, we are going to have a confrontation with them. I suggest we exploit our advantage right now. After all, Mr. President, they have had a hand in all of this." Leonce pleaded.

"Let's wait everybody and let this thing play out."

"Mr. President, you are taking an awful chance here; millions of American lives are at stake," General Miller added.

"I don't believe that, General! These people are not that foolish. They may have secretly supported suicide bombers, but I don't think they are willing to commit suicide today!"

"God, I hope you're right, Sir!"

A young staffer knocked on the door and entered the cabinet room.

"Mr. President, the TCC wants to come up on video immediately. Would you like me to connect?"

"Yes, please."

"What is it now?" General Miller said, disgusted.

After a few minutes, the screen splashed to life. The image of the person that came up looked vaguely familiar to the cabinet members, but the President recognized him instantly.

"Mr. President, this is Supervisor Tripp. Can you hear me okay?"

"Yeah, Ed, we hear you just fine. What's going on?"

"Well, Sir, I wanted to give you the news myself, because I'm on duty. Mr. President, I'm happy to say there's been a military takeover in Malaysia. The new government is communicating that they have President Putra in custody and many of the top members of the ruling government, and they need instructions."

Doug sat in disbelief. "Could the plan have actually worked?" he thought.

Suddenly, loud cheers went up in the Situation room. Everyone stood up and started applauding and slapping each other on the back. "We did it!" they yelled. Even the usually stoic Bart Foster let his head drop slowly to his hands and stared straight down at the table as tears welled up in his eyes… "Thank God," he whispered.

"Mr. President, Mr. President," Ed broke in again, "I have some additional communications to read to you!" The image on the screen of Ed Tripp looked haggard and unshaven, but calm.

"Go ahead, Ed, what else?"

"The TCC has just spoken to diplomats with the People's Republic of China and they are telling us they are turning back to port with their naval force as we speak!"

Another round of cheers went up in the Cabinet room. "*It's over*," Doug thought. "At least for now."

He sat down in his chair. He had a mild case of the shakes, which he was able to hide from everyone in the room. Events had happened so quickly it had left him totally drained, but elated.

"Gentleman, let's all calm down. We still have more work to do."

"Ben, we need to get in touch with Syria while the iron's still hot!" Doug said.

"Yes sir, Mr. President. I'll contact the TCC immediately!"

Doug steadied himself for the next round of this war—

"What about China?" Leonce asked.

"Trust me, this administration will make our position clear." Doug said.

"What are we going to do to even the score with China?" Leonce asked.

"We are going to depend on our missile defense shield while we demand those individuals in the Chinese government that participated in this massacre be turned over to us!"

"What if they don't?" Leonce pressed.

"You already know the plan," Doug said forcefully.

"I was hoping you would say that, Boss." Leonce said, as he pulled a cigar from his pocket.

45

Friday February 22nd 2013
Mississippi Sound, Horn Island

The President stood on the bow of a twenty-two-foot flats boat in the misting Mississippi rain. He handled the custom-made nine-foot fly rod like a pro as he repeatedly cast the fly towards the shallows. This was his first day of fishing and his first trip back down south since his election. He could have traveled to a more "Presidential" location to get away from it all, but he had decided going home would be a better place to unwind. The President just wanted to spend time fishing and visiting with his family and friends before going back to the rigors of what was certainly turning out to be one of the most difficult presidencies in history. At the moment, stalking redfish along the flats on the western tip of Horn Island was more important, though.

Small fleets of accompanying vessels were patrolling along a parameter that extended a mile from the area of the President's boat. The entire area had been sealed off for a mile around the circumference of Horn Island. Several fire teams were on the island itself ensuring there wouldn't be any snipers taking aim at the President from the dense shrubs of the shore line. A couple of United States Army Blackhawk helicopters noisily flew just far enough to the east and west to not disturb the fishing but were clearly audible to the President far below. It was no secret that terrorist elements around the world wanted this American President dead, more than any of the others that had served. The Secret Service wasn't in the business of taking chances and had asked for the assistance of the United States Army, Navy, and Coast Guard to help protect him. Everyone was walking a fine line by allowing the President to choose the place and time of his recreation, but he was President. The Secret Service was committed to doing everything in its power to keep the President from putting himself in grave danger, so the protection in place was unprecedented.

The crisis was over for now; however, Doug wasn't convinced that the Chinese had learned their lesson and wouldn't try to undermine the United States again; in fact, he believed they would. Measurable progress had been made in Malaysia. The new government there had decided on a new, open and friendly policy towards the United States. Elections would be held in March and the world fully expected a free and Democratic government to take power. The country had been purged of many of the radicals belonging to the terrorist group Jemaah Islamiya; in fact, the generals had outlawed the terror group. Over seven hundred and fifty terrorists had either been killed or arrested and turned over to the United States. Hundreds of others were scheduled to stand trial before a military tribunal in Malaysia for taking part in the fatal attack in New York. Of course, there had been many who had made it out of the country, but the CIA was attempting to hunt them down one by one. The TCC continued to communicate with countries where Malaysian terrorists could surface, warning them that if they were found to be hiding in their country, they would be on a war footing with the new administration.

The hum of the electric trolling motor joined with the sound of small wavelets slapping against the hull as the boat moved over the flats that extended out in front of them.

"Boss, have we heard anything from the Syrians?" Tony asked, from the stern of the boat.

There was a long, pronounced silence. Tony wasn't sure if the President was concentrating so hard that he hadn't heard the question. The cloudy gray mist that hung in the air was now turning to a light rain. A cold front was moving in from the Northwest, and Tony expected the wind to begin to clock around from west to north in the next hour or so, then the wind would increase and close out the fishing for several days.

"I think they're ready to discuss how to rein in some of their malcontents," the President finally said, slowly still concentrating on placing his fly in front of where he saw tailfins protruding above the water's surface.

It was obvious to Tony that Doug had been concentrating on fishing, because he spoke only after he began to reel in his line and moved the boat to a new position to cast. That was good, Tony thought. Before he opened his big mouth about business, Doug hadn't been thinking about world affairs at all, only fishing, nothing could have been better.

"Has Syria changed their minds about letting terrorists hide out in their country?" Tony asked, as he, too, whipped his fly into the shallows.

"If I wanted to talk about international policy, we wouldn't be out here chasing redfish around, would we? I'd be back inside the beltway meeting with the Joint Chiefs right about now!" Doug said, never turning to look in Tony's direction.

"Sorry, Boss, just trying to find out what's going on from someone who knows," Tony said, apologetically, knowing he had interrupted Doug's concentration.

"I can tell you this. We've gone out of our way to make it clear to the Syrian government that, if an attack takes place on American soil that can be traced back to Syria, we'll have to give them the same options we gave Putra! The TCC is working with them, if you want to call it that. But we do want them to understand all military options will be on the table unless they start rooting out these radical elements inside their borders. We have also warned the Chinese that any attack by a Muslim country against our country could trigger an attack on their homeland if we find out they are involved."

"Sounds like the gloves are off!" Tony said.

"Yeah, they're off, and they are going to stay off! The world can't endure nuclear terrorism, and it's outrageous that China conspired to help these people. As you know, Tony, I'm still an isolationist. You also know, if I could, I would choose to stay out of world affairs, as strange as that sounds, and maybe, in the near future we can do that. However, that doesn't mean we're going to put the "Big Sticks" in the closet either; there has to be respect for our way of life," Doug said. As he began to fish again, his yellow fly line moved in a large, arching loop above his head.

Tony made another looping cast into the shallows as the drizzle slowly turned to rain. For the moment, at least, time stood still. This could have been any fishing trip, on any given day, two friends casting their lines and casting their cares into the gentle waters of Mississippi Sound.